ESCAPING THE WHEEL

ESCAPING THE WHEEL

A NOVEL

ERIC ARTISAN

ESCAPING THE WHEEL

www.EscapingTheWheel.com

This is a work of fiction. Any resemblance to
actual persons or events is coincidental.
However, the many books mentioned do exist
and the author hopes you read them all.
The phenomena described are real.

Published in the United States of America
Also available as an e-book

ISBN-13: 978-1500561871
ISBN-10: 1500561878

Book Design by Jim Arneson

Some of the hypnosis language used is from *Clinical
Hypnotherapy,* by the late Dr. Allen Chips, DCH, Ph.D.

The "dark and devious ways" quote in Chapter 37 is from
Joseph Campbell's *Hero With a Thousand Faces.*

Hemi-Sync is a registered trademark
of the Monroe Institute.

FOR THE SEEKER IN ALL OF US

Come, come, whoever you are, wanderer, worshiper,

lover of leaving; come, ours is not a caravan of despair.

Though you've broken your vow a thousand times,

come, come again.

~ Rumi

PROLOGUE

THAT'S BETTER, HE THINKS. There's nothing like the sight of gold to get a man's attention.

The coin spins across the wide, wooden tabletop, wobbles lazily, then finally comes to rest amidst the twelve men gathered in the hotel's dining room. Whitley stands at the head of the long table, his compatriot from the Mint sitting opposite him at the foot: places of honor as guests in this burgeoning town. There is a respectful silence now as all eyes are either on him or on the dully shining doubloon in the center of the table.

"Our business here, gentlemen, is gold. The very gold you have so much of in your hills." He points damningly at the coin. "And to put an end to the likes of this."

Whitley catches the eye of a man he does not yet know but who must be someone of importance to have been invited to this gathering; he motions to him, says, "Please. Examine it and tell us what you see."

The elderly man slides the gold piece toward him and holds it closely to his mutton-chopped face, inspecting it carefully. His surprise is obvious. "Why, it is . . . It is quite unique, I must say. It's not like the Spanish variety at all." He passes a swift glance around the table. "Is this the 'Eagle' we have heard so many rumors of lately?"

"No, indeed it is not." Whitley removes two more of the same coin from his waistcoat pocket, hands one to each man beside him. He sees Harris, his stern and silent counterpart across the table, do the same. "Please pass these around. I would like for everyone to see what we are up against."

"It's quite heavy," says Muttonchops. "I had assumed it at first to be Spanish. But the eagle and shield . . ."

"'*E Pluribus Unum*,'" reads the man immediately to Whitley's right, Mr. Morgan, an old friend of his father's. "That's our nation's motto, is it not? And is not the eagle and shield our national symbol as well?"

"It is. You are correct, of course," Whitley says. "But the coin is not one of ours. See the date."

"1787 . . . Ah, I see."

"These coins are made by a jeweler and goldsmith in New York, a man named Brasher. Washington's neighbor, actually."

"The president?"

"Yes. A coincidence, I'm sure."

"A hefty weight," someone says.

"They are the same weight as the heaviest of the Spanish doubloons: eight *escudos*."

"I particularly like the image of the sun rising over a new land," says a stranger next to Harris. "But the workmanship appears inferior." He peers closely. "Is this the man's name?"

"Yes, it is," Whitley says, "as are those his initials stamped into the other side. To authenticate each piece, I presume. That, and I believe him to be full of himself."

He gets to the point: "Mr. Brasher wishes to replace the Spanish doubloons with his own. He's produced a number of these coins since '87 and continues to do so. To accomplish this, of course, he needs a great many depositors of gold—depositors who should now be rightfully contributing to *us* instead."

"You wish to create a national currency, then." This from the hotel's owner, James Burke, Whitley's closest friend from childhood—before the war, before their sudden falling out. Politics will forever prevent their reconciliation, it seems. "Are you also for a national bank," he says, "as is Hamilton and his Federalists?"

This is stepping into dangerous territory, he knows, but Whitley answers without hesitation: "Of course. Or would you have every goldsmith like Brasher producing his own currency?"

"I see nothing wrong with it. Gold is gold. Why must we have a national currency at all? Are we Spain or France? A monarchy? No. We stand for the individual rights of man—for personal liberty and free enterprise. I say the government should have nothing to do with the production of currency, nor with the allocation or distribution of it. Unless, of course, one wishes to see the *government* become the wealthy, ruling class."

Whitley bristles, taking this as a personal affront to his honor, as if he had joined the government solely as a means to obtain wealth and power. He does his best to keep his temper, especially with such an important task at hand—and his father's friends watching carefully.

"To the contrary, sir. I myself fought in the war as a young man, as you well know, alongside General Marion himself. And now I want nothing more than for my newly founded country to prevail. But to do so—to be a sovereign nation indeed—we must be free from our debts. And to pay the enormous debts we have incurred, it is imperative we form a national currency."

"I do not understand your reasoning," Burke says. "Why not simply send gold, regardless of who coins it? It is the weight that matters."

Whitley tries a different tack: "What about foreign trade? Are we to deal with other nations without our own currency to offer?"

"Again, your logic escapes me," Burke argues. "What the Continent wants is our lumber and cotton and other resources, or bullion, not our precious coins of King Washington. They could care less whose face is on them, I'm sure."

This comment provokes much grumbling and shaking of heads. A fellow at Burke's side whispers what must be a warning into his ear, but Burke only grunts and exchanges wary looks with a few other men at the table.

A dapper young gent from the Cavanaugh family—much too young to be seated at such a prestigious table, Whitley thinks—brandishes a Brasher doubloon with a grin. "Why not take all of these and melt them down, turn them into your own?"

"That is exactly what we are doing," Whitley says, glad for the break in the discussion. "These pieces are destined to be converted like the rest, when we eventually return to Philadelphia. However, to do so we must first locate them all—and others like them—and exchange them for like kind of our own . . . These!"

With a dramatic flourish, he lifts the small, canvas satchel from his chair and drops it onto the table before him. Its heavy thud and the unmistakable clinking of coins lights the greed in every man's eyes.

"As you know, we have only just begun minting gold this past year. I have the first of the coins with me now." Whitley indicates his partner. "Mr. Harris and I have brought more than enough for a sample for each of you, if you'd like. For the proper remuneration, of course."

"Of course," someone says soberly.

Whitley removes handfuls of gold and silver coins, making a large pile in front of him, smiling at the excited murmur around the table. Then, one by one, he selects a coin and slides it swiftly and unerringly down the table to each man in turn.

Twice.

This is the moment he's been waiting for all day. He can sense the group's admiration and respect for him growing as the coins are quickly snatched up.

"Compare these with the inferior coins of Brasher's," he says proudly, finally taking his seat, "or with a Spanish doubloon, if you have one." Two men signal they do. "I pray you will find these well worthy of a national currency."

He holds up both coins: "The thicker, heavier one is termed the 'Eagle' and is worth ten silver dollars. The other, half the weight, is termed the 'Half-eagle,' of course."

"Of course," someone echoes; and the men laugh as they examine the newly minted coins, turning them over in their hands, commenting amongst themselves.

"What's a 'dollar'?" asks young Cavanaugh, ignored.

One gentleman holds a gold piece in the palm of each hand. "The Eagle weighs less than the doubloon. Why is that?"

To Whitley's relief, Harris speaks up finally: "They are not intended to be equal," he says. "The standard denomination for our new currency is the 'dollar,' a term unique to our republic. It is from the German '*thaler*,' I believe. Each gold Eagle is equivalent to ten of these silver dollars."

Without the flair displayed by Whitley earlier, Harris places his identical satchel on the table. Methodically, he unclasps the buckles and turns back the flap, counts out two stacks of silver pieces and slides them to his left and right, giving each man there a nod. "Like the gold pieces in your hands, these are the first dollars to be minted. From October of '94, only a year earlier."

"It's like a piece of eight!" exclaims Cavanaugh excitedly, holding his high to catch the light. "How many coppers does one make?"

"What kind of bird is this?" asks a Mr. Stewart, examining his coins critically.

Whitley cringes at the observation. He'd hoped to avoid this aspect of the coins' appearance, for reasons becoming fast apparent.

"Yes, is this supposed to be an eagle?" someone says. "It looks more like a Phoenix. And a scrawny one at that!"

"Or is it Ben Franklin's turkey?" quips another.

"It looks like ol' Ben won that battle after all!"

Everyone but Harris joins in the laughter, even Whitley, to be a good sport. The eagle on the reverse of the coins *is* a bit sickly looking, he has to admit. Many people have commented on it since their striking.

"Lady Liberty's hair is a right mess!" says Mr. Hargrove, a prominent merchant and longtime friend of the family. "And what is this on her head, a turban?"

Whitley laughs good-naturedly. "Come now, Mr. Hargrove, that is but the wind of freedom blowing through her hair."

This brings more laughter as the men gleefully play with their coins. It's a heady feeling, even for Whitley, who has been working at the Mint since its inception in '92.

Harris again: "Our former director, David Rittenhouse, gave the bullion for the dollar coins himself from his own stock of silver. Two thousand were struck; but unfortunately, two hundred and forty-two of those were found unacceptable." He gives a quiet cough into his fist. "However, the process has been improved upon, I am happy to report. We've had a much better success rate with the gold. Finding depositors, however . . ."

"I am simply amazed by how . . . remarkable they look in comparison with the Spanish coins," says Muttonchops, barely containing his mirth. "Lady Liberty is a splendid choice and rather well done, but you really must do something about the eagle, you know. I fancy it a duck."

There's the murmur of agreement around the table.

Whitley needs to get the conversation back on track. "I'll make mention of it to Mr. Scot, the Mint's engraver. Thank you, sir . . . Now, gentlemen, let us discuss the reason for our visit."

Once again, he has everyone's attention. He almost stands but decides against it: he needs to win these men over, and it would be best done, he thinks, on their level, as an equal, not as the representative of a government many worry might become as heavy-handed as the one they just recently fought for independence.

Besides, he was sent to Charlotte not so much for his standing at the Mint as for his having been raised here, within a prominent family with plenty of connections. Still, he's proud to have been selected for a mission of such importance. Accomplishing this task will surely boost his status in Philadelphia and bode well for his future in government.

Whitley clears his throat, suddenly nervous now, feeling every bit the rambunctious youth many of these same men once scolded during his adolescence. "We're here because this is where the gold is mined," he says simply, his carefully prepared speech forgotten. "This is where we need to build the next Mint."

HE'S WEARING NOTHING BUT his nightshirt when she comes to his door that night. Her candle's flame illuminates the striking features he once loved so long ago: the emerald Scottish eyes and rosy lips, the sharp Cherokee nose and high cheekbones, the tawny complexion and long, black hair in a braid to her waist.

The years have been more than kind to her, he thinks, as she slips silently past him into the room.

If only it could have been different. If only it wasn't for my family . . .

That was then. Now Whitley is a married man with a family of his own, and a home far away in the nation's capital. But seeing her now—even from behind as she stands in her work dress, setting her extinguished candle beside the lamp on the desk—he is nineteen again, home from the battle of Cowpens, the last he fought in the war.

She doesn't move from the spot, doesn't speak. It's only when he finally comes forward and places his hands upon her waist that she turns and faces him, her eyes looking up into his, searching—for what?

For a brief, foolish instant, Whitley wants to ask her why she's come. But instead he says the name that has haunted his dreams for so many years:

"Sarah."

"I knew you would come back," she says softly. "When they told me, I . . ." She looks down, as if embarrassed by such emotion.

He lifts her chin with a finger, gazes into those shiny, reflective pools . . . and kisses her, tentatively at first, then hungrily, overcome with passion. After much tugging and tearing, Sarah's dress is on the floor and her undergarments soon follow, his own nightshirt already gone and forgotten.

They make love standing, her legs wrapped around his waist, as they first did in Gordon's Pond—before the war, before his family's admonishment, before he left for what has seemed like forever.

WHITLEY AWAKENS TO A persistent rapping at his door, Harris calling that his presence had been sorely missed at the morning's meal. He shouts a "Thank you, I'll be right along!" and gets out of bed, naked, the smell of sex—Sarah's smell—all over him. He breathes it in, smiling at the memory of last night.

Her furtive glances as she served him and the others dinner that evening had led him to believe she might want to see him alone as much as he did her. But she had disappeared afterward. The men had retired to the hotel's lounge, where Burke himself served them drinks and cigars.

The man runs a decent hotel, despite his political leanings, thinks Whitley, happy for his old friend. And he's glad Sarah has been able to find work in such a respectable establishment. He hadn't expected her to still be in Charlotte. He knows it must have been difficult for her as an unwed mother.

It occurs to him only now that she said nothing to him of the child. He had not thought to ask. His family has never made mention of it in any of their letters these past fifteen years.

Why, the child is nearly a man by now! Or a woman, of course. He'll have to look into the matter today. Surreptitiously. With Sarah's good looks and his intellect, their child may have a future in government. Perhaps a position can be found for him somewhere; or a suitable marriage, at the least.

And perhaps Sarah will return to Philadelphia as his mistress. The thought makes Whitley's member stir. It's not too late for them, he thinks. His wife never need know.

As he washes in the basin, Whitley's eyes casually scan the desk and the papers he has already had signed. It will take a few more meetings like the one yesterday to ensure the cooperation of enough businessmen in town to finally move forward. He knows that what matters most is the quality, not quantity, of investors taking part—land and mine owners being most important of all.

Today's clothes hang ready on the wall, as equally impressive, he thinks, as the gabardine suit he'd purchased in New York and worn yesterday for the first time. The cambric 'kerchief is a nice touch, as is the new beaver felt hat. Thankfully, the finest clothing is still imported from the Motherland. And such a pleasure to wear again! It's so nice to be free of those filthy, traveling clothes for a change.

Below the suit rest his new Hessian boots, polished to a shine. And beside them . . . nothing.

What? My bag! The small, canvas satchel with the newly minted gold and silver coins—given to him by the Director himself for safekeeping—it's not there. It's not where he left it last night.

Last night! The realization floors him, makes his head spin; he has to sit on the bed for fear of fainting. Whitley looks again about the small room. There is nowhere else it can be. There is no one else who could have taken it.

BURKE IS SPEAKING WITH Harris and a group of other men in the foyer when Whitley accosts him.

"James! Your serving wench has stolen my coins!" He is beside himself with anger for having been taken for such a fool. "Bring her here immediately! If she is at home, you must summon her at once!"

The group is shocked into silence. Whitley knows he must look a sight in only his trousers and undershirt, but he'd rushed out of his room. Sarah could be fleeing town at this very moment; they must take swift action.

Burke looks equally alarmed. He turns to the young woman behind the counter: "Bring Martha and Jenny, please."

"No, it's Sarah I mean," Whitley says. "It's *she* who took the coins."

"Excuse me?"

"Sarah. The one who served us dinner. She came to my room last night—unbidden, I might add."

Burke levels his gaze at a point over Whitley's shoulder, his voice suddenly cool. "Surely you are mistaken, sir."

"I am not. I know the woman. I know her intimately."

The muscles in Burke's jaw visibly clench, his color rises, his hands become fists at his sides. He turns away, clearly suppressing his anger.

A more level-headed man would have perhaps recognized the signs, but Whitley is far too upset to notice. He continues brashly: "She came to my room for the sole purpose of seducing me, then robbing me blind."

Burke's arm comes around in a blur and the blow sends Whitley staggering to his knees. His head is ringing. He's slow to get up, shocked at being hit for the first time in decades.

Burke takes a step forward, face red, eyes bulging, his voice barely controlled. "The lady you speak of is *my wife,* you fool! I demand an apology! This instant!"

It takes a moment for this to register. *His wife?* That's impossible. Burke is a distinguished name in Charlotte, much like his own. Whitley stands shakily. "But she's a half-breed," he says without thinking.

Fortunately for him, Harris steps between the two men as Burke advances with fists raised. Whitley's coworker pushes him backward, holding him tightly by the shoulders. "There must be a mistake, Richard," he cajoles. "We'll figure this out together. Come along, let's go to your room."

"The purse is gone, Harris! *Gone!* She's the only one who could have taken it. She was there all night." Whitley looks past Harris to Burke, who has murder in his eyes. If Sarah is his wife, then . . . his former friend . . . "Your wife is a thief and a whore!" Whitley shouts, newly enraged. "And you're her handler!"

Half the men from the group are now holding Burke back, trying to calm him, hopelessly. "I demand satisfaction!" he roars. "Today! You arrogant bastard! You—You piece of dung on my boot! You shall not get away with this!"

"I want my coins, James!" Whitley yells back. "You can have your damn Cherokee squaw!"

THE DUEL IS HELD AT NOON. Harris, along with Whitley's father, his brother, Robert, his younger sister, Emily, and other members of the community do their best to talk him out of it; but he will not be budged: it is a manner of honor.

Sarah cannot be found, which lends credence to Whitley's story and seems to further infuriate Burke. More than one person has commented that this is what the man gets for marrying an Indian—and the daughter of a witch, at that.

The people of Charlotte haven't seen a duel like this in nearly a year, and the fact that it involves such prominent families brings out a crowd. They are gathered on Collingswood Green, keeping their distance from the two men standing back-to-back, pistols drawn, awaiting the count.

Whitley is confident in his aim, although it has been many years since he fired a pistol. This one is from a set of Mr.

Morgan's, engraved with ancient symbols from the Motherland; it had been tested earlier and shoots true. As does its twin, he thinks ruefully.

Seven paces, turn, fire . . . Seven paces, turn, fire . . .

He can hear Emily crying tearfully on Robert's shoulder. He cannot believe the position he is in. But it feels right somehow. Although he didn't call for the duel, it is *he* who has been wronged.

When this is over, he'll find Sarah and the coins himself. God help him if he doesn't kill her, too.

"On my count!" hollers the constable, standing well away. "One! . . . Two! . . . Three! . . . Four! . . . Five! . . . Six! . . . *Seven!*"

As Whitley steps and turns to his left, he realizes too late that turning right would have allowed him to bring the weapon to bear sooner. Burke is standing with only his side exposed, arm extended, a burst of smoke obscuring the man's face an instant before Whitley pulls the trigger.

And then he's falling, slowly, having somehow spun around. The ground is surprisingly soft beneath him; the tall grass tickles his face. There's the loamy smell of earth, the metallic taste of blood, Emily screaming from miles away.

PART ONE

Men never do evil so completely or cheerfully as when they do it for religious conviction.

~ Pascal

1

HE IS A POINT OF CONSCIOUSNESS in space. He registers this with the usual surprise and elation. It's when he feels the most alive, the most aware.

He's moving, flying, and within seconds there is the Earth, the Mediterranean Sea, a nondescript village square. A bird's-eye view.

He takes in the scene and knows instantly what is happening: one-story buildings, dusty beige like the ground; a crowd of people in robes—ancient Middle Eastern garb—surrounding a large, roughly made, open, wooden container, no one standing too close; Roman soldiers milling about the perimeter; the box is full of weapons: swords, knives, axes, spears; the village has been conquered, its residents told to give up their weapons here.

This is not a dream; he is in the actual past. He knows this with an absolute certainty. He has once again traveled through time.

With an inner *Whoop!* he dives into the container of sharpened steel, flying in circles through and around the countless blades—laughing!—ecstatic, knowing that none of it can hurt him.

This is what I really am! he silently crows. *This is who I really am!*

From the box of weapons he flies to where a soldier stands over a villager cowering on his knees. He hovers a moment beside the young Roman, taking in his features, the military dress, then is suddenly drawn inside.

He is now looking out of the soldier's eyes, thinking his thoughts, feeling the contempt he holds for the sniveling Jew at his feet. He can only watch as his own sword arm raises.

But it's a feint. He kicks the villager, instead, knocking the man over, laughing with his fellow soldiers.

AAAY! There's a sudden, sharp, burning pain in his lower back, and he whirls with a cry.

A small boy with tears on his face and blood on his blade stands with defiance blazoned in his eyes.

He recognizes the boy's spirit within.

Then once again he is flying—still ecstatic, still amazed, as always, at the condition he has found himself in—each time bringing new experiences, new revelations. All around him is a blur, then blackness as he travels infinitely faster than the speed of light: the speed of *thought*.

He *is* thought. And energy. He is an independent, individual form of Consciousness, part of a greater Whole. Without knowing how he knows, he knows without a doubt that he is an eternal, "spiritual" being, without beginning or end. In his true form, he exists outside of time or space. He knows that right now he is experiencing the being—the *soul*—who occupies his physical, human body. And he knows that he hasn't even begun to fully experience or comprehend this awesome reality.

He slows. There is the Earth; central Africa; a wide, copper-colored river. Tall, muscular men, their blue-black bodies ritually scarred, pole a long, floating barge filled to capacity with people from a neighboring tribe: slaves to market. The captives' moans and wails carry across the water. Those living on shore say a silent prayer, thankful it is not them on board.

Too quickly he feels the lash of rope across his back, his arms, his legs before he is pushed roughly aside. He is a *she,* rather; fifteen years old; her name is Ngozi; it means "being a blessing."

Her mother lies curled in a ball, weeping, beside her. Ngozi had watched her father and brother killed today by the man who just hit her, who now turns back in anger.

"What did you say?" the man snarls.

"Devil!" she spits. "You have no soul! You are evil!"

There is no trace of fear within her. She knows and accepts her fate, choosing it over the alternative.

Wrists tied, the girl raises her hand in the most insulting gesture she knows.

He watches her death from above. He recognizes the spirit embodying the brutal slaver and reaches a new level of understanding.

Then, like a rushing wind, he is moving again—a blur to black—exhilarated, reveling in this unlimited but temporary freedom.

The Earth, the North American continent, a densely wooded forest. An elderly native sits beneath a tree, eyes closed, barely breathing, his long gray hair touching the ground, naked but for a strip of buckskin about his waist and a small, leather bag hanging from his neck. Shafts of light pierce the canopy above, bestowing upon him a mottled glow. The last wisps of smoke rise from a fire long gone cold.

All around him are arrayed animals of the forest: squirrels, raccoons, badgers, skunks, rabbits, beaver, deer, boars, foxes, snakes, birds . . . A raven comes down to land softly upon the old man's shoulder.

As if pulled by a magnetic force—a familiar feeling now—he is drawn into the Indian's body . . . But the transition is different this time: there is less of a change; he is awash with a tremendous feeling of love for all life, for all creation; he feels a peace beyond words—and a *power*.

Hello, Poor Bear, he hears Raven say. *Good, good.*

• • •

THIS TIME, DARKNESS TURNS to starlit sky as he slows. Above, a crescent moon lounges heels up, unconcerned. Below, the prison rec yard.

Home.

He floats high over the walls and razor wire. The red-brick buildings are dark inside. Only the outside fences are lit. A cigarette flares briefly in a guard tower. He circles the sprawling compound once, twice, then is diving through a window, through walls, corridors, prison cells.

His own small cell is a six-by-nine-foot cement box with one wall of bars. In it is a single metal bunk, a toilet, a sink, a shelf full of books. This is segregation—solitary confinement—and what he prefers as it gives him the opportunity to meditate for hours on end, as he is doing now.

For a moment he watches himself sitting cross-legged on his bunk, eyes closed, back upright against the wall. His year-round attire: a pair of white boxer shorts. He has a shaven head and pale white, sun-starved skin over muscles well-developed through years of rigorous yoga practice. Covering his chest is a large tattoo: a circular star with wings, symbolizing his soul's upward progress through good thoughts, words, and deeds.

Footsteps sound far down the hallway outside.

WITH A JERK, HE IS BACK in his physical body. Josh's eyes open as his ego, his human personality, quickly takes back the reins. As always, his mind recovers first; his hands and arms twitch, slow to respond to the brain's commands.

He has to get moving: this is the big day; this is the moment. The slow cadence of footfalls in the hallway grows louder, closer. He's just able to turn his head, wet his lips; then the guard is there in front of his cell, clipboard in her hand, counting heads, taking inventory.

"Officer. Excuse me, officer." His voice is only a raspy whisper, he'd been gone so long. "Officer."

She either doesn't hear or ignores him and continues on.

"Officer! . . . *Officer!*" This last is a shout and the force of it brings his entire body back into wakefulness. "*Officer!*"

She appears again before the bars. "What's up?" she asks, not unkindly. This is one of the good ones, one of the few guards who treat prisoners like fellow human beings—a rarity—and this is why he's picked her.

"Um . . ." He balks. *You can do this*, he tells himself. *You have to do this.* "Thank you, ma'am. I just wanted to say goodbye. And God bless you."

Josh picks up the bare razor blade resting in his lap and raises it to his throat. Their eyes lock and he watches her scream as his blood sprays across the opposite wall.

The guard drops her clipboard and frantically, pointlessly, begins pulling on the cell door. Then she runs, still screaming, calling out for help.

Josh tentatively fingers the gaping wound in his neck, presses his palm over it. The blood pulses out in a sheet beneath his hand with every slow heartbeat. He's surprised it doesn't hurt more.

"Shit," he says, leaning his head back against the wall. He may have just screwed up. Royally.

But he isn't afraid: he knows that, no matter what happens, he—who he *really* is—will never die.

Josh closes his eyes. And waits.

2

ERIN ENTERS THE HOSPITAL ROOM pushing an empty wheelchair, its seat holding a cardboard carrying tray with two paper cups of coffee. In a white lab coat nearly dragging on the floor, she looks every bit the doctor. Her name tag reads S. WALLINKSY, DO. A curly, blond wig and platform shoes add six inches to her petite frame.

"I thought you might like this," she says loudly. She holds out a cup to the barrel-chested guard who had obviously been dozing in his chair.

"Oh! Uh, hello, doctor, uh . . ." He stands abruptly, flustered, clearly embarrassed at being caught so unaware.

"It's coffee," she says.

"Oh, yes, thank you, ma'am, I appreciate it." He takes the cup and smiles sheepishly.

"It's a shame you're not allowed to bring some reading material in here with you," she says. "It's obvious he's not going anywhere."

Erin gestures with her cup to the patient handcuffed to the bed frame, his neck wrapped in thick bandages, an intravenous line connecting his near arm to a ruby red bag of blood hanging above his head, wires going to the vitals monitor beeping quietly, slowly, beside him. His skin is deathly pale.

"I'd be happy to bring you some magazines from the lounge," she offers.

"Oh, no, that's all right, I'm fine." The guard swallows a grateful gulp of caffeine. "I could probably use another one of these, though, later on. It's gonna be a long night." He raises his cup in toast and takes another drink.

Erin smiles. "I'll be sure to bring you one."

They stand sipping their coffees in silence.

"It's good," the guard says after a while.

"Yes, it is, isn't it. Not too much sugar?"

"No, no, just right."

Erin approaches the hospital bed, studies the tragic figure lying there. He appears deceptively peaceful. His face is badly scraped on one side and there's a large knot on his forehead.

"You almost didn't make it," she says softly.

"Yeah, that's what I hear." The guard has joined her at bedside. "Really did a number on himself. Lost a lot of blood."

"Were you one of those who brought him in?"

"No, no, not me. That was second shift. It happened about ten o'clock tonight, or last night." He slurps his coffee. "I'm glad I wasn't there. Scared the hell outta the lady that saw him do it. She's a mess. Did it right in front of her."

"I'm sorry to hear that." Erin reaches out and takes Josh's hand in hers. "It must have been a terrible thing to witness." She squeezes his fingers with no response.

"I've seen my share," the man boasts, "but usually they hang themselves. Gotta cut 'em down. Or else they jump off 'three-row' onto their heads . . . The ones that cut themselves? At least the ones that cut their wrists? They usually don't mean it." He pauses to take another drink. "This guy, though? He was dead serious. No pun intended." He chuckles.

Erin turns to the guard, looks at him closely. "How's your coffee? About done? Shall I get you another one?"

"No, no, I'm fine, thank you, ma'am—er, doctor."

"My pleasure, enjoy, drink up." She's noticed his speech has begun to slur. It won't be long now.

Erin steps to the vitals monitor, unscrews the cable connecting it to the wall, to the nurses' station far down the hall. Then she turns back to the bed, takes the syringe from her pocket. It contains epinephrine, a powerful stimulant similar to the body's own adrenaline, very fast acting—much like the chloral hydrate she'd used in the guard's coffee. She expertly inserts the tip into the IV's catheter.

The guard steps forward to watch what she's doing. He stumbles and has to catch himself on the monitor's stand.

Now. She depresses the plunger.

Immediately the monitor begins to beep faster. The guard stares at it openmouthed as if he were the cause, swaying unsteadily on his feet.

"I need the keys," Erin says, holding out her hand.

"Huh?"

"I need the handcuff keys. Where are they?"

"Oh." He goes to reach into his pocket, tries to switch hands but fumbles the cup of coffee, drops it. "Oh. Sorry." He bends to pick it up and falls forward.

Erin has to jump back.

She crouches over him. The keys must be in his right pocket; she hadn't seen any hanging from his belt. But now he's lying on his right side. *Shit!* He's a big guy and it takes all her strength to roll him onto his back. His eyes follow her sleepily; he's scared, she knows. "Sorry," she says. She digs in his pocket and finds the keys.

The heart monitor is beeping furiously now, dangerously fast. Josh's chest heaves as he hyperventilates, his eyes darting rapidly behind closed lids. Erin moves quickly to unlock the cuffs attaching both his wrists and ankles to the bed. Then, with a loud gasp, he opens his eyes—wide and panic-stricken.

She grabs his arm. "Josh! I'm here!"

He tries to talk but only coughs instead.

"Hush, it's okay." She helps him to sit up, holds his face firmly in her hands, forces him to focus on her. "Are you ready?"

His eyes are intense, frantic, but comprehending. He smiles weakly and nods his head.

"Good, because we're getting the hell out of here."

3

JUDGE HARDEN RAISES A HAND to the security guard as he drives through the main gate. The man isn't someone he recognizes, but that isn't too unusual: people can't be expected to last long at such a low-paying job.

Harden doesn't approve of the lavish Christmas decorations on display at the entrance, especially the life-size nativity scene. Exclusive communities like theirs are above such things and should hold themselves to a higher standard. But complaining is beneath him; he'll make sure Allison says something about it at the next homeowners' association meeting.

She's no doubt worrying about him arriving home so late. But conferences of the State Judicial Council are held only once a year and are not to be missed; it's *the* time for playing politics and rubbing elbows. Allison will understand.

What she won't understand, however, he knows, is his inebriated condition. How many times has she lectured him about drinking and driving? Even *he* can smell the bourbon emanating from his pores, and that's saying something. The car smells like a distillery after the two-and-a-half-hour drive from the capitol building in Austin.

It doesn't help that he had to get into his stash of Chivas in the trunk on the way home.

He plans his entrance: from the garage to the laundry room, straight to the shower in Sean's old bedroom, then a quick sandwich, and it's off to sleep in front of the television in the den. *Thank God it's Friday.*

Looking back on the evening, Harden realizes that he actually enjoyed himself this time. He'd felt relaxed and confident, secure in his newfound status. And the Christmas spirit seemed to have had an effect on everyone; there wasn't the usual partisan bickering and grandstanding so typical of these events. Instead, a feeling of camaraderie had prevailed. Or maybe it was just him. Maybe it was the copious amounts of alcohol imbibed by all.

Still, there's no denying that something in him has changed this past year. He's finally become the man he's always wanted to be. He's reached the pinnacle of his career. He's always held the power of life and death in his hands, but never so absolutely.

Now, as district judge, his word is law. And no one can ever take that away from him.

As much as Harden enjoyed his many years as district attorney, they had been difficult ones, full of high-tension and controversy. Truth be told, what he misses most is the constant media attention that surrounded him as Texas's most "Tough on Crime" prosecutor.

He'd been infamous. His conviction rate was always second to none. And no one produced such lengthy prison sentences as he did, no matter how minor the offense. He'd sent well more than his fair share to death row. So what if a few innocent people got caught up in the process—that's what appeals are for. What mattered was that folks knew not to commit a crime in *his* county.

Now he's no longer in the spotlight, but less than a year on the bench and he's already furthered his reputation. One *Houston Chronicle* reporter recently called him "Hanging Harden." He hopes the name will stick. He's determined to become more respected and feared than ever before.

As he navigates the curving, manicured streets, Harden can't help but be impressed by the sight of so many large, beautiful homes decked-out for the holidays. Their neighbors, however, unfortunately, have overdone it again, covering their house with so many colorful, blinking lights it looks as if the place is on fire, especially set back so far from the road.

His own house is very tastefully done, of course—understated, as befits a man of his stature and profession. Their driveway is illuminated by dozens of frosted white, snowflake-shaped lights posted every few feet to the parking circle and garage.

Though right now they are also illuminating a large, blue, ten-speed bicycle lying haphazardly on its side in the middle of the drive.

Unbelievable! Who could have done such a thing? Certainly not someone who knows who he is. And it's clearly an adult's bike, not the fault of some child. Teenagers? He doesn't know of any in the neighborhood. What he does know is that this bike has no business being on his property.

For a moment Harden considers running over it—*That'll teach 'em!*—but that would probably damage the car somehow. Plus, he has some important neighbors: there's a good chance it belongs to someone whom he had better not piss off.

Shit!

He stops the car only inches away from the bike and gets out. He'll throw it in the trunk and tomorrow have Allison find out just who in the hell it belongs to. *Inconsiderate assholes.* The thought crosses his mind that it could be stolen, but no, never in this community.

As Harden bends to lift the bicycle, he feels a quick, sharp pain in his thigh. "Ow!" He's been bitten by something. He reaches back to grab at the spot and his hand closes around a small, cylindrical-shaped object with bristly "hair." He quickly pulls it out.

What the . . . ?

It's a clear syringe—a dart. And it's empty.

He rubs his leg, looks around to see where it may have come from. The azalea bushes? He sees no one—just a dark van, approaching slowly on the street, its headlights off.

Harden runs twenty feet toward the house before collapsing onto his hands and knees, then falling to his side. His whole body is going numb; he's paralyzed; even his tongue refuses to respond. He can only grunt and groan, and this he does profusely and with as much righteous indignation as he can muster, as a strong pair of arms clad in black lifts and drags him backward down the drive.

4

GLORIA HURRIES DOWN THE STEPS of the courthouse; she doesn't want to be late for her meeting with a potential client—a very *wealthy* potential client. It's a long drive to the restaurant and she still has to swing by the printer to pick up the programs for next week's Christmas service.

She and Rochelle have finally put together a youth choir worthy of their efforts, and their first big performance will be then. They've chosen three contemporary Christian "rock" songs popular with the kids today, as well as a few of the traditional holiday tunes. Some parishioners are sure to criticize them for their selections, but Gloria knows the church needs to attract the younger generation if it hopes to keep growing.

Her own choir will be performing only two pieces this year: one at the beginning of the service and one at the end. But each is a real foot-stomper. They're going to knock the congregation's socks off! They've really outdone themselves this time. Thanks to her leadership.

Gloria has sung in church her whole life; but she began singing in earnest when she was in college, since she left home at seventeen. She'd tried a variety of churches when she moved to Houston for law school, but none do it quite like Mount Zion Baptist. Their choir has won the Mighty Gospel competition three years running now, and they're set to do so again, this spring.

Both her children—Michaela, eleven, and Gabriel, nine—are following in their mama's footsteps, both stars in the youth choir. Each will be singing a solo on Christmas day. She is so proud!

Her husband, Dwayne, no longer attends church, but he damn well better be there next week to hear their babies sing. Gloria hopes this might be a chance to get him involved in the church again, like he was when they were first married. Before the accident at work . . . before the pain pills, before the booze, before the even more crippling depression.

If he doesn't change his tune, she's going to leave him, she swears . . .

PRAISE JESUS! She's making excellent time. The print shop has done a wonderful job on the programs. She'll drop them off at the church tomorrow, first thing in the morning. She still has plenty of time to make it to her meeting; there's no need to rush. She can even stop for a mocha latte. God is truly looking down on her today.

As she drives, Gloria thinks about the poor boy she's likely seen for the last time as his court-appointed attorney. Hector was a seventeen-year-old Hispanic boy tried as an adult for theft of a motor vehicle and possession of narcotics and firearms. She believes he had no idea the drugs and guns were in the trunk (the car's registered owner is a notorious gang-banger and drug dealer), but possession is nine-tenths of the law, as they say, and putting it all on Hector and his friend was the easiest road to a conviction. So she'd negotiated a fifteen-year sentence: a plea bargain with the D.A.

At least Harden doesn't still have the job, she thinks, or the kid would have gotten fifty.

As it was, the new D.A. had started at twenty-five. So, in a way, Gloria figures she's done Hector a favor. But she knows he doesn't deserve hard time for joyriding in a stolen car. She knows that, had he been a paying client, she could have gotten him probation, or two years state jail. She feels guilty about it, but not as much as she used to. Today's justice belongs to those who can afford it. It's like she learned in law school: *Si nummi immunis:* He who pays goes free.

Approximately one-fifth of her caseload these days is for the State as a public defender. Every registered criminal lawyer and member of the Bar is obligated to take on their share of such cases, representing those who can't afford their own attorney. Cases are randomly assigned (supposedly) and it's next to impossible to get out from under any particular one (at least for her).

Usually, they're not very difficult; she only has to do the bare minimum required by law; and only rarely does one ever result in a trial, as about ninety-five percent of all cases are decided by plea deals.

Regardless, it's best to get them over with and out of the way as quickly and easily as possible. Almost always this means simply giving the district attorney's office what they want: a conviction. It's not hard to do. Most people are guilty anyway. And after all, it's the State who's paying her salary in such cases. Plus, if she plays her cards right, she can also win some concessions for her *paying* clients. "You scratch my back, I'll scratch yours": it's how the game is played.

What matters most, of course, is pleasing her paying clientele; and this meeting promises to land her a very good one.

A valet greets Gloria with a "Merry Christmas" as she pulls up to the restaurant. This is a welcome surprise: she doesn't remember such service here before. She accepts her claim ticket and goes inside. She's early. The hostess leads her to the bar to wait for Mr. Martin to arrive.

Although Gloria normally doesn't drink alcohol (and never at home), she orders a cocktail—to celebrate, she tells herself, but also because she's nervous about taking on such an important case.

She'd gotten the call only two days ago: A wealthy man's son had shot and killed a friend by accident, then panicked and hid the body. The son plans to turn himself in, but only after Gloria meets with Mr. Martin, the family's tax attorney, and begins work on the young man's defense. She'll learn the family's name today if she decides to accept the case, as of course she will.

It will be up to her to first arrange bail and later get any murder charge lessened to involuntary manslaughter. If the killing really was an accident, then manslaughter is doable. Either way, this case is sure to result in many billable hours, especially if it goes to trial, which, unfortunately, is highly unlikely. Then again, the new D.A. may have an agenda, an axe to grind; it depends on who the family is.

It's been too long since Gloria has had a high-profile case, and *that* one hadn't been a winner by any means. Just the opposite. If this family is as wealthy as she's been led to believe, such a murder case is bound to make headlines—especially if the boy's friend was also rich. It will be excellent advertising for her and may attract a whole new set of clientele.

Who knows, maybe she can get the son acquitted: it could have been self-defense. God has performed greater miracles in her life. And she's due for one about now.

Gloria can't wait to learn all the details of the case.

But apparently she'll have to. Shortly after she finishes her drink, the hostess comes to tell her that Mr. Martin has called to cancel the reservation—and, therefore, their appointment. He sends his apologies.

"That's it?" Gloria asks, bewildered. "He didn't say anything else? About rescheduling? Anything?"

"No, ma'am, I'm sorry."

"But . . ." She remembers now she doesn't have the man's phone number. *Damn!* She can't recall why or the excuse he gave, she'd been so excited.

"Damn it!" It had been such a great opportunity for her, she thinks.

And it still very well could be. He'll call again. He has to. Right? . . . Or maybe he had second thoughts. Did he find someone else? Is it because she's a woman? Is it because she's black? He had to know . . .

Damn! Damn the man to hell!

The valet greets her with another "Merry Christmas," but Gloria is no longer in the mood for pleasantries. As her car is being fetched, she chides herself for ever getting her hopes up. She's had murder cases before, of course—she's defended every type of criminal over the years—but her paying customers still tend to be low to middle class, who can't afford the exorbitant fees charged by the "best" attorneys. This had been her chance to finally be one of those "best"—to prove herself, to join their ranks—and to charge accordingly.

Damn! Damn! Damn!

Driving away, she realizes she forgot to tip the valet. *Oh well, it's just everyone's bad luck today, isn't it?*

And her luck seems to be getting worse. At the bottom of the hill leading to and from the restaurant is a dark blue van blocking the road, "City Maintenance" on its side, orange traffic cones scattered about. A worker in a bright orange-and-yellow safety vest is flagging her down.

Lord, what next?

The worker approaches her window. It's a woman, and Gloria is surprised at how pretty she is: such smooth, flawless skin, like porcelain, with a smattering of freckles, and even with the construction cap, the most lovely mop of curly blond hair. She motions for Gloria to roll down her window.

"It'll only be a few minutes," the worker tells her, "but please go ahead and turn off your engine, okay? I promise, it will only be for a little while." She attempts a smile. "I'm really sorry."

Gloria sighs. "All right, if I have to." The woman does look sincerely sorry for the delay; it's in her eyes.

Still, it's a hassle. Gloria can't help but hit her fists against the steering wheel in frustration as the worker walks away. She would beat the hell out of that Mr. Martin, too, right now, if she could get her hands on him.

She sits watching the woman collect and stack the plastic cones. What had she been doing out here all by herself? Gloria wonders. Whatever it was, it hadn't taken very long: she wasn't here when Gloria arrived.

A strong, sweet, chemical smell suddenly permeates the car. It must be coming from outside.

Ah, a gas leak, that's what she's been working on.

There's a rustling from the back seat. As Gloria turns, a damp cloth is pressed to her face and her head is violently forced against the headrest. She manages to let out two muffled screams, her fingers clawing at the leather gloves at her face, before her world goes black.

5

DANIELLA—"DANI" TO HER FRIENDS, if that's what you want to call them—paces the floor of the hotel suite, waiting impatiently for her fix. Barry's late, as usual.

Not for the first time, she considers leaving him. As if she had a choice. But Dani has to admit: for the past three years this is the best she's had it in a long, long time. Barry might be an asshole, but he's generous. And he always manages to score the best dope, no matter where they are.

Barry has connections all over the city. He has his fingers in a lot of pies, as he likes to say, as an investor and "silent partner," hoping somebody else will eventually come up with the Big Idea that will set him up for life. Until then, he has his girls, like Dani.

She knows she should feel lucky, but she's so tired of being used. She's been some man's plaything and property since she was a child. Still, not many women have it this good; every man but one has kept her well fed and in nice clothes and jewelry, not to mention all the smack she can shoot.

Tits and ass, not her dazzling personality, has gotten her this far, she knows. And she still has it goin' on. But even a boob job can't hide all the signs of aging. She's getting older, and lately *feeling* older than her thirty-five years. Dani once believed heroin would keep her young and wrinkle-free forever (no stress, you see), but that was just another lie she kept telling herself. It's a good thing there are many older men who prefer a "mature" woman; it's the reason she's working tonight, and hopefully will be for at least a few more years.

Dani often thinks about that once seemingly far-off future. And it scares the hell out of her. Who will take care of her? How will she get high? When the time comes to retire, she figures she'll most likely just give herself a hot shot and leave the world wrapped in a warm, silky blanket of oblivion. That's a comforting thought, at least.

Until then, she'll keep living it up—if that's what she's doing, this so-called life with Barry and the girls.

She does love her "sisters," though (except for Cherryl, that bitch). And she misses the hell out of Mariah, her closest friend in the bunch, who sadly, last month, learned the ultimate lesson of picking up your own trick online: Evil really does exist in the world. Finding her body was the closest Dani ever got to running away, to getting out of the business for good.

But right now she just wants her fix, goddamn it.

This is such a classic Barry move: leave her in the room for hours by herself, jonesing and wigging out; then when he comes with the john, she'll be oh-so-ready to party and to please. The son of a bitch; he knows her too well. He *owns* her—in more ways than one.

At least tonight's going to be very laid back, she was told. The guy just wants a little female companionship on Christmas Day. And get his freak on, too, of course. A businessman: import/export to the Middle East or somewhere, wherever it is they grow opium, make heroin. He's supposed to be bringing some of the pure shit he smuggles into the country.

Barry is already creaming in his pants, hoping to get in on the action. If things work out, he says, he'll take her to Disney World: it's where Dani has always dreamed of going. After all, it was *her* photo spread online—not Cherryl's or Paulette's for a change—that got this businessman's attention.

Finally! There's the knock on the door.

Barry's got the key but he likes for her to play hostess and greet the "guest" as he arrives. There's a certain protocol they follow: When it comes time for the appointment (the "party"), Barry always meets with the john beforehand; they have a drink, maybe a few lines; then, if everything's cool, if the guy's legit, Barry escorts the gentleman up to the room; where Dani follows their leads—subservient, submissive, indulging whatever whims and fancies they've arranged.

It's always a nice room in a nice hotel, since the cost is always included in the price. She never knows exactly how much a client pays but has been told enough over the years to know she sees only a tiny fraction of it. She's being screwed, in every possible way. Even tips are supposed to go to Barry, for "safekeeping"; and if he catches any of the girls holding back on him, he puts them on dope restriction: something she never wants to go through again. She'd rather die first.

Dani opens the door to a pleasant surprise. Standing beside Barry is a tall, good-looking man in a sharp gray suit, a classy purple tie; no older than herself, maybe; well-built; thick, wavy, brown hair; a square jaw with a full, trimmed beard; a nice smile; and the most striking gray-green eyes—eyes she is sure she's seen somewhere before.

Her breath had caught for a moment (he'll be flattered) but now she's playing her part: "Hi, handsome, I'm Dani. Please come in. May I take your coat?"

"No, thanks, I'd better hang on to it."

"Okay, suit yourself." She gives her most alluring smile, turns, and sashays into the room, knowing she's being watched and admired.

She hears the door close behind her, and Barry's booming voice: "Dani! Dani, my dear, I'd like you to meet Blake, Mr. Blake Martin. It's my great pleasure to announce that we'll be doing great, great business together." His words are slurred; she can tell he's been drinking already—a *lot* by the sound of it.

Dani reaches the center of the room and spins on her toes, striking a pose. She knows she looks particularly spectacular tonight. Barry had insisted on it, even buying her a new outfit, something he rarely does anymore. She's wearing a shimmering, aqua blue evening dress that shows plenty of everything. She's barefoot: she knows most men find this sexy, and she's too tall in heels; plus, it's just more comfortable this way.

Barry leads the john into the room, a hand on the man's shoulder. It almost looks like he's leaning on the guy, holding himself up.

Holy shit! How much has he had to drink? Dani's shocked at the sight of Mr. Cool shitfaced.

"Blake, I present the best of my girls: my most special, my most sexy, my most—Daniella." And with that, he pushes off, launching himself a dozen feet to the couch. He plops down heavily, arms and legs spread wide. He beams back at them—drunkenly, sloppily, but beaming nonetheless—obviously very happy with himself. Their business talk must have gone very well indeed.

Dani looks to the john—Mr. Martin, Blake—and offers her hand.

He takes it gently but firmly, smiles. He doesn't look the least bit fucked up. "Hi, it's nice to meet you. I'm Blake."

"It looks like you two have already started without me," she says. She hopes Barry isn't too far gone to fix her a hit. Soon. Like in the next five minutes.

"Yeah, we were just downstairs, getting to know each other a little bit. Barry here is a pretty bright fella."

Was that a smirk? "He is. And I hear you're pretty smart yourself. In the importing business?"

He nods. "Uh-huh. Trading mostly with Afghanistan and Pakistan. We import a lot of"—he makes quotation marks with his fingers—"flying carpets." He gives her a conspiratorial smile. "Would you like to sample some of our merchandise?"

He really does have a gorgeous smile, Dani thinks. And those eyes . . . *Where do I know this guy from?*

"Why, absolutely," she says, smiling back, incredibly relieved. She waves him to the couch and its large, glass coffee table.

The couch is L-shaped. Barry has taken the shorter section for himself. He still sits splayed out, with that stupid grin on his face, his eyes clear but glossy. Dani has never seen him like this, so out of it, so . . . docile. She kind of likes the change. This john may end up being good for the both of them.

Yes! Disney World here I come!

Blake takes the middle seat next to Barry, and Dani sits down beside him. He reaches into a pocket of the charcoal-colored overcoat he's brought with him and removes a small, black satin drawstring bag. He opens it and slides out its contents onto the glass: two needles; a silver spoon; a ball of cotton; an eye-dropper; a thin, silver lighter; and a length of purple, satin cord.

The cord is a nice touch, Dani thinks, but she herself won't need it: she goes between her toes these days, or on her ankle—to hide the needle marks, mostly, but also to find fresh veins.

She picks up the cord and runs it through her fingers. *Soon, it'll be soon, only minutes away now.*

Oh, wait! Without Barry to prompt her, she'd forgot: "Can I get you a drink, Blake? There's a full bar."

"Please," he says, only glancing at her, preoccupied with setting up. "A ginger ale, or a Sprite, 7-Up, whatever's easiest, thanks." He rummages in his coat again, shoots her a look. "And a glass of water, too, please."

"Of course. Anything." Dani stands and looks to Barry, but he just gazes back dumbly, smiling with that dopey expression. "Can I get you anything, Barry?"

He flicks his hand dismissively: nothing for him.

Ooookay. That's a first.

She brings Blake the glass of water right away. On the table now with the rest of it is a tiny bag of light brown powder. He's taken off his suit jacket and is rolling up his sleeves.

Pouring their drinks at the bar, Dani can't quit thinking about where she might know this guy from. Is it her imagination? No, she's sure it's from somewhere. She must have had him as a client, but years ago, before Waylan got rid of her. That's it, it must be. And that's why he's contacted Barry this time: he really enjoyed himself then; he likes her.

When she returns, he's cooking the dope with a flame beneath the spoon.

"Here you go, Blake." She sits and places their drinks on the table. She's poured herself a vodka-cranberry but only has eyes for the bubbling liquid in Blake's hand. Just watching him prepare the fix has a calming effect on her.

"Blake, have we ever met before?"

He glances at her and goes back to work, now drawing up the dope into the syringe, filtering it through a piece of cotton.

"Why? Does it feel that way to you?"

"Well, yeah. You look really familiar for some reason. Like I've known you before, or something."

"You ever been to Seattle?" He holds up the syringe, taps it, lets out the air bubbles along with a glistening droplet that runs down the needle's side.

"Um, no. Is that where you're from?"

"Mostly. I spent a long time here in Texas, though, once. Too long. Here you go." He places the quarter-full rig on the glass in front of her. "This one's for you."

Dani knows that etiquette dictates she wait for him to also fix his own, but shit, it's been way too long for her today already; she really can't wait.

It's all Barry's fault. She looks over at him for permission, but he just sits there with his head lolled back, smiling at the both of them through slitted lids. *What the hell is he on, anyway?* Usually, Barry's the one who gets the conversation rolling and the action started, breaking the ice and getting the john comfortable before eventually taking off.

But tonight it doesn't seem to matter. Blake is clearly the strong, silent type; he doesn't seem to need or want a lot of chatter. He's confident and relaxed, and this puts Dani at ease as well. She feels like she's going to enjoy his company tonight. But first:

Let's get this party started!

"Thank you very much," she says. "Don't mind if I do."

Dani places a bare foot on the edge of the coffee table, her newly polished nails glistening cornflower blue. She chooses a thick vein in her ankle, has just enough time to shoot it all and set the needle on the glass, before she has to close her eyes, lying back in her seat.

The drug flows quickly to her brain, filling her entire body with a smooth, tingling ecstasy beyond description—filling the "want," the "need." The sensation becomes her entire universe—it's all there is—obliterating the outside world, erasing all worries and cares, all tensions, all thoughts. All that matters now is this incredible, overwhelming *feeling*. Dani sinks further into the cushions, lets out a contented sigh. *Wow, this is some good shit.* And then she's gone, rolling in warm waves of liquid mercury, through the sparkling cosmos that is her own inner being.

A sudden, loud, crackling sound—like the zap of a million volts of pure-blue electricity—wakes her abruptly from her dream state.

What was that? Her eyelids are like heavy weights. She rolls her head to the side. *Where's Barry?* His seat is empty. She's alone on the couch. *Where's the john?*

She's able to focus on some movement across from her, on the floor, on the other side of the coffee table. *Oh, there they are.* The john is crouched over Barry, who's lying flat on his stomach. It looks like the john is tying Barry's arms behind his back.

Dani knows she should do something—get up, run away, scream for help, *something*—but any action right now is beyond her; the effects of the drug are too great.

Oh, well . . . She closes her eyes.

6

THE CLUB IS PACKED for New Year's Eve. Only one hour till midnight.

Santos commands an elevated corner booth away from the dance floor. His wife and his two closest *compadres* and their women have accompanied him tonight. Their table is covered with glasses, buckets of ice, champagne, several bottles of the best liquor, and a large crystal ashtray for his cigars.

Right now the ladies are dancing, or fixing their hair, or socializing, or whatever the fuck it is women do. He hasn't seen them in a while. Neto, his bodyguard and occasional enforcer, is face down, hoovering a thick line of coke. Luis is at the bar, searching for the "Lady in Red."

The three men had grown up together in *Segundo*, the second ward, a notorious *barrio* in Southeast Houston. As boys, they had their own gang, ran with a bunch of *cholos* for a while, until finally being assimilated into the Texas Syndicate in their early twenties—half a lifetime ago.

For a dozen years Santos has been in charge of the Syndicate's sports book operations. He has seven men who report directly to him, and they in turn have hundreds more. It's an enormous enterprise. And he's got it all under control. The organization has done extremely well since he began running the show. He has a lot to be proud of.

Tonight he, Neto, and Luis are celebrating their most profitable year yet, and what promises to be an even better year to come.

Chewing on his cigar, Santos scans the crowd, looking for the voluptuous little redhead who propositioned him earlier. Their waitress, Melina (and the only one allowed near their table), had given him the note and pointed the woman out. In it, the Lady in Red came straight to the point: she wants to get laid at the stroke of midnight, to bring in the New Year. For good luck, the note said. She'd waved once before disappearing into the crowd.

This isn't too unusual. After all, he's an important man. And rich. He's got *senoritas* throwing themselves at him all the time—something his wife, Consuela, doesn't appreciate. And sometimes he gives in to temptation. Discreetly. Consuela is tolerant but only up to a point: she's also proud and won't condone any of his flings being made public knowledge. And since she is the daughter of a *very* powerful man in the Syndicate, it makes sense to keep her *very* happy.

But there's definitely something special about this sexy *mamacita* with the note, that piques his interest. He'd noticed her earlier when they first arrived, her standing alone by the entrance, leaning against the wall. Their eyes had met and locked before she smiled coyly and turned away. For one thing, there's that wild, red hair. He's always had a thing for redheads (who doesn't?), and this girl is a natural, he can tell: that pale, almost translucent, white skin with golden freckles can't be faked, nor can that special shade of eyebrows. He'd pay a lot of money to see that beautiful bush of the same color downstairs. And the body on this girl: petite with outrageous curves. Those *chichas* were all natural, too.

She's definitely a "10" in Santos's book. But is that enough to risk the wrath of Consuela? Especially tonight? He doesn't think so. Besides, he'd want more than just one midnight quickie with this lady. And they'd need a hotel room to do it right; he's tired of screwing in bathroom stalls. Tonight's out of the question anyway: his wife would notice him gone for sure.

But he's curious. As Luis so tactfully pointed out without insulting him: what's her game? Why him? She could have anybody she wanted. She didn't really look like a hooker, but if she is, she'll be damn expensive, he knows. Though right now he'd be willing to pay whatever it takes. Her little note has had its effect; he's practically talked himself into it. It just can't be tonight.

Where the hell is she? Santos cranes his neck, scrutinizing the crowd.

"There's Luis," says Neto, rubbing the remaining cocaine on his gums.

Luis, at six-foot-four, is easy to spot. He's looking their way, pointing over the heads of a bobbing group of dancers. The Lady in Red is at the edge of the stage, moving to the beat, sipping a drink through a straw, eyeing the scene.

As Santos watches, a young *vato* in last year's style saunters up and starts hitting on her. She shakes her head and ignores him and eventually has to walk away. But the dumb-ass follows her, still talking his game.

Santos raises his arm, signals for his friend to get her.

When the little redhead sees Luis, she stops, apparently recognizing him. Watching the *Don Juan* trailing her is comical: he almost bumps into Luis, his jaw drops and he stares, then he can't get out of there fast enough. *Smart man.*

Luis speaks to the woman, turns once to raise his chin toward Santos in the booth. Then together they come over, skirting the dance floor, weaving through the tables.

And in a minute she's in front of him. Her face shines with perspiration; her lips are a natural deep pink; she needs no make-up whatsoever. *Ay caramba!* She gives him a seductive smile, waiting.

"You're very bold, miss."

"I know."

She just stands there, smiling at him, knowing the effect she has.

God *damn* but this woman is sexy. Her tits are ready to burst from her brown, leather vest. Her faded blue jeans—decorated with colorful, intricate embroidery—are painted on. In those dark red boots, she's like a high-fashion biker chick from heaven.

"Have a seat," Santos says finally, aware that he's probably drooling.

Neto slides over, making room for both her and Luis, who sits last, blocking their visitor from escape.

In Spanish, Santos says to Luis, "If Consuela says anything, she's with you. She works for you in accounting."

To her he asks, "Would you like a drink?" Hers is nearly empty. He points to each bottle in turn: "We have cognac, vodka, scotch, tequila—"

"I'll have tequila, please," she says. "I love tequila. But I've never had this one before." She picks up the bottle, reads the label: "Casadores."

"It's one of the best. You'll like it." He passes her an empty glass. "That was a very tempting offer you made," he says as she pours. "But I have to ask you: Why me?"

The woman takes her time recapping the bottle. "Well, it still stands. And I'm glad you like it." She gives him that bewitching smile again. "And I hope you're more than just tempted." She takes a drink, swishes the tequila around in her mouth before swallowing, like tasting a fine wine. She exhales loudly, with obvious pleasure. "Wow! This *is* good. Very good. Thank you."

"My pleasure." A girl who likes tequila this much has got to be wild in the sack, he thinks. But she still hasn't answered his question.

She leans back contentedly, looks up at the hulks of both Neto and Luis to either side, giving them each a more timid smile. She takes another drink, a big one.

"I'm Irish," she says at last. "This is a custom of mine. For luck. It's always worked wonders for me. I do it every year, wherever I am." She points her glass at him. "What's important is finding the most lucky guy to do it with, you see? And as far as I can tell, *you* are the luckiest guy I've seen in quite a long time." She raises her glass in toast and drinks, swishes. "Aaahh!"

"Ha!" Neto barks. "A fuck for luck!"

Santos's look quickly silences him. "Luck, huh? How am I lucky, you think?"

She indicates the space around them. "You have the best seat in the house, for starters. You have people fawning all over you, so you must be someone very important, which I'm sure you are. Bottles of the best stuff—ice, champagne, the works—here at your table, when everyone else has to order it." She pauses to give her breasts an adjustment. He'd like to rip open that vest right here. "And I saw those women you're with, all decked out in designer clothes. And I'll bet those are real jewels they're wearing. That alone . . ." She stops and looks out at the people dancing below. "And it's obvious people are afraid of you, too. I saw the way that man ran off when your buddy here showed up."

It's Luis's turn to laugh. "Shit, he was afraid of *me*. I gave him the look." He shows them the look.

Looking Santos directly in the eyes, the woman says, "I want some of that power—that respect—even if it means just having you inside of me for a while."

They stare at each other over the table. Then she smiles again, happily, and raises her glass. "Anyway, here's to the luck of the Irish." She downs the last of her tequila.

Santos continues staring. He'd have to be a fool to turn down such an incredible piece of ass. "Where are you from?" he asks. She doesn't have a southern accent.

"L.A. I travel a lot. Scout out commercial real estate for some investors. I'm in Houston all the time lately."

So he could see her again. "Does it have to be tonight? What about later, like tomorrow? We could get a nice room, wherever you want." Then it occurs to him: "Where are you staying?"

"The Sheraton, downtown. But yes, it definitely has to be tonight. I need to bring in the New Year with a bang."

Neto laughs and she joins him, looking up, exposing that soft, white throat—so vulnerable.

"Ideally," she continues, "we'll both be coming at the stroke of midnight. But we can go for as long as you want." She playfully kicks his leg, under the table.

Santos is getting hard just listening to her talk like this. He has to reach down and adjust himself this time. She gives him a knowing wink, clearly pleased with herself.

Santos exchanges glances with his boys. *Go for it!* their looks say. He looks at his watch: 11:35. *Ay, ay, ay!* They need to figure something out quick. "How do you wanna do this?"

"I have my rental outside," she says eagerly. "It's a van. Parked where no one will bother us. There's plenty of blankets and pillows from the hotel. It's perfect." She looks ready to go.

He feels nervous, like a naughty boy, much more so than usual. In the parking lot? What if Consuela finds out? She's going to miss him at midnight for sure, at the countdown to the New Year. But he has an idea: Luis can cover for him, say he ran into an important business associate, say he'll be right back—ten minutes, no more. Fuck that: twenty.

"All right," he tells her. "I'll meet you outside in a few minutes. But we have to make it look like we're not together. *Comprende?*"

"Great!" She holds out her hand to shake on it. "I'll be waiting. The model of discretion."

SANTOS SNEAKS OUT with plenty of time to spare. There she is, alone, waiting a good distance away. There are a few small groups of people standing around, talking, near the entrance. No one seems to notice him. The fiery little vixen motions with her head for him to follow, and begins walking away through the rows of parked cars.

As he trails her, Santos looks back: Neto has stepped outside and follows behind. He'll watch his back but also give them their space, their privacy; he's done this before.

Her van takes a minute to reach; it's parked in the far corner of the lot. She's chosen a good spot, where the streetlamp is out; it's comfortably dark.

His Lady in Red is waiting for him. She looks more nervous now than she did inside, more fragile, insecure.

When he gets to her, his hands go immediately to her breasts, pushing her up against the side of the van. She gasps and lets out a small cry. He bends down and covers her neck in kisses, bites her roughly, tastes her sweat. He could eat her alive.

"Wait," she says breathlessly. "Let's go inside." She puts her hand on his crotch and squeezes. "Oh my!"

Reluctantly, impatiently, he lets her go. She turns and slides open the door. He takes the opportunity to grab her ass as she climbs in, then hurriedly enters after, shutting the door behind him.

It's dark in the van. Too dark; he wants to see this beautiful creature naked under him, riding him, bent over. He looks around: something must covering the windows. He can't make her out at all in back. "Hey," he says.

As if in response, a brilliant white light goes on from the front seat beside him, only a few feet away. Santos turns and is instantly blinded by it shining directly in his face. "Aaahh!" His hands go up reflexively. He hears a "*Pfft!*" sound and feels a pain in his thigh.

"Fuck!" he shouts, more in surprise than anything else. Has he been shot? Stabbed? *What the fuck is going on?*

In the next moment, the light is gone and the van's engine roars to life. Santos, still blinded, is thrown backward and to the floor as the van lurches from its place; he slides to the wall as it turns sharply.

Gunshots crack over the sounds of the engine and squealing tires.

Neto!

He tries to push himself up, only to collapse as his muscles refuse to respond. The shout he makes comes out like a squawk. He can't speak; he can't even move his lips, his tongue. Helplessly, in the dark, he's rolled by momentum to the opposite side of the van, then is bounced a foot in the air and falls hard as the vehicle leaves the parking lot.

On a smooth road now, a straightaway, Santos's forehead rattles painfully against a bolt in the metal floor. He's pissed and shit himself, which shames him completely.

Oh, fuck, Neto, Luis. I've let you down. I've let everybody down.

The van picks up speed. He can hear the freeway.

Avenge me, he prays.

7

HARDEN WAKES. He's famished. His mouth is dry, pasty.

Oh, what dreams he had! He's flown in dreams before but never like this. It was the most wonderful feeling. It seemed like he traveled the entire world, the entire galaxy. But already the memories and images are fading and nearly gone. He keeps his eyes closed, trying to will back the experience, the sensation, maybe fall back asleep.

But it's no use, he must have overslept as it is. He feels well rested, supremely content. It's a strange feeling; he wants to stay like this for a while, savor it while it lasts. He's lying flat on his back, arms straight at his sides, a position he never sleeps in.

Wow, I must have been really tired, he thinks. *Or really drunk.*

He senses Allison's absence beside him. It has to be the weekend. She's probably out canvassing the community for her latest charity project, or over at the Lansfords' or Montgomerys'. Will she be upset with him? he wonders.

For the life of him he can't remember what he did last night; he must have blacked out. *Shit, not again.* But he doesn't feel hung over. Actually, just the opposite: his mind is sharp, extra clear. It's his body that feels lethargic, like it weighs a ton and will be hard to move. But he has to get up: he needs to take a leak; and he *really* needs a glass of water.

Harden opens his eyes, immediately takes in the foreign ceiling and the walls directly to his right and behind his head less than a foot away. They're made of corrugated metal, whitewashed white, covering (or intended to cover) what used to be a rusty maroon.

Huh? What in the . . . ?

He makes to sit up, but his muscles are incredibly weak, as if he has been lying there for days instead of hours. He manages to get his elbows propped up underneath him and looks around.

He's in a small room, like a metal box—a storage container, it looks like—about eight-by-ten. A set of cargo doors makes up the wall across from him. He lies upon a thin mattress on a narrow bunk; he's covered with a sheet and a dark gray blanket. To his left, against the back wall, is a shiny metal toilet/sink combination. A metal shelf runs the length of the wall opposite the bunk. There's a square, recessed light in the center of the ceiling; a small, circular drain in the cement floor; and a vent high in the back wall. That's it; there's nothing else in the room.

Where the hell am I? Why aren't I at home?

He pushes himself up, notices a small square of cotton gauze taped to his forearm, a spot of blood in the center of it. He pulls it off and examines his arm: there's a sizeable puncture mark, not quite healed, over his vein.

He's confused. Is he in a hospital, a clinic, somewhere?

Was I hurt?

The memory comes to him in a flash: the driveway, the bicycle, the dart . . . *Oh my God!* He'd been attacked!

In a wave of panic, Harden goes to get up. He throws back the covers to find himself naked. Slowly, gingerly, he places his feet on the floor. Then he quickly runs his hands over his body. Where is he hurt? Shit, where is his *hair?* Not that he had much to begin with, but there's nothing but stubble there now, and about a week's worth of beard on his face.

A week? A week! He can't even imagine it. He's lost weight, too, that's obvious, and not such an unwelcome surprise. After a cursory search, he can't find any scars, any sign of an operation, any injuries at all.

Harden braces himself and stands shakily. Taking baby steps, he makes his way to the toilet and pees. Above the sink, bolted to the wall, is a polished piece of metal, a mirror, reflecting back a worried, scared, and now bald-headed man. But his gaze is clear and shining; the dark circles are gone from under his eyes.

Two push buttons are located on either side of the sink above and behind the toilet. He chooses the left one correctly and the bowl flushes with a resounding roar. It's powerful; you could put almost anything in there, he thinks. The other button lets out a thin stream of freezing cold water into the sink. He greedily puts his mouth to the hole, scoops up handfuls of water, and splashes his face repeatedly.

Standing there with water dripping onto his chest, Harden registers the chilly temperature for the first time. The air-conditioning must be on full blast. He shivers and wraps his arms around himself, steps over and puts his hand in front of the vent but feels nothing blowing out. He retrieves the blanket and places it over his shoulders, hugs himself tight. It's terribly scratchy but will have to do.

He tries the doors. They're locked, as he was afraid they would be. He pounds on them with his fists, calls out; but it's a feeble attempt, and the effort soon tires him.

So: he is being held somewhere. But for what reason? As a patient or a prisoner?

Harden looks over the room once again. It's so small and claustrophobic, with not even a window.

He now notices a pile of clothes on the floor, at the foot of the bunk. He crouches down and inspects what's there: two pairs of socks, two boxer shorts, two T-shirts, two sweatpants, and at the bottom, a thick sweatshirt with a hood—all of it an ash gray except for the boxers, which are white.

Harden sits on the edge of the bunk and gets dressed, putting on both sets of clothes against the cold.

Done with that, he sits with his hands folded in his lap. Nothing to do now but wait. Someone will have to come, eventually. And then he'll find out what's going on. Allison must be worried sick, he thinks. She's sure to have called the police by now.

He feels his beard again. How can he have been gone so long? Has he been unconscious this whole time? How has he been fed?

With the thought, Harden's stomach growls loudly and he starts; he's never heard it do that before.

Across from him are a few things on the shelf he hadn't noticed earlier. One is a book on its side. Another is a white coffee cup with something sticking out of it. He gets up to investigate.

Beside the plastic mug is a folded hand towel and a washcloth, a bar of soap, a miniature toothbrush no bigger than his little finger. Protruding from the cup is a piece of paper. He takes it out, sees that it's rolled around a sturdy, plastic spoon.

The paper is a photocopy of a newspaper article. The headline: "Navarro's Killer Gets Life." The defendant's photo is prominent.

Harden doesn't need to read the article: he remembers the case well, knows it inside and out. It had been a big one, the murder of a Mafia boss. He prosecuted it himself eleven—no, twelve—years ago. It had essentially won him the election for district attorney a week later.

He stares at the man's photo: Joshua Rostam—a drug addict, a nobody, not someone to be missed. A very intelligent guy, though, Harden recalls—a computer whiz in spite of his addiction. The man had written his office for years afterward, proclaiming his innocence. But Harden knows the truth of the matter.

Then, as the realization slowly dawns on him, whatever remaining strength in his legs gives out and he slumps to the floor.

He clutches the paper in his fist, his back to the wall, his eyes looking at nothing.

Oh, shit . . . oh shit oh shit oh shit oh shit oh shit . . .

The level of anxiety he felt before is nothing compared to what he's experiencing now. He's afraid—very, very afraid. With a doomed sense of certainty, Harden realizes the fate that has befallen him.

Rostam escaped from prison about nine months ago. He has yet to be found.

Until now, it seems.

PART TWO

*As long as you are not aware of the continual
law of Die and Be Again, you are merely
a vague guest on a dark Earth.*

~ Goethe

8

"OKAY, YOU'VE DONE VERY WELL. You have every reason to feel good about yourself. You've done something very special here today. You're not the same person you were before, and you'll continue to grow and change as you integrate all you have learned into your daily life . . .

"As you relax comfortably in your beautiful garden—your sanctuary of the mind—know that you can easily return here anytime. Just breathe deep and fill yourself with life energy as you did before, then simply *will* yourself back to this special place—simply imagine yourself here. It will be just as you left it . . .

"As I count from one to five, you will return to normal consciousness, feeling wide awake, refreshed, and alert . . . *One*—step firmly and fully into your physical body, remembering all you have experienced . . . *Two*—feel your breath expanding, your circulation increasing, returning sensation to your arms and legs . . . *Three*—feel your body and mind adjusting to what's best now, coming up to your fullest potential . . . *Four*—reenergized, revitalized, feeling good in every way . . . And *five*—open your eyes now; you're wide awake, refreshed, happy."

As always when he leads a particularly good session, Josh himself has gone into a slight trance. He sets his notebook aside and gives his earlobes a few tugs: his own posthypnotic signal to come fully awake.

Payton, a nineteen-year-old recovering meth addict and Josh's only session for the day, sits beside him in one of the Center's donated, overstuffed recliners, their chairs angled toward one another. He places a hand on her forearm, as much a friendly gesture as a way to help ground her, help bring her back to the here-and-now.

"How do you feel?" he asks.

She takes a moment to respond, her eyes still unfocused. "Umm . . . fine." She blinks a few times, licks her lips. "I mean, great. I'm so relaxed. Wow." She gives him her one-hundred-watt smile.

"Good. Here." He hands her a tall glass of water from the end table between them and picks up his own. "We had a really good session today."

"Thanks, Doc." Her eyes sparkle and she's keeping them locked on his. Her expression can mean only one thing.

Uh-oh. Erin had warned him that Payton has a crush on him. It's a huge boost to his ego and he doesn't mind some harmless flirting once in a while, but any kind of sexual relationship is out of the question. The Center's patients are here to get their lives back together, and what Payton needs most right now is a friend, not a lover. Besides, he's twice her age, though he knows he doesn't look it: One of the unexpected benefits of prison life—of the monastic life in general—is that it preserves you.

Josh takes a long drink of water, way overdue. "You were finally able to go really deep," he says. "I'm happy for you. Next time maybe we can try a little regression work."

"What's that? You said something about it before. Is that, like, where you go into my past, or something?"

"Right. Your memories. Your subconscious holds the memories of everything that's ever happened to you."

Payton's smile dims. "Why would I want to do that?"

"Well, there are lots of reasons. Mostly, though, it's because your history affects your present, you know? All the things you've been through before shape the person you are today. And we can look at these things and see how they've made a difference in your life." Josh can tell she's not enthused.

"How they messed me up, you mean," she says, looking away. "I don't want to remember any of that stuff."

"Well, it's something to think about, at least. It can be really helpful. It was for me."

Payton stares at her lap, begins fidgeting with her hands. Not the best sign.

"I'm sorry. I didn't mean to upset you."

"You didn't."

"It's just that —" How can he say this? "It can help to see things from a different point of view sometimes, you know? There's a part of each of us—the *super*conscious—that's super smart and wise. And when that part of us looks at a problem—or something bad, maybe, from our past—it can better understand it and tell the rest of us—the other parts of our mind—not to worry about it, not to let it bother us so much. To forgive it. Maybe even how to fix it."

Payton keeps her head bowed. Josh knows he hasn't said anything that makes a lot of sense yet, so he keeps on:

"Right now, your subconscious, where a lot of your memories are stored, has some pretty screwed-up ideas about some things. They're screwed up because you and I both know that what's past is past—it's over. The present is what matters. *Now* is what matters. Right?"

Silence. A slight nod of the head.

"But the subconscious keeps these old programs running that affect us in the present. Like it thinks these past events are still a problem, when they're not. With hypnosis, the smart part of your mind—the more rational part, the *now* part—can tell the subconscious to chill, to let it go, to stop reminding us all the time—to think about it differently."

He can't help but sigh. After six months you'd think he'd be better at explaining all this by now. "Am I making any sense at all?"

"Mmn-hmm." Payton quickly glances up before looking back at her lap. At least her hands are at rest now. "You want me to forget," she says.

"Well, no, not really. It's not about forgetting. And it's not about changing the memory, or anything like that. It's about changing the way the memory affects you, how you react to it today."

As Josh takes a drink of water, he thinks of a good analogy: "It's like when you were five. Some things that may have been scary to you back then—or traumatic even—you can look back on now and laugh about, right? It's all a matter of perspective. I'm not saying we should always laugh at our past problems or fears, or anything like that, but it does help to look at them objectively, as if they happened to someone else. Because, really, that's who it did happen to, in a sense—someone else. We're not that same person anymore."

Payton looks at him now. "I understand. I'll do it. I trust you. It's just that —" She hangs her head, gives it a shake. "There's some things—There's some things I'm embarrassed about."

"Yeah, I know what you mean. But don't be. That's how we become better people: by making mistakes, then learning from them."

Payton doesn't answer; she has her head turned, looking out the window now into the trees, lost in thought.

Josh wants to turn the conversation around. He doesn't like to sound preachy, and now is not the time for a lecture on Forgiving Yourself and Your Past.

"Hey," he says, "what'd you think of those CDs I lent you? You try 'em out yet?"

Her head swivels back around; there's that smile again. "Oh my God! They are so awesome! Thank you!" She scoots forward and places her hand on his. "I listen to them and it's like I'm flying. I didn't really at first, but now—like three nights in a row—it's, like, Wow! I'm out of my body, or something."

Her enthusiasm is contagious and he laughs. "You are! You *are* out of your body. Pretty cool, huh?"

He gives her hand a quick squeeze then stands, breaking contact. "Look, I've gotta go find Erin, get the grill started. Same time, same place?" He means their next session. Payton is relatively new and still has about seven weeks remaining in her stay.

"Uh-huh, you bet. Wouldn't miss it for the world, Doc." She jumps up, all her usual energy now. They shake hands.

Then she's hugging him, hard, her face turned against his chest. He's all too aware of her breasts pushing against him. Then just as suddenly, she's gone, without a word, out the door and into the sunshine.

Hoo-wee. That was nice, he has to admit.

Josh stands in the doorway a moment, watching her walk away down the wide dirt road through the trees. She's an attractive girl, there's no doubt about that. Hell, after almost twelve years in a prison cell, they're *all* beautiful. But he isn't about to let himself get caught up in any kind of romance. Especially not with one of Erin's patients. And especially not now, with so many more important things on his mind.

Thank God for Sheila, who doesn't seem to care if he pays her a visit once a day or once a week. In her profession it doesn't make sense to get attached to any one man, and that suits him just fine.

Josh doesn't know if he'll ever be able to have a romantic relationship with a woman again. It would mean putting his heart in someone else's hands. It would mean being open and honest. It would mean revealing the truth about himself; and that's something he just can't risk. Not ever. Besides, a relationship would be counterproductive, anyway. His goal is to have no attachments, no desires—no reason to return.

* • •

IT'S A LOVELY SUMMER DAY. A mild breeze has the tree branches swaying, creating a shimmering dance of shadow and light on the path ahead. Josh is in no hurry and walks slowly, keeping an eye out for any wildlife. Something as commonplace as a blue jay or a squirrel is a major treat to someone who has been shut up in a dark cage for over a decade. If only people could experience a *month* of what he went through, he thinks, they'd appreciate their lives and everything in it so much more.

As he gets closer, Josh can hear some of the commotion. Because of the holiday, more people than usual are visiting the Center today. Its location, nestled high in the foothills above town, provides the perfect view for tonight's fireworks. Replacing the usual hammering and sawing and other construction noises are music and people's laughter. A folk band is here for the occasion. As are friends of Erin's, friends and family of some of the patients, and locals from town who know a good time when they hear of one, or who just know about the view.

A lively scene greets him as he comes around the last bend and leaves the forest behind. Children! At least a dozen of them, running all over the place, with dogs at their heels. A few are carrying hotdogs, so someone must have started the grill early, without him. All the better.

One kid on the grass has a kite flying high and far out over where the lawn drops off to the thick trees below. The kite floats in a perfectly clear blue sky. It abruptly darts and dives as the wind shifts direction, and Josh gets his first whiff of hickory smoke and barbecue sauce.

It's going to be a great day for a party—his first in way too many years.

Josh heads straight for the Big House, the prodigious, two-story main building, where he knows he'll find Erin.

Its sprawling flagstone patio isn't as crowded as he thought it would be. Most folks are out on the grass, sitting or lying about on blankets. Many are inside.

He spots Erin with Donna and a small group of people he doesn't recognize. Erin's wearing a flowery, long-sleeved summer dress and her big, floppy, straw hat to protect her from the sun. Her long, curly, red hair flashes at him from across the lawn.

She has the dogs with her. Honey lies sprawled on her back, getting her belly rubbed, as usual. Pooch is gnawing on something large, hopefully a bone.

There's a short line to the grill, where Ronald, a patient newly arrived, is busy with a pair of tongs and a spatula. His sister, visiting for the weekend, has her arm around his waist, laughing at something he's said. It looks like someone has brought sausages, maybe bratwurst, and their spicy aroma makes Josh's mouth water.

Two long picnic tables are crowded with potluck dishes. Coolers and ice chests are overflowing. Everyone who's come must have contributed something to the feast. They'll be having leftovers for days.

The band is set up in the far corner of the patio where a wing of the building juts out. This creates a nice sort of amphitheater, projecting the music outward. A spirited bunch is dancing nearby in the grass, and Josh plans to join them as soon as he can. A promise he often made to himself in prison was that once freed, if ever, he would listen to good music and dance every day. It's a promise he's kept, for the most part, though usually he dances alone. This live music is a real treat and he can't help but move to the rhythm.

"Hey there, Doc."

Josh opens his eyes; he was really gettin' down there for a minute, off in his own little music world. A tall, burly guy with a bushy, brown mustache stands beside him, grinning hugely.

"I like your moves," the man says. "For an old-timer, you dance pretty well."

Josh laughs: the guy is clearly his own age, if not older. "Old-timer, huh? Well, stick around, youngster, and I'll show you a thing or two. We call this one the 'Funky Chicken.'" He sticks his elbows out and struts in a tight circle, giving his best rendition of a rooster on crack.

The good fellow laughs heartily. "I like it, I like it! Where I come from, we've got the 'Boxing Kangaroo.'" He then proceeds to hop about and flail his arms like a maniac, attracting the attention of everyone nearby, especially those most in danger of getting clobbered.

They keep it up until both men are doubled-over with laughter. "You're crazy, man," Josh says, catching his breath.

"*I'm* crazy? Look who's talking!"

With a bark, Pooch is there, jumping in place two feet off the ground, his whole back end wagging furiously. He wants to play, too.

Josh crouches down to a face full of kisses. "Hey, my friend. Hey, little stinker." He gives the dog a quick, vigorous rubdown and stands up. Pooch takes off like a rocket back in Erin's direction. Josh knows he'll be running back and forth between them a few times in his excitement.

God love him.

Pooch and Honey, like himself, are relatively new additions to the Center. Josh had found them both at the local animal shelter a few months ago. If he could, he would have brought *all* of the dogs home. The sight of so many poor souls being caged—their despondency and fear so plain and so familiar—broke his heart. Having a pair of dogs—one to always keep the other company— was another promise he'd made to himself behind bars.

Pooch is a rambunctious mutt, less than a year old, with a patchwork coat of many colors. Honey looks like a Golden Retriever-Labrador mix, maybe six years old, according to the vet. Though not officially trained and certified as therapy dogs, both have wonderful people skills, and their presence lifts the hearts and minds of everyone they come in contact with. Like all dogs, their ability to express and demonstrate unconditional love is a much needed and much appreciated quality here at Fresh Start.

"That your pooch?" his dancing partner asks. He has a British accent—or no, probably Australian, hence the kangaroo reference.

"Yep. Uh, what'd you say?"

"That your doggie?"

"No, I mean, yes, he is. Did you say Pooch?"

"I did. It means dog where I come from."

"That's his name: Pooch."

"Oh! Well, it's a mighty fine name, then, isn't it." The man extends his hand. "My name's Gavin. No last."

"Huh?" Josh is a pretty big guy himself but his arm is getting shaken like a noodle.

"No last name. Gave it up. No use for it anymore. Just Gavin."

"Oh, all right, I gotcha. Good to meetcha, Gavin. I'm Trip. No last for me either."

"Trip" had been Josh's nickname in prison, known only to his fellow inmates. After so many years, it became who he thought of himself as. Only Erin calls him Josh now, and only in private.

"Trip it is, then. I take it you're a doctor here."

Josh laughs; he knows why Gavin might think so: "Doc" is what a lot of the patients call him, especially the younger ones. "No, I'm just a regular mortal," he says. "Erin is the only doctor I know of around here—besides a patient or two sometimes. I do hypnosis. And cook. And clean the toilets." There's something about this guy, a friendly vibe, that makes Josh want to laugh and joke around. "You from Australia?"

"Good God, man! No! I'm a Kiwi. New Zealand. Why would you think I was from Australia? Crikey! We just met and already you're insulting me."

Gavin's hearty laughter is infectious; he puts his whole body into it. He could be the Laughing Buddha, Josh thinks. "But they don't have kangaroos in New Zealand, do they?"

"No, 'course not. But I couldn't very well do the 'kakapo' dance, now, could I? You already snagged the bird."

"Huh?"

"Why do they call you 'Doc,' then? I only got here Sunday and all I hear is 'Doc this' and 'Doc that.' You must do a bang-up job on the toilets."

"The trick is to flush while you scrub; get in there up to your elbow. Use a squeegee on the seat. No bleach, that's for amateurs." He says this with a straight face, which earns him a laugh. "No, really it's just a name they've given me. Maybe someone figured I must be a psychiatrist or something to do hypnosis, but anyone can do it. You don't need to be certified or licensed, necessarily, to help someone. Though it's good to be trained, or at least study and practice a lot."

"Ah, so you use hypnosis to help people quit the drugs," Gavin says. "I've heard it works good for smoking."

"Shit, it works good for everything. But my specialty, actually, is spiritual hypnosis—past-life regression."

A beat. "*Spiritual* hypnosis? I've never heard of it."

As much as this is Josh's favorite subject, he's hungry for a grilled sausage sandwich, with the works—plus, he doesn't want to bore his new friend—so he gives the quick version of his spiel: "It's been around forever. Most hypnosis works with the subconscious mind, which is just fine for most things. However, spiritual hypnosis is a way to reach the *super*conscious, or the soul, or what some call the Higher Self—the eternal, 'divine' aspect of each of us. What I do is essentially a guided meditation that takes people deeper than normal, so to speak. By accessing the superconscious, we can explore other lifetimes—both past and future—and our life *between* lives in the spirit world, in 'Heaven,' or whatever else you want to call it."

Gavin just stands and stares back at him, like a statue.

Josh is used to a variety of responses to the description of his chosen life's work—everything from enthusiasm to downright disbelief—but this is a reaction he hasn't encountered before: catatonia.

They stand facing each other like this for an interminable moment.

This has got to be a joke, Josh thinks. Then, just as he's about to say more, Gavin slowly begins to pivot, turning away as stiff as a board, eyes straight ahead. At the ninety-degree mark, he takes off running. Josh's jaw drops in astonishment as Gavin rounds the corner out of sight. He can't believe it.

"Well, that's a first."

INTRODUCTIONS ARE MADE all around. The others sitting with Erin and Donna are Donna's friends and coworkers, getting their first glimpse of the "radical" rehab center they've heard so much about.

Balancing his heaping plate of food, Josh commandeers Honey's spot beside Erin; but the dog doesn't seem to mind: she bounds off after Pooch, now chasing a Frisbee.

At a break in the conversation, Josh leans close: "I just met your newest patient. A guy from New Zealand."

Erin's face lights up. "Oh, that's Gavin. I saw you two talking. He's the one I was telling you about."

"Who's that? When?"

She checks to see that the others aren't paying them any attention. "The cancer," is all she says.

And it's all she needs to say; he well remembers their conversation now. "Oh. I thought he was from Pennsylvania."

"He was working there. A geologist, I think."

"Wow, I can't believe it. He seems so happy, so full of life. I mean, we were totally cracking up just a minute ago."

"I know, I watched you two goofballs. Where'd he go?"

"Uh, I'm not sure. I don't think I made a very good first impression. He freaked out about the spiritual hypnosis bit."

"Really? I'm surprised. I would have thought he'd be more open-minded than that. At least he seemed that way to me when we talked. But, then again, he *is* a scientist. I know what they can be like." She laughs. "Did you really scare him off?"

"'Fraid so." Josh looks around hopefully, trying to spot the guy. *Aha!* But of course. "There he is. Dancing."

As they watch, Gavin spins his partner and catches her up again. They're doing a kind of swing dance, clearly improvised, both grinning from ear to ear.

"It's hard to believe, isn't it?" Erin says.

"Yeah." He knows she's referring to the fact that Gavin is sure to die soon. Pancreatic cancer is no joke. "How far along is it?"

"It was diagnosed about a month ago, I think. An early stage but inoperable, irreversible."

"Wow." Josh is impressed: this man's courage—to literally laugh in the face of death—is admirable. "He's a brave soul."

Erin nods in agreement, sighs. "If only we *all* had such a positive attitude toward life."

"Yeah, well, we've got to make the most of the time we're given," he says, "especially if there's just a little bit of it left, I suppose. 'Seize the day,' and all that."

Uh-oh. Erin is eyeing his plate of food on the blanket, between them. "Hey, hold on a—That's mine! Seize the *day*, not my lunch!"

But it's too late: she's already scooped it up and holds it just out of reach. "What? You didn't get this for me? You know how much I love coleslaw."

"Ah, but you don't love bratwurst." She lets him snag his sandwich, at least.

They eat in silence for a while, watching the festivities. Erin shares a few bites with Donna, busy talking with her friends. A few of the others go to get their own plates of food.

The band begins a slower melody, with only the guitar and violin. Josh smiles to see so many couples pairing up to dance, Gavin among them.

This is exactly the kind of gathering he'd fantasized about attending again someday, given the chance to be free.

What Josh missed most while in prison was simply regular people—anyone but the motley assortment of gangsters, thugs, and psychos he was normally surrounded with. Sure, there were plenty of good, decent people like himself—people who had just been caught up in the System, or who had simply made a mistake and had already learned their lesson—but the vast majority of prisoners were idiots and assholes, misfits and losers, the dregs of society who deserved to be there.

Regardless, it was thousands of men out of their element, crowded into a cramped, filthy, noisy place, struggling constantly with their anger and frustration and fear. It was a different world. A different set of rules applied. A different culture prevailed. Even the kindest, most friendly person eventually became a hardened convict capable of the greatest violence; the most scrupulous man, a thief; the most religious, a hateful bigot. Prison changed a person, and too often it was for the worse.

Josh had done all he could not to succumb to the negativity that prevailed in there. He tried hard to make the best of a bad situation, as impossible as that was to do sometimes. Every day—every *hour,* it seemed—provided a new set of challenges to overcome, a new lesson, a new opportunity to control his thoughts and actions.

He was extremely fortunate to have had some money stashed away—money the police never discovered. And this money had (at one point, finally) provided him with books—countless books, on everything from history and science to spirituality—which helped him retain his sanity and expand his mind. Thanks to these books, Josh had been able to change his life for the better, in spite of his hellish environment. He became more knowledgeable, and in the process became a better person.

Through his reading, he discovered the true nature of Reality and his place in it. He learned who and what he really was as a spiritual being and why he was here on Earth. He learned the Truth, and the Truth had set him free. Because he learned how to *experience it* for himself, through meditation and hypnosis. And with these tools he could escape the walls of his confinement.

It was this he had tried to teach his fellow prisoners for years, and the reason he earned his name: "That dude is a *trip*," they would say, with all his talk of past lives and out-of-body experiences.

Now, sitting on the thick grass, listening to beautiful music, surrounded by warm, wonderful people and his best friend in the world—his soulmate—Josh closes his eyes and gives thanks. More than words, his prayer is a feeling of tremendous gratitude. *Thank you, thank you, thank you so much.* The prayer is to his Highest Self, the Source, All That Is—God by whatever name. And for a time, he is totally immersed in the feeling, oblivious to his surroundings.

When Josh finally opens his eyes, Erin is looking at him with a touch of concern. She reaches out a finger and wipes away the tear rolling slowly down his cheek.

The transition into the free world hasn't been easy for him this past year, and Erin has done her best to help him when she can. However, in this instance, she has no need to worry, and Josh assures he's fine by giving her a smile and her knee a gentle squeeze.

"Here," she says, "I saved you some."

The once heaping plate of food is nearly clean. There's maybe one bite of coleslaw left. And some olives, which don't count.

He laughs. "You were hungry! It's a good thing there's enough food here for an army. We need to throw a party more often."

But at the sight of the empty plate, it registers that he's lost time somehow. Again. He notices the music has changed to a lively tune. They're the only ones left on the blanket. He wonders how long he was "gone" this time.

Erin is watching the dancers. "Well, it looks like this one will be an annual thing for sure," she says. "I was thinking about maybe having a party for Halloween, too, this year. By then the first floor should be finished. It might be a good time to show the place off to the bank. Butter 'em up for 'round two.'"

As if making the payment on the first loan isn't hard enough for her already, Josh thinks. "You think you'll be ready for that?"

"Well, now that Gavin is here, we should be able to meet our obligations for the next few months." She glances his way, gets interested in the folds of her dress all of a sudden. "And then there's his hospice care, which should last a little while, at least."

"Huh? Hospice care?" This is something they haven't discussed.

"Only if things work out with his treatment. Which of course they will," she proudly adds. "He says he may want to stick around for a while. Spend his final days here, too, instead of at some hospital somewhere. It's either that or go back to New Zealand, and I guess that doesn't appeal to him, as much as he loves it there. His family disowned him a long time ago."

"Wow, that's some news." And it's something else he and Gavin have in common besides addiction and a goofy sense of humor: total rejection by their loved ones. But somehow Gavin has managed not to go broke. The only reason Josh had any money at the time of his arrest was because he stole it: self-payment for services rendered. "I take it he has some money, then," he says.

"Stocks, I think. Oil and gas. I don't think he's had to worry about money for quite a while now, to hear him tell it. But it also allowed him to live the lifestyle, you know what I mean?"

Josh nods sagely. Of course he does, only too well. Money can be the greatest curse if it's used to fuel an addiction. There was a time when he himself had too much money for his own good. His early success as a computer whiz kid had ruined him in the end, before he was thirty.

"You think you're up to something like that?" he asks. "Hospice care has got to be a lot of work."

"It shouldn't be too difficult," Erin says. "What's most important is having a supportive environment, I think. And we do have the facilities. And the medication, should he need it, which he probably will."

"How long would he stay?" Josh is not sure he likes the idea of someone else becoming a permanent fixture around here.

"I don't know. I wouldn't expect him to last much longer than six or seven months. It all depends on him, I suppose—his will to live."

Erin reaches out and takes his hand, fixes him with a look. "Josh, he's not going to get in the way. He'll be just like any other patient, only bedridden most of the time. It'll be okay."

She gives his hand a squeeze and smiles happily. "And he's paying *triple* the rate!"

"Holy shit!" That does make a difference. Having a paying client is a big deal in itself, but this is a godsend. "We need to keep him alive for as long as possible!"

Erin laughs and pats his leg. "We'll see. It's not a sure thing yet. What's important now is making Gavin's last days addiction-free."

She jumps up and holds out her hands. "Come on, let's dance!"

"It's about time."

THE BAND HAS CALLED IT A DAY. Now a nice mix of relaxing music is playing softly over the sound system. Everyone is waiting for the fireworks to start.

People walk in and out of the main building, the "Big House" as the patients call it, referring to it jokingly as their "prison." Josh takes no offense, of course; no one has any idea of what he's been through. All of the lights are on inside, both upstairs and down. Erin is leading a tour for some local businesspeople, and a few patients are showing off the facilities to latecomers.

The children and dogs have worn themselves out and lie scattered about the lawn or nestled snuggly in their parents' laps.

Josh reclines in one of the chaise lounges on the patio, Honey and Pooch to either side. With one hand he takes turns scratching them behind the ears, and with the other he holds a tall strawberry daiquiri he only half wishes contained alcohol.

He's just finished a long talk with Lincoln, a twenty-four-year-old patient he's known for ten weeks and who is soon going home. They'd discussed Lincoln's plans for afterward and his worries about avoiding "friends" he used to get high with. If Josh is good for anything, he figures, it's giving good advice. After all, if it's true you learn from your mistakes, then he must be a genius by now. He'd spent nearly twelve years in prison reflecting on his "education."

Now he sits alone, watching the fireflies float up from the grass to get caught up in the sparkling lights of Eureka Springs, far below.

"Hiya, mate." Gavin takes the now vacant seat beside him, gives Pooch there a pat. "I reckon it'll be time for the fireworks soon."

"Hey there . . . Didn't mean to scare you off earlier."

"Oh, I was just having a bit of fun with you . . . But honestly, I've had enough 'spirituality' in my life—people trying to force their beliefs on me." Gavin pauses to take a drink. He also has a virgin daiquiri, only twice the size in a plastic pitcher. "I'm not saying you would, but . . . I guess I was a little disappointed, that's all. I thought I'd gotten away from all that crap."

"What crap?"

"You know, the 'Twelve Steps,' a 'Higher Power,' 'Jesus died for my sins,' all that higher-than-thou, holy-roller malarkey."

"Yeah, I know what you mean."

Josh is actually a big fan of Alcoholics Anonymous and their twelve-step program. He'd been resistant to any kind of counseling himself at first. But in the end—after going through weeks of the most horrific withdrawals imaginable while in jail—going to that first AA meeting was the best thing he could have ever done for himself. Although he eventually outgrew it, personally, it made him really consider for the first time the existence of something out there greater than himself; it had put him on the Path. But now isn't the time to debate the issue.

"Don't worry, you won't hear any of that stuff from me," he says. "But hypnosis *is* pretty cool. It's different. And I'm here if you ever want to check it out. That's all I got to say."

Gavin takes a hearty drink and smacks his lips. "Thanks. Who knows, I might take you up on it."

They sit in companionable silence for a time.

Then: "I'm staying on for a while. Did Erin tell you?"

"Yeah, she did," Josh says. "I think what you're doing is admirable, by the way."

Gavin snorts. "Well, I'd rather spend my last days out here in the beautiful Ozark mountains than in some sterile, sickly hospital, where I probably couldn't even go outside . . . Too many rules, too, I imagine."

"Yeah. You'll like it here. It's pretty laid back."

The two sip their drinks, watching the sky grow subtly darker.

"So how long you been in the States?"

"'Bout ten, eleven years. Why? Does my accent give me away?" Gavin says this last with a thick southern drawl.

"Just wondering. I'm surprised, though: I thought you Kiwis were always on 'walkabout,' or something—couldn't stand to stay too long in one place."

"True enough. I've sure been moving around lately, that's for certain. Doin' my bit to help them find all that oil and natural gas in the ground, you know." He pauses to take a drink. "You ever hear of 'fracking'?"

"Yeah, sure, that's where they drill down deep and use high-pressured water or whatever to break up the rocks underground—the shale—to let all the oil out."

"Close enough. The 'whatever' is chemicals, and particulates. You hear what it's done to the environment? To the groundwater?"

"I know some people aren't happy with it. Say it's causing earthquakes or something."

Gavin laughs bitterly. "It's doing a whole lot worse than that, let me tell you. It's the reason I quit. Or tried to: it's the only game in town anymore." He sounds disgusted with the business.

"Well, you're out of it now." Josh regrets the words as soon as they're out of his mouth.

It takes Gavin a moment to respond. "You know, I found a big deposit me very self. Years ago," he says finally. "Smack dab under an elementary school. Only I didn't know it was a school there, at first, you know. They just give you data and whatnot to work with, right? But I found out soon enough. Didn't tell a soul about it. Or about some other ones. Can't have 'em putting up a well in the middle of the playground, now, can we?"

The pause goes on and on, so Josh finally has to ask: "So, what happened?"

"They put up a well in the middle of the bloomin' playground! Four of them, all around. The school's still there. You can light the tap water on fire now. Kids have started twitching: some kind of nervous disorder."

"But you didn't tell them."

"No, I got canned. They found out anyway, of course. I guess I wasn't the only lackey they had working on that spot." Gavin takes a long pull from his pitcher, turns to face Josh for the first time; his bushy mustache is covered with strawberry slush. "I went and got myself wasted for three months after that. Don't remember half of it." He shakes his head and turns back to stare out at the night sky, now completely black. "Tried to work again after a while and got hired on a few times; but I'd work a few months then quit, go on a binge another few months. Whiskey, coke, speed, it didn't matter. Three months on, three months off … Word got around pretty quick, so I tried other places: Alabama, Georgia, North Dakota, Pennsylvania." He sighs. "But it didn't matter where I went. I couldn't escape *myself*, now, could I?"

"I can relate." Josh is sure Erin has told him that he, too, is a former addict and alcoholic. He knows she spoke to Gavin a lot this afternoon, put in a good word for him. "What finally got you to wise up, come here?"

Gavin clears his throat loudly and wipes his mustache on his sleeve. He sits thinking, petting Pooch, who lifts his head to lick Gavin's hand. At last, in a voice much softer than before, all the bravado absent from it now: "I want to die with dignity . . . I want a modicum of self-respect before I go . . . I want to be the man I used to know and love before hitting the bottle . . . if that's even possible anymore."

It's clear he's about to say more, when people begin streaming out of the kitchen behind them, chattering.

"It's almost ten o'clock," someone says cheerfully. "Time for the show to begin!"

The men exchange a look and a thin smile; they can pick up this conversation again later. Josh is looking forward to getting to know this guy. What he's doing is important, spiritually.

Erin pulls up a chair beside them. She immediately relieves Josh of his drink. "Aahh! Where was I when they were making these?" Honey gets up and puts her head in Erin's lap: mama's girl. "I know a few people have spiked theirs," she says. "I could smell it on their breath. None of ours, though," she's quick to add. "I made sure of that, believe me."

"I guess it's got to be expected," Josh says.

"Yeah, we had more of a problem with it last year. Lots of weed, too." She gives him a quick, guilty glance: besides an occasional beer or glass of wine, a joint once in a while is Erin's only other indulgence—research aside. "It's up to me to tell them not to bring it next time," she says. "These folks were new but should have known better. You just don't bring vodka to a rehab clinic! Sheesh!"

Gavin coughs into his fist. "Sorry," it sounds like.

"What's that?" Erin has to lean forward to better see him reclining on the other side.

Gavin raises his pitcher sheepishly. It's empty. "I had a wee bit myself."

Erin makes a noise but Gavin holds up a hand to stop her.

"I caught this young bugger out at the garage, with a bottle. And I told him in no uncertain terms that what he was doing was wrong, that he was a bloody fool for having it here." He gives them a mischievous smile. "And that if he didn't fill my glass, I'd report him at once."

Josh laughs. "You didn't!"

"Oh, I did, I did. Hell, it's my last day of freedom."

Erin just shakes her head. Josh can tell she's trying not to laugh. "Your *second* to last day," she says. "You don't go to sleep until the day after tomorrow."

"But tomorrow is tests and counseling and who knows what," Gavin growls. He upturns the pitcher over his mouth, tries to shake out the last miniscule drop before giving up, stares morosely at the emptiness of it in his hand. "This is an historic moment," he says thickly. "The Last Drink—no matter how puny it may have been, goddamn it." He raises the pitcher high, in toast. "May God help me!" he roars. "There will never be another!"

Erin raises her own glass to this as the first of the fireworks explode in the sky: a grand opening—red, white, and blue. The darkness sparkles before them.

Josh puts his hand on Gavin's shoulder. "Amen, brother," he says quietly. "Amen to that."

9

ERIN SITS CURLED UP on the couch, a pad of paper in her lap, her pen caught between her teeth. She stares at a point in space, lost in concentration. Even with two new patients paying their own way, she won't be able to repair the roof on the Big House this summer *and* meet their monthly obligations. But she hates the idea of putting it off till next year. Once again, it looks like she'll have to dip into her own savings, as meager as they are.

Then again, if she postpones replacing the plumbing in *her* place . . .

She hears the screen door open and shut, catches a glimpse of Josh walking past in the hallway, carrying the "tool box."

"He's still not eating," he calls out as he goes by.

A pointless act of defiance. *Let the asshole starve,* she thinks, surprised at how much she's let herself come to despise the man.

She can hear Josh in the kitchen, washing the empty trays.

Soon he's leaning in the doorway, taking a huge bite of a veggie burrito. He grins, chewing, a couple of alfalfa sprouts clinging to his beard. "He doesn't know what he's missing," he says through a mouthful of food. "This is good stuff."

Erin slaps the well-scribbled notepad onto the end table beside her; she's through worrying about finances for the evening. She can use a glass of wine but doesn't want to drink by herself in front of Josh. "I don't know what he's trying to prove," she says.

"That he doesn't need us. That he still calls the shots . . . It's about all he *can* do," Josh says. "Besides tear up books." He takes another bite and closes his eyes, obviously relishing the taste.

Erin believes he'll appreciate every bite of food he takes for the rest of his life. She remembers their first meal together—a salad bar in Fort Smith—and how Josh had cried, he was so happy, silent tears running down his face. Salads and fruit had been what he missed most in prison—besides women.

"Well, he *is* losing a lot of weight," she says. "That'll be good for him. But it's one hell of a diet plan. How many days has it been?"

"Just six. Don't worry, I've done more than that. And he's still drinking plenty of water. He's not trying to kill himself, or anything. His ego's too big for that. It would mean we won."

"I'm not worried. He'll come around eventually." Erin stretches and lays out fully on the couch, props herself up with the pillows. It's been another long day. "What's on the menu for tomorrow?"

Josh stuffs the last of the burrito into his mouth. He raises his eyebrows at her and holds up a finger—*Just you wait*—then heads back to the kitchen.

Since Josh arrived, the Center's meals have improved dramatically. He's become their resident head cook and dietician. Erin knows a lot of it has to do with their "special guests" and the effort that's gone into planning their stay, but she's still grateful for his expertise.

The menu varies, depending on the patients' whims and on what's at hand. Most everyone takes part in creating the meals, using the large, renovated kitchen in the Big House and sharing recipes. For the most part, it's a high-protein vegetarian diet, with chicken or fish served twice a week for those who want it. This is done as much for budgetary reasons as anything else. Rice and beans go a long way. And they're delicious with the right herbs and spices.

Two local co-op growers deliver bushels of vegetables and some fruit each week for a modest charge; and Erin hopes to have their own garden by next summer, as well. Josh has promised to put one in beside the Long House, or the "chicken coop" as it's come to be called now.

All things considered, they eat like royalty and she has no reason to complain—or to trim a single penny from the food budget, thank God.

The health benefits of such a diet are also evident. Her patients either lose or gain weight as their bodies require. Their skin clears up, their digestion improves, and many of the medical conditions they come in with virtually disappear within a couple of months. All thanks to a healthy, natural diet without processed foods or sugar. (Their weekly dessert doesn't count, thank goodness.) Over the past few years, Erin has even seen moderate cases of diabetes completely cured by the time her patients leave. The handful of medical doctors who volunteer their services for the pre- and post-physicals are always amazed at the progress they see in her patients, and she has to attribute much of it to the simple foods they eat.

Josh returns carrying two plates of his homemade cheesecake. Erin has to laugh: *So much for simple foods.*

She groans unconvincingly and rolls her eyes at him. "Donna's gonna kill me."

"I like you fat. You're jollier." He hands her a plate and fork and takes a seat on the floor, resting his back against the couch, near her feet.

She studies his profile: he looks well tonight, untroubled. "You sleeping okay?" she asks.

"Uh-huh." He takes a small bite and leans his head back on her leg, eyes closed, chewing slowly.

"Is the ketamine still helping you?" Josh had had nightmares and difficulty sleeping his first many months at the Center, dreaming he was still "inside." She'd given him the drug to knock him out for hours, and it worked.

"No, I haven't needed it for a while now. It's too powerful anyway: I can't remember where I've been . . . I've still got some, though." He raises his head and gives her a look. "Why? Do I look like I need more sleep, or something?"

"No, no, not at all. I guess I just like to worry about you, that's all; and I haven't had anything to worry about lately." She takes her first bite of the cheesecake; it melts in her mouth. "Oh my God, this is *sooo* good."

"Shall I make it every week?"

"No!" She's full-figured enough, especially for her size. Five-foot-nothin' leaves little room for expansion.

"Just one more, then, for your birthday," he says. "Boston cream pie."

"Aw, you remembered. You spoil me."

"You deserve to be spoiled. I promise it'll be better than the truck stop version."

"That was actually pretty damn good." It had been one of the happiest and most exciting nights of her life. Nearly a year ago, August 10. It marked the end of Josh's sojourn in the woods following the escape. He'd appeared at the truck stop looking like a mountain man under that scruffy beard and dark tan. It was her thirty-third birthday, and they had celebrated it and Josh's newfound freedom late into the night.

"How's Gavin doing?" Josh asks.

"Just fine, sleeping like a baby. It's his last day tomorrow. Dr. Waterhouse was up from Fayetville today and watched me do his second blood treatment. She about flipped. She'd always thought ozone was a poison or something bad. Sheesh! So I sent her home with some material by McCabe to read up on. It's like if it doesn't come out of the *New England Journal* it's not real medicine. I just don't understand their thinking; they're like sheep, or lemmings." She calms herself with a particularly large bite of cheesecake.

"It's safer to be a skeptic," Josh says.

"No kidding." Skepticism is something Erin is used to. Her treatment methods are unconventional, to say the least, so it comes with the territory. But a medically induced coma is nothing new; it's been around for decades. To apply the procedure to treating drug addiction seems like a no-brainer to her. So why is she facing so much resistance from the medical community? Especially when her results are so positive?

The concept is simple: Addicts become both mentally *and* physically dependent upon a drug; they go through the most horrible withdrawal symptoms without it. It's during the initial withdrawal phase, which usually lasts about two weeks or so, where a person trying to quit the drug is most likely to relapse, because the "need" is so great. It's this period where the pain—both physical and mental, both real and imagined—is the greatest. And it's the period where the most danger lies: Often an addict must be weaned off of a drug slowly or face serious health problems, like heart attack or seizure.

Placing an addict into a medically induced coma—the "Big Sleep" they call it at the Center ("coma" tends to freak people out)—and treating the person appropriately while in that state, removes the distress, the danger, and the likelihood of relapse. It essentially bypasses the withdrawal process.

Only recently, Erin has also been incorporating other therapies, such as blood filtration combined with UV and ozone treatments. By cleansing the circulatory system and hyper-oxygenating the bloodstream, she is able to more quickly heal and repair the body and reduce the time necessary for the entire process to ten days. Any shorter period than that just isn't possible, she feels.

Patients are far from cured of addiction after their long sleep, but they've certainly gotten through the worst of it. They now have more than a fighting chance. Erin does her best to see that every patient leaves Fresh Start addiction free following their twelve-week stay.

Counseling, of course, is a necessary part of the program, too. Addicts have often made a mess of their lives, for one thing; and their minds aren't used to thinking rationally, for another. Being clean and sober takes some getting used to. It's a big adjustment to make, especially when one suddenly wakes up and the cravings are simply gone.

Josh has suggested using headphones and "positive" recordings during the sleep period, to make use of the time and to help prepare them—program them, essentially—for their recovery. It's something she has to think about. It's a good idea.

The psychological aspects of recovery aren't her specialty. Thankfully, however, there's no shortage of caring students and local professionals who are more than happy to help.

Donna is one of them. If she could afford to, Erin would have Donna become a full-time counselor and Fresh Start's Director of Psychology.

Lately Erin's been considering the idea of partnering with her *personally* as well as professionally. But it's too soon, really, to be thinking about such a commitment.

Besides, there's Josh's project to consider; it isn't something she can share with her girlfriend, or with anyone else for that matter. It will have to be kept a secret indefinitely. Three years? More? She hopes it will end sooner than later.

Erin sighs, and Josh mistakes the reason:

"Don't worry," he says, "once everyone reads your next book, they'll *all* be jumping on board, saying how much they agreed with you all along. And then you'll be training *them* how to do it, too."

Erin does once again hope to revolutionize the field of addiction treatment with her published findings but has no illusions as to how realistic that hope is. "It's not that difficult," she says. "Anyone can do it. But look where the first book got me. How many chronic alcoholics today are being treated with LSD? None. Zippo. Unless they're treating themselves . . . Face it: it'll always be an illegal drug, and it'll always be near impossible to use or to even study anymore, no matter how much it may help people."

"But this is different," Josh says. "What you're doing now isn't illegal at all, by any stretch. It's just a new approach. And like you said: anyone can do it."

"But will they? That's the question. It's like your work with hypnosis. It's repeatedly been proven—*proven!*—to get the best therapeutic results in the shortest amount of time. But it's still too far-out for most people. They're scared of it, or something. All the Hollywood bullshit. Until it becomes mainstream, it's just another 'radical' method."

"And that's exactly why you've got to continue bringing what you're doing to the world's attention. For as long as it takes." Josh lifts another bite of cheesecake to his mouth as Erin watches enviously (she finished hers way too soon). "Just watch," he says, closing his eyes, losing himself in a moment of sugary ecstasy, "by the time you're a hundred and two, the Big Sleep will be as commonplace as hair-of-the-dog for a hangover."

"Whatever," she says, sneaking the last small piece off his plate with her fingers. "Just so long as I get all the credit."

ERIN STACKS THE FOUR blue, plastic trays left to dry and places them out of sight in the "tool box" for morning. Making up and carrying the full trays directly from the Big House to the Shed would bring undue attention to the building, so food is brought from the main kitchen to her house, where the trays are prepared. This is Josh's job each day, as is anything else having to do with his project.

Erin's done her part. She'd arranged delivery of the storage containers and the rest during the first months of preparation. She played her role in each person's capture, at considerable risk to herself. And, with Josh's help, she had subjected each of his guests to the Big Sleep, moving the necessary equipment temporarily. Now it's out of her hands. It's not her responsibility. She has plenty enough to do just to keep the Center going.

Erin takes her glass of wine back to the couch, where she left her notepad. Without sitting, she stares glumly at the figures written there. The property tax is due in September, just over a month away. How could she have forgotten? It's always something else. She'll have to file for an extension, and in the meantime find the money somewhere.

Having the old sawmill land donated to the cause was a real blessing; it had made her dream possible, after all. But the costs to renovate the property and buildings have put her greatly in debt. And unless she can refinance the loans, it may be insurmountable.

With a shake of her head, Erin turns out the lamp. She considers treating herself to a bubble bath, letting her worries go down the drain, but decides to cuddle up with a good book instead.

On the way to her bedroom, she pauses in the hallway before a series of drawings she had framed years ago, sometime after meeting Josh. He'd sent them to her from prison: detailed sketches of defining scenes from past lives they have shared. Now, as always, looking at the pictures brings up vivid images as clear as anything from *this* lifetime.

In the first, they are children, no more than six or seven. They're fleeing a fire, a raid from a neighboring clan. Their entire village is destroyed, their families killed. They had been relative strangers until that moment but now must rely on each other to survive in a brutally dangerous world. It's somewhere in what is now northern Europe; the year unknown, maybe 1500 B.C. They didn't fare so well then, she recalls.

The second picture shows a happily married couple in their old age, which for that period—about 350 B.C.—was probably around fifty, given the hardships they faced. In that lifetime, she was the *he* and had been badly crippled at the quarry where he worked. Josh, as the wife, had taken on the responsibilities for keeping them alive. Life was a constant struggle for the both of them. But they had each other and that was all that mattered. This was somewhere in the area of southern France today.

Of course, all the pictures—all the memories—are special to her, but it's the fifth one she enjoys remembering the most. In it they are both men—powerful men—captains of their own trading vessels plying the eastern Mediterranean, or simply the "Sea" as it was known then. They'd been based out of Alexandria, Egypt. They were rivals, driving each other to always work harder and smarter each year. There was a grudging respect between them. Then, in the year 1169, Josh had been captured by Cyprian pirates and held for a ransom that could not be met. Risking his life and that of his own crew, Erin boldly rescued him, getting injured in the process. But rather than become pals, they continued their adversarial, yet venerable, relationship for the remainder of their lengthy careers. An exciting and satisfying life, indeed!

There are eight framed sketches on the wall, but Erin knows there are countless other lifetimes they've shared, both here on Earth and elsewhere. She and Josh are part of the same spirit family. They're soulmates.

It had taken some persuasion on Josh's part to finally convince her to undergo hypnosis and explore her past lives. As an academic and a scientist, she had automatically assumed such a thing was ridiculous, poppycock, just some far-out New Age idea. Bullshit, basically. After all, if there was any truth to it, she would have learned about it in school, right? But she finally relented and paid a visit to a hypnotherapist Josh had recommended, in Springfield, just over the border, in Missouri. And over the next many months, she underwent a number of sessions with a number of different practitioners. All with identical results.

And what Erin experienced changed her life forever. It caused her to alter her perception of reality, to reconsider everything she thought she knew about science, about human existence, about life in general.

Before, she had been so sure in her beliefs. But afterward . . .

She realized she had never really given the concept of re-incarnation any serious thought at all: it would have been like pondering the existence of the Tooth Fairy—a pointless exercise. But once she knew—once she had *experienced* the truth for her-self—it opened the doors to whole new levels of understanding. *So this is what they mean by "karma"!* she would suddenly realize; or, *So that is the relationship between evolution and intelligent design! Amazing!* She found herself contemplating ideas she never would have previously. And the revelations came quickly, building upon one another.

With this new awareness had come new responsibility as well. She now saw her life from a "higher" perspective. She wasn't simply Erin Pearse, the human being, solely looking out for her-self, anymore. She was an eternal, spiritual being and part of the greater Whole, with a connection to every other person, or soul.

It was this realization that had been the catalyst for Fresh Start. Her previous research into psychopharmacology and treat-ing addiction had introduced her to a legion of lost souls, each one needing help in this life—"salvation," so to speak. Her mis-sion was now clear.

But what became even more apparent was her connection and responsibility to Josh—or, more correctly, to the fellow spiritual entity she now knew as Josh. They had been there for each other throughout countless lifetimes, and this one would be no excep-tion. She would do whatever she could to help him, no matter what it took. It was her spiritual duty.

Hence her present dilemma: She is harboring a known fugi-tive; she has helped him kidnap four people and is now holding them captive on her own property; she risks prison and destroy-ing everything she has worked so hard for. Compared to this, her financial troubles are nothing.

If only I'd never responded to his first letter . . .

Erin has had this thought many times before, but she can't say she regrets knowing him. Quite the contrary: meeting Josh was the beginning of what has now become an eight-year journey of self-discovery and enlightenment. She wouldn't be where she's at today if not for his influence. He's already inspired her to accomplish a dream with Fresh Start. The very least she can do is see him through this project of his which means so much to him, despite her misgivings about it.

From her bedroom window, Erin can see the light on at the Shed, flickering, a quarter of a mile away through the trees. She knows Josh prefers to be alone out there, that as much as he enjoys the company of good people, his years alone in a cell have conditioned him to solitude.

It's all the more conducive to his yoga and meditation practice, too, she supposes. She's watched him from a distance as he meditates in a small clearing near the meadow. She once came back *hours* later to find him in the same position, eyes closed, slightly smiling, sitting there like a statue.

Josh has become known as something of a "guru" among her patients. A number of mystical qualities have been attributed to him, and she knows a few aren't far off the mark. Like his ability to "speak" with the dogs. It always amazes her when all he has to do is *look* at them and they come or go or do exactly what it was he had in mind. Or how he often seems to appear out of nowhere, at just the right moment, to say or do exactly what's needed at the time—and then he's gone again, just as quickly. It's uncanny, she has to admit.

But most astounding to Erin by far is Josh's ability to leave his physical body, which she knows he does on a regular basis.

She's tested him on this once—and only once: She suggested he look in on her that evening at nine o'clock, and then the next day report on what she'd been doing. Her plan was to begin stripping the paint from all the old doors in her house, only she ended up going to Donna's place that evening, unexpectedly. Still, the following day, Josh was able to describe (with a roguish smile, she recalls) *exactly* what she had been up to at the time, including a detailed description of Donna's apartment, where Erin knows for a fact he's never been. How could he do that without actually being there? And how had he found her? She'd told no one but that night's interns where she was going.

Now she doesn't doubt for one second when Josh describes some of his more fantastical-sounding out-of-body experiences.

It's in a similar way, he told her, that he's able to view his previous lives on Earth. He'd discovered their connection this way, although this hadn't occurred until *after* he first wrote to her, months before. Finding her own obscure book in a stack of many donated to the prison, they both feel, is a perfect example of serendipity—of cosmic forces at work in their lives.

Erin climbs into bed. She picks up her latest book, *The Biology of Belief,* but soon has to set it aside. The wine has softened the edges of her worried mind, and the pull of sleep tugs at her gently, coaxing her into its world of dreams. Her last thoughts of the day are still of her friend—his handsome, bearded face smiling warmly at her, his eyes radiating peace and love.

Perhaps he's actually projecting himself here right now, to say Good night. The thought comforts her.

It's true: Josh *is* on another level. But for the most part, she thinks, he simply exudes the aura of a gentle monk, and that is what most endears him to her patients. He's so easygoing; he always has a smile and a kind word; he listens rather than talks; and it's obvious he's sincere in wanting to help people, however he can.

And he *is* helping. For those who want to try hypnosis as a way to reduce their psychological dependency on drugs and alcohol, or to improve their lives in any way, he's there for them. And from what Erin has seen and heard for herself, he's doing a remarkable job. Then for those who want to experience a *spiritual* hypnosis session, Josh is more than happy to oblige them, of course. She appreciates that he doesn't preach about what he believes (or *knows,* actually, as she does, too, now) or pressure people into these sessions; he just lets them know he's available if they're interested. And quite a few are, it seems.

Plus, Josh is a great help in working around the Center. It's like having her own handyman on call twenty-four/seven. Then of course there's the cooking and the cleaning and the foot rubs . . .

It's simply a blessing to have him around.

Why, then, can't she shake the feeling that Josh is such a danger to her? And not just because he's an escaped convict. Erin knows his prison experience has left him unstable in some ways; she knows he has the potential for violence (she's seen him in action); but she also knows he would never hurt her intentionally. It's something more intangible, more unearthly, she is afraid of.

What Josh is doing, he says, will put an end to his continuous cycle of death and rebirth. It will change the lives of everyone involved, including her own. Now and into the future. For all eternity.

He's playing God, it seems to her. He's toying with the Universal Laws that govern the destiny of souls.

And perhaps what scares her most, Erin thinks as she drifts off to sleep, is that she knows he'll succeed.

10

HER WHITE SHIFT BILLOWS around her waist, so she presses it down so it clings instead. She's nervous. And excited. Happy to have finally found her home, her people: true Christians.

The Reverend places a hand to her forehead, the other to the small of her back, gently pushes her backward. The water is cool and she holds her breath as it washes over her completely, as it washes away her sins, her old self. Born again . . .

Gloria blinks as the light comes on overhead. As usual, she'd slept fitfully off-and-on all night.

Her breakfast—the first of the two meals served during the day—will arrive in exactly two hours. She's counted the seconds and minutes and hours enough times to know the schedule never varies. She is fed every twelve hours, as the innumerable soap marks on the walls can attest. Soon a sturdy, blue, plastic tray will be slid through the slot at the foot of the doors. Her last meal will be delivered two hours before the lights go out for the night.

No words are said by her captor. None. Never. Not once this entire time. Gloria has pleaded with him, screamed at him, to release her, to at least tell her why she's here.

But she already knows; that old newspaper article made it clear enough: Revenge. Apparently Rostam feels she is somehow responsible for his murder conviction. The predictable conclusion of a deranged mind.

Gloria has gone over the case endlessly in her memory, and she can't see how she could have done anything differently. Rostam had been a court-appointed case for her. For all the money he stole, he supposedly couldn't afford his own attorney. Or at least the authorities couldn't find the money. It was a ploy, of course; he had millions stashed away somewhere. Navarro's death had landed him at least that much; and the crime was certainly not his first like it. The only reason he'd been caught this time was because of an informant: someone had seen him dump the body.

Rostam claimed he was innocent, of course. They all do. He'd been framed, he said; and he had proof: records, witnesses, an alibi. If so, where were they? Rostam's case had been headline news, so why didn't any of his so-called witnesses step forward? Did he expect her to go wasting her time on a wild goose chase to track them down? Did he expect her to fabricate evidence? No doubt.

It's always like this, Gloria thinks. These sociopathic criminals never want to face responsibility for their actions. It's far better for their inflated egos to blame their defense attorney, the prosecutor, the judge, the D.A., the cops, the victims, society. Never can they admit their own guilt, not even to themselves.

The two times she met with Rostam prior to trial, he'd been arrogant and demanding. Why hadn't she done this, why hadn't she done that, why didn't she return his calls and letters? She tried in vain to convince him to confess, to come clean, that it would go so much easier for him if he did so; and he'd gone into a rage. She was afraid to be alone with him after that.

At the trial, at Gloria's insistence, in fear for her safety, Rostam had been forced to wear handcuffs. He eventually had to wear a gag, as he would not stay quiet. He railed against the "injustice" and the "lies" and the "conspiracy" between her and the D.A.'s office. As if *they* were the ones who had committed such a heinous crime. In the end, he was such a distraction to the jury that he had to be removed from the courtroom. Hours later, he was read their verdict in a holding cell.

However, the following day, she remembers, during his sentencing hearing, Rostam had been quiet and withdrawn, never once even looking at her, or at anyone else for that matter. He seemed contrite, apologetic, but she knew it was a ruse. He realized he was beaten and would now have to pay for his evil deeds, so he played humble and meek, repentant, trying to sway the jury into sparing him the death penalty.

And it worked, obviously. Unfortunately. Rostam should have been killed a long time ago, Gloria thinks.

Her current predicament testifies to what an evil creature he is. It's not enough to physically torture her, as she first expected him to do; it's apparent he's more diabolical than that. Instead, he plans to brainwash her, corrupt her mind—drive her insane.

As an agent of Satan himself, it's clear he intends to turn her away from her Lord and Savior, Jesus Christ. Gloria knows her soul is the very prize Rostam seeks. This is her greatest test. She must stay vigilant.

Dear God, have mercy on me, a sinner, and deliver me from this evil.

She prays constantly for the strength and courage to withstand the trials and tribulations sure to come. If she must, she's prepared to die for her faith.

But for the sake of her family, if not for herself, Gloria is playing along with Rostam's game. For now. She knows she must do whatever it takes to appease him if she is to have any hope of being released some day. And she must hold on to this belief that release is possible. If this means reading his stupid books and pretending to be swayed by them, then that's what she will do.

The books come once a month.

The first, *Mastering Your Hidden Self,* had been in the room when she arrived, when she'd finally woken from whatever drugged sleep Rostam had put her through for however long.

She hadn't touched it for days, but curiosity and boredom finally got the better of her, and she read the book nonstop in one sitting. Then, sure that Rostam would be testing her on the material, she had read it again, more slowly. Three times in all.

It was interesting, Gloria has to admit. Different. There were some good ideas in there, like tips about quieting the mind. Don't focus on any one thought, the book said, but let each one go, like a cloud on the wind—acknowledge it and just let it go. She likes that analogy, the peaceful image it takes on for her when she tries it. But it's impossible to keep up for very long. How can she meditate when she is so full of fear, of worry? As much as she strives sometimes to practice what the book preaches, she can't help but dwell on her current predicament. Try as she might, her constant terrors won't turn into fleeting clouds.

Fortunately, there hadn't been any tests after that first week, or the first month, or still. But she's determined to be ready—even now if it means faking it.

The seventh book arrived eighteen days ago. And whatever suspicions Gloria has had about Rostam's agenda are a certainty now: he wants to convert her to his religion.

She can't fathom his reasons for doing so, but then trying to understand a sick and twisted mind is a pointless exercise, she knows. And she's not even sure what his religion is, just yet. The books he's given her have covered everything from Hawaiian mysticism to Zen Buddhism to Hindu Yoga to New Age philosophy. There's no consistency to it, no theme, and certainly no dogma. It's a free-for-all of beliefs and ideas. Spiritual anarchy.

None of the books have appealed to her, but this month's has really put her on edge. She hasn't been able to stomach it at all; it's simply too much to take. She could hardly get past the introduction.

Gloria has never heard of such a thing: "past-life regression." She knows that people from some eastern religions mistakenly believe in reincarnation—that they've lived before as other people, or animals, or whatever—but this book purports that *everyone* can recall their past lives. Through hypnosis.

It's ridiculous! she thinks. It would be laughable if it wasn't such a dangerous belief system. To believe that one lives again and again is to refute the teachings of the Bible.

Some of the previous books had mentioned reincarnation, but in an abstract way. They were basically harmless, simply too outlandish to be believed. Even the one about children remembering their previous lives could be written off to fantasy or imagination—children say a lot of things. And they lie, just like everyone else.

This latest book, however, is serious trouble: it has the power to corrupt people's minds. It's apparently written by a prominent doctor of psychiatry, for one thing, which is sure to sway many gullible readers. The "evidence" he claims is startling but has obviously been manufactured to suit his agenda. Like most pseudo-scientific assertions and theories, it is based entirely on obfuscation and deceit. To say that each and every one of us has lived before in another body and will do so again is a downright lie! It's sacrilegious!

Gloria refuses to waste another moment of her time on such nonsense.

But now, at least, she knows one thing: Rostam's religion promotes the belief in reincarnation, which is anathema to her own.

According to Christianity, man is given only one life before he is called to be judged by God. That is what she was taught and it's what she believes. It's what she teaches the children in her Sunday Bible School classes. At the Rapture (which could happen any day!), when Jesus Christ returns to take up his rightful position as King of kings and Lord of lords, every single believer in Him, whether dead or alive, will enjoy eternal life by His side. Those who don't believe in salvation through the Blood of Jesus Christ face eternal death. It's as simple as that. For the Bible tells her so.

And the Bible mentions nothing about reincarnation. If it did, she would know. That's one book she knows backwards and forwards, as well as it *can* be known.

More than anything else, Gloria wishes she had her Bible with her to read now, instead of this heretical trash Rostam keeps foisting upon her. She can only imagine what titles will be next in the months to come.

Months! The very thought terrifies her. It would depress her if she let it.

True, she has spent entire days in her bunk, wallowing in self pity, and she has to sometimes force herself to get out of bed; but all it takes are the images of her kids' faces to keep her going. She has to get through this for *their* sake.

Finished with her morning ablutions, Gloria stands before the "mirror," the thin piece of polished metal bolted to the wall above the sink.

Her hair has grown out considerably since the beginning of this ordeal. It was the first time in her life she'd ever been bald. Even as a newborn baby, she was told, she had a fine head of hair. Only now it's a matted mess. She has no comb to tease it or untangle it with, nor any means to cut it. Though she can wash it as often as she'd like in the sink. Lately she's resorted to simply wetting it and plastering it back away from her face. Still, no matter how careful she tries to be, her hair is becoming full of dreadlocks.

It's perfectly natural, she tells herself. But the thought of looking like a pot-smoking hippie or Rastafarian makes her cringe. So she avoids the mirror as much as possible these days. Out of sight, out of mind.

However, besides her hair, Gloria is pleased with the overall changes in her appearance. She's lost a lot of weight in the past months. She can really see the difference in her face: her features are more pronounced; her eyes appear larger, more lively, as they were in her twenties. She's lost inches from her waist. Where the elastic in her "prison issue" sweatpants had been much too tight, now she wishes for a way to take up the slack.

Dwayne won't believe his eyes!

Tears come at the thought she may never see her husband or children again. They are the only things besides the Church that mean anything to her, that she's proud of in her life. She may not have been the best attorney, she may not have worked hard enough for her clients, but she has always been the best mother those kids could ever have.

Lord knows there are too few examples of decent parents these days. Although Gloria herself has raised her children right: to respect their elders, love the Church, and get a college education. Neither Michaela nor Gabriel has ever done drugs, and they never will. They don't aspire to run with any gangs or other bad characters. And there's no way they'll turn out like so many of the young hoodlums she sees traipsing through the courtroom. No sir, not if *she* can help it.

Oh, my babies! Gloria falls to her knees and cries, leaning her arm on the metal toilet. Without her, they're lost, she knows. They're at that impressionable age where peer pressure has the most influence, and without her guidance and steady hand to steer them straight, they'll soon be acting up and getting into all sorts of trouble. It isn't their fault, of course—she's taught them the difference between right and wrong; they know better. But their fellow classmates, dressed like so many gangsters and prostitutes, are animals; they're sure to sense "fresh meat" and the chance to corrupt her innocent children in her absence.

Lord knows Dwayne isn't any help. He hasn't been a worthy role model, let alone parent, since the accident. Just the opposite. She'd tried to keep the drinking and the pills hidden from the kids, but anyone can see he's wasted half the time. And not being able to work is no excuse; there are still plenty of things he can do. He can become a deacon in the Church. He can be there for his children. There's more to a man's life—his worth—than just *work*, for God's sake. She'd done her best to try to talk to him about it, but it's obvious he doesn't give a damn anymore. Dwayne cares more about those damn pills now than his own family.

Gloria can't bear to think how they must be struggling to get along without her, without her income to put food on the table, pay the bills. Dwayne's disability checks can only go so far.

Almost seven months! Does she still have a house? Has the Church taken them in? Has the State intervened and put the kids in a home somewhere? These depressing thoughts make her weep all the harder.

There have been few days since her kidnapping when Gloria hasn't cried like this. She realizes it's a weakness, that it shows her lack of faith in Christ and her lack of trust in God's plan. But every day she bemoans her fate and runs through the myriad possibilities that could affect her and her children.

If only she could know when she is going to be released—if she is *ever* going to be released. And what is expected of her? This not knowing is the hardest part.

Gloria knows she should sleep. It's only then she doesn't worry or despair, when she's not afraid. In her dreams she is free. But sleep comes hard for her, and only in short increments.

By now Gloria realizes it's fruitless, but she *has* to be awake when Rostam comes to feed her. Or when he finally comes to get her, to release her. She has to let him know she's been reading the books, that she's doing what he wants her to do. And she has to know he's still there and hasn't left her to die, to starve to death.

What if something happens to him? she often worries. The thought terrifies her. As much as she prays for God to strike him down, to banish him to the fires of Hell, Gloria also says a little prayer of thanks twice each day when Rostam silently comes to her door.

If that's even who it is. She has no real way of knowing. But who else could it be? Someone he's paid with his ill-gotten gains to destroy her life? No, it has to be him. It's the most obvious answer; it's the only thing that makes any sense. Why else would that newspaper article have been left here for her to find?

Gloria had heard of Rostam's escape when it happened, of course, but hadn't worried too much about it. Most likely he would be caught right away, she figured. And he certainly had no reason to hold a grudge against her. Or so she believed.

She once received a letter from Rostam six or seven years after his trial—the only time she'd heard from him again. He forgave her, he said. As if *she* was the one needing forgiveness!

Gloria had screamed at him months ago through the steel doors, "Is *this* how you show forgiveness?"

She has been relentless in trying to elicit a response. And lately she's changed tactics: She thanks him profusely now for the meals, for the books, for the bars of soap, the toilet paper, the tampons. She says "God bless you" and tells him she's praying for him. Yesterday she had even told him "*Namasté*" as it says in one of the books he's given her. If Rostam wants her to switch to his religion before letting her go, then that's what she'll have him believe she is doing.

Apparently his religion does believe in a god, just not the *real* God. According to what Gloria has read so far, his god has no laws, no morals; people can do whatever they want because there's no judgment in Heaven, no punishment—no Hell.

She doesn't understand how such a belief system could be conceived; it invites lawlessness, chaos. Unless, of course, it's simply a way for some people to justify their abhorrent behavior. If God is only love, as it seems these books are saying, then people can do whatever they want without repercussion. Until the *next* life, that is. Instead of a conscience, a moral compass, they have "karma," some kind of cosmic rule of "cause and effect" that affects them when they reincarnate. So they don't have to worry about their behavior in *this* lifetime at all. It's outrageous! It's hedonism in the guise of religion: exactly what a criminal mind like Rostam's would be attracted to.

But Gloria will do whatever it takes to win his trust, even if that means pledging her allegiance to whatever pagan cult and "gurus" Rostam follows. She knows God will understand; He knows where her heart *really* lies, and that's all that matters.

Right? . . .

Or would she be making a mistake somehow? Perhaps, instead, she's meant to demonstrate her faith, to *prove* her devotion to Jesus. After all, aren't all of God's chosen servants tested like this in some way?

Gloria wipes her eyes and picks herself up off the floor. She looks once again in the mirror, does her best to put on a courageous and determined face.

She needs to pray for guidance.

She folds her blanket and places it on the floor, beside the bed. She kneels, leans forward on her elbows, bows her head.

Dear Lord, please help me. Please help me . . . Oh, Lord, why have you forsaken me? . . .

But further words fail her. She's cried herself out; she's exhausted; it's just too much for her to think anymore. Her mind is a blank.

After some time of kneeling like this in silence, Gloria sits back on her heels, lays her head to the side, her eyes closed, her breath softly stirring the hairs on her arm. There is nothing else. Any thoughts are simply gone.

There's no telling how long it's been when she feels the change: She's suddenly filled with an indescribable feeling of peace and tranquility. She feels protected, watched over, safe and secure, as if she is being held gently in the loving hands of God . . . Then a warmth flows through her and she is engulfed in *fire*—in a light more brilliant, more colorful, more blazing than the sun.

All is well . . . Everything is going to be all right . . . Everything is for a reason . . . You are not alone . . . Be at peace . . . The message is as much in words as a *feeling* in her mind.

Gloria knows she is in the presence of Christ himself.

Then, just as quickly as it came, the light, the sensation, is gone.

Gloria lifts her head and looks about her. "Jesus?"

He had been there with her, she's certain. He had come to give her hope. He has never forsaken her.

She gasps at the realization and begins sobbing anew, this time for sheer joy.

Thank you, Jesus! Oh, thank you, *Jesus!*

Gloria turns and sits on the folded blanket, brings her knees to her chest, cradles them in her arms. She closes her eyes, trying hard to recall the feeling of the Holy Spirit as it had descended upon her.

Never in her life has she felt—ever experienced—such *Love* before. For a brief, unforgettable moment she had known what it was like to be truly cherished and loved unconditionally as a child of God.

She relishes the memory; and after a time, Gloria becomes aware that she is singing.

11

BLITHELY NAKED, HEALTHY, still reveling in her newfound freedom from addiction, Dani stretches for the upper corner of her cell. Soapy water trails down her arm. She's just able to reach the near invisible spider web hanging there; no sign of the little critter that made it—must have scared him off.

The walls and floor are shiny wet. A newly laundered sheet hangs across the empty shelf, and wet clothes hang to dry off each corner. The warm air circulating between the vent and the slot in the door will have everything dry in no time.

It's "Book Day" and one Dani likes to celebrate each month with a little spring cleaning. Today, however, she's gotten off to a late start. Usually she'll wait until the cleaning is done, letting the anticipation build, before ever opening a new book; but the title and cover of the one that arrived this morning—the eighth so far—was too intriguing to put aside for later: *Journey of Souls,* by Michael Newton. Such a warm and wise face the author has in his photo, like the father she always wished for. She'd read the first four chapters without stopping, unable to put the book down. Now she's looking forward to picking it up again soon.

This subject of reincarnation fascinates her. She had never given it much thought before. As far as she knew, you got this one shot at life, for no particular reason, and then you died. That was it. End of story. But from what she's learned so far, there *is* a meaning to life, and we go through a *lot* of them. Apparently this is common knowledge to some people.

Dani loves the idea that her physical body is really a "vehicle" for a spiritual being to experience life—that *she* is actually a spiritual being, who wears her body like a set of clothes for this lifetime. When her physical body dies, she simply discards her "clothes" and goes home. And then she comes back, but only if she wants to. To learn and grow, by experiencing stuff. That's the whole point: to learn and to grow.

At least that's what the books all say.

Dani had never been much of a reader before this, but she finds she enjoys it a lot. Of course, being high or wasted the majority of the time before didn't help matters any. And besides, the TV was always there and easier, anyway.

Amanda was always reading, Dani remembers. Romances and thrillers. She liked the adventure, she said, the fantasy—to lose herself, to escape her own life for a while.

Dani had chosen the more popular escape: the needle.

She has no idea why she hasn't gone through any withdrawals since she woke up here. But she does know she was "out" for a long time before waking up. She'd lost some weight, and that doesn't happen overnight. Even her breasts had been a little smaller, despite the implants.

Now, though, she's back to size and a little heavier than she's been in many years. It looks good on her. Even the hair is looking nice, now that it's grown back; she hadn't seen its real color in ages. She only wishes for a brush and a full-length mirror to take it all in. *Ah, vanity;* she knows it's a sin; but when you've got it, you've got it. It's just a shame there's nobody else but her to appreciate it.

Maybe Josh will pay her a visit soon, Dani thinks, who knows? She's pretty certain it's him who abducted her. Besides the newspaper clipping, she has a sort of "sixth sense" about it, like she can almost see him in her mind sometimes, behind the doors. Plus, there were those *eyes* that john had: she can now vaguely remember them belonging to Josh from way back. The beard had thrown her off. Not to mention that he was supposed to be in prison—for, like, forever.

She has no clue how he got out, but he sure as hell did apparently. It's incredible. And kinda scary.

When Dani first saw that article—"Navarro's Killer Gets Life"—here in this tiny room, she was so afraid. She thought for sure Josh was going to kill her. Or rape her. Or rape her, then kill her. Or sell her into slavery or something, like when she was little. For days she couldn't stop thinking of all the terrible things he would probably do to her.

After all, Dani had thought at the time, she deserved it.

What Santos did to him—what she *helped* do to him—was horrible. Josh had done his job and done it well. And he never suspected a thing. She still doesn't know why it went down like it did. Santos wasn't about to explain himself to her, a mere pawn in his grand scheme. Maybe he didn't want to pay Josh, once it was done. Maybe he didn't want any loose ends. But, then, why not just kill him, like he did Navarro?

But it doesn't matter what she thinks now. She's as guilty as Santos is, really. She's the one who sold the scam to Josh in the first place, made him fall all over himself to do it for her. Shit, he would have done it for *free,* she'd been that good.

Dani had actually enjoyed the time they spent together—getting high, having sex, getting high again, while he did his work. And Josh was pretty cute, too, for a geek; and that had made her job all the easier.

How many days had it been? She tries to remember but they all just run together in her memory. No more than a week, she figures; enough time for Navarro's accounts to get emptied, the stocks or whatever to sell, and the money transferred offshore. She knew that much, at least; Josh had explained it to her. It hadn't taken a whole lot of computer time, she recalls, mostly just days of waiting. And shooting up and screwing.

The thought of doing either right now is making her wet. Dani isn't sick, her body isn't craving a hit, physically, but she would love one just the same. Old habits die hard. She can't recall ever *not* being on dope. Since she was thirteen, at least. Since the Syndicate found her and put her to work. Twenty-two years ago.

My God, that's a long time!

What Dani remembers most vividly of her time with Josh is a feeling she had. It had felt so good—so empowering—to be the one with the dope for a change, the one in control. Part of the deal was that Santos would provide everything: the laptop, the hotel, the food, the drinks, the dope, and of course, *her.* She has always had the power of the pussy over men, but then—for that one short time with Josh—she had something even greater: something he wanted even more. He was broke, and needy. And she made him beg for it. Just like she had been forced to do by so many men, so many times before. He'd thanked her profusely each time.

Now, as reluctant and ashamed as she might be about facing Josh again, Dani wants to thank *him* this time.

She is sure he means her no harm. The many life-changing books he's been giving her attest to that. Not to mention the food: so delicious and healthy and made with such obvious care each day. There's even a dessert once a week. No, if Josh intended to hurt her for what she did to him thirteen years ago, he would have done so by now.

Lately Dani's beginning to think he may even be trying to save her: from pimps like Barry, from the dope—from herself.

Josh won't talk to her yet. She's long stopped trying to get a reaction from him. But she knows eventually the day will come when they'll meet again. And then she can apologize to him properly—thank him for changing her life for the better (even if it is a bit cramped and lonely at the moment).

Then he'd better fucking let me go.

Dani laughs to herself, realizing what a novelty that cuss word has become. Before, she wouldn't even have noticed it; she and everybody else she knew cussed like sailors—or at least like hookers, dealers, and pimps. It wasn't anything to use three or four cuss words in a sentence; you just didn't think about it. And it really wasn't anything bad—unless you meant it, of course.

But she knows differently now. One of the many things Dani has gotten from her reading these past many months is that thoughts are actual *things*. Important things. They create the world. Everything—*everything*—first began as a thought, she's learned. Including words. Words are thoughts made physical, so to speak, and are just as powerful in shaping a person's life.

Thoughts are important. What a simple concept. Dani almost feels stupid not to have realized it before, not to have given it any—*thought*. So now she pays attention to what she's thinking about all the time, especially the constant background stuff, the "dialogue" she seems to always be having with herself.

And the thoughts never stop.

Besides thinking about what she's been reading lately, Dani mostly thinks about her past. And unfortunately, most of these thoughts aren't so good. Or at least the memories aren't. She's trying not to let them get her down. She's been making a real effort to make her thoughts in the present as good as possible: if not positive, then at least neutral—anything but negative. And it does take effort sometimes. She can only imagine how hard it will be to do once she's out in the world again.

Dani has learned so much from her new books. She considers them her friends. They "speak" to her; and sometimes she'll even talk back, commenting on something she's just read. What she particularly likes about her books is that they accept her as she is; they don't care if she struggles over some of the words, or if she can't read very fast yet. They just want to be read and enjoyed. She's been through a few of them twice.

Right now they're all on her mattress, wrapped protectively in the blanket, away from the excess humidity in the air on cleaning day. But since the walls and floor are nearly dry now, and the laundry almost there, Dani decides to uncover her friends a little early.

She sits cross-legged on the bunk and arranges them in chronological order, from the first she received to the most recent, fanning them out before her in a colorful array of knowledge. Each one is special in its own way. Each one has been her favorite from all the ones before, and today's is no exception.

She goes leisurely through each one in turn, stopping at the dog-eared pages that mark special sections. She wishes she had a pen to make notes, or even a notebook to record her thoughts.

Mastering Your Hidden Self had been the first. Dani didn't know what to make of it at the time. It was the only thing in her little room that really stood out, besides the newspaper clipping. She didn't touch the book for at least a week, too afraid of her new situation, her new surroundings, too unsure of her fate. But when she finally opened it and began reading, it was as if she'd been transported: the metal walls around her and her frightening predicament just disappeared . . . for a short time, at least. And then for longer and longer periods as she was able to concentrate more and give herself over to the book for hours on end. It became her refuge. And she read the whole thing before the next one came.

What she learned had been so profound to her then, Dani remembers. But it was just a stepping stone for what was to come:

Conversations With God
The Power of Now
Autobiography of a Yogi
The Seat of the Soul

Each book expanded upon the one before, exploring spirituality and what it's really about, and how we can *experience* it for ourselves.

Dani had no idea before, none at all. And in her ignorance, she'd never cared.

Now her life will never be the same.

The first five books were real eye-openers, but the next two had totally blown her mind. Both were about reincarnation: the continuous cycle of birth, death, and rebirth. It's her favorite subject now. *Life Before Life* covered over forty years of research into children's memories of previous lives. *Same Soul, Many Bodies* discussed reincarnation through the lens of hypnosis, or past-life regression.

Dani's intrigued. She wants to someday explore her own past lives. She has no doubt it's real. The last book included a lot of word-for-word excerpts from recorded past-life sessions; and it's obvious the people aren't faking: you can't make that stuff up—not like that. Plus, Dani can't see any reason why the authors—both such well-respected doctors—would want to lie to their readers. What would be the point? It's plain to see they just want to help people by spreading knowledge and improving people's lives.

Now today's book, *Journey of Souls,* promises to be the best one yet. Instead of previous lives, it talks about *between* lives—how people remember it during super-deep hypnosis. The author has, like, thirty years experience doing it. He says that, regardless of a person's religion or culture or beliefs, everybody—every single person, no exceptions—reports *exactly* the same things, the same "steps," in the spirit world before coming back to Earth.

It's amazing! And this book has a lot of transcript sections, too, which she likes the best.

She finds the place where she stopped reading earlier. She can't wait to start again soon. She'll read this one a few times at least, for sure.

Dani stacks her cherished books together, admires the irregular rainbow their spines make, hefts their considerable weight.

Time to go back on the shelf . . . Except for you, new guy.

Dani gets up to check on the laundry. Everything is bone dry. She has no idea how long she spent sitting there. As usual, the space around her just disappeared when she's reading, focused inwardly but not on herself—on a journey—exploring limitless possibilities in a world so much greater than she could have ever imagined.

She stops in the center of the room, stands quietly with her eyes closed, "listening" with her mind . . .

Wow, the time has really flown by: Josh is coming with her last meal of the day.

How she knows this with such certainty, Dani can't explain. It started happening sporadically about four months ago. Now it's constant and it never fails. It's just a sense, a knowing, nothing more. She's pretty sure it has something to do with the intense "flying" dreams she's been having since then, too. In them she is awake as she is now—more so, even, if that makes any sense.

There he is. Outside the door comes the sound of something heavy being slid out of the way.

Dani crouches down to accept her tray as it slides through.

"Hey, thanks again for the book," she tells her not-so-anonymous keeper. "I really like this one."

She isn't expecting a reply so is shocked into silence when it comes:

"You're welcome," the voice says. It's a man. But Josh? She can't be sure.

Following the tray slides a thick, purple notebook. Then a pen. A fat piece of bubble gum.

Dani is speechless. This is a first. She picks up the notebook reverently and flips through its many blank, lined pages—each one waiting eagerly for her thoughts and ideas to be shared.

She has to close it quickly as the first tears start to fall.

12

SANTOS IS COVERED IN SWEAT as he does dips off the side of his bunk, hands braced behind his back, legs stretched out in front of him on the floor. His arms burn with the effort.

". . . forty-eight, forty-nine, fifty."

He stands and paces his metal cell, swinging his arms, counting again, quietly, to himself: one minute between sets.

Counting keeps him sane. When his thoughts begin spinning out of control, when his anger reaches the boiling point, Santos goes to his numbers: sequencing primes, combining square roots, inventing new complex equations to solve in his head.

Right now it's "the game": Any number can be written as a combination of prime numbers (those that can't be divided by any other number except one); and there are one hundred and sixty-eight prime numbers between 1 and 1000 to play with. He's chosen the problem number at random: 6,545,448 . . .

. . . It takes him fifty-five seconds this time to find the solution:

$$2^3 \times 3^5 \times 7 \times 13 \times 37$$

Whew! That was a close one!

It hadn't taken long for Navarro, head of the Syndicate's sports book operations in Houston, to take notice of Santos's mathematical prowess: it could be invaluable to him. And it was. Santos could calculate interest rates and percentages in split seconds. He could determine odds better than Vegas. He could store multiple databases of figures in his brain. Statistics was child's play. And eventually, he became Navarro's right-hand man, with him wherever he went, privy to his every move—his secrets.

Inadvertently, Santos discovered that his boss was embezzling a little here and a little there (adding up to a lot) to invest in the drug trade—Navarro's own private enterprise on the side. Santos knew that if *los Generales* found out, Navarro would be history. Executed. But, ironically, telling them would mean Santos couldn't be trusted as a confidant and partner anymore: no matter how honorable his intentions, he would be labeled a "snitch." So he had quietly done the job himself, getting rid of both Navarro and the millions he stole from *La Familia,* assuming it all for himself. And, as he hoped, filling the vacuum Navarro's death had created.

Then Santos had run with the ball. He managed to increase profits dramatically soon after he took control. His future with the Syndicate was assured.

I would have been a General *myself someday.*

Having reached the end of his count, Santos drops to the floor, begins doing pushups. "One, two, three . . ." The counting keeps him from thinking of what he's lost, of what might have been.

He knows his prolonged absence has left the entire organization in chaos. Ortega would be in charge now. The man's capable enough, but only Santos knows where all the bodies are buried, so to speak—the "bodies" in this case being bank accounts located throughout the Caribbean.

One of these is his own personal account, known to nobody else, and set up for him secretly four thousand, seven hundred and seventy-one days ago by the *pinche gabacho* who now has him locked in this fucking box.

He should have had Rostam killed immediately afterward; he should have done it himself; he realizes this now. But there had to be a fall guy. There had to be a plausible explanation for Navarro's disappearance, and for the disappearance of all his money—and the Syndicate's. Too many people close to Navarro would have suspected Santos, his trusted assistant—his fucking gofer and punching bag. There had to be somebody else to take the blame.

Rostam had been the perfect sucker: he was smart, he was a computer guy, and he was totally unconnected to Santos and his circle. Even more, he was a fucking junkie: he would do anything for his drugs; he'd follow instructions unquestioningly. And Dani had him wrapped around her little finger.

". . . forty-nine, fifty." Santos hops to his feet and resumes his pacing, his quiet counting. But the game doesn't help this time; the simple exercise in numbers can't keep him from thinking about *her*.

Dani had been Navarro's whore, his *puta primera*. Santos had serviced her whenever the old man wasn't paying attention, which was practically all of the time. He'd been—what?— twenty-eight, twenty-nine then. Her maybe ten years younger. She was love struck; it hadn't been too hard to convince her to help him.

And keeping Dani quiet afterward hadn't been too difficult either. She knew what the price would be if she told anybody. He'd laid it out for her. Besides, she was as complicit in the deal as he was. She couldn't expect a reward from the Syndicate, or from Navarro's family. Plus, no man would ever trust her or keep her again if she went and shot off her mouth—if she even survived.

Santos had briefly thought of arranging her death as well (an overdose would have done it easily enough), but the coincidence would have been too hard to overlook, especially by Ramón, who's never forgiven Santos for letting his father be kidnapped and murdered right under Santos's nose.

Santos is sure there are some people to this day who suspect him of the crime. *Let them*, has always been his attitude. *And let them fear me for it.*

And he's sure there are also plenty of people happy to see him gone, out of the way.

Fuck. He can just see their gloating faces now.

"FUUUCK!" he yells at the top of his voice.

Santos steps to the steel cargo doors making up one wall and side-kicks them with all his might. *BOOM!* He switches legs. *BOOM!* He does this over and over again until he can't anymore. It's his favorite exercise of the day. It vents his frustration. And the incredible echoing noise makes his head ring after a while, dazes him, oddly helps to calm him down.

Afterward, he's breathing heavily and has to sit on the bunk for a moment to rest. He's in better shape now then he's been in many years, but he still has a long way to go. He'd let himself get soft. He'd let himself get complacent. He'd gotten too sure of himself. Despite having Neto and Luis constantly by his side, he'd dropped his guard just enough. He can see now that there had been many other times prior to New Year's Eve when he could have been captured or killed. Things will be different when he gets back out there, he thinks. He'll carry a gun, like when he was younger; he'll get him an armored car; and he'll stay in fighting shape till the day he dies.

Santos is sure he'll be released eventually. Pretty sure, at any rate. Rostam is obviously holding him for ransom, wanting to be paid for all those years behind bars. And Santos can't say he blames him, really.

Maybe Rostam has also told them the truth about Navarro's death. But who would he tell, exactly? Ramón? Pancho? And how? Besides, he doesn't know anything . . . Then again, Rostam had apparently found out it was he, Santos, who was behind it all. How the fuck had that happened? . . . He must also know about Consuela. But does he know who her father is? Who else could he go to for the money? And why is it taking so fucking long?

Santos has gone around and around with the same questions for months. If only the cocksucker would talk to him. And Santos has tried. It shames him now to think of how he had begged for any information at all, how he promised Rostam all the money he had to be set free. He'd felt so desperate at the time. He even came close to giving Rostam the new pass codes to the Antigua account, but had stopped himself just in time.

What if that *is what Rostam is really after?* Santos thinks. *And what would keep him from leaving me to die once he had the codes?*

Or worse, what if *this* is Rostam's plan: to simply make him suffer like *he* had suffered in prison? This thought scares Santos more than any other. He can't imagine another eight months of this miserable existence—this boredom, this hell—let alone another eight years. Or more.

His breathing back to normal, Santos goes to the sink for some water, fills his plastic mug, notices some torn pieces of paper still clinging to the inside of the toilet bowl. He flushes it again.

What is up with these fucking books?

Today's had been the ninth one he's ripped to shreds. Rostam obviously hadn't gotten the message when he shoved the remains through the food slot, or filled his empty tray with confetti; so now Santos just flushes the damn things down the drain as soon as they arrive. Why even bother opening them? What would be the point?

In the mirror, Santos admires his bushy salt-and-pepper beard, now grown a good few inches past his chin. He might keep it when this is over, he thinks—trim it, though.

He takes the rag and new bar of soap and begins washing himself in the sink. He starts with his face and matted head of long, black hair and works his way down, kicks his boxer shorts out of the way. He'll wash those next.

The boxers are all he's worn these past few months in this fucking oven of a metal box. He'd kill (literally kill) for a fan right now. It was too damn cold when he first arrived, and now it's too damn hot. But the days are finally starting to get cooler again. Santos doesn't know where he is, but it sure as hell ain't Houston. The air coming through the vent smells different, too, like pine-scented air freshener or something.

He can't hear a sound from outside the walls. Sometimes he thinks the overwhelming silence will drive him insane.

Every once in a while, when he's on the shitter, he can feel (but not hear) another toilet being flushed somewhere. He's emptied the water out of the bowl and shouted into it, but has never gotten a response.

He's gone over every inch of the cell, looking for weaknesses or anything he can use as a weapon. But there's nothing. The recessed light fixture had seemed promising at first, but its metal frame and Plexiglas have proven to be unbreakable.

And he has spent hours looking for any kind of video camera. Santos knows that if *he* was the one on the other side, he would want to keep an eye on his prisoner. But he hasn't found any sign of surveillance. He's considered the vent but can't see how a camera could see through the fine steel mesh there. Still, he's thought of covering it up, just to make certain, but then he'd probably suffocate in here for sure. So instead, he's had to be content with plugging up any suspicious-looking holes in the walls, with soap.

Of course he's explored the slot at the base of the right-side door, where the food trays come and go. Just outside the door is a wooden compartment just deep and wide enough for a tray to fit. This is where he leaves his empty tray, in order to receive a full one at the next meal. It hadn't taken him too long to figure this out. Though once, he didn't return his tray for a whole seven days. He'd been trying to get a response of some kind, some answers, some attention—anything at all—but with no luck. He must have lost at least five pounds that week.

Santos has known many men who have been to prison. They've described it to him and he thinks this must be the same. Without all the fucking *changos*, though, of course. *Gracias a*

Dios. As lonely as it's been, at least it's not overcrowded; at least he's got the place to himself. At least there's no asshole guards hassling him all the time. It could be a lot worse.

When Santos is finished washing, he begins to masturbate, handling himself roughly. It's as much a part of his daily routine now as kicking the doors. After all, what else is there to do? Use it or lose it, right? He closes his eyes, thinks of the Lady in Red. *That cunt!* She's become his fantasy now, his unobtainable dream, the prize that had been so unfairly dangled in front of him, then snatched from his grasp. He doesn't care that he may be building her up to be more than she really is; it gets him off. No other thoughts entertain him like these do. In them he's raping her, violently, giving her everything she asked for, and more.

Tease him? Humiliate him? She'll pay for that some day. He's going to do everything in his power to track that bitch down once he's free again . . .

Rostam will tell him.

By the time Santos is done with him, Rostam will tell him who she is and where she can be found . . .

Rostam will tell him everything.

Oh yeah. Rostam will tell him everything as he's taking it up the ass . . .

13

ON THE SCREEN, JOSH WATCHES Santos pacing like a caged animal, swinging his arms in circles, moving his lips.

"What's he saying?" Erin sits in the recliner beside him, nervously chewing on a strand of hair curled around her finger.

Josh's laptop computer is open on the small end table pushed forward between them.

"He's counting," Josh says. "He waits a minute or so between sets."

As they watch, Santos stops, places his hands on the floor near the wall, kicks his feet into a handstand, begins doing inverted pushups.

"Wow." Erin's clearly impressed.

Josh, not so much. "He's cheating; he needs to go all the way down to the floor."

"He's lost a lot more weight. Is he still eating?"

"Every meal."

The "hunger strike" had gone on for seven days; not bad for a rookie. Josh once went for twenty, although his was a spiritual fast. His meditation during the final week had been extremely productive—a breakthrough for him.

"But he hasn't been reading," Erin says.

"Nope. Destroys the books as soon as he gets them."

"What are you going to do?"

"I don't know. I guess I need to have a talk with him." This is what Josh has been dreading; he hates confrontation. And he has to admit: Santos frightens him.

"Is that safe?"

A good question. "Probably not. Not right now. But what else is there to do? He's got to come on board. This whole thing won't work without him."

"Can you drug him first?"

"That's your answer for everything. No, I need him lucid, able to reason. He's got to decide on his own that it's in his best interest to cooperate."

"Well, at least take the dart gun with you," Erin says worriedly.

"I can zap him with the Taser if I need to."

"Oh yeah."

On screen, Santos is swinging his arms, pacing again, back and forth.

"So is this all he does?" Erin asks.

"Pretty much. Here, this is what I wanted to show you."

Josh clicks on the "fast-forward" icon in the corner of the screen. Santos speeds through his routine, then appears to suddenly rush the camera. Josh clicks "stop," then "play." The image, now normal speed, shakes violently. Santos is up close at the bottom of the screen, kicking at the doors.

"Wow! He is *pissed!*" Erin gives a nervous laugh. "And he does this every day?"

"Yep. It's how he finishes his workout. This is earlier."

"What's wrong with the picture?"

Dark bands have formed at the top and bottom of the screen and are getting progressively wider as the image shrinks and continues to shake.

Shit. Here we go again.

"The camera's come out of its bracket. It happens every time," Josh says, standing. "Hold on, I forgot to fix it before."

He crosses the room—his "office," where he meets with Erin's patients—and opens the door to his private living area, much smaller. Both rooms are "rustic," with bare wooden walls and floors, but comfortable. The ceiling is high, with exposed wooden rafters. Only two walls are new sheetrock, painted white: the shorter separating the office from the bedroom, and the longer dividing the front of the building from the much larger area in back, where the containers are stored. The Shed, as the old building is called, used to be the sawmill's main storage area. It had been lined with shelves and was full of old junk and equipment before Josh cleaned the place out and remodeled it to suit his needs.

In his quarters, in the bathroom, he unlocks a narrow door to what looks like a closet. When it's opened, he's faced with a battered, metal sign a few feet away—DANGER! HAZARDOUS CHEMICALS—meant to deter anyone who, on the off chance, happens to come snooping around. But there's no real danger of that happening.

Josh takes a left, then a right, and enters the center aisle running the remaining length of the building: thirty feet long and four feet wide, with ten-foot-high walls of plywood on either side. Near the corner stands a stepladder left for his purpose.

He climbs it, inserts his arm past the elbow into a hole cut in the wall. The straw separating the wood from the container pokes at his bare skin, reminding him for the umpteenth time to install a section of tubing at this point.

The camera has come almost completely out of the bracket holding it in place, so he pushes it back into position. It's installed in the thin gap above the doors, invisible from inside. Gluing the camera in place, as he's been considering doing lately, would prevent the doors from swinging open at any time without damaging the camera; so, for now, Josh goes through this daily routine sometime after Santos's own.

When he returns, Erin is staring at the screen, her hand over her mouth. She looks up at him, eyes wide. "This guy has some *serious* issues."

"Tell me about it." Josh takes his seat, sees that it's still this morning's recording: the screen is fully dark but for a thin band of light across the center. But now the sound is on and he can hear Santos's voice loud and clear, reverberating in the cell:

". . . you asked for it . . . Oh, yeah, I'm gonna give it to you good . . . fuck you like you want it . . . Oh, you like that, don't you, you —"

Josh quickly mutes the sound. "Sorry about that."

"Not your fault," she says, blushing. "I couldn't see anything, so I figured I could at least listen in. But yikes! It's a good thing the camera slipped. I don't *even* want to know what he was doing."

"I would have stopped it before then if I was here." He laughs. "Just another part of his workout. He likes to finish with a bang."

Josh clicks on the screen, opens the program file. "You wanna see what he's up to right now?"

"Uh, I'm not sure. Probably not."

The screen changes. Santos is lying on his bunk, with his hands behind his head, staring up at the ceiling. His foot is shaking, burning off unused energy.

They watch him in silence for a while.

"You think he's ever going to mellow out?" Erin asks.

Josh considers this for a moment. "He has to. Eventually. Maybe after I talk with him a bit."

"Good luck with *that.*"

He moves the cursor over the "Camera 2" icon. "You ready to switch?"

"Please."

Santos instantly disappears, but the image remains basically the same; it's the same layout and perspective. Here, though, on the bunk is a large lump covered with a gray blanket. Only Harden's head is visible, facing the wall.

"This is all he does," Josh says. "Sleeps all day."

"But he's reading, right?"

"Yep, I'm pretty sure he's read them all. But I can't tell if he's spending any time contemplating them. Unless he does it while he sleeps."

"Maybe he's not sleeping but thinking."

"Could be. Part of the time anyway." Josh shakes his head, disappointed. "I haven't seen him meditate once, though."

"He's depressed."

"No shit. So was I. So is everyone who gets locked up. All I wanted to do was sleep, too, at first, just to deal with it— or not *have* to deal with it. But not for *nine months*. This is ridiculous."

Erin catches his eye, grinning devilishly. "Maybe he needs an attitude adjustment."

"You can say that again."

She taps on the screen. "All right, if there's anyone who needs an attitude adjustment, it's this guy."

They watch Harden's still form for another few seconds. Then, with a sigh, Josh switches to Camera 3.

Gloria is sitting at the head of her bunk, pressed into the corner, knees pulled to her chest, rocking slowly, rhythmically.

"Listen." Josh turns up the volume.

Erin leans forward. "She's singing . . . It's pretty."

"She has a beautiful voice."

Neither speak for a minute. Then he turns off the sound; he rarely likes to listen in.

"She's been doing that a lot lately," he says. "Just sitting and rocking like that, singing softly to herself."

"I feel sorry for her." Erin looks to him, concerned. "Do you think she's okay?"

"She's fine. She's doing better now than she was, at least. She's stopped screaming at me and crying every time I feed her . . . And it looks like she's sleeping better." He shrugs, not sure. "She's adjusting, I suppose . . . Shit, it took me *three years* to get my head on straight."

"And she's reading, you said."

Josh snorts. "Oh yeah. And she makes damn sure I know she is, too. Not that I've actually seen her do much of it, though." But he has to agree: she does look pitiful. "I know it can't be easy for her," he says. "The reading, I mean. She's a Bible-thumper. Hardcore Baptist."

"Oh. Well, she's from the South. A lot of people are."

"What? From the South?"

"No, silly. Baptists. Fundamentalists. At least she's not Pentecostal, speaking in tongues and all that. Or dancing with rattlesnakes."

Josh nods. He'd spent long enough in Texas to know how strongly people there feel about their religion, about their Holy Book. To them, everything else is heresy. It's the Bible's way or the highway—to Hell. Other philosophies or religions, like Buddhism or Yoga, are a joke, contemptible even. It's the southern cult of Christianity, or nothing at all.

The two friends sit in silence for a while, each with their own thoughts.

"Not much fun to watch, is it?" he says.

"No."

"Not much fun to *do,* either, believe me."

He moves the cursor and clicks. Now Dani is there, lying on top of the covers, reading, the book propped up on her chest. She's made a pillow out of her extra clothes. It's easy to see her expression.

"Is she *laughing?*" Erin says.

"Sure looks like it." Josh has to laugh himself. "I know she digs the books."

"Yeah, I'll say. Which one is it this month?"

"*Healing Lost Souls,* the one about spirit attachment. But that's not what she's reading now. I went ahead and gave her my own copy of *Destiny of Souls,* by Newton, she liked the first one so much."

Erin motions to the screen excitedly. "All right! Finally some-one who's into it! At least *she'll* be ready for Stage Two, don't you think?"

"I hope they *all* will." But Josh already knows that won't be the case. "I'm going to have to do something about Santos, though, for sure. But I'm still gonna wait till the end of the year."

"I know." Erin places her hand on his arm, looks at him so-berly. "He probably just needs an attitude adjustment, too."

He sees that she's serious this time. Maybe she was before.

An "attitude adjustment." This is their pet term for an acid trip: LSD (lysergic acid diethylamide). And if there's anyone who knows how to administer one properly, it's Erin.

Josh has read her book on the subject, of course, and they've discussed the treatment at length. She had even given him a therapeutic (large) dose of acid following the escape, to save for later, until he'd grown comfortable in the woods, calmed down a little. The idea was that, after almost twelve years in prison, a serious change in perspective—an attitude adjustment—was in order.

It was just a little piece of blotter paper, less than a quarter inch square, dyed a bright purple. The LSD is in liquid form and is absorbed into the paper, although it can easily be put into any-thing. This wasn't the same stuff Erin had used in her research, years ago, as then every micro-amount had to be accounted for along the way. She had obtained this batch from a psychiatrist friend, she said. She'd tried it herself with Donna and proclaimed it "kick ass."

Josh finally took the acid at his camp beside a small stream, deep in the mountains southwest of Eureka Springs. He'd been in the same spot then for almost a month. Erin's only instruc-tions had been, "Be in a pleasant environment and a pleasant state of mind. Only *then* do you take it. Promise me." He promised. And he'd tripped his balls off. For eighteen hours straight.

It was a shamanic experience, that's the only way he can describe it. His ego vanished completely. Gone were the slightest barriers to experiencing his Higher Self. He truly became One with the Universe. He was able to "clear out the cobwebs" of his mind like so many years of focused meditation in prison couldn't do. He had incredible insights into his own psyche and the world's collective consciousness as a whole. He visited other realms and was given messages from more advanced entities to take back with him. He was allowed incredible glimpses into the mysteries of Nature all around him. He was changed, for the better.

And when it was over, he slept for just as long, flying outside his body as he had done so many times before, carefree and limitless, like a magical bird.

Josh blinks. Erin is looking at him expectantly, wearing that patiently bemused expression he's seen all too often before. He clears his throat and looks out the window, embarrassed. "Was I *away* again?"

She pats his shoulder. "Not too long. A couple minutes. Gave me time to go to the bathroom," she says, making light of it.

It bothers him that his mind wanders like it does. He knows it's probably due to so many years in prison—in solitary—sitting in meditation, traveling astrally, letting his mind go where it would, escaping each day the only way he knew how.

Until Erin had helped make the real thing possible.

Josh looks back at the screen. Dani has rolled onto her side, her head propped up on an elbow, clearly enthralled with her book. Her toes wiggle enthusiastically as she reads.

She'll be all right.

He clicks on Camera 3: Gloria still sits in her corner, rocking, singing softly to herself.

Click: Harden only faces the other way in bed, eyes open, staring.

Click: Santos sits on the edge of his bunk, his face in his hands.

It wasn't part of his original plan, but Josh has to agree: maybe an "attitude adjustment" is just the kick-in-the-pants these guys need.

"Let's do it," he says.

14

REGRETS, SO MANY REGRETS. If only . . .

Judge Harden—*former* judge now, he has to keep reminding himself—lies on his bunk, under the covers, thinking, as
he has done all too much of these past ten months. Reflecting.
Pondering. Contemplating. Dragging up the past. Judging his
own actions for a change.

That's all he's done is *think* since he's been here.

And read—which just leads to more thinking.

He's tried to meditate, as the books encourage, but it's no use:
he can't stop his mind from churning, from incessantly nagging
him with worries and the memories of each and every mistake
he has ever made, no matter how small—and feeling remorse for
each one, learning from each one.

He'd risen to nearly the highest level within his profession—to
the highest level within society for that matter. But at what cost
to his soul?

Everything Harden's read recently has led him to the conclusion that he does indeed possess a soul—that foremost he *is* a
soul. There's no question in his mind anymore; he's convinced.
He's examined the evidence. All that remains is for him to *experience* it for himself, as so many others have apparently done
and have been trying to describe and teach for thousands of
years.

Now, personally experiencing his Higher Self is his only reason for living anymore. After all, what left is there? He knows with a certainty he is never leaving this "prison" cell alive.

For that is exactly what it is, isn't it? Rostam evidently wants him to suffer as he did.

And why shouldn't I?

And the books. Perhaps there's a modicum of altruism strangely incorporated into Rostam's quest for revenge. Harden can only guess that the man read the same books himself over his many years in prison.

And perhaps, through them, Rostam had come to the same conclusion: What is life for if not to learn and grow from our experiences? And what better way to learn than from our mistakes?

To suffer and learn a lesson, one pays a high price, he muses, *but a fool can't learn any other way.*

Not for the first time, Harden thinks that maybe Rostam is imprisoning him for his own good, out of some twisted form of love for his fellow man, to "enlighten" and change him this way, make him a better person. That it could be revenge by itself makes no sense, considering the books.

He'd given up trying to talk with his captor—to question him—months ago, in June—or what he *thinks* was June.

Harden doesn't know how long he was out of commission before finally waking up in here; but he knows it was at least long enough to get over the usual alcohol withdrawals. He's had them before and they're not something you'd miss: the shakes, splitting headaches, nausea, cold sweats, high blood pressure, anxiety, irritability, nightmares, suicidal thoughts—hell on Earth, essentially. He figures he was unconscious for at least a week, maybe two—maybe longer. A scary thought.

Although Harden doesn't physically crave a drink, he sure would like one: anything to ease his overburdened mind. He could use a few fingers of Glenlivet right about now. Just the thought of that smoky, amber liquid going down his throat sends a flood of warmth throughout his body and cheers him a little.

Ah, the power of imagination!

Still, he's grateful to be clean and sober for a change. Not that he ever had a serious drinking problem; he wasn't an *alcoholic* or anything. He only wishes he could share the novelty of his sobriety with Allison. She hadn't said as much (she never really complained), but he knows she disapproved of his drinking, and not just when he drove afterward. She wouldn't recognize the introspective philosopher he's become lately.

They had a good marriage, Harden thinks, looking back. He's sure she misses him and had cried a lot at first. But now . . . Like him, she's bound to know he's never coming home.

At some point, the insurance company, too, will determine he's dead and cough up the money Allison is entitled to under his policy. It's a small consolation, at least, knowing she'll be taken care of, still living in the manner she's accustomed.

And the kids? They'll be fine without him, of course; they always were. Sean in California—a *massage therapist,* for Christ's sake! (and after attending one of the most prestigious universities in the country)—he won't mourn for very long, if at all. They haven't spoken in over three years—four now—since Sean's outrageous choice of a career. His new wife is a yoga instructor (or so Harden's heard) and a vegetarian to boot, undoubtedly turning his son into even more of a tree-hugging, pacifist hippie. She's probably the one to blame for everything in the first place.

And Claire: Daddy's girl. She should have graduated college in May. That's something he really misses having seen. She wants to be a teacher; probably is one by now. There's nothing wrong with that, Harden supposes, but it's not what he would have chosen for her, of course. Yet she had been firmly against law school. She saw what it did to *him,* she said, what assholes it made out of people. (Gee, thanks, honey.) But she still loved him, in spite of that, she was quick to add. She's probably teaching some first-graders at this very moment. She probably has her own place now, too; hopefully somewhere close to home, for Allison's sake.

Harden knows he was neither the husband nor the father he could have been—should have been. Replaying his life now, he's able to see so many things he wishes he had done differently. All that time and energy spent on work instead of his family is what rankles him the most. Could he have advanced so far in his career otherwise? Probably not. No, definitely not; his drive and ambition are what made all the difference. But now he can see how wrong his thinking had been. His wanting to "succeed" had taken precedence over everything else: his family, his friends, his own well-being. He sacrificed his morality, his character, his integrity—for what? Not money, but power. Ego.

But what has affected Harden's conscience and kept him awake more nights than any of his other failings is how he had abused that power in the courtroom. His reputation, his entire rise to fame, had relied on his unrelenting stance on crime: There were no excuses, no mitigating circumstances: you do the crime, you do the time—and the more years behind bars, the better. So what if he had to sometimes break the rules himself in order to see justice served. It was his prerogative. It's what his constituents wanted and it's what he delivered. Besides, the criminals he prosecuted didn't vote—at least not anymore.

Now, though, he has a different perspective: He's experienced for himself what nearly a year of imprisonment is like. And how it can change a person. Even without Rostam's reading material, Harden can see how just the "time out" alone can make a difference. For someone who has never been locked up before, a short period—maybe one year, no more than three—would be enough to set them straight, he thinks.

Repeat offenders? He can't fathom the idea, although he knows it happens, of course. Much, much too often. But why? Why would anyone want to undergo anything like this again? Who could stand it? It could make a person insane . . .

With this thought, a light goes off in his head: Perhaps the prison system—the way it's constructed now—isn't a solution at all but only exacerbates the problem; perhaps it only serves to make people crazier, more unstable, more criminally minded than they were before. Harden already knows from his many visits to the county jail how dehumanizing the experience is; how actual attempts at rehabilitation went out the window decades ago; how prisons, for whatever reasons, have become nothing more than warehouses for the living dead. But he never once considered the possibility that prisons are actually *contributing* to the crime problem in the long run, rather than alleviating it.

Why else are there so many returning to prison each year? Did the experience make them worse off? It certainly didn't help them, apparently; it certainly didn't change them for the better, turn them into law-abiding citizens.

And Lord knows the increasing numbers of people in prison are ruining states' budgets. Perhaps they're also ruining local communities and the greater society as a whole. Too many parents gone, for one thing, creating a whole new generation of prisoners to follow in their wake. A pointless "War on Drugs" creating more and more people embittered and disenfranchised and damaged by a police state and its heartless and inhumane "correctional" facilities.

But when he examines his own situation, Harden has to ask himself: Has my time in here made a difference? Has it been productive? Am I a better person because of it? And the answer to all three, he has to say, is a resounding "Yes."

Thanks to the books. Especially for the books.

But what about another year? Another five? Another ten? Is there a point where a person begins to go downhill, to lose whatever gains one has made—to lose one's *mind*? Certainly it wouldn't take long of such an existence to become unfit to reenter society.

Harden doesn't think he can take much more of this himself. He's so depressed, it's all he can do to get out of bed most days. After all, what's the point of living if it isn't "life" anymore at all? Only the thought of his eventual release had kept him going at first, but now . . . There's no hope for that any longer.

The only—the absolute *only*—thing left for him now, he believes, is his spiritual growth. But that is such an intangible goal. And a difficult one. Meditate? Clear his mind? Go within? Good luck with that; it's impossible. Maybe in a few years, though, who knows? Maybe after all the memories and regrets and remorse have run their course. Maybe once he's a nutcase.

Harden's stomach growls.

Shit. He needs to eat, which means he needs to get out of bed, put his feet on the cold cement floor . . . And the tray is too far away. The food is cold, it's been sitting there so long . . .

He rolls over. Forget it, it can wait. But . . .

Damn. Now he has to take a piss.

Grumbling, as he does every morning at the futility of it all, Harden goes through the motions. At the sink, he splashes some water on his face—ice cold when he first arrived, then warm for a time, now much cooler again: the only changing of the seasons for him now.

Breakfast is the usual blue-tray special: two hard-boiled eggs, oatmeal, raisins, a bran muffin, an apple (sometimes an orange). It's one of the highlights of his day. The other is dinner. And then there's his reading, which he always enjoys, and which allows him to forget himself, his circumstances, if only for a while.

He forces himself to eat slowly, consciously, savoring every mouthful while it lasts. Today he puts aside both the muffin and apple for later.

He pushes the empty tray out the slot. It'll get picked up and replaced with the next meal this evening. As always, without a sound from his jailer.

Harden gets back into bed, snug under the covers, gets a whiff of something sour. He considers washing the sheets again (it's been a few months) but opts instead for the latest book, retrieving it from the floor beside him.

Backwards, by Nanci L. Danison. He's impressed with it. It's his second time through. The author, a high-powered attorney like himself but in the medical field, had died in the hospital, following surgery, and come back to tell about it. She's put her excellent writing skills to good use here.

Reading the book by itself, Harden knows, wouldn't have nearly the same impact if he hadn't already read the others leading up to it. Having done so makes what she says so much more believable. It would be harder to do otherwise: The continued life after death she describes sounds just too good to be true. But it's totally in line with everything else he's read so far.

Harden had grown up as an atheist with ambivalent parents. To him, believing in God was one of the most foolish things a person could do. God was akin to Santa Claus. ("He knows when you are sleeping, he knows when you're awake; he knows if you've been bad or good, so be good for goodness sake!") Heaven and Hell were equally dubious concepts, as was any form of an "afterlife." If it didn't work for modern science (Einstein, the mystic, not included), it didn't fly with him: there was no use investigating the matter.

And this belief (or unbelief, rather) had shaped the way he lived his life: You only live once; take what you can get; he who dies with the most toys wins; power is might; survival of the fittest; every man for himself. "Materialism" he believes it's called. Spirituality was for the naïve: suckers, dreamers, fools, sheep. It played no part in his thinking. And why should it? It was all just myth and superstition.

But now he knows better.

Harden's problem now is grasping the enormity of it all. It's almost—or maybe it very well could be—beyond human comprehension.

How can so many be right and so many be wrong about something so fundamentally important? he thinks.

What if he had known the truth about all this from the beginning? Not abstract theology, not some belief system, not religious dogma steeped in elitism and ancient history—but the plain and simple *truth* about what happens to us when we die, and why we are here in the first place.

How would my life have been different?

He had always been told that such "divine" knowledge was impossible to discover, and that anyone claiming to know such things was to be considered either an idiot or a charlatan. But apparently that is merely an aphorism spouted by the ignorant to protect their self-esteem. Because some *do* know what lies beyond: people have been "dying" and living to tell about it for ages. And their stories are all similar, if not identical.

So who should we listen to: those who have been there personally, or scientists and priests who haven't?

As Harden ruminates over such things, it occurs to him that he stopped reading some time ago, without being aware of it. The book lies open in his lap. He's been staring at the same spot ahead of him for quite a while now, transfixed. He feels anchored, rooted in place, very comfortable and warm, sitting propped up there against the wall, with his small pillow of clothes. He has no wish to move, nor does he think he can if he tried, being so fascinated all of a sudden with the shifting patterns on the doors, like a blank movie screen where colorful images are taking shape then receding, merging into the next. It's spellbinding.

Harden shifts his eyes, the muscles in his neck much too relaxed to turn his head. The walls are doing the same thing: shimmering, undulating, pulsating with light and energy. Swirling rainbows of colors dance across every surface.

Over time (though time and all else is forgotten), the colors seem to become even brighter, the changing patterns more complex.

With a gasp—*Was that me?*—he watches as a dozen bright, blazing, red crystal globes ricochet wildly off every corner and come crashing together before his eyes with an infinitely echoing explosion, like the tinkling of broken glass and tiny bells. Every particle of space around him now vibrates and glitters in tremendously intricate geometric shapes and colors, like being an inch away from a color television, its pixels alive with a consciousness of their own, each radiating intelligence and a joy for the individual part it plays in Creation.

On impulse, Harden's hand rises, lazily waves an arc through this sparkling sea of life energy, an elongated stream of peach-pink effervescence trailing in its wake. Then with both hands now, he makes snaking patterns in the air before his eyes, delighted with his spontaneous designs, elated, entranced, full of wonder at this newfound magic.

He looks at his hands, radiating their own inner light; and with the flick of his fingers, he can send sparkling stars floating across the room, which seems to have expanded greatly in size, there no longer being any boundaries at all that he can see, only light, energy, color, motion, sound.

He hears the whistle of a train in the distance, coming closer. Intuitively he realizes it's the means to escape his confinement, to return to the outside world, to rejoin the hustle and bustle of civilization. But even before it arrives, Harden knows he's going to let it go by. He doesn't need to catch that ride anymore. Everything is fine. No worries. He's right where he needs to be right now.

Bloom where you're planted.

Happily surrendering to the euphoric feelings overcoming him, still safely enthroned upon his cozy flying bed, Harden soars into a wide, swiftly rotating tunnel of brilliant colors and sounds. Continually forming kaleidoscopic patterns take shape and spin away as he rushes onward, into the unknown, into unlimited thought, one mind-blowing instance after another.

• • •

HOURS — DAYS? — LATER, Harden finds himself in miniature, spiraling up and around what he recognizes as a double-helix of DNA: the unique genetic fingerprint within every cell of every living thing. It's much longer and twistier than he remembers it being portrayed in textbooks. He feels a conscious intelligence emanating from the structure as it receives and sends information, issues commands. The individual sections making it up, connected like criss-crossing chains of iridescent bubbles, glow with an ethereal light from within.

Melding through the membrane, becoming even smaller, Harden travels inside.

He is surrounded by atoms—neon blue, bright violet, deep purple—vibrating, moving so fast that it's all he can do to keep up. Each one clearly knows what it's doing, ceaselessly interacting with its neighbors, busily combining, giving, taking, exchanging what's needed when, vibrantly playing its part within the greater whole.

Then, with a sudden tremendous movement, he has gone even further still. Within the atoms are countless other particles—miniscule, brightly white, almost invisible in their incalculable speed—buzzing by, zipping around him as he stares in jaw-dropped awe.

"I AM HERE," says the booming voice reverberating through his skull.

And in the utter silence that follows, Harden has two revelations at once:

First, God is within *everything;* He *is* everything. He is as much Harden the man as He is the smallest particles within Harden's body, as He is the very air Harden breathes, the very thoughts Harden thinks, the energy around him. There is *nothing* "outside" of God.

Second, Harden realizes that he has lost his mind much sooner than he anticipated.

15

ANGEL WINGS ENVELOP HER, and within them she is safe and warm. Erin could stay like this all night but knows it's not possible. Any moment now she'll have to face the man and make her pitch. His decision, she's sure, will determine if Fresh Start ever reaches its potential or forever languishes in debt.

"Come on, I'm getting cold," says Donna, her chin resting on Erin's head.

Erin sighs. She's been staring out at the lights of the town and the stars and the shiny, silver moon above it all for quite a while now. She had come out onto the patio to gather her thoughts. And her courage. Donna had found her shivering.

Now Erin turns within Donna's silky, white wings, looks up into the face of her guardian angel, says, "Thanks." She lets her eyes communicate the rest.

"No problem. It's what I'm here for," Donna says with a kiss. "Now get in there, you little devil."

They enter the kitchen hand in hand. Erin knows they make a cute couple: a tall, beautiful angel in sparkling white and a short, red devil complete with tail and pitchfork.

Most everyone inside is also dressed for the occasion. Even her patients, many far from home, are wearing their favorite costumes. Months ago she had arranged with a businessman in Jonesboro to provide the costumes for tonight's party, in exchange for treating his son for cocaine and alcohol addiction.

Much of what the Center has, Erin has been able to obtain through the barter system. The extra effort to arrange these deals saves Fresh Start and herself a lot of money neither has.

The kitchen has been turned into a medieval torture chamber. "Bloody" knives and cleavers lay upon countertops covered with gore (much of it just colored dough and jello). A scantily clad, partially dismembered mannequin lies spread out on the butcher-block island in the center of the room. Its severed head, wearing a werewolf mask, will surprise anyone looking in the fridge. Erin's very own full-size skeleton from her school days ("Dr. McCoy") hangs suspended in paper shackles on the wall. A black leather whip is coiled like a wreath on the pantry door. *Now where did* that *come from?*

Only a handful of people are hanging out in here. Donna and Erin say "Hi" and pass through into the Big House's main living and recreation area, where all the noise is coming from, the talking and laughter much louder than the music.

The place is packed. To Erin it seems like even more people have shown up while she was outside. Not everyone is dressed for Halloween but it doesn't matter. They all appear to be having a good time.

Stringy cobwebs, hairy spiders, and vampire bats hang in a jumble from the tall ceiling. A dozen glowing pumpkins line the walls. Much of the decorations were provided by Mrs. Asibi's fourth-grade class, and Erin plans to have them all up in the summer to pick as many blackberries as they can carry home in their buckets. Her patients have spent the past couple of days putting it all together. Josh has even made a bunch of ghosts from some old, rotten, canvas tarps he'd found while cleaning out the Shed; and these are scattered around the property: in the courtyard, on the roofs, in the trees.

With her girlfriend in tow, Erin makes her way to the bar (nonalcoholic, of course) to warm up with a glass of hot cider. She has the chills from being outside for so long.

One of the Three Musketeers, a local coffee shop owner, serves them with a flourish. "Ah, such lovely ladies! And which to choose, the naughty or the nice? Methinks *both* would make the perfect companion."

Erin smiles. "There's no yin without the yang."

"So which one are you?" Donna asks. "Wait, let me guess . . . D'Artagnan!"

"Why, I'm the good-looking one, of course," he says with a bow. The huge feather in his hat neatly dips into the punch bowl.

Laughing, Erin turns and blows on her steaming drink, the tall glass warm in her hands. She surveys the crowd, spots the Phantom of the Opera across the room. She shivers, and not just from the cold. The man intimidates her. And it's he who she has to most impress tonight.

The majority of guests are friends and local business owners, here to lend their support to the Cause, whether emotional or financial. Every person here, Erin believes, knows at least one person suffering from some sort of addiction or who has been treated at Fresh Start. Except, perhaps, for "Mr. Perfect," the Phantom this evening and chairman of Mountain Valley Bank. The irony is not lost on her that the Center's biggest source of funding is also its greatest critic.

Well, it's now or never, she thinks. She's put it off for too long already; there's no telling how long he'll be here tonight.

Donna is in conversation with a portly Peter Pan, her boss from the Social Services office. Erin catches her eye and raises crossed fingers. Donna gives her an encouraging smile and a big thumbs-up.

Mr. Worthing, the Phantom, is conversing with a couple of his peers when she approaches. The witch, Erin knows, is president of First Security Bank; the Mad Hatter, not much taller than herself, is head of the local Credit Union. Both banks (with their regrets) had refused to loan Fresh Start any money. The risk was simply too high, they explained, and they weren't in the business of lending to nonprofits. Every other bank had told her the same.

Only Mr. Worthing's bank had taken the chance on her and the Center, but only as a favor to his long-time friend and fellow alumnus from the University of Arkansas, Russ Shepherd, Erin's professor and mentor during her graduate program.

Russ has been like a father to her since her parents' tragic death during her sophomore year. He also donated the old saw-mill land, which had been in his family's name forever. If anyone has faith in her and Fresh Start, it's Russ.

With the property as collateral, Erin had secured a substantial construction loan from Worthing's bank to refurbish the existing buildings and improve the land. A smaller loan provided for all the essential medical equipment and supplies needed for a small number of patients at one time. This one she has recently managed to pay back in full after three years.

However, all the rest of the money has been used up. So Erin hopes now to obtain another small loan or refinance the big one in order to get the funds needed to complete the second floor above them. This would allow her to accommodate more than three times the number of patients currently, both paying clients and research participants. She figures she can raise the money for the additional equipment and supplies through donations down the road. Otherwise, unless she can service more people, Fresh Start will continue to struggle financially. As it is now, Erin doesn't see how the Center will survive.

Mr. Dreyfus, the Mad Hatter, has just wrapped up a story about his recent trip to Israel, when the dogs break into their circle, laughing silently, tails wagging. Pooch makes a little jump and catches himself in time before putting his paws up on Erin's waist. Miraculously, he's still wearing his furry lion's mane. Honey is dressed as a bumble bee, though she's lost one of the antennae somewhere along the way. As always, the dogs inspire plenty of smiles and good cheer, and the bankers reach down to pet them.

Only Worthing is immune to their charm. He eyes Erin stonily from behind his white half-mask.

"You've managed quite a lot in three years, Ms. Pearse," he says. "I have no doubt Mr. Shepherd is very proud of you."

"Thank you, Mr. Worthing. Yes, I just spoke with Russ this morning. He wanted me to shake your hand and wish you a 'Happy Holidays' on his behalf. And he said to tell you that he'll definitely be there for your son's wedding."

Worthing accepts her outstretched hand. "And my best wishes to him. And to you, of course."

Erin greets the other two bankers, nods to another man she hadn't noticed, dressed as a cowboy. Mrs. Gardner, the witch, makes the introduction: "Ms. Pearse, this is Dr. Arthur Moore, an acquaintance of mine. He's an anesthesiologist. He was interested in seeing your rehabilitation clinic for himself. Dr. Moore, this is Erin Pearse, the clinic's founder and director."

"Pleased to meet you," Moore says. "I've heard a lot of good things about what you do here."

"Thank you. It's a challenge but we think we're making a difference."

Worthing harrumphs and coughs into his fist.

He doesn't have to make his disapproval so plain, Erin thinks. He had made his views known early on: drug addicts are not to be coddled; they should be treated like the criminals they are and "rehabilitated" in prison, where they belong. Already Erin would like to smack him in the nose, if she could reach that high.

Worthing motions to the room. "You have many friends, it seems, Ms. Pearse. How many people here are your patients?"

"Nine. Well, eleven, counting the newest two asleep at the moment. That's the most we can accommodate right now."

"Asleep?" Dreyfus says.

"Only eleven?" Gardner looks surprised. "I thought from your loan request it was to be a lot more."

Erin hopes her discomfort isn't obvious; she can feel her color quickly rise. "Well, the work on the buildings and property was a lot more than we anticipated. There was all the new plumbing and electrical and the foundation repair and—"

"All things that should have been taken into consideration initially," says Worthing unsympathetically.

"You're right," Erin concedes. "Nonetheless, we still have a lot to do." She throws up a quick, silent prayer. "With the second floor finished, we could increase the number of patients at any one time to thirty-three, possibly thirty-five."

Gardner nods thoughtfully. "That's a big difference."

"You say 'we,'" Worthing says. "Is there more than only you running the facility?"

"Er—I guess 'we' is just a figure of speech," Erin replies nervously. "I'm including all of the people—all the patients and volunteers—who help with the work around here. It always feels like a group effort."

"I see. I thought you might be referring to the gentleman who's been living with you this past year. I understand he works here, as well."

Uh-oh. "Oh, yes, that's Trip. He's a good friend of mine, from way back. He's offered to help out for a while—a regular jack-of-all-trades." An idea strikes her, one Worthing might appreciate: "He's become invaluable, a real asset to the Center. And he works for free; he's already saved us thousands in labor costs."

Worthing looks skeptical. "He isn't some sort of counselor here?"

"Um, well, yes, he's that, too. But only informally, and only to those patients who request it." Clearly Worthing has been talking to someone, Erin thinks. He probably knows just what it is Josh does, too. "He practices hypnosis."

"Ah, *hypnosis!*" Behind his mask, Worthing's eyes grow wide in mock surprise. "Yet another unconventional practice to add to your repertoire."

Erin doesn't appreciate his tone, or his line of questioning; but what can she do? She pauses to take a drink of cider, then: "Actually, it's hardly unconventional. Hypnosis is a tried and true way to help people quit doing drugs, and recover from addiction afterward."

Dreyfus says, "Of course, of course, like smoking. Or weight loss. I've heard about that."

Worthing waves his hand dismissively. "I'm referring to the more . . . unusual kind of hypnosis. Isn't that what your friend, Trip, practices?"

Erin would like to slap that smug look off his face, but instead attempts her most disarming smile. "He practices the more conventional hypnosis to treat addiction," she says, "and he does spiritual hypnosis as well. He's been a minister for many years."

Dreyfus: "Oh, a minister, I see . . ."

"*Spiritual* hypnosis?"

"It's completely optional, of course," Erin hastens to add. "Sometimes a patient will request spiritual counseling as well as psychological. We have many therapists and counselors who regularly volunteer their services, and every once in a while we'll get a visit from someone from a church or ministry in town, but not that often. So Trip is available if they'd like."

"What denomination is he?" This from Moore, who looks genuinely interested.

"Well, I'm not sure how to—"

"The Truth," says Josh, standing beside her all of a sudden.

How does he do that?

His friend, Sheila, is with him, dressed provocatively as a Middle Eastern belly dancer.

"Interfaith, really," Josh continues, addressing them all. "No particular group. After all, 'There is no religion higher than the Truth,' as the Theosophists say."

There's an uncomfortable pause. Then Dreyfus says, "Well, you must belong to *some* church, don't you, to be a minister?"

"Was Jesus? Was Buddha?" Josh's costume is of a Roman soldier. It looks authentic, and he looks formidable with his tanned, well-defined muscles and trimmed beard. The raised, white scar across his neck and the many others on his face, arms, and legs only add to the effect. He cradles a red-plumed helmet in his left hand, and his right rests upon a short plastic sword at his hip. His friendly smile is incongruous with his appearance. "My church is the brotherhood of mankind," he says. "Everyone qualifies."

"This is the twenty-first century, sir," Worthing says haughtily. "Certain legal requirements must be met to counsel the public."

"No, not really," Josh responds. "'Freedom of Religion' and all that, you know. Still, I understand what you're getting at. I've created my own official organization: Mystic Ministries."

"Oh, that sounds interesting," Dreyfus says.

Josh points across the small circle to Gavin, who has sidled up between Gardner and Moore. "This is my Chief Evangelist."

"I was lost but now am found!" Gavin booms with an irreverent laugh. "I'm born again!"

If Erin didn't know better, she'd think the man was drunk; but Gavin has been clean and sober for more than three months now, since his Big Sleep. He's dressed as a baby, wearing nothing but a diaper with giant safety pins and a bib that barely reaches around his burly neck. The unlit cigar stub clenched between his teeth sets off the ensemble.

At least he has on sandals, Erin thinks, shaking her head with a smile. She's grown very fond of Gavin.

However, she would prefer that both he and Josh were somewhere else right now.

"We were just discussing your unique brand of hypnosis, Mr. Trip," Worthing states, after looking down his nose at Gavin's costume. "Tell us, how does it work, exactly?"

"I assume you mean the spiritual hypnosis. It isn't too widely known about, really, but people have been practicing it for thousands of years. Regular hypnosis—"

"How do you know that?" Worthing interrupts.

" . . ."

"How do you know that it's been practiced for thousands of years? Where is this documented?"

Josh gives Erin a look that says, *Who is this asshole?* Then he patiently answers, "Well, there's the ancient Egyptians, for one; it was part of their spiritual practice. There's their famous *Book of the Dead.* And the Tibetans, going back just as long, with their book of the same name. And the Hindus and their *Upanishads,* which go back thousands of years. And then there's the ancient Greeks and their 'dream temples,' where they practiced hypnosis 'religiously.'" He makes his fingers into quotation marks. "This is all thoroughly documented. But really, it's indigenous to all the ancient peoples of the world. Many shamanic cultures still practice variations of spiritual hypnosis to this day—like in the Amazon, and in Indonesia, Africa, Scandinavia, Siberia, the aborigines of Australia, Hawaii . . ." He shrugs and smiles. "I'd be more than happy to discuss it at length with you sometime, if you're really interested."

Erin has seen Josh debate this subject before. He won't lose his cool and he won't lose, period. But she hopes it won't come to that; she would really like to steer the conversation away to something else, something safer.

But apparently Worthing has an agenda: he must have heard of Josh's work from someone, and he's skeptical. Nothing new there. She sighs inwardly, resigning herself. She'll jump in to save things. If she can.

The others seem interested, if a bit confused by the topic of conversation, but Worthing just rolls his eyes. "And with this hypnosis you claim to be able to visit people's former lives, is that correct? As in *reincarnation?*"

"Yep."

Gardner gives Erin a questioning look, eyebrows raised. Erin just smiles back with a shrug. *What can I say?*

Worthing looks around the circle with a smirk. "Aren't people very susceptible to suggestion during hypnosis?" he asks. "Couldn't you perhaps be encouraging them to see these past lives? Couldn't you be putting these thoughts into their heads?"

"Nope, not at all," Josh says. "In fact, with many practitioners, not just myself, the clients bring up their past lives without any prompting. For example, I might simply say, 'Go back to when this problem first began,' and the person is suddenly describing a life in the sixteenth century."

Gardner says, "But how do you know this isn't their imagination?"

"In transpersonal hypnosis, people aren't accessing their present-day ego, or imagination or fantasy, but deep-seated memories. And they do not lie."

"*Do* not or *can* not?" Worthing asks belligerently.

"Both. They simply report things the way they see them—or remember them to be, actually."

It's Moore's turn to jump in: "So people tell you about living before, in other lifetimes?"

"Yep. All the time," Josh says. "Every one of us has had many lives, often thousands."

Worthing scoffs at this, and the others exchange looks of polite disbelief.

Gavin speaks up: "Hey, I know I don't look like the paragon of virtue or anything in this getup, but believe me, it's true. I was the biggest skeptic you'd ever want to meet. But now . . ." He raises his arms, tilts back his head, and in his best southern gospel, hollers: "I have seeeen the light!"

Erin cringes. She *has* to do something about this. "Can I get anyone a drink?" she asks hopelessly.

Gavin looks seriously now at each person in turn. "Literally . . . I have *seen*. The *Light*." But then his wide grin is back. "Hey, look, you guys, you can say the lake is empty all you'd like; but if millions of people are fishing from it every day . . ." He spreads his hands. "There's a reason why the vast majority of people around the world believe in reincarnation: it's the truth. It's the way it is, whether you like it or not. And really, there's nothing not to like, you know what I mean? So just go with it. It actually makes a lot of sense, too, when you think about it for a while."

There's no response to this. Everyone stands staring at the half-naked, hairy baby in front of them.

Gavin chews on his cigar for a moment, then raises a hand goodbye. "Listen to this guy," he says in parting. "Everything he tells you is true." He gives Erin a quick salute.

Erin hears Josh chuckle beside her. From the corner of her eye, she can see him looking at her, but she pointedly ignores him, hoping he'll get the hint.

She notices a sizeable crowd has formed around them—probably because of Gavin's antics, she thinks, or maybe because folks just like a good showdown.

"You have *one* convert, I see," Worthing says. "But tell me: If there was any real evidence for reincarnation and past lives, wouldn't we have learned of it by now?"

Josh is unflappable. "What would you like to discuss first? The evidence, or the reasons why you haven't heard any of it?"

"Let's hear the evidence," says Moore.

"Okay, well, we could be here all night, covering it all," Josh says, "so I'll try to keep it brief." He moves his helmet to the crook of his arm, holds up a hand as if to tick off the points on his fingers. "Also, I'll stick to only past-life regression—hypnosis—and not the thousands of cases of spontaneous recollection reported by children every year. First—"

"Wait," Dreyfus says, "what's this about children?"

"Some of the most powerful evidence comes from the mouth of babes," Josh says. "As soon as they can speak, they begin describing the life they lived before this one. They ask about their former families and towns and what-have-you. They tell about how they died, and in some cases, even who murdered them. And pretty much in every case where the facts can be checked, it all pans out."

Gardner: "These are all documented studies?"

"They are," Josh says. "There are people who have dedicated their lives to the research, traveling all over the world to study reports. And there are plenty of good books on the subject, with hundreds of case studies." He shrugs. "These children know things they couldn't possibly know without having lived the lives they describe."

Erin can see that many of the people around them now are also interested in the discussion. There's a buzz.

"Tell us about these kids!" calls out someone behind her.

Josh's face is lit up with enthusiasm for his favorite subject. "All right, here's just one: A little boy, from really early on, he always had these really horrible nightmares; he would yell and thrash about in his sleep, kicking like crazy. Then, when he was finally able to talk, he described being shot down in his fighter plane and drowning, unable to get out of the cockpit. Scary stuff! Well, of course, as is almost always the case, his parents didn't know what to make of all this. But how could he be imagining it, with so many details, when he's only two or three years old?"

"Television," Worthing says.

Josh ignores him. "Anyway, one day his mother picks up a little toy plane in the store, and the boy is able to name all the parts of it. The mom points to some things underneath the wings and says, 'So what are these? Bombs?' and the boy says, 'No, those are auxiliary fuel tanks.'" Josh grins and looks around, clearly enjoying the reaction.

"Plus, at four, the kid can draw a perfect picture of a World War II Mustang—including the *inside of the cockpit.*" He pauses again for dramatic effect, waves his hand nonchalantly. "So anyway, when all was said and done, he finally got to meet with all the surviving members of his squadron and recount old war stories with his buddies about flying, getting laid in Okinawa, all that stuff."

Gardner looks incredulous. "Are you serious? You're not just making this up? I mean, this would be, like, *proof* he lived that life."

"Exactly!" Josh says. "This kid knew every detail about being a fighter pilot in the islands of Japan during the war. Before he could even *read.* Plus, there's the verification from his war buddies. They *knew* it was him after talking with the boy. He knew their old nicknames and could describe their tattoos before they even took their shirts off."

"Bullshit!" barks a man humorously.

Josh smiles back in his direction. "No, it's a true story. Just one of many, of thousands. You can read all about it in a book called *Soul Survivor.* His parents wrote it."

"You see," says Worthing over the exclamations around them, "here is a perfect example of a child's parents using him to get rich and famous. The whole thing, I'm sure, is a fabrication."

"Well, sir, I suggest you read the book," Josh says calmly. "And also maybe ask yourself how some of these young children can speak foreign languages fluently without being taught. Or play the piano. Or draw perfect maps of places they've never been."

He holds up his five fingers again. "But let's get back to the subject at hand: past-life regression, my specialty."

He gives Erin a wink and she rolls her eyes: she's heard it all before.

"First: transcripts. Countless past-life sessions have been recorded and transcribed over the years, word-for-word. And fortunately, some of the best have been compiled for us to read. I can give you a list of books to check out if you'd like."

"That won't be necessary," Worthing says.

"Actually," both Gardner and Moore say at the same time, each holding up a finger. They laugh at the synchronicity.

"You got it. I'll send one to both of you." Josh taps the next finger. "Second, many of the details reported in these sessions can be verified by historical records."

Worthing makes a skeptical noise, which Josh again ignores.

"For example, someone may describe the life of a Mongol warrior during the time of Genghis Khan: the various battles fought, the politics, and the types of trade along the Great Silk Road of China during that period. These kinds of things can be fact-checked. Or the name and description of a place, or anything else, that no longer exists anymore, when there's an historical record of it somewhere. That kind of stuff."

Moore says, "But aren't these things people could have heard about, or read somewhere before?"

"Right, that's taken into consideration. But so many of the details reported are so obscure, and so outside anything they may have ever seen or heard of before, that it lends credibility to it being an actual recollection of a past life. For example, a farmer in Nebraska today, with a grade school education, describing in detail the crew and cargo manifest of a Portuguese sailing ship that sunk in 1502. And he's speaking in old nautical terms, when the guy's never even *seen* the ocean in this life."

"Do you think a simple farmer in Nebraska, then, can't pull off a hoax?" Worthing says heatedly. "Is he so *stupid?*"

Josh pauses, stares. "Sir, Mr. . . . ?"

"Worthing."

"Mr. Worthing, with all due respect, until you've at least studied the matter a little yourself, I think it's best to keep an open mind, don't you?"

Worthing looks affronted and grumbles something under his breath. For a moment Erin is afraid he's going to stalk off.

"Third," Josh continues, "peop—Oh! Wait! They actually found the remains of that ship, by the way—exactly where the farmer said it would be, off the coast of Africa." He happily taps a finger: "Third, people reporting past lives are able to describe places they've never been in this lifetime, and in great detail. Cities, countries, jungles, deserts, you name it. They can describe the architecture, the vehicles, the manner of dress, and so on. And remember, these descriptions are of the past, the way these places *used* to be, often hundreds of years ago. And again, their descriptions can be checked through the history books, or sometimes by visiting the places today."

Mr. Dreyfus: "So if someone said they lived at the time of Christ, they could describe Jerusalem, even if they've never been there? In this life, I mean."

"Yep. That is, if they'd been to Jerusalem and spent much time there. They'll describe whatever they can remember of it." Josh shrugs. "It's like any other memory: you have to have experienced it for it to be there."

"Very interesting." Dreyfus nods, looks to the others for their reactions as well.

"Fourth," Josh says, "people exploring a past life are able to speak in the local dialect and in the slang of the period. They're able to speak in languages they've never spoken or even heard before, like Russian or Farsi or even 'extinct' languages, like ancient Aramaic or Chippewa Indian—whatever they were speaking back then."

"You're joking!" Gardner exclaims.

"Nope. Happens all the time." Josh laughs. "You have to ask them to switch to English to be able to understand them."

"That's incredible!" says a woman in the crowd. Others agree.

"I don't believe you," Worthing says.

Josh shakes his head. "That's too bad. You probably also wouldn't believe the hundreds of audio and video recordings of this happening."

Worthing points a finger: "So *you* say. I have yet to hear you mention one credible source to back your claims."

"Check out *Regression Therapy: A Handbook for Professionals*, by Lucas," Josh recommends. (A little too cockily, Erin thinks.) "The bibliography of research alone in Volume Two is enough evidence to quiet the loudest critic. Not that I expect you to actually look into it, though."

Worthing's reply is a cool stare.

"Fifth—and finally, before I bore you all to death—" Josh grins and looks around him, hamming it up. "People reliving their past lives are able to access the knowledge and skills they had then. So, even someone with little or no expertise in a particular subject in *this* life, can still discuss complex medical procedures, or the movements of the stars, or incredible feats of engineering, like how to build a suspension bridge in the early 1900s. Or they can explain how to make colorful, permanent dyes from various plants and minerals, or how to best prepare a buffalo hide . . . And it's not just limited to things they could have learned from books. For example, people with absolutely no interest in or aptitude for art in this life—even people *blind from birth*—are able to describe painting a masterpiece, including the *feelings* they had while doing so."

Moore holds up his hand with a question: "Wait. People blind from birth? I don't understand. How can they—?" He falters, at an obvious loss for words.

"That must be so wonderful for them!" says Gardner excitedly. "To see for the first time, even if it's only memories of another life. That's just amazing."

"I agree," Josh says. "I'm amazed every time I have a session with someone."

"I'm going to need to study this further." Gardner opens her small handbag and looks inside. "Do you know how to reach me?"

"I do," pipes Erin, glad to be of help. With any luck they can wrap this up and move on to financial matters.

"Rats! I didn't think to bring any cards," Gardner says. "Do you have your phone?" she asks Josh.

"Sorry."

She looks to Erin: "Will you make sure I get this list of books he mentioned?"

"You bet," Erin says. "You can borrow some of mine if you'd like. I have most of the titles, I think."

"Thank you." She turns to Moore: "I'll make you a copy, I promise."

Dreyfus clears his throat conspicuously.

"And one for you," Gardner says with a smile.

"Anyway—" Josh makes a gesture and fumbles his helmet, almost dropping it. He looks at it curiously, as if he's never seen it before, then puts it on his head.

Erin has to laugh. *What a goofball.*

"Anyway, the evidence goes on and on," he says, spreading his hands wide." Like I said, we could be here all night and not cover at all."

"Yet it still begs the question," Worthing says resolutely. "Why has the public—the vast majority of us ignorant dupes, as you so think us—never heard of this so-called evidence."

Josh doesn't hesitate: "The Church. Politics. Power."

"Ah, so it's a conspiracy, then. Why am I not surprised?"

"It's always been about power, and control over others," Josh says with feeling. "And greed, of course . . . What is the Church but a political organization? After all, it was first created and ruled by emperors. And later it was the Church who decided who would become King and who would be allowed to remain on the throne. According to them, *they* were the voice of God and His only authority on Earth. So to defy the Church, or the government, was to defy God Himself.

"Organized religion was first meant to *unify* the populace," he goes on, "then to *control* it. In time, the Church's number-one job was to keep the masses in fear and in reliance on them. If the people ever knew how powerful they were themselves as genuine spiritual beings—as powerful and important as the Emperor himself!—they wouldn't have a need for the Church. They wouldn't obey the laws, was the fear."

Worthing shakes his head, makes an impatient "get on with it" gesture. "So how is the Church responsible for us living in ignorance today, then?"

Josh doesn't reply right away. His look is unfocused, as if recalling a memory—as if looking back into the distant past. "There was a time when reincarnation was common knowledge," he says at last, more slowly. "It was simply a fact of life—of life, death, and rebirth—as it still is today—as it *always* will be . . . And the knowledge was passed down from generation to generation—within families, communities . . . Not everyone knew about it, or understood it, though, of course. Back then, maybe five percent of the people could read or write, so they had to rely on what they were told—or on what they experienced for themselves.

"But then, one day—" He pauses, clearly making an effort to get a hold of himself.

Erin's surprised: For the first time, she can see Josh getting worked up over the issue. She knows he's relived many lives where he was persecuted for what he believed, and at least one where he was forced to convert to Christianity, and where he was eventually killed. She hopes he can keep his passions in check.

When Josh resumes, there's a measure of anger—of disgust—to his voice. "But then one day, in the year 325, it was suddenly made the *law* that everyone had to be something called a 'Christian.' It was now a crime *punishable by death* to believe or teach anything but what the Church *told* you to believe. So for the next few hundred years—the next thousand—anyone who shared their belief in reincarnation was killed if they were discovered. And whatever writings on the subject were destroyed along with them. Most of it, but not all."

"So Christians are to blame, is that it?" Worthing sputters. "Why not the Jews, while you're at it?"

Josh continues as if he hadn't heard. "For ages, reincarnation had to be taught as 'secret knowledge.' Mystery Schools were created all over Europe and the Middle East to disseminate the Truth . . . They had to be kept hidden from the Church and its murderous Inquisition. . . . Later, many great thinkers, like Michelangelo, Francis Bacon, Leonardo da Vinci, and Isaac Newton became leaders of these 'subversive' groups."

Clap! Clap! Clap! Worthing applauds slowly, deridingly, insultingly. "Thank you, Mr. Trip. But we don't need a lecture."

Josh blinks, seemingly startled from his reverie. "You asked," he says.

Worthing waves him off, like shooing a fly, an unwanted nuisance. He appears more than fed up with the subject. "Your fervor is admirable, but misplaced. You would do much better at the local community college, I'd say. Your ideas are very . . . entertaining, to say the least."

Josh stares. "You mock me?"

A heavy pause, Worthing's cheek twitches. "I do."

The men glare at one another. The crowd around them is quiet. There's nothing but the soft music in the background, people chatting in the distance.

"People mock what they don't understand," Josh says. His voice is cold, deadly.

Erin can't believe this. Josh has actually allowed himself to become angry—furious even—something she never thought she'd see. He stands stock still, radiating malice. If looks could kill . . .

Erin finds she's been holding her breath and she lets it out slowly, her eyes fixed on Josh. When his hand goes to the sword at his hip, plastic or not, she is quickly there in front of him, standing close.

"It's okay," she whispers, "let it go."

He looks down at her at last and his face softens into a smile. "Sorry," he mouths.

"It's all right. He's a jerk."

Worthing breaks the silence that has descended upon the group: "Ms. Pearse, surely you don't go in for this nonsense."

Erin turns to see that Worthing is standing alone; a space has formed around him. She sees some of her friends gesturing to her, shooting her warning looks.

The last thing Erin wants to do is ruin her only chance for a new loan—to jeopardize the Center's future in any way. But she isn't about to lie to this man. To do so would be to lie to everyone else here tonight—her patients, friends, volunteers, other supporters. So in a firm voice she says, "Yes, Mr. Worthing, I do. I do believe in this 'nonsense.'"

He throws up his hands. "But you're a person of science!"

Something like courage flares within her.

"Actually, I don't believe in it, sir," she says, stepping forward. "I *know* it, for an absolute fact. I've been through numerous past-life sessions, which is a lot more than *you* can say. I have experienced the truth of the matter for myself, and there is nothing any 'person of science' can tell me to change that."

As these words pass Erin's lips, a thought strikes her for the first time. She looks Worthing in the eyes, full of surprise behind his mask. She can just imagine how she must look to him in her devil costume, brandishing her pitchfork "menacingly," and she laughs out loud.

"As a matter of fact," she says, "it seems like Science today has become in many ways like the Church, claiming to have all the answers, claiming to be the only *real* source for knowledge"— Erin thumps her chest with her empty glass—"when the answers have always been right in here."

16

THE WATER IS COLD and invigorating. She prefers it to the tepid, almost hot, water of summer, though bathing is now a bit dicier. Gloria splashes her face twice more and examines her reflection in the mirror. She likes what she sees: the face of a younger, healthier woman.

She's lost even more weight in the past few months. For a while she hadn't been able to wear her sweatpants without having to constantly hold them up with one hand, until, using her teeth and nails, she managed to make a belt out of the elastic from one pair. She uses the other pair's elastic to tie back her hair, which has become thick with dreadlocks. She likes the look when it's pulled back as it is now.

Gloria hangs the washcloth on the edge of the sink to dry. She's broken in the brand new bar of soap that came this morning, using it sparingly. A new mini toothbrush and some tampons also arrived, along with the weekly roll of toilet paper.

She's happy; she can't help it; she looks forward to "delivery" days. It's like getting a package, a present, each month. And it helps her keep track of the countless days she's been here. If she's right, it's November now.

Ten months! My God, so long!

There's also the latest book, which she doesn't care for at all. This month it's *Seth Speaks*, a thicker, heavier one than normal.

Gloria doesn't give a damn about what this Seth character has to say.

But she *is* intrigued with what's come with the book this month: Sitting beside her breakfast tray at the foot of the bed is a portable CD-player with headphones—fully loaded, batteries included.

As curious as she is, Gloria is even hungrier, so she eats first, taking her time, savoring each bite as she eyes the device. She's already inspected the CD inside: *Deep Time Dreaming* with *Hemi-Sync*. She knows exactly what it is, it's obvious: a brainwashing program. Mind control. Apparently we've come to the next step in Rostam's sinister plan.

The luminous rainbow reflection on the back of the disc had immediately grabbed her attention and kept her entranced for some time: an aftereffect from her recent infusion with the Power of God. A week later and Gloria can still sense the lingering euphoria such grace had bestowed upon her. Occasionally, she'll see streaks of light on the outskirts of her vision, flashing red and blue balls. Everything in the room—herself especially—has an aura, as if containing an inner glow. She can still see the trails of light and color her hands make as they move before her eyes.

She had been praying at about this same time of morning when the Power first descended upon her. It was nothing like the peaceful, loving presence of Christ she experienced months before. This, instead, had been a powerful energy—an all-consuming, holy force beyond any imagination. For hours she was anchored to one spot, on her knees, unable to move, overcome with the mighty Power of God Himself, as revelation after revelation had been imparted to her. By the end, she had been presented with the Secrets of the Universe.

Gloria has no idea why her prayers were answered in this way, or why she had been chosen to receive such divine inspiration, only that it was an incredible blessing. She is eternally grateful. She feels she has had a taste of what the greatest saints themselves must have experienced. And she would love to experience such virtuous, omnipotent power again.

She's since resumed her prayers with renewed vigor.

At one point she had been given the power to travel to other worlds, other dimensions. And in the land of Darkness and Despair, a blazing red sword of Divine Light had materialized in her hands. With it she fended off the legions of demons who reigned there; she did battle with the very Forces of Evil and sent them fleeing back to Hades. Surprisingly, she'd felt no fear at the time, only fury—and the triumph and jubilation of a spiritual warrior. It had been mostly an exciting adventure.

In fact, there is nothing that scares her now: not demons, not Rostam, not her current predicament in this man-made hell. With the Power of God on her side, Gloria knows she can conquer anything. Even this latest attempt of Rostam's to conform her to his religion holds no fear for her, only contempt. And a fierce curiosity.

After sliding the now empty tray through the door, she settles into bed, tucks the blanket around her, places the CD-player on her newly flat stomach, the headphones over her ears, hits "play."

At first she can hear nothing at all, only a soft humming, so she turns up the volume. There's the sound of a crashing surf, first only in her left ear, then in both, then only on the right, then back again. She can hear the faint sounds of harp strings and the tinkling of chimes; a low-blowing flute—first to the left, then the right, back and forth, from one ear to the other. A drum begins to beat softly in the distance, like a heartbeat, louder, then diminishing again. Then a voice—*Is it a voice?*—high and sweet, running through a complex set of scales she can barely follow.

It's so beautiful . . .

And now, behind all this, she can make out the sound of water, a bubbling brook flowing over stones . . . a song unto itself.

Gloria lets her eyes close, enjoying the delightful music. Her last conscious thought is that she must stay awake, alert, vigilant against the agents of darkness who use such things of beauty to hide behind, insinuate themselves . . .

SHE IS WALKING AMID crystal towers shining from within—a crystal city, illuminating a dark blue-black sky above. She can see other people moving through the streets as well. The majority appear to be converging on one building, a giant, clear dome, like an indoor arena. Even from a distance, Gloria can see hundreds, perhaps thousands, of people inside. It's very bright in there.

She moves in that direction herself, drawn by an invisible force as much as the desire to know.

As she gets closer, she becomes surrounded by other people. She wants to ask someone where they are going and why, but she's too timid, too unsure of herself. Then a smiling young girl in pigtails floats around her in a circle and grabs her by the hand, pulling her along, emanating joy.

For the moment, Gloria is happy to be acknowledged and accepted, and she allows herself to be led. But as they approach the dome's entrance, crowded with bustling figures, she becomes afraid. *What's inside?* she asks the girl, who doesn't answer but only beams back. *What's inside?*

She pulls away and is left standing alone, the crowd milling around her. For the first time since she arrived, Gloria studies the people filing past. There's something unusual about them . . .

They're floating! It just occurs to her. *She's* floating! This must be dream. But she feels so awake—more than awake: hyper-alert, all her senses alive.

On an impulse, she rises straight up into the air, high up to the tops of the buildings. *Left,* she thinks, and she moves left. *Right,* and she moves right. *Wow, this is pretty neat!* Gloria focuses on a pointed crystal spire in the distance, protruding even higher into the dimly lit sky; and with a thought, she's moving toward it, circling it, faster and faster. *Whee! This is fun!* She feels so free and light.

Someone is calling to her. But no, it's not that—it's the pull she again feels from inside the lighted dome, only stronger this time. People are still entering, and from her vantage point Gloria can see just as many exiting the other side. It must be safe, she reasons, and so she floats down to the brightly shining entrance.

Inside, she is shoulder to shoulder with countless others, people of all types and ages. Most everyone appears happy, smiling—beaming, literally, as if there is a glow to them.

Is she? Gloria looks down at herself: she's wearing her favorite Sunday outfit. *How nice! She reaches up: Even the hat!* But she isn't glowing like some of the others.

She lets the crowd carry her along. They seem to be converging upon a brilliant orb of light—sparkling white, blue, silver, and gold—hanging suspended in the air. As she gets closer, still some distance away, Gloria can feel a tremendous presence and a feeling of incomparable peace and love emanating from this light. It's identical to a sensation she has experienced only once before . . . months ago, in the little room.

Christ Jesus!

She has to be near Him, touch Him, speak to Him! This must be his second coming! she thinks excitedly. And she's being called to His side!

In her impatience, Gloria pushes her way through the crowd. The closer she gets, the more radiant the light and the more she is filled with its divine grace. She's weeping from happiness, shaking with anticipation.

Finally she is there before Him, blinded by a light a thousand times greater than the sun. She drops to her knees, throws up her hands: "Take me, Jesus!"

But there is only silence. And radiating Love.

Gloria stays there, kneeling, floating before Him. She has only once before experienced such a level of peace, her mind as clear and untroubled as a newborn baby's, as she basks again in Christ's presence. She never wants to leave.

Eventually, however, after an undeterminable amount of time, Gloria begins to wonder, to worry. *Why hasn't He taken me? Am I not worthy?* She begins to consider all the reasons why she might be rejected: She's been vain, she knows, and judgmental . . . selfish, self-righteous, self-serving, conceited, egotistical, deceitful, intolerant, hateful, unforgiving . . .

Oh, Lord!

But she has never once doubted Him. She has never once lost her faith . . .

Or has she . . . ? Hasn't she been swayed by the reading she's done lately? Hasn't the thought crossed her mind at least once that there may be some validity to the concept of reincarnation? Hasn't she at least marveled at the idea that she herself, along with All of Creation, *is* God?

The guilt Gloria feels now is staggering.

But those books had been forced upon her! It's not fair! She'd been tricked! There was nothing else to do! Oh, if only she had been stronger, braver, hadn't succumbed to Rostam's treachery!

Gloria is sure now she's failed the test God has put before her. Rostam—Satan—has won.

But can't she redeem herself? Isn't there any way, any hope, for her at all? "Please, Jesus, I beg of you! Forgive me!" she cries. She'll do anything to make it up to Him. "Just one more chance!"

She can feel the love and forgiveness pouring forth from His being. But she knows it's not enough. She still must prove herself worthy to join Him. She must prove her devotion to Him alone. Gloria swears then and there that she will dedicate herself to serving only Him, forever—that nothing shall ever again come between them.

"My child." A tender voice above her.

Gloria's eyes open wide with hope and wonder. "Jesus."

"No, my child, it is only I." Standing beside her is an elderly man with a silver head of hair, a thin gold band with colored lights wrapped across his forehead. He's wearing a light-blue, futuristic jumpsuit. He smiles at her and holds out his hand for her to take.

He seems kind enough, and Gloria is too emotionally drained to resist. She makes a final, silent promise to Jesus as the man gently leads her away. Together they pass through the milling crowd. She had forgotten there were so many others here, too. It seems like forever ago when she first arrived.

They reach an open spot and the man asks her, "Why are you so distressed, my child? This is a place for joy and celebration."

His kindly eyes elicit a truthful response, as shameful as it is to say: "I was expecting to be taken up with Him. But I'm not worthy. Not yet." Gloria hangs her head, barely suppressing tears.

"I understand. I have seen it many times before. But you are mistaken. This awesome being we visit is not Jesus Christ, nor is it God."

Gloria looks up, suddenly wary.

"It is *you*," the old man says. He pats her hand consolingly. "It is your Higher Self. Though not your *highest*," he adds with a quiet chuckle. "And all of these people you see here"—motioning to the multitudes—"are you as well. As am I. We are all individual aspects of our Higher Self, separate personalities, living in different times and places—other worlds, even. We are each a soul, but we are still One, do you see?"

So soon, Gloria thinks, swiftly gripped by fear. She hasn't even left the building and already her faith is being tested. Again.

She pulls her hand away. "Thank you," she says politely, "but I know the real truth." She looks frantically about her for the exit. "I have to go now, goodbye."

And with that she is dodging people as she heads for a nearby archway in the crystal wall of the dome. Many others are moving in the same direction; she gets caught up in the flow.

As she noticed before, most everyone looks happy, but now Gloria can spot a few others who seem as anxious as herself. She also notices now how differently everyone is dressed; some are even naked, and she averts her eyes. There are women and men, girls and boys, of every color, shape, and size. Quite a few *do* appear alien and otherworldly to her, but to think for one moment . . . She banishes the thought and chides herself for not staying diligent against such a heretical notion.

Gloria is still deeply affected from her audience with Christ. But now she wants only to put this place behind her and return to the natural world. She understands now that the many temptations and challenges to her faith are actually *opportunities* to demonstrate her unwavering devotion to her Lord and Savior.

She literally flies out of the exit when she can, at last. The softly glowing, crystal buildings are no longer beautiful to her anymore.

What if there's no way home! she fears—even if "home" is currently only an eight-by-ten-foot metal box.

Gloria doesn't know which way to go. A dark blue glow extends to the limit of her vision in every direction. Above is only blackness.

She panics, flying faster and faster but seemingly gaining no ground.

Perhaps this is the Catholics' Purgatory, she thinks, horrified, where she has been condemned to wait for Jesus's next return.

But no! He is to come again only once!

In desperation she calls out, "Help me, Lord! Help me, Jesus!"

She speeds on, fraught with terror. The ground below has turned to a churning red, orange, and black—a steaming cauldron of molten lava roiling beneath her. Without warning, a searing tower of flame leaps into the air beside her. Incessant tongues of fire flick at her teasingly as she tries in vain to fly higher, away from the tumultuous inferno.

Then, one by one, shapeless demonic forms come at her from out of the darkness. She's assailed from every side. Each time, Gloria is barely able to avoid their attacks, their teeth and claws rending her Sunday clothes to shreds. She screams at them, curses them, but to no effect. Oh, where is the Power of God she had wielded against them before?

Black wings beat furiously against her as she falls from the sky, somersaulting helplessly, a lake of bubbling fire rushing up to meet her . . .

Gloria wakes screaming on the floor beside her bunk, thrashing wildly, headphones askew, knuckles white against the CD-player still clutched in her hand.

She takes in the relative safety of her cell, the familiar, bare metal walls. She's back.

"Thank you, Jesus!" she sobs between breaths. "Oh, thank you, Jesus!"

17

A BRIGHT GIBBOUS MOON, riding low in the sky, casts an otherworldly light over everything Dani sees. The bare trees of the forest glow like ghosts.

The little woman is all bundled up in a winter coat and scarf and a colorful, fuzzy stocking cap, some red curls escaping here and there, her hands thrust deep in the coat's pockets. Her breath steams as she walks by with the dogs down the wide, dirt road through the trees and past the old, wooden building from where Dani spies from the roof.

It must be cold outside but Dani feels none of it. She's not really sure how she came to be here, but it's nice to finally be free from the confines of her little room. She's thinking maybe this woman can help her—she seems friendly enough, surrounded by a pink-yellow aura.

Dani drifts down to alight on the road a short ways behind. "Hello," she calls out softly, not wanting to startle her. "Hello, can you help me, please?"

The woman continues on, oblivious, but both dogs stop and turn their heads.

Louder, Dani calls out again: "Hello! Excuse me, please!"

This time the woman does stop, but it's only to address the dogs: "Come on, guys, let's go."

The dogs return to her side. The smaller, motley-colored one looks back again and gives a soft bark.

"What's the matter, Pooch? You see a ghost?" The woman glances back, still walking, and though she must have seen Dani standing there, keeps going on her way.

Without thinking how she does it, Dani is suddenly standing twenty feet down the path in front of them now. "Hi, I'm sorry to bother you, but—"

Both dogs give a bark and stop in their tracks. The woman, obviously alarmed, stops, too. She follows the dogs' gaze, peering down the road ahead of her. "What's up, you two? What do you see?"

Maybe she's blind, Dani thinks. But no, that can't be the case. The woman scans the darkly lit woods around them and looks again at the dogs, both of whom are sitting and watching Dani intently.

"Please don't be afraid," Dani says. "I just want to talk to you, if that's okay."

"Now you've got *me* spooked," the woman says. She hugs herself through the thick woolen coat and rubs her hands together briskly. Then she shrugs and turns away. "Come on, fellas, let's go get mama some cocoa."

Dani can't understand this woman's behavior, but she doesn't dwell on it. Instead, she flies ahead of her down the road.

The wide path curves through the trees, and soon a trio of buildings appear, spread out around a large, open courtyard. The buildings are painted pale yellow and white and glow brightly in the moonlight. An expanse of grass makes up the far side, where it appears to drop off. She can see a small town beyond, down below and far away, sparkling like so many scattered jewels. The dirt road she is on starts up again on the opposite side of the circle, as if heading for town.

The larger, two-story building to her left is alive, its many tall windows downstairs spilling light into the courtyard. This is where she heads now.

Up a few stairs is a wide, covered porch and the entrance.

Through a window beside the door, Dani can see an expansive room with a tall ceiling. To the left are two raggedy, old couches and a pair of mismatched recliners. To the right is a long dining room table with at least a dozen assorted chairs. In back is a pool table and stools, along with another couch, some beanbag chairs, and a large, flatscreen TV. A wide staircase leads upward in the corner. Colorful artwork, bookcases, and tall green plants line the walls. In the center of the room is a faded Persian rug covering the hardwood floor. A small circle of people are sitting cross-legged upon it. She counts nine. Their eyes are closed; they appear to be meditating silently.

It's fascinating: Dani can see an aura of light surrounding each person individually, and a soft, golden glow around the group as a whole. Many of the people have bright white beams of "laser" light steadily shooting out from them in every direction.

What are they doing? she wonders.

One person, facing away from her, has a different colored aura than the rest; his is a light green with sparkles of yellow and silver.

Dani enters through the window and moves to the right of the circle, keeping her eyes on the green man. No one seems aware of her presence.

The recognition doesn't surprise her at all: it's the john who got her high and abducted her. And underneath the beard and added years, she now recognizes Josh, the hint of a smile on his face. He doesn't appear to be breathing, he sits so still.

Dani wants to kneel beside him and tell him she's sorry. She wants to explain everything and plead for his forgiveness. She wants to ask him to let her go. But intuitively she knows that now is not the time; she doesn't want to bother him during his meditation or whatever. She can wait awhile longer.

She'll explore a little and come back later. She wants to learn more about this place she's being kept.

Dani moves swiftly through the building, clockwise, down the hallway to the left, looking through open doorways or stepping through closed ones for a quick peek. First there's a large office cluttered with books and papers; then a hospital-like room with four beds (two of them occupied) and various pieces of medical equipment on trolleys; a large, tiled bathroom with a bunch of sinks, toilets, and showers; a laundry and storage room; then, in a row on either side of the hallway, all the way down: ten small bedrooms about the same size as her own, but each with a real bed, a nightstand and lamp, a chest of drawers, a tiny wooden desk and chair, and a curtained window in those rooms on the left (only one has anyone in it and she's sleeping); then it's through a bedroom wall and into a kitchen pantry and the kitchen itself with antique appliances and miles of counter tops and cupboards; then back into the great room, where the circle still sit peacefully all aglow. Nothing has changed in the short time she's been gone.

Skirting the group, Dani now travels up the wide, wooden staircase, turning twice on a pair of landings. Upstairs it's dark; but as everywhere else, everything is subtly illuminated with a soft white glow. In this case it's only the walls, floors, and ceiling, for each room is bare, save for an ancient, lion-clawed, porcelain bathtub in one. Many of the walls have gaping holes in them, their plaster crumbling or missing in large patches, exposing the framing underneath. The ceiling is in no better shape. Only the plank wood flooring, though marred, seems to have withstood the test of time. Dani can't understand why things haven't been remodeled up here as down below. It's a question she might ask Josh if she gets the chance.

Then just that quick, as if she's summoned him with her thoughts, Josh is standing with her across the large, empty room. He no longer has the same light-green aura as before, but his body still seems to sparkle.

"Hi," he says.

"Hi."

Dani's not sure what to do. After a moment's hesitation, she walks slowly forward, nervous about the reception she'll receive. But to her instant relief, Josh smiles warmly and holds out his hand.

Dani takes both of them in hers, tells him everything she's been wanting to for so long. It all comes flooding out, the river of guilt and regret finally undammed. And through it all, Josh never stops smiling kindly at her; there's not even a hint of the anger and accusation she so expected and feared. And this encourages her to tell him more: how she's changed, how happy she is to be finally living drug-free, how grateful she is for what he's done for her, regardless of his methods.

In the end, they embrace. Dani feels so relieved to have finally unburdened herself to him. "Can you ever forgive me?" she asks, hugging him tightly.

"Of course," Josh says. "Thank you, Dani. I only hope you can forgive *me.*"

They remain holding each other like this for a long time. It feels so good to her, so comforting and empowering at the same time. She wishes it will never end. It's definitely the best hug Dani has ever had, not that she can remember that many others in her life.

Finally, she can feel him pull away.

"Dani, you have a gift," he says, looking her in the eyes. "You may not know it yet, but you do."

"What do you mean?"

"This. To be here now, in this body, separate from the physical." He takes her hand and holds it up between them. "Do you see? Can you see the difference?"

She shakes her head, not understanding.

"Look closely. What do you see?"

Dani gazes intently at her palm. Then it suddenly becomes clear: "It's like glitter," she says in awe, a smile spreading across her face. "Like a zillion tiny stars." This must be the light she's been seeing in everything all evening; she'd just taken it for granted. "Is this what you mean?"

"Yep. Right now we're in our energy bodies, or 'etheric' bodies. Not fully in the physical and not fully in the astral either— kind of in-between."

Josh lets go of her hand and takes a step back. "Watch this," he says. He continues walking backward and waves to her as he passes through the wall behind him.

Dani lets out a gasp but really isn't that surprised: it seems almost natural to her for some reason. And hadn't she done the same thing herself earlier, without thinking it anything special?

Josh reappears, smiling. "We're *in* the world but not *of* it, so to speak. But, then again, I guess that's always the case, isn't it." He laughs and holds out his hand, which she gladly takes. "But in *this* body, at least, the physical laws don't apply anymore . . . Come on, let's go downstairs. The express route this time."

Then before she even realizes what's happening, they're passing through the floor and hovering in the air above the meditation circle. The sudden change from darkness to light is disorientating and Dani blinks reflexively. She grips Josh's hand tighter and grabs his arm as they float softly to the floor.

The golden aura surrounding the group almost reaches them. Dani holds out her hand to it but feels no change.

Seeing Josh still sitting there on the rug with the others while also standing beside her is a shock at first, until she recalls what he said about this being another body, separate from the physical.

Where am I, then? she thinks. *In my room? I wasn't meditating, was I?*

"We're praying for the victims of the earthquake in Iran," Josh says. "Doing so in a group magnifies the energy a hundred-fold. 'Where two or more gather in my name,' and all that." Pointing, he adds: "See those rays of light? That's positive energy—Love, basically—going out to anyone who can use it. It really does help. I can show you how it works sometime."

With a tug on her arm, Josh turns her to face him. His eyes are bright and alive with energy, but his expression is somber. "But what I'm doing is different. I'm there now ... Do you wanna come? You can, you know. And I could use your help."

Dani considers the implications of what he just said. What does he mean he's "there now"? Where? Iran? He's here—but in two places at once—or at least in two bodies. Can he also be in still another one, somewhere else?

The idea of traveling with Josh, wherever it is, is a scary but exciting proposition. She's sure to be safe by his side, though, right? ... And he did say he could use her help ... This is what decides it for her.

She nods once. "All right. I'll go with you."

"I'm glad. Thanks, Dani." His smile is reserved, still serious. "Just follow my lead. We're only going to give directions, explain a few things, that's it." He gives her hand a reassuring squeeze. "We're going to be one step further into the astral plane. Things work a little differently there. Just remember: like here—like anywhere—your *thoughts* create the reality, okay? Only faster. Your thoughts have real power, meaning *you* have real power. Always remember that and nothing can harm you, or shouldn't even scare you ... Got it?"

Now she's having second thoughts, and Josh must be able to see it in her face.

"Don't worry," he says, "you'll be fine, I promise. I'll be right there with you. Unless you decide to leave, of course. You can do that anytime you want. But I think you're going to dig this." He gives her a big smile this time. "You ready?"

Dani gathers her courage and returns the smile as best she can. "Ready as I'll ever be."

"Good. One last thing: Don't worry about talking or about being understood when we get there. Just think. And feel. Thought and emotion are all that matter."

And with that last bit of advice, in the blink of an eye, they're standing in the midst of a catastrophe.

It's daylight, early morning. Dust fills the air, blown by sudden gusts of wind. A whole mountain appears to have collapsed around them in the past few hours, destroying a small town or village. Buildings are crushed and buried for as far as her eyes can see. A few of the survivors are staggering about, still dazed, but most are yelling for loved ones missing in the rubble, digging impotently at the mounds of debris. Some stand simply crying.

Oh my God! Dani is thinking. *The poor people!* So many must have died. And all so suddenly, without warning.

She looks to Josh beside her, still holding her hand. He's lost form somehow; he looks insubstantial, like a ghost; only his face is clear to her, but even that has a transparency to it. He waves a phantom arm, indicating the entire tragic scene, and Dani takes it in: the vast devastation; the few survivors; the harsh, unsympathetic wind; the red, dust-covered sun on the horizon; the fast-moving clouds overhead, oblivious to the human drama unfolding below.

They stand there silently for another moment, then Josh's voice sounds in her mind: *"Now."*

Instantly, as if a veil has been lifted, Dani can see dozens—no, hundreds!—more people climbing through the wreckage. Like the ones she saw before, most are walking about in a daze. Others cry or scream or try vainly to move the rocks covering their once-was town, their once-were homes, their once-were friends and family.

Dani cries out herself at such despair, and lifting her hands to her face, realizes she is no longer connected to Josh. She looks around, finds him talking to a small group of people atop a plateau of fallen rock some distance away. He is no longer ghostly in appearance but as solid-looking as the rest and dressed in similar clothing. A faint green glow sets him apart from the others and makes him instantly identifiable to her.

With just the thought of being near him again, she is there by his side. The people around him jump at her sudden appearance.

"They will meet you there. There is no point in waiting. Many have already left," Josh is telling them, though not in any language she has heard before. Picture images fill her mind, and an instantaneous knowing translates his words.

"How do we know that what you say is true?" shouts one man close by. Others echo the same question, and a ripple goes out through the crowd.

"Look to the Light!" Josh says, pointing to the sky above them.

Dani looks up with the rest. A brilliant white light—a swirling vortex—bigger and brighter than the sun, fills the dome of the sky. To her amazement, many far-away figures are floating upward through the air toward it, as if pulled by an invisible force, diminishing in size to little specks before finally winking out of sight.

"But I am not dead!" shouts another man. "I am alive as when I woke this morning, before the earth shook and the mountain fell!" This sentiment, too, finds resonance within the crowd, and many loudly proclaim their own good health as well.

"That's right, you are correct," Josh responds to them all. "You are *not* dead, nor will you ever die. Only your physical bodies are gone now, buried beneath these stones. You do not need them anymore."

"Then what is this?" asks a young woman at his elbow, pinching her bared arm. "Is this not my body? You talk nonsense!" She turns to leave but there are too many in her way.

Josh raises his voice to be heard above the murmuring crowd: "Will you heed my words and join your loved ones in Paradise, or would you wander the Earth as a wraith—a restless spirit—for all time?"

He pauses and Dani can see that this has gotten their attention.

"I tell you this as a brother," he continues, "as someone who knows and who cares. Your place is not here any longer but in your true spiritual home, *there*"—he points—"in the Light!"

"I am not worthy!" cries an old man, meekly, tremulously, a tear sliding down his weathered cheek. "I have never had faith. I drank; I whored; I was not a good Muslim."

Josh opens his arms wide. "*Everyone* is a child of Allah and is dear to Him. No one is turned away." To the old man crying openly he says, "We are here to learn and to grow from our mistakes. You will not be judged. In Paradise there is only love and understanding. Only *you* will judge *yourself.*"

A little girl, a child no older than five, pulls on Dani's pants leg. "Are you dead, too?" she asks.

Dani crouches down and holds the girl gently by the shoulders. Everything she's recently learned from her books comes to mind. "We are all as alive or as dead now as we ever will be," she says. "There is really no such thing as death . . . You don't feel dead, do you?"

The child shakes her head. "No."

"Well, then, there you go. It's just that when our life here is done—no matter how long or how short it was—it's time to go home. And then we can come back again later if we want."

People around them have been listening, for this last comment sparks mutterings of "heresy," "pagan," and "Sufi."

"Will I see my mother and father?" the girl asks. "Will Mehr be there?"

"They're not here now?"

"No, I can't find them."

"I *know* they'll be there," Dani says with a smile. "For sure. And I'll bet they're all waiting for you right now."

"Can I go now?"

"Of course you can." She points to the massive Light swirling high above them. "You see the Light? That's the doorway home. You can fly there right now. I can go with you a little ways if you'd like."

Dani has no idea where her words and confidence have come from. She feels inspired.

The girl smiles back at her timidly and holds out her hand. "Okay."

And then they are both rising slowly through the air, to gasps of astonishment from the crowd. Dani holds the girl's eyes with her own and keeps a reassuring smile on her face, despite her own apprehension.

Soon they're far above the disaster below. The little girl looks upward in wonderment, her face resplendent with light. "Mommy! Poppy!" she cries happily. Dani releases her, and without a backward glance, the child floats rapidly away.

As Dani descends to the ground, she recognizes some of the other people from the crowd rising past her, alone or holding hands.

From high above she can see Josh talking to even more people who have come out of curiosity or need. On the outskirts of the crowd are children—so many children!—wandering about, lost and ignored, many crying for their parents.

With a sense of great purpose, Dani knows what to do.

SHE WAKES IN HER ROOM, propped up with her makeshift pillow, fully dressed as when she fell asleep. The headphones are still in place, but the recording, *Shaman's Heart,* had to have ended long ago.

The light is on: it must be morning.

Dani sets the CD-player and headphones carefully on the floor, pads over in stocking feet to retrieve the book that had come with the new CD yesterday. The book's title, *Adventures Beyond the Body,* is an apt description of what she has just experienced so vividly.

Was it a dream? She doesn't think so.

Dani splashes some water on her face and drinks a cupful. In spite of the night's work, she feels well rested.

Breakfast hasn't arrived, so it must still be early. Maybe she can ask Josh about their astral adventure, if that's what it was.

Though the most he ever says to her through the door is "Hi" or "You're welcome."

However, last night's meeting—if it really did take place—has to have changed their relationship. She's certain of it.

Will she be allowed to leave now?

Is she even *ready* to leave? Where would she go? Surely anything is better than being held captive; but life on the streets, she knows, can be much worse than this. She can go to a shelter, maybe, or a church. There are always caring people at churches. Or so she's heard.

He's coming.

Dani fusses with her hair in the mirror (a pointless gesture, of course) and sits at the foot of her bunk to wait.

Within a minute she hears the heavy, sliding noise, and her tray is pushed carefully through.

She goes to her knees and moves the tray aside. She speaks through the slot: "Josh."

There's no answer, no movement she can sense.

"Josh, was it real? Tell me. Please."

She waits and is about to speak again, when he replies:

"You did good, Dani. Real good . . . Thank you."

And then he's gone.

18

SANTOS OPENS HIS EYES. He was dreaming, but something has woke him up.

Krunk! Pop! Squeak!

The doors!

In an instant he's thrown off the covers and is crouching on the floor, adrenaline rushing through his system.

For the first time in nearly a year, Santos sees the steel cargo doors of his cell part. They open only a crack, an inch, nothing but darkness beyond.

"Santos." It has to be Rostam.

Santos doesn't answer; he doesn't move. His animal instincts have completely taken over—nerves sharp, muscles tense. Waiting.

"Santos, I have a gun, and I *will* use it. Don't do anything stupid."

He considers rushing the doors.

"I can see you," the voice says. "Do us both a favor and back up. Sit on the floor by the wall."

Santos is raging inside, torn by indecision. This is his one chance, he's sure. How many times has he seen chumps get fucked because they hesitated? But the gun . . .

There's no way anybody can aim through that crack.

"All right," he says finally. "Hold on."

He slowly begins to rise, then like a missile, his legs like pistons beneath him, he launches himself at the doors. He hits them with his shoulder, right in the center, his full weight behind him. *WHAM!* And is stopped cold. The doors have opened maybe another inch.

Santos staggers back, collapses to his knees. His head is ringing, purple lights flashing before his eyes. A part of him knows he should be feeling pain, but there's nothing, only his heart beating like a drum in his chest—and the urge to attack again.

He puts his right fist on the floor, his left leg beneath him, begins to stand, when it all—

OH, FUCK. He hurts.

He goes to raise a hand to his head but there's a sharp pain in his shoulder that makes him stop. *What the . . . ?*

Santos opens his eyes, sees the ceiling; he's lying on his back, on the floor, his head a foot away from the toilet. Dark spots fill the room; he blinks to get rid of them, gives his head a shake— *Ow! Bad move*—closes his eyes against the pain. He'll just lie here for a while till it goes away.

With a start, he remembers the reason for his painful condition. He quickly sits up, bracing himself with his good arm.

His head spins; he can't seem to focus very well. But it's obvious he's not alone: a man is sitting in a chair by the doors, bent forward, elbows on his knees, looking at him calmly.

Santos's first reaction—to attack—is suppressed by the object the man is holding in his hand: a Taser.

He looks the guy over as his vision clears: a *güero*; with a short, thick beard and long, messed-up hair; good sized, well built; dressed in a blue fleece pullover, faded jeans, and hiking boots. A fucking lumberjack. It's nobody he's ever met before. It doesn't look like the junkie he framed for murder, but that was a long time ago.

They study each other for a while.

"That your *gun?*"

"Yep."

There's nothing I can do, Santos thinks after a moment, *not right now.* He'll have to wait; an opportunity may present itself. He scoots back against the wall, below the shelf, cradling his left arm. His shoulder hurts like a bitch. He stares at the man staring back. He waits. He's gotten good at waiting.

Let's see what this motherfucker's got to say.

"Why haven't you been reading the books?"

Not what Santos thought he'd say, that's for sure. And definitely the wrong question to ask. "Fuck you and your fucking books."

The guy shakes his head, sits up in his chair—one of those small, metal, folding ones. "You know who I am, right?"

"I don't give a fuck who you are." But of course he knows: it's Rostam. He was right, it's him, after all.

"You probably think I'm pissed at you," Rostam says.

Santos snorts. "No shit."

"And I was, believe me. For a long time." He spreads his arms wide, the Taser in his lap. "I mean, I could never figure out why you did it. It's not like I'd ever done anything to you to deserve that, right?"

Rostam pauses for too long. What? Does he really expect an answer? Fuck him.

"But then one day I understood. I *had* done something to you. A long time ago. Lots of times, in fact . . . In other lifetimes."

Santos searches Rostam's face for any hint of a smile, that he's joking; but his eyes give nothing away.

He can't be serious . . . Can he?

"I can tell by your expression you don't believe me," Rostam says. He shakes his head. "If you'd only read the books . . ."

The stupid asshole doesn't get it; and Santos isn't about to clue him in. "Are you crazy?"

"What I'm saying is true. And I can prove it to you if you give me the chance."

"Fuck you."

Rostam picks up the Taser, turns it over in his hands. Santos tenses, ready to throw himself to the side if he has to.

"No, I'm not crazy. Not anymore . . . But what *is* crazy? Not thinking like other people?" Rostam shrugs. "Then, who knows, maybe I am."

There's another long pause as they stare at each other. Santos wishes he'd just get on with it, say something that makes sense.

"What do you want?" he asks. "How much?"

Rostam looks disappointed, like Santos has failed a test or something. "Money's got nothing to do with this," he says. "This is about something much, much more important . . . If you'd just read the books . . ."

"Fuck the books!" Santos yells. "Don't tell me about your fucking books!" He slams his good elbow against the wall, making the whole box shudder.

He looks away. *Damn!* He lost his cool. And he's hurt his other arm. He can feel his face getting red, his head beginning to throb again. He can almost watch his left eye swelling shut; there's nothing but a slit to see out of now.

"Oh, shit . . ." Rostam says quietly. "You can't read, can you?"

Santos rests his head against the wall, closes the one eye that isn't already. How many years has it been since he's heard somebody say that to him? It isn't something ever repeated.

"I'm sorry, I wish I'd known."

"Shut up."

"All these months . . . A whole year . . ."

"Shut the fuck up!" Santos's hand shoots out uncontrollably, grasping at air. If he could reach him, he'd rip this motherfucker's heart out.

He needs to relax, get his shit together.

He needs to get the fuck out of here.

So he leans back again, takes a deep breath, lets it out slowly. "Just tell me. Please. What—do—you want?"

"I want you to forgive me," Rostam says.

This is so off-the-wall, so far from anything Santos ever expected, that he's left dumbfounded. He can't believe his ears.

"I want to end this cycle we're on," Rostam continues, "of ruining each other's lives. We need to forgive each other, once and for all. But it's not going to happen until we both realize what's going on."

Santos is suddenly tired. The adrenaline has worn off and left him feeling drained. "What are you talking about?"

Rostam leans back in his chair, stretches his legs, rests his hands—the Taser—on his stomach. "You and I have lived many lives together before," he says. "Hundreds. More . . . We don't really interact in all of them; and when we do, it's sometimes for the better and sometimes for the worse. But in way too many lately we are seriously affecting each other, either directly or indirectly. And it's not good . . . We've started this vicious cycle of 'I hurt you' then 'you hurt me.' It's like we take turns, over the centuries. It's a pattern we're stuck in, a rut . . . karma."

This takes a moment for Santos to absorb. By the look on Rostam's face, he means it. He really is insane.

"This time you hurt me," Rostam goes on. "I'm not sure where it all started, exactly, but I've traced it back to at least nine different lifetimes . . . The one just before this one was in the 1920s and 30s during Prohibition. You and I were both smuggling booze out of Canada into Buffalo, New York. We were competitors, but we never met, though. I think you were Mafia, I'm not sure; you and everyone you were with were always dressed real nice—expensive-looking clothes . . . Anyway, in the end, I set you up and you went to prison; I don't know for how long. I ended up getting killed, right after."

For the first time since he got here, Santos is craving a drink. And a cigar. Bad. He'd almost forgotten he ever enjoyed such vices, but Rostam's story has triggered something in him. He bursts out laughing. "So this time *I* sent *you* to prison, huh? That's great. Now we're even."

"I wish," Rostam says. "As far as I'm concerned, you're forgiven, we're done. But what about you? When *I* die, I'm not going to have any residual feelings against you at all. In fact, I'm going to love you, like a brother—like the spiritual brother you are to me."

Santos scoffs. "Spiritual brother? Don't feed me that crap. We're not brothers, you stupid prick. No fucking way."

"We are, though. We're part of the same spirit family. There's seven of us."

Santos motions to the tiny cell around them. "Is this how you treat a brother?"

"I'm trying to help you."

"You're full of shit."

"I'm not talking about our physical selves but our spiritual ones—our souls."

"What the fuck you know about souls? You a priest now? You get that jailhouse religion?"

"I know that that's who we really are." Rostam picks at his pullover. "These bodies are like clothes we discard when—"

"Where do you get this shit? From a fucking *book?* How do you *know?*"

Rostam sits up and leans forward. "Because I've experienced it. I've *experienced* myself as a soul. And that's what I want you to do, too."

"You're fucking *loco,* man. You got your mind messed up with all them drugs. I know you." Santos is disgusted. He knows he should be humoring this fool, but he's always hated drug addicts. It's why he got out of that end of the business as soon as he could. It's why he'd lost respect for Navarro, for screwing with it. The only thing worse than junkies, he thinks, are Bible-thumping hypocrites. And now he's talking to both at the same time.

But Rostam is emphatic: "No, no, I'm done with all that; I'm done with drugs. That's why getting locked up was the best thing that could have ever happened to me. I haven't touched any drugs since then, not even a beer. Thanks to you."

"Thanks to me, huh? You crack me up. So what was that shit you put in my food the other day? That wasn't a drug? Yeah, right. Fuck you."

Santos has sampled a lot of different drugs in his life—it came with the territory, the lifestyle, growing up—but never anything like *that*. Whatever that was Rostam gave him is on a whole other level entirely.

Usually drugs messed up the numbers; but on that stuff his brain had computed the mathematics of the universe. It was like his genius could reach out and process infinite amounts of data streaming freely through space. He'd had one extraordinary insight after another—more than he could possibly ever remember. Though there were some he will never forget. Like the one with his favorite "mathematically perfect" number: 6—or in this case, 666:

He knew it can be written as the first seven primes squared:

$$666 = 2^2 + 3^2 + 5^2 + 7^2 + 11^2 + 13^2 + 17^2;$$

but not also as palindromic cubes:

$$666 = 1^3 + 2^3 + 3^3 + 4^3 + 5^3 + 6^3 + 5^3 + 4^3 + 3^3 + 2^3 + 1^3$$
$$\text{(in the center is 6 x 6 x 6)}.$$

This little gem had tickled him; it never occurred to him before. But there was another problem Santos solved that had eluded him all of his life until then—a feat worthy of the mathematical history books: He'd calculated that there *is* a limited number of "twin" primes—something he had only speculated on before. He would need paper and pen to work it out now, but while on that drug his acuity knew no bounds: his mind was the only blackboard he needed.

However, for a time, after so many hours in that heightened state, Santos had thought he was going insane; he almost couldn't handle it. He didn't know if he would ever come down. He can see how this junkie Rostam had "experienced his soul": he was fucking hallucinating.

His jailer sits quietly now, staring at his lap, turning the Taser over and over in his hands. Obviously, what Santos said has struck home.

Finally: "Yeah, that might have been a mistake, to use it without telling you." Rostam looks up in earnest. "But it helped you in some ways, right? Opened your mind? Gave you a new outlook on some things? I mean, it definitely calmed you down."

"Do I look calm to you, asshole?" He wants to tear this fool's head off. "I was scared to eat anything after that. Thought you were going to drug my fucking oatmeal again, or something."

Wait, he thinks. *How does he know it calmed me down? He has to be watching me somehow, after all.*

"I tell you what," Santos says, "you do that again, I'll kill myself, and you won't have anybody to ransom." A bluff, of course.

"I told you, it's not about money."

"Right, 'karma'; it's about saving my fucking soul. What do you want me to do? Forgive you? All right, you're forgiven. How's that? I'll forget *all* this shit. Just let me go."

"I'm talking about real forgiveness, Santos. At the soul level. It's not something you can just say; you've got to actually *feel* it, sincerely, and mean it." Rostam waves an arm. "And it's not about forgiving me for this, but for all the things I've *ever* done to you—in other lives. So we can finally break the cycle."

"Right, right." *Just play along; do whatever he wants for now; bide your time.* "So how the fuck am I supposed to do that?"

Rostam visibly perks up. "We're going to visit your past lives, through deep hypnosis. You'll be able to see and feel and experience these lives, as if you were actually living them again." He holds up a finger. "But only the ones where you and I have issues.

So we can see the pattern and figure it out. Then you can forgive it—me, yourself, the whole thing—because you're able to see it from a higher, spiritual perspective. And then we won't have to go through it anymore; there won't be any point . . . But we *both* have to do it, we both have to forgive each other *all* of it, whatever it is—or it won't work."

Santos doesn't believe in any of this "spiritual" bullshit, of course, but he can see Rostam's logic behind it, no matter how twisted. There's just one thing he needs clarified: "Did you say *hypnosis?*"

"Yep. Transpersonal hypnosis, or 'spiritual' hypnosis I call it, past-life regression. It's where we access not just your subconscious but your *super*conscious—the part of you that lives forever."

"You have got to be fucking kidding me. You think I'm gonna let you go fucking around in my brain? You must think—" And then it comes to him; he figures it out in a flash. "Oh, you're *good.* You're a fucking genius, aren't you? But so am I . . . But you knew that already, didn't you?"

"What are you talking about?" Rostam actually looks confused. The guy can act.

"I'm not stupid, motherfucker. I might not be able to read your fucking books, but I can run a business, I can manage an organization . . . Dani told you, didn't she?"

"Told me what?"

"Don't fuck with me! You know what I do."

Santos has the numbers. He has the Syndicate's entire sports book operation inside his head, the offshore account information. And one account the Syndicate doesn't know about: the one Rostam set up for him so long ago. The one he wants now.

Now it's Rostam who looks agitated for a change. "Man, I don't give a damn about your business, or what you 'do.' I keep telling you: this isn't about money. How many times do I have to spell it out? I don't care anything about your money. I don't care anything about the material world at all anymore." He throws up his hands, one still holding that damn Taser. "That's the problem! People get hung up on the *material* things. They get so attached to the physical world and all its riches—all its drama—that they forget about the spiritual one all around them all the time. The spiritual world is the *real* world; it's our greater reality. It's why we're here in the first place: to evolve, spiritually."

"I'm not letting you fuck around in my head, freak."

Santos means what he says. He has too many secrets, too much critical information, in there. His life would be as good as over if any of it ever got out; he'd be better off left in here. But either thought scares the hell out of him.

"Look, it's nothing to be afraid of," Rostam says. "You'll be in total control the entire time. It only works if you want it to. You can stop at any time, I swear. All it is is going back in time and looking at memories. You don't even have to reexperience them, really; just watch them from outside your body, like watching a movie."

Santos is tired of the bullshit. "I've got a better idea. Just get me a computer, or a phone and fax, and I'll wire the money wherever you want it. A million, right now. All right?" He can spare that much.

"A million dollars."

"Yeah. Just think what you could do with all that money. You could set yourself up anywhere. Get you a commune for all your hippie friends. All the ice you wanna shoot—or smoke, whatever. Or, what do you do, heroin? Check this out: I know somebody who can get you a *lifetime* supply. Straight from Sinaloa, as pure as you can get, no middle men. And I'll throw that on top of the mil. Extra. A bonus. What do you say?"

Rostam just stares straight ahead at the wall above Santos's head, not saying a word. It's clear he's playing hardball, holding out for more. But two can play at this game, and Santos is a pro.

Neither of them say anything for a full minute. Then two. Three.

Finally Santos has to give in: "All right, a million-five. I can't go any higher than that; that's it. I already spent what we got from Navarro a long time ago, and then some. Besides, I don't have that account any more," he lies. "But I can get it from someplace else."

Nothing, no response. It's like Rostam has become a statue in his chair. His eyes have glazed over.

Ay caramba! He's out of it; he's got to be on drugs.

Santos goes through the motions, in his head: brace with his right hand, lift up, shoot his legs underneath, push off the wall, tackle the son of a bitch, grab the Taser, kill him, leave. He counts another eleven seconds to make sure.

Now!

He's up and launching himself off the wall. Rostam doesn't move, doesn't blink. Santos grabs the hand with the Taser as he tackles him, the chair clattering away as Rostam goes over backward. Santos has him pinned now beneath him. Pain shoots through his shoulder as he wrenches the Taser free. *Mine!* His other hand grabs Rostam by the throat.

Then there's a sudden blur and he's instantly blinded, excruciating pain exploding behind his eyes. He lets out a yell, pushes the Taser against Rostam's side, fumbles with the trigger. But then his windpipe is hit with such force that his head is snapped to the side. He collapses, both hands going immediately, reflexively to his throat. The pain is immense. He can't breathe. He can't do anything as Rostam pushes him away but fall to his side, gasping for air.

Rostam's hand closes over his own, presses the metal points of the Taser against his neck.

NO!

And in the next instant, Santos's whole body is shaking violently, uncontrollably, as his nerves are fed hundreds of thousands of volts of electricity. This is an altogether different kind of pain: enormous, agonizing, like being stabbed everywhere all at once with millions of small, searing knives, over and over again. He has no control over his limbs jerking spasmodically, his hands and feet scrabbling on the floor. He's pissing himself now.

Gracias a Dios! Thank God! It's stopped.

Santos hasn't been able to draw a breath in so long that it's only by sheer necessity he finally sucks in some air, wheezing thinly as he does so. He can taste blood in his mouth from where he's bit his tongue. He tries but still can't move. His one good eye is locked open, staring.

He's lying crumpled in the corner, his back to the partially opened doors; he can feel the overturned chair against his leg.

Rostam stands over him to the side, at the foot of the bunk. Two thin, coiling, silver wires hang between Santos's neck and the Taser in Rostam's hand.

They stare at one another, Santos's breath rasping, his hands and feet beginning to twitch as they regain movement; he can blink finally. Every inch of his body is racked with a lingering, burning pain.

Rostam wears a sad expression, like it hurts him to do this.

The smug bastard. He's got the upper hand now, but one day . . .

"I'm going to kill you," Santos croaks. "I'm going to fucking—*AAARGH!*"

His body is abruptly once again on fire, his muscles convulsing with electricity, his skull rattling against the metal wall. Santos's eyeballs skitter in their sockets and eventually roll up into his head as the pain goes on and on and on . . .

19

A DUSTING OF WHITE POWDER covers everything, sparkling like countless tiny diamonds as the morning sun tops the trees. It's the first real snow of the season and Josh intends to enjoy it. His footsteps crunch beneath him as he hikes the winding trail into the mountains south of the Center. He plans to be gone all day.

Through the trees he can see Honey with her little red backpack, exploring on her own but keeping pace. He knows Pooch is far ahead, searching for game to chase, but will be returning to check on him shortly. The dogs' packs contain plenty of food and water for the day, and Josh is carrying his own, too. Still, they're traveling light and making good time.

Josh hopes to get to the lake by noon and relax there for a while, think things over. They left at eight o'clock, right after serving breakfast. He'll be back in plenty of time for this evening's meal. It's spaghetti and garlic bread tonight, and that should make everyone happy.

He's been taking special care lately with his guests' meals. It's the only way he knows how to possibly make up for putting the LSD in their food. It was a pretty big dose. It's one thing to know what's coming and to prepare yourself for it, as he had done, and something totally different to be surprised with, having no idea what's happening or why. He's lucky no one hurt themselves.

Erin had warned him, too, even though it had first been her idea. But Josh had been adamant about not talking to any of them until the year was up—until Stage One was over. He would at least adhere to that much of his original plan.

However, the acid appears to have done the trick.

Harden has clearly come out of his depression. He isn't sleeping the days away anymore. He's been bathing regularly and doing laundry for a change. Plus, it looks like he's meditating now and even doing a little exercise every day. All starting immediately after his trip, as if a switch had been thrown in his mind. Whatever insights Harden had have certainly turned him around.

Gloria, too, has been out of her stupor since that day. Instead of just rocking and singing softly to herself in the corner, she's also been spending time meditating, it seems, sitting quietly, peacefully with her eyes closed. It's like she and Harden both received a similar message. Now when she sings each day, it's loud, giving it all she's got. It's pretty impressive; the lady's got some pipes.

Josh had worried at first that the others could hear Gloria singing, but when he's stood outside her container, he can barely make out the words. And if that's with only one straw bale between them, then the three between containers must mute the sound completely. Besides, what does it matter if they know someone else is there, too, so long as they can't communicate. But ideally, he feels, it's best if they remain in complete isolation and not distracted by any outside influences. He'd accomplished the most himself during his many years in solitary confinement.

And getting there, Josh recalls, hadn't been easy.

Only those prisoners deemed a constant threat to other inmates or to the guards, or who were in imminent danger themselves, were placed in segregation. Here they were locked up alone for twenty-three hours a day, with one hour allowed for "recreation," where they might stand alone in a small cage outside or take turns watching television. It's not the place most inmates wanted to be.

But after three years in general population, Josh had had enough of the constant noise and overcrowding. Most of all, he hated having to share a cramped, smelly cell with another prisoner—usually a gangsta from da 'hood or some deranged psycho. So he decided to do something about it.

His first few fights hadn't gone so well. He'd never been a violent person and had been in only two other fights in his life—both as a kid, where no one really got hurt. In prison, however, fights were serious business and could mean a man's life.

Josh had seen enough already to know what he was getting into, so he trained, he got fit. All those wasted years as an alcoholic and addict had made him weak and out of shape. It took him a full year of strenuous, daily workouts before he felt he might be ready.

At first he confronted those he pretty much knew he could beat: the smaller thugs and gang-bangers with more mouth than muscle. Then he took on the ones he wasn't so sure about. And he actually won more fights than he lost, which built his confidence. Within another six months of constant fighting, Josh had made a name for himself: "Don't fuck with that dude; he *will* go off on you."

But respect wasn't the goal. He wanted solitary.

After most big fights, those involved were put in isolation for fifteen days at a time, the usual "punishment." But as it became clear to prison officials that Josh would just be coming right back within a few days, they eventually began leaving him there for longer and longer periods. Each time they let him back into general population he would kick someone's ass. Badly. He targeted the drug dealers and sexual predators—those who he felt no compunction about hurting, those who he felt deserved it.

Josh has to laugh at himself now, at the sheer audacity and balls it took to pull it off. And he grimaces at the memory of some of the worst beatings he took. But thankfully—miraculously—besides a whole lot of cuts and bruises, he had never once broken his nose or lost even a single tooth. Being able to *dodge* punches, he learned early on, was just as important, if not more so, as landing them.

His reasons for wanting to stay in solitary confinement had been a complete mystery to everyone but himself. Despite the still constant noise and occasional interruptions, it was the only way he could find to meditate in peace. Meditation, Josh had learned through his reading and through personal experience, was the best way to obtain spiritual enlightenment—to experience his spiritual Self—which was all he cared about anymore. After everything in his life had been taken from him—after he'd done such a poor job of living it himself—there was nothing else that mattered. Discovering his true spiritual nature and learning the Truth with a capital T had become his one driving ambition.

Now, of course, he realizes what a blessing his arrest and incarceration had been. He knows he would never have been able to quit the drugs and alcohol on his own without getting professional help or getting locked up first. He would never have even considered rehab for himself, being in denial that he had such a serious problem—being so *insane,* essentially. And like most people, he had never heard of the "radical" and hugely successful treatment methods like Erin uses today—not that he would have tried them without someone forcing him to do so.

Josh takes heart in that, if one good thing results from his current project, it will be that Dani is saved, as he was, from a further life of addiction and the hell on Earth that goes with it. He can feel good about that, at least, no matter what happens.

Dani, too, has been meditating a lot more since her trip, balancing it with her avid reading. When he checks in with her on video (which, he has to admit, he does more often than necessary), he'll occasionally see her sit and spin one of the CDs, shiny side up, over and over again, while she gazes at its rainbow reflection, lost in thought—or non-thought, as the case may be, which is even better.

Josh is really happy with Dani's progress. He's looking forward to talking with her about the books and all she's learned. He can't wait to present her with the next one personally. And he especially wants to hear what she thinks about her "astral" adventures lately. Dani clearly has a special affinity for traveling out-of-body. It took him years to reach the level she has in months. Even with the Hemi-Sync recordings, which make it so much easier, it's an amazing accomplishment what she's been able to do already. At least what he's *seen* her do—it could be a lot more.

Pooch comes bounding down the trail. The dog looks Josh full in the face, imparting his message, before settling in beside him.

Someone's coming.

Josh gives a whistle to call Honey over.

It doesn't take long. Within a couple minutes he can make out two people, a man and a woman, descending in single file, each carrying a large backpack.

"Hey there!" Josh calls out early. "Don't mind the dogs, they're trained."

They spend a minute chatting, then each party is on their way again. The couple had spent only the weekend at the lake but said there were other groups staying longer. For Josh, it's nice to know that more people are out and about, enjoying nature, even in winter. As much as he likes his own company, he cherishes interacting with other people, for however long. He has too many years of loneliness to make up for.

Within an hour, the trio crest the ridge, the small, spring-fed lake spread out below them in all its alpine splendor, its deep azure blue a stunning contrast to the freshly white-speckled forest. They head due west, off the beaten track, on their way to a secluded beach Erin had shown Josh soon after he arrived in August, the year before. Since then, he's been back many times, to many different parts of the lake, with Erin and some of her patients.

Everyone at Fresh Start is encouraged to make the trek at least once during their stay. Mother Nature has her own special way of touching the heart and mind. It's easy for Josh to see why She has been so revered throughout the ages. He's counting on Her magical, rejuvenating powers to aid him today.

It's New Year's Eve. Tomorrow marks one year since his project officially began. Now Stage Two begins, and Josh has his work cut out for him.

Santos aside, this is where he'll finally confront each of them face-to-face and discuss the reason why they're here. It could only happen after they had a chance to calm down, only after they studied the books and digested the material, only after they had time to contemplate their lives and recognize the need for change. Only *then* could they move forward.

Over the coming year, they'll revisit each and every lifetime they've shared that resulted in a negative karmic imbalance for either party, and resolve the issues. It will be for their own good as well as his. And if one year isn't long enough, then Stage Three will just have to wait. This is the core of the project.

The trees have thinned out considerably; there's nothing but a clear, powder-blue sky above them as the threesome traverse the ridge. To their right are a series of rock ledges stair-stepping down to the forest and the water beyond. Josh pauses above a particularly large, flat rock where he and Sheila had spent a few hours this past summer. It has a great view. The spot had called to them and they couldn't pass it up. After making love (for that's what it is now, he fears), they'd lain on its sun-baked surface and watched a pair of red-tailed hawks riding the warm thermals of air directly above them. They told each other then of their childhoods, but that was about as far as they got. Both of them obviously have secrets and pasts they would rather keep to themselves. It's something else they have in common besides a love for sex and the outdoors, particularly sex *in* the outdoors.

Their business relationship has evolved into something more. He's not sure what to call it—friends with benefits, maybe. Love? He hopes not; that's one attachment to this world he really doesn't need: it's a sure-fire way of wanting to come back, he thinks.

And of getting one's heart broken.

When Josh first arrived in Eureka Springs, after being introduced by Erin, he and Sheila had seen each other almost every day, then once a week, then only twice a month as his money quickly ran out. He hadn't taken a trip into town for over a month when Sheila had shown up at the Center one day this past spring. She missed him, she said. That was their first hike together. Now a week doesn't go by when they don't meet for a few hours of nature loving. No charge, of course.

Josh has managed his money frugally, except for in that one area. And you really can't blame him, he feels, after spending almost twelve years—the prime of his life!—in the company of only men. There is not a single moment with Sheila that goes unappreciated. Still, he can't help but miss the huge amount of money he so willingly spent for her attentions. He's blown his budget.

Nearly sixteen of the twenty thousand dollars he stole from Santos and kept safely hidden in his own numbered account, offshore, had been waiting for him after his escape. After writing Erin for well over a year (shortly following her first few past-life sessions), Josh had given her the account information and pass codes to retrieve the money. It hadn't accumulated much interest over the years, after the bank's annual fees, but it was still there.

With the money, Josh asked Erin to send him books—glorious books!—all the titles he'd been wanting for so long—to supplement his reading from the prison library, which he'd already exhausted. And for the next four years, she sent him at least four or five books a month, whatever he requested, and sometimes her own selections as well.

Erin purchased many of the same titles for herself, and they would discuss the books in their letters. Almost all had something to do with "spirituality," be it theology, comparative religion, the occult, metaphysics, quantum physics, parapsychology, meditation, yoga, hypnosis, reincarnation, karma, spiritual healing, or simply spirituality in general. Other books (always the most well-regarded titles, if they could help it) covered science and history, particularly religious history, which seems to make up the most of it anyway.

In this way, Josh had become a veritable scholar in his lonely cell. When he wasn't studying, he was meditating or practicing his yoga.

So when he and Erin finally stopped writing, and the books stopped coming, he had ramped up his meditation efforts, spending many hours at a time—often entire days—in trance. And his efforts had been rewarded.

Looking back now, those were actually some really good years, Josh thinks, in spite of his really not-so-good environment. He always enjoyed learning new things, and each day had offered the thrill of discovery within the pages of his books, or from adventuring within. And having Erin to share it all with, albeit remotely, for a time, had made it even that much better.

When it was all said and done, he figures he spent about five and a half thousand dollars on books during that period. A very worthwhile investment.

Now, after financing his project to this point, including personal expenses, Josh has less than a thousand dollars left. With this he can purchase books and supplies for maybe another seven months—eight, tops. He's going to have to start making some money somehow, and soon.

The sun says it's eleven-thirty when they finally arrive at the lake. Pooch rushes headlong into the water, pack and all, but it's waterproof, so that's okay. Honey stands patiently for hers to come off before she, too, jumps in. The day is warm enough, despite the snow, for Josh to think about joining them.

He removes his own pack and takes out his lunch and the book he's brought with him: *The Language of Miracles,* on loan from their neighbor and fellow animal lover, Jem. Like Josh, Jem and his brother, Milo, also believe they have a special connection with their dogs. This book, Jem says, is the best he's found on the subject of telepathic communication with animals. And from what Josh has read so far, he has to agree. The author is the real deal and a great writer. He may just have to add this one to his "required reading" list; it's that good.

Josh hasn't been reading nearly as much as what he did in prison. Rather, he has been doing his best to put all he has learned into practice, applying it to his daily life, as the knowledge is intended, working on himself and interacting with others. He knows it would be much different and much more difficult if he was out in the world, instead of sequestered here at the Center. But all in due time, he thinks. In a couple-few more years, once he's accomplished what he's set out to do here, he'll gladly immerse himself within society and take on the challenges and responsibilities that go with it. He considers his time now a transition period.

All in all, he's proud of himself: he's come a long way from being the person he once was prior to setting foot on the Path.

Gazing out over the lake, its surface broken into a million glittering facets by the breeze, Josh gives thanks.

THEIR RETURN TRIP down the mountain is at a more leisurely pace. It's now late afternoon, the trail is in shadow, but they still have plenty of time before the sun goes down completely. They're almost home. Both dogs have nearly tired themselves out and stay close by Josh's side.

It's been a very enjoyable day. And productive: he's gotten a lot of thinking done.

The Santos problem has been really bothering him. The others all have their roles—their importance—in this, too, of course, but Santos is the key: *he* is the one who put all the drama into motion this time around. And he'll continue to do so time and time again until the matter is resolved, one way or another, if ever. However, it's obvious Santos won't cooperate.

The only solution Josh can think of is a risky one. But what other choice does he have? And if it works . . .

He believes he's also found a solution to his money problem: By September, when he'll *really* need an income, most of the work for Stage Two should be completed, and he can begin focusing his attention on work outside the project. By then, too, most of the remodeling and construction work for the Center will be finished for the summer. He can begin advertising his services as a hypnosis practitioner around town. He can practice officially as a "spiritual counselor" as a minister with Mystic Ministries, the nonprofit Erin set up for him in her name. Just so long as people don't look too closely into his assumed identity.

Which is another problem not so easily overcome in today's world. Establishing a new identity isn't as simple as it was many years ago. Still, it can be done, as thousands of illegal immigrants every year can attest. He'll take his cues from them—maybe take a trip to Atlanta or Miami to obtain some "legal" documentation. It shouldn't be too difficult. If he has to become "Pedro Gonzales," then so be it.

Josh's only real worry is that it may still be too soon; he's only been free now for a year and a half. His mug shot and prison ID photo had been all over the news nationwide for months following his escape. "Armed and dangerous," they said; a reward for any information. He's done his best to stay out of sight. So far, he's spent all his time at the Center, besides visiting Sheila at her place occasionally. The thought of going to work and putting himself in the public eye scares him. However, he realizes it has to be done eventually; he can't just keep hiding forever.

But Josh also knows the Law never gives up looking for escaped convicts. He'll have to stay wary for the rest of his life. And keep the beard—although it's starting to grow on him.

He laughs at his pun, breaking the silence on the trail. The dogs look at him and wag their tails, their tongues lolling, smiling, laughing with him. It's a good time to stop for a quick biscuit and water break, he thinks. Finishing the last of the water will also lighten their loads.

Erin had bartered for the dogs' packs and other items, along with a lifetime of free health care, with a local veterinarian.

Not everyone comes to Fresh Start for the full twelve-week stay. Some arrange for the Big Sleep by itself, especially those who can't afford to spend more time than that away from their work. Plus, there's also the shame factor. Addiction doesn't discriminate between social classes. Josh has seen quite a few upstanding citizens—like the vet—enter anonymously, off the books, for the relatively short stay. Each time, they arrive late at night, dropped off by a taxi or a spouse. These are always paying clients, of course, and Erin is always more than happy to oblige them.

Then again, Erin is always willing to help *anyone*, regardless. Hence her many *pro bono* "research" patients, and her financial woes. The woman is a saint, as far as Josh is concerned.

He would still be languishing in prison if it wasn't for her. She had risked everything—her life, her freedom, her career, everything she's worked so hard for—to help him escape. And she is *still* risking it all to see his project come to pass.

Erin is really coming through for him in this lifetime, as she has done so many times before. He feels he owes her for all she's done for him. However, being "indebted" isn't a factor for either of them on the spiritual level. They have both reviewed dozens of lives they've shared together, but never once have they considered "keeping score," tallying the times one has helped the other. They have always been there for each other equally, forever.

Finding Erin in this lifetime and discovering for himself who she was to him had been a "game changer." For the first time since Seattle, since he was in a loving relationship, Josh had a reason to live beside himself; he had purpose. As soulmates, he had a responsibility to be there for her, regardless of his own situation, and he vowed to do whatever he could from behind bars.

Educating Erin—reminding her, rather—about her own true nature as a spiritual being is the greatest thing he could have ever done for her—for anyone—in any lifetime. That alone is reason enough for his being on Earth this time around.

But if he can do this one additional thing—his project; if he can pull this off—it will benefit not only their current lives, but all those to come—for *all* of them, Erin included.

It's worth the risk. He knows she understands that. There is absolutely nothing more important than their spiritual evolution.

What Josh will accomplish here has the potential to end his continual cycle of death and rebirth, and shorten it for the others. Of course he'll still have some work to do on himself once the project is finished, but having his karmic "family feuds" settled once and for all will leave him with no reason or compulsion to return.

No attachments, no desires. No guilt, no regrets. No drama, no lingering emotions. No unfinished business, no unresolved issues. No reasons outside oneself to return. *This* is what is required to finally escape the Wheel of Life, to leave it all behind.

POOCH RUNS AHEAD with a sudden burst of energy as they leave the trail and step onto the old logging road winding through the Center's property. From his still-elevated position on the mountainside, Josh can see the slate roof and upper story of the Big House, where he'll soon be ensconced in the kitchen, helping prepare the evening's feast for their New Year's Eve party tonight.

And what a feast it will be! He's hungry after the day's hike.

Ten minutes later, he and Honey are passing the Long House, the building where full-size tree trunks were once stored to dry when the sawmill was in operation. Josh had spent nearly a month removing its old, rotting floorboards, and then another turning the whole place into one giant chicken coop. The thirty-three hens, six ducks, two geese, and one rooster have plenty of room to nest and peck and mozy around in there, as well as in their little yard outside. He'd cut out a number of tall windows to let in the sunlight and air, and he lined the whole thing in chicken wire to protect them from predators. It's definitely one of his best ideas and his proudest accomplishment at the Center so far.

Collecting the day's eggs each morning is always a treat for Erin's patients, and they usually make it a group event. Many of Fresh Start's interns and volunteers go home with any extra eggs.

Josh is thinking about checking on the birds, when Pooch comes running back. He barks twice, something he rarely does, and makes a few starts and stops back down the road. He looks anxious. The message is clear: something unusual—potentially dangerous—is up ahead.

Josh picks up his pace but stays wary, keeping his eyes and ears sharp for anything on the road or in the trees around them. When the Shed comes into sight, he crouches down and takes a moment to inspect the area; but Pooch is impatient with this, indicating that it's safe, that whatever it is is further along.

Josh quickly removes the dogs' packs and his own and stashes them beside the building. Then, communicating with a thought and a gesture, he sends the dogs on without him.

Josh had learned over his many years in prison to attune himself to any portents of danger, and right now his every nerve is on edge. His "sixth sense" is sending him a warning.

Rather than continue on the road, he angles off into the trees, intending to circle around to where he can get an unobstructed view of the Center's courtyard.

It takes him almost no time at all, running soundlessly through the forest, to reach an elevated vantage point among some bare blackberry bushes. The courtyard is in shadow but he can see clearly, thanks to the porch lights and the light spilling out from the windows of the buildings.

Parked to the side of the garage is a plain, gray sedan. And standing talking with Erin on her veranda is a man dressed professionally in a brown suit and tie; he holds a fedora in his hands. Josh doesn't see anyone else with him, no one waiting in the car.

He's just a salesman, he tells himself, somehow knowing it's not true.

Erin is wearing the long, mint-green lab coat she often wears at the clinic during the day, her hands in its pockets. From this distance it's impossible to see her expression, but Josh can tell from her posture she is not happy.

They talk back and forth, Erin repeatedly shaking her head. Then she shrugs resignedly and turns and goes inside. She's thrown the screen door open wide behind her, and the stranger catches it before it shuts. He pauses in the well-lit doorway and, facing out, slowly scans the courtyard and other buildings before following her inside.

Ohhh, shit.

What worries Josh now, more than simply the man's presence, are the holstered gun and badge on the man's belt.

20

ERIN'S HEART IS POUNDING as she enters the living room. She stops. *No, not in here!* This is where she and Josh most often hang out; he may have left something incriminating behind.

She can almost hear his voice now, laughing at her: *What, a hair? Calm down, Erin. Relax.*

Yeah, right. She heads to the kitchen instead.

She lights the burner under the kettle, sets out some mugs. She can't think of anything else to do. She knows she has to act normal, like she has nothing to hide.

He only wants to talk. Routine visit. Be cool, be cool.

From the hall: "Ms. Pearse?"

"Here I am!" She sets out three different kinds of tea on the small, wooden table. "I'm afraid I don't have any milk or sugar," she says as he enters the kitchen, hat in hand.

"That's okay. I apologize again for intruding so late in the day."

"What's your name again?" He had shown her his ID when he first arrived. U.S. marshal.

"Frazier. Michael." He motions to a chair.

"Please, have a seat." Erin takes off her lab coat and hangs it over the back of a chair, but instead of sitting, leans against the counter by the stove, waiting for the kettle to steam, waiting to get this over with and this man out of her life. Hopefully. She crosses her arms—a defensive posture, she knows, but she can't help it.

"So, Ms. Pearse, like I said, just a few follow-up questions. I know you went through all of this before." He's laid his hat on the seat of a chair and now takes out a small notebook and shiny, silver pen. "The most obvious first. I know you already told me, but let's start from the top, okay? You haven't seen him." More a statement than a question: they'd been over this outside.

"No."

"And you haven't heard from him."

"No, not at all."

"No letters?"

"None."

"You were pen pals once."

"Not for many years."

"What ever got you to write each other in the first place?" he asks. "You didn't know Rostam prior to his arrest, did you?"

The questions are all too familiar, but harder to deal with this time, so out of the blue like this. "No. I'd recently earned my doctorate and published my research, a book, about nine years ago now. He read it and wrote with some questions about it, some ideas of his own."

"Like what?"

A heavy sigh escapes her; she can't help it. She had been grilled so many times in the days, weeks, and months following Josh's escape, always by different investigators who never seemed to share her answers to the barrage of questions they posed. Or maybe they did, Erin feared, and were looking for her to make a slip of the tongue at some point, catch her in a lie. She'd thought it was all behind her. She should have known better.

"The book was on treating alcoholism," she says, "using a unique approach. Rostam was a former addict, so he was interested in it. He suggested I explore some other treatment methods as well."

"Such as?"

"Hypnosis, mainly." From the beginning, they agreed she would tell the truth whenever possible; there was no need to lie when it wasn't necessary.

"And did you?" Frazier asks. "Explore hypnosis?"

"I did. Although it was already a widely used practice for treating addiction. Very successful."

"Huh. Why was he interested in hypnosis, do you think? He was a computer programmer, wasn't he? Software design?"

"Yes, I believe he was, when he was younger—though we didn't often discuss his past." She shrugs. "He'd done some reading on it, apparently. By the time he wrote me, he'd used hypnosis with a number of his fellow prisoners. And it helped them, he said."

"Hmmm." Frazier flips through his notebook, reads something there. "So you corresponded for how long?"

Erin is sure he already knows the answer. He knows every answer, of course; he can't be new to the case. "Five years."

"And you discussed treatment methods for addiction—hypnosis—this whole time?"

"No, we covered a lot of things; he had many interests and ideas. He read a lot, and he liked to share the things he learned. I looked forward to his letters . . . At first," she hastens to add.

"What else did he write to you about?"

"Just the things he studied, mostly: history, science, spirituality."

"Did he ever mention any friends, family?"

"No. Well, not really. He mentioned it only once and I didn't pry. He said his parents disowned him when he was younger, when he dropped out of school. He was fifteen, I believe."

"Pretty young," Frazier says, almost caringly. "Any friends? Anyone he might go to for help?"

"Not that I can remember. He didn't tell me much about his past. Just that he had been on his own for a long time, and that he was originally from Seattle."

"Did he tell you why he came to Texas?"

"Some girl, a girlfriend—maybe his fiancée, I don't know. She met another guy and ran away to Houston. He followed her there to try to win her back; but it didn't work out." Erin throws up her hands. "So he sought solace in drugs and alcohol. Like a lot of idiots. Self-destructive behavior."

"Did he ever have a girlfriend in Houston?"

Erin pushes herself off the counter, turns up the flame under the too-slow kettle. She lets a little exasperation into her voice—just enough, she hopes, to cover the lie. "Like I said, we mostly discussed my research and his own studies. That's all. We weren't friends, necessarily."

"I see." He looks back to his notebook. "And you wrote how often?"

She hesitates. The kettle gives a soft whistle beside her. Perfect timing. As she pours, Erin takes the time to recall the correct response. This is where the lies really start.

"Oh, it varied," she says. "He wrote me much more often than I wrote him. More at first, then less as time went by. Maybe once a month, on average."

She'd always worried about this, but Josh assured her that the prison mailroom was much too busy to keep track of their letters or what they discussed in them; he wasn't "red-tagged" for such scrutiny. Although they obviously made note of her as a regular correspondent: It was her previous address, the one in Fayetville, before Fresh Start, but regardless, the authorities had tracked her here immediately.

In reality, she and Josh had written more like once a week, even daily, especially during and after her regression work. Too often for casual pen pals.

Erin avoids Frazier's eyes as she sits and dips her bag of Lavender tea: something to sooth her nerves.

"Were they long letters?" he asks.

"His were. Mine were usually pretty short. I was busy."

"So, what happened? You wrote the warden. Rostam started harassing you, all of a sudden?"

She stares at the steam rising off her mug. "Yes. Sexual comments. He wanted that kind of relationship, he said . . . I put an end to it."

"So you weren't interested?"

A pointed and insulting question, Erin thinks. She can look directly into his eyes now; let this truth make up for the rest.

"I'm not attracted to men . . . Besides, this man was in prison. For *life*. What do you take me for?"

A beat as Frazier stares back. She can see he's not surprised, or shocked, or even amused. *He already knew,* she thinks. *He probably knows everything about me.* But there must be something in her expression: he blinks and looks away.

"Excuse me," he says, "I didn't mean to—" He pretends to consult his notes. "So you stopped writing."

She takes a calming sip of tea. "Yes, that's right. I imagine they stopped his letters to me, as I requested. There was only one after that, a couple of months later. I didn't read it but sent it straight to the warden, like the others."

"You sent him *all* the letters?" Frazier actually looks surprised, as though he'd missed something earlier.

"Uh, well, no, just the sexually explicit ones—three total. I wanted them to see for themselves. I wanted them to stop him from writing me."

"Of course." Frazier follows her lead and takes a drink from his mug. "Oh, this is good. What is it?" He looks at the box closest to him. "'Linden.' I've never had this before. I like it. Thank you."

"I'm glad. It's good for the nerves, and muscle tension."

Frazier nods, takes another sip, asks nonchalantly, "Ms. Pearse, do you know anyone in Bentonville?"

"Well, sure, I guess so. I mean, I went to school at the University of Arkansas; it's pretty close. There must be at least a few people I know who live there."

"But no one in particular?"

"No, why?" Erin's gut is twisted in a knot. If they have pictures of her . . . video footage . . .

"Rostam sent a lot of mail there, to one of those private mailbox places. It started shortly after the two of you stopped writing each other." Frazier's look is clearly suspicious.

"Oh. Well maybe he found some other woman to pester, to send him money."

Frazier arches an eyebrow. "He asked you for money?"

Shit! "Yes, in the end. I think that may have been his plan all along, I don't know." She's winging it now; she's never mentioned Josh asking her for money before; she hopes she isn't blowing it. "You've never seen the letters?"

"No."

"Well, they may still have them somewhere, I don't know; do you think?" She hopes not.

Oh, God, what have I done?

"They're bound to be somewhere," Frazier says. He scribbles something in his notebook. "I'll look into it." He doesn't appear too concerned. But then his brow creases. "Why so many packages?"

"Pardon?"

"Packages. Books, it says here. They all came from different places, but I assume it was you who sent them."

"Yes. Books."

"Why? Why so many?" He tosses down his notebook, leans back, begins twirling his pen slowly between his fingers.

Erin can't help but fixate upon the pen. "He asked for them," she says. "It's all he had to do with his time: read . . . study."

"So you cared for him, then."

"Yes. Yes, I did. At one time."

"It seems like you two were friends, after all."

"We were, I suppose. For a while. But not in the end."

"You were before he came on to you."

"That's right. He showed his true colors."

"And you stopped writing, stopped sending him books, because of that."

"Yes." Erin tears her gaze away from the shiny pen, looks briefly at the man before sipping her tea. She nods, suddenly wary.

"And that was the last time you ever heard from him."

What is this? "Yes, as I told you before, as I've told you—well, not *you*, but your agency—all you people, years ago—it's been, what?"

"Twenty months."

"I just don't understand why I have to be bothered with all of this again."

Frazier pauses, takes another drink. He looks at her skeptically, twirling his pen. The silence is unnerving; the seconds go by like minutes. Then finally: "Ms. Pearse, do you have a man living here with you? Someone who works for Fresh Start?"

Erin can feel the blood drain from her face. So this is it. This is where it ends, after all their careful planning. They thought they were so smart . . . Josh is going to have to leave immediately. Tonight. No, not tonight, they'll be watching . . .

"Ms. Pearse?"

He's waiting. But what can she say? He already knows the answer.

"Yes . . . A handyman."

Frazier is nodding his head, looking at the pen twirling in his hand. "Does your handyman also perform counseling for your patients? Hypnosis, maybe?"

She wants to cry. He can probably see it in her face; but she won't give him the satisfaction. She takes a long sip of tea as she tries to recover; but she knows it's too late. Her hands are shaking. "He's also a minister," she says.

Frazier is tapping his pen now, and once again Erin can't pull her eyes away from it. This must be some kind of interrogation technique they teach them at Quantico or wherever: pen tactics.

"Is he here now?" she hears him say. "Can I meet him, please? Is he next door?"

She saw the dogs return earlier. She knows Josh is here somewhere. Frazier has to leave, she thinks. As soon as possible.

"Do you have a warrant?"

The pen stops its movement, is placed carefully beside the notebook. Frazier puts his hands together, fingers interlaced, places them on the table. He leans forward. "Ma'am, we are searching for an escaped convict—one who we have every reason to believe has kidnapped at least two people and likely tortured them to death. If I have any reason to think he is here, I could have helicopters landing right outside within twenty minutes and every inch of your property gone over with a fine-tooth comb. My *word* is all the warrant I need."

Erin knows she's lost, that it's all over now; but she can't go without at least a token fight. "I see. Just like you did before. Repeatedly . . . Then why don't you? I mean, you obviously suspect something, or you wouldn't be here."

"A man matching Rostam's description was said to be here at Halloween." He picks up his notebook, flips through it, reads: "'Debating the issue of reincarnation.' Your handyman."

Who could have said something? Worthing? "Matching the description? What's that? What's he look like?"

"You don't know?"

"Well—"

"You visited him in prison."

"Once! Only once."

Frazier makes a visible effort to let this go. "I'll ask you again, Ms. Pearse: Can I meet this person you have working here?"

"Er—Um, I don't know . . ."

Erin is startled by the toilet flushing in the bathroom next door, down the hall. It sounds like the door is open. If the Fed is surprised, he doesn't show it. There's the sound of running water in the sink. Then a booming voice from the hallway:

"Wow! That was an *amazing* shit!"

Gavin walks in, drying his hands on his flannel shirt. "Oh, hello! Company, have we?" He extends a hand to Frazier, who hesitates a second before shaking it. "Name's Trip," Gavin says. "Just Trip. But some people around here call me 'Doc.' How do you do?"

Without waiting for a reply, he gives Erin a wave and a sly wink as he walks past. "Hiya, girl. Hope you don't mind me using your loo. Had me a bit of an emergency, you know. The ones across the way were plum full up." He opens the fridge, begins rummaging around.

Frazier is looking at her expectantly.

"Uh, Trip, this is Michael Frazier . . . We were just talking about you." She's too afraid to say anything else.

Gavin turns with a big, green apple in his hand. "Oh, that's nice. Are you planning on joining us, then, Michael? Couldn't have picked a better place—or a better doctor." The apple crunches loudly between his teeth. He settles back against the counter, chewing, smiling widely.

He's looking a lot better since this morning, Erin is happy to see. She's surprised to see him out of bed.

Frazier just sips his tea, looking from one of them to the other. Then: "No, I only stopped by for a visit . . . What do you do here, Mr. . . . ?"

"Trip. Just Trip. I do a little bit of everything around here, I suppose. Help my girl, Erin here, keep the place running. Cook, clean, you name it."

It's obvious he's doing his best to tone down his accent. Still:

"Where are you from, Trip?" Frazier asks. "Australia?"

"Christ, no! Wouldn't be caught dead there! New Zealand. Totally different world." He points with his apple. "Say, you're not from Immigration, are you?"

Frazier chuckles. "No, not me. Ms. Pearse tells me you're a minister."

Gavin nods, chewing obnoxiously. "For a small fee, you, too, can be saved."

Frazier smiles and holds up his hands, begging off. "Actually, I'm more interested in hearing about your methods. What do you do, exactly? Hypnosis, is it?"

Gavin doesn't miss a beat: "I lift people's spirits and soothe their souls," he says resoundingly in true televangelistic style. "I introduce them to their Higher Selves. I teach them that the Kingdom of Heaven—the Kingdom of God—lies *within,* and that *they* are in fact embodiments of God, with the same power to create and to love."

Gavin is clearly enjoying himself, Erin can see. He grins at her and she can't help but smile weakly back, her spirits buoyed for a moment. Maybe—oh, maybe—they can pull this off.

"But my main specialty," Gavin continues in a normal voice, "is guided meditation—what some people may call hypnosis, I suppose—where I lead folks on an exploration of their past lives and the life between." He takes another huge bite of his apple and gestures earnestly. "Once people experience themselves in this light—once they experience the *truth* about who and what they really are as eternal, spiritual beings of intelligent Light energy—their lives are forever changed."

He sounds just like Josh. If Erin wasn't so petrified, she'd clap.

Frazier looks a bit taken aback. After a moment's pause and a long drink, he says, "So you believe in past lives—in reincarnation." Yet another statement-but-still-a-question.

"Absolutely!" Gavin's face lights up like Erin hasn't seen in weeks. He had taken a bad turn in November, his health failing rapidly. But now he's like a new man. He pulls out a chair, spins it around, and straddles it, resting his arms on the back, his apple forgotten. "You too?"

"I'm a Christian," Frazier says.

"Good place to start. Which kind?"

A beat. "Catholic."

"One of the twenty-four percent who believe in reincarnation?"

"Uh, I'm afraid not."

"Well, that's all right; you know what they say: 'If you don't believe in reincarnation now, don't worry, you probably will in your next life.'"

Erin laughs nervously and sips her now tepid tea.

Frazier also laughs, says, "So, Trip, you live here on the grounds?"

"I do. I have my own little place out back. The 'Shed' we call it, where I can keep an eye on all the tools and things. It's not much, but it's all I need."

"How long have you lived here?"

Gavin looks to Erin for confirmation. "How long has it been? About a year and a half? Not quite that long, I don't think. I remember I got here right on your birthday, in August. Wow! Time flies!" He shakes his head, notices the apple core in his hand, pops the whole thing in his mouth.

Erin studies Frazier, who is studying Gavin, a.k.a. "Trip." Maybe it's her imagination, but the man doesn't seem nearly as suspicious anymore. But it's probably just wishful thinking on her part.

He turns to her. She just smiles and shrugs, as if to say, *Yeah, I know, he's a character, isn't he?*

Frazier continues to stare at her. She's too tired to look away.

Then Frazier quickly lifts his mug and downs what's left. He picks up his notebook and flips through it to a blank page, places it on the table. The pen starts twirling again. "How long do you plan to stay, Trip? I take it you have a work visa."

Gavin nods, appearing suddenly concerned, the consummate actor. "Are you sure you're not from Immigration?"

"No, not Immigration, but I *am* with the federal government."

"Oh, I see." Gavin sits up straighter, a sober expression now.

"Well, sir, I did have one, but I let it expire. So much to have to do here at the Center, you know. But I'll be leaving very soon, I promise. I'd prefer to stay longer, but—" He gets a catch in his throat and coughs wetly into his fist. "Um, uh, I don't know when, exactly, but it won't be long. Maybe a couple a months, I imagine, at the most."

"Do you have any identification I can see?" Frazier asks.

"Uh, well, sure." Gavin reaches into his front pocket, takes out a thin, leather wallet. "Don't leave home without it," he quips. He slides two pieces of ID across the table.

Frazier studies them carefully, glancing up to compare the photos with the man before him. "'Trip' is a nickname, I take it."

"Yes, sir. Since my university days."

"You look different with a beard."

"An improvement, I hope. I was shooting for 'wise and sophisticated.'"

Frazier smiles. "So where will you be going?" he asks, copying down the information. "Back to New Zealand?"

"Well, uh . . . I'll be going *home,* sir." Gavin turns to Erin and holds out his hand, which she takes. His eyes are moist, his sad smile sincere. He's speaking only to her when he says, "And believe it or not, I'm actually looking forward to it."

This isn't acting now, she knows. Tears come to her eyes, and she gives Gavin's hand a squeeze. It's so much frailer than it was only a month ago. She sends him her love with her gaze—and something more: extreme gratitude. They hold each other like this with their eyes, both on the verge of crying, it seems.

Frazier is watching them, Erin can tell, but she's put him and her problems aside for the moment. *This* is what really matters right now. Gavin has been a role model to her and to Josh and to all of her patients who've known him. He's shown them what true courage and fortitude are. He's become a real friend. She's going to miss him greatly.

Finally, after some time of being ignored, Frazier pushes back his chair. He's left Gavin's IDs on the table. "Well, Ms. Pearse, thank you very much for your hospitality. I won't trouble you anymore tonight. I know you both have your dinner and your party to get to."

He's already put away his notebook and pen and reaches for his hat. Erin and Gavin both stand along with him. She wipes away a tear.

"I appreciate you answering my questions," Frazier says as he makes to leave.

"Glad to help," she says. Her knees are shaking; she's wiped out; all she wants to do is lie down.

"Oh, and Trip . . ." Frazier turns and points his hat at Gavin. "I'm glad you've enjoyed it here, but things have to be done legally. I'll be back around in a few months to check on your work status. Will that be long enough, do you think?"

Erin can see the toll Gavin's performance has cost him; he's lost the energy he had earlier. He makes an obvious effort now to smile and put on a pleasant face. "Yes, sir, I think that'll be fine. Plenty of time. Thank you. I'll be gone by then for sure."

"Take care," Frazier says. He seems to hesitate, then: "God bless."

Erin walks him to the door.

Outside, he hands her his card. "If you do hear from Rostam, please contact me immediately."

"Of course. But I won't. I mean, I won't be hearing from him. I would have already by now, don't you think?" She really needs to shut up.

"You never know," he says.

Was that a suspicious look?

At the bottom of the stairs, Frazier turns. "He's sick, isn't he?"

He means Gavin, of course. "He's going to die soon," she says.

Frazier nods somberly. "I thought there was something . . . How long does he have?"

"You guessed it about right: maybe a few months, not much longer than that. Maybe less, I don't know."

"I see . . . Well, thank you again, ma'am." At his car he tips his hat to her. "Happy New Year."

"You too."

Erin doesn't go back inside until she sees his tail lights blink out of sight, down the hill.

Gavin is on the couch in the living room when she comes in. He pats the seat beside him.

She flops down and lays her head back, closes her eyes, exhausted. It's all too much to process right now. She wants to believe they're safe, that they've successfully dodged a bullet. She wants to go to sleep for a while but knows it will be impossible. She wants to find Josh.

"Erin." Gavin touches her gently on the arm.

With an effort, she rolls her head to the side and opens her eyes. He looks as worn out as she feels. And as worried.

"Lady, what in the hell is going on?"

PART THREE

After all, it is no more surprising to be born twice than it is to be born once.

~ **Voltaire**

21

KRUNK! POP! SQUEAK!

Harden acknowledges the sound and lets it go—without a thought, without a ripple. His mind is like a still pond, deep and unfathomable, reflecting infinity. Occasionally, an image moves across the surface, and this he does pay attention to, extracting whatever message or meaning it may have before releasing it back into the ether. Always an emotion is attached, no matter how subtle. Emotions convey the most meaning, he's found.

A glimpse of Rostam in the courtroom flickers across his inner vision. The emotion is guilt.

"Harden."

His name, a man's voice, a ripple across the water.

"Harden, just stay where you are. I'm coming in."

Now a veritable wave of images and emotions flood his mind. *Oh my God! He's here!*

His eyes open to see a tall man with a beard much shorter than his own walk across the room and set up a folding chair opposite him against the wall, beneath the book shelf. He looks like an outdoorsman: fit, rugged, sun blown. He sits down, facing him. In his hand is something Harden recognizes instantly: a police-issue Taser gun.

The man looks nothing like Rostam, the pathetic drug addict he prosecuted for kidnapping and murder so many years ago, and for a moment Harden is confused: has he been wrong about the reason he's here?

"Hello, Mr. Harden. You probably don't recognize me. I'm Joshua Rostam." He has a deep, rich voice, like an actor—the first Harden has heard outside his own in a year. "But I bet you remember my case."

Harden takes a deep, centering breath, let's it out slowly.

And so it begins . . . Finally.

"Hello." He has to clear his throat; it's been a long time since he's spoken, even to himself. "Hello, Mr. Rostam . . . Yes, of course I remember your case."

"I didn't kill that man Navarro."

Harden closes his eyes, to temporarily escape as much as prepare himself for what he knows is coming, what he knows he has to face.

"I know . . . I'm sorry."

Rostam's eyes have grown larger, but he stays seated, remains calm. There's no rage, no assault, no violent retribution. Not yet.

"You know? What do you mean, you *know?*"

"I know you didn't kill him. I knew. I knew then . . . I'm so sorry."

Rostam appears confused; he sits there dumb, uncomprehending, for a full minute. Then: "Uh, what? You knew? . . . Why did you do it, then? Why did you make me out to be such a dangerous criminal? A killer."

Harden has given this a lot of thought over the past year. He knows why he acted the way he did. And he's ashamed. Although he's finally comes to terms with it. He takes another calming breath before beginning:

"Yours was my first big case as district attorney. I was only appointed to the position at the time, to fill Anderson's seat when he took the bench; I hadn't been elected yet . . . I took your case to trial two weeks before the primaries. I was up against some stiff competition. I had to—I *wanted* to make a name for myself, make headlines."

He can't meet Rostam's eyes. There is another long silence. Too long.

"But why me?" Rostam says at last. "I could have given you the real killer, maybe, if you'd just listened to me for a minute. Or at least pointed you in the right direction."

"There wasn't time. We needed—" He catches himself again: honesty, especially with oneself, is a difficult thing to police. "I wanted a big conviction before the election. I wanted to win that primary."

"But you knew I didn't do it . . . How?"

"There was video footage of you and a young woman at the hotel where you stayed—where the Internet connection was made, where you made the transactions. It's clear you never left the hotel. But *she* did, early on the last day. With the laptop . . . According to the medical examiner, Navarro was killed at some point while you were still there."

Rostam looks dumbstruck. "So this video *proved* I didn't kill him?"

Harden nods. "I'm sorry."

"I can't believe this . . . This—This changes everything."

Rostam looks fixedly at a point over Harden's shoulder. He just sits like this, staring, occasionally shaking his head, for the longest time.

Harden doesn't know what to say; he's afraid to open his mouth.

Eventually Rostam turns his head and glares. "You *knew!*" he shouts. "You *knew* I had nothing to do with it! Yet you sentenced me to life! . . . *Life!*" He throws up his hands. "You tried to have me executed!"

"But you did have something to do with it," Harden says cautiously. "Your prints were all over the laptop. You emptied his accounts."

Rostam stands abruptly, sending his chair skidding into the corner with a clang.

Here it comes. Harden braces himself for the attack. He's still sitting with his legs crossed on the bunk, his back to the wall, as when Rostam first entered. He presses his hands firmly against the mattress to either side and looks straight ahead; he'll take his beating like a man.

Rostam paces a few feet in both directions, the limit of the cell. His face is growing redder by the second. He stops and points the Taser.

Harden flinches and puts up his hands.

"How could you?" Rostam shouts. "I *told* the cops I liquidated his accounts and moved the money offshore. It's what I was *hired* to do. There was nothing illegal about it."

Harden stays quiet. When Rostam begins pacing again, he lowers his hands. He can feel his heart pounding. He closes his eyes and takes a conscious breath: He needs to calm the man down, and he needs to be calm himself to do it.

"Mr. Rostam, did you ever think for one moment that it wasn't actually Navarro who was hiring you?"

Rostam stops his pacing. He throws Harden a look of disgust and turns away. He slowly runs his finger along the spines of the books on the shelf, takes one down, flips through it, puts it back. "No, I never did," he says. "I was an idiot . . . Didn't question a thing . . . His assistant—" He turns back and shrugs. "She had me convinced. At the time—I mean, she was *incredible*. Like a dream come true . . ."

Rostam grabs the chair and takes his seat again. He leans back, massages his brow. "And then there was the dope, of course. I was an addict, you might remember. I would have done anything for it back then." He levels his gaze, his cool gray-green eyes serious, and sincere. "Except hurt someone. Or kill. I would *never* do that. I had no idea, believe me."

"I do believe you," Harden says. And he does. He'd always known the poor computer-whiz-kid-turned-druggie had been used, then framed for the murder. It's what makes Harden's guilt and shame so much harder to take. Having finally confessed to the man has helped. But he hasn't told him all of it.

"It was because you were a drug addict," Harden explains. "That was part of it—why we—*I* considered you disposable. As you were, you were nothing but a drain on society, if not an actual menace. If I hadn't locked you up then, you would have gone on to commit further crimes—maybe violent ones—to support your habit."

Rostam sits with his hands on his knees. The Taser is out of sight, Harden notices, probably in the pocket of his pullover.

His jailer stares at him incredulously. "For *life?* . . . What you did to me was the equivalent of murder, as far as I'm concerned. You took my whole life away."

"I understand that now. And I'm sorry, I really am, more than I can ever express." He raises his hands in what he hopes is a sincere gesture. "I'm not trying to justify what I did, only come clean with you. Full disclosure."

Rostam makes a scoffing sound. He just shakes his head, staring coldly.

Harden's mouth is incredibly dry. He points to the sink, makes a drinking motion with his hand. "If you don't mind . . ."

He was only asking for permission to move, to get a drink of water, but Rostam gets up and fills his cup, brings it to him.

"Thank you."

But Rostam won't look at him; he goes to sit back down.

Harden drains the cup. "I don't expect you to ever forgive me for what I did to you," he says. "I'm having a hard time forgiving myself. Though I know that's what I have to do." He motions to the row of books above Rostam's head. "Thank you for the books, by the way. I've learned a great deal. They've really helped . . . If it wasn't for them—" He shrugs. "I don't know . . ."

"What? Kill yourself?" Rostam gives a jagged laugh. "Do you have any idea how many times I thought about killing myself in prison?" He leans forward and looks Harden in the eyes. "Every. Single. Day."

Harden is appalled. "No, no, that's not what I meant! I didn't mean to imply—I thought I would lose my mind."

Rostam sits back, crosses his legs. "Well, losing your mind isn't such a bad thing, if it's the small mind you lose . . . But don't sit there and tell me you never thought about it—about offing yourself. It happens to all of us who have to live like this."

Harden doesn't answer right away. Of course the thought has crossed his mind—many times in fact. But it's not something he wants to talk about; it depresses him—scares him, really—and he doesn't want to go back to that dark place.

"Have you noticed how there isn't much of anything in here to kill yourself with?" Rostam asks, more sympathy now in his tone. "It's because the temptation can become too great. I know. Death is infinitely more appealing than sitting alone, rotting away in a cage, isn't it?"

He pauses, slaps his hands on his knees and stands, begins pacing again—but slowly this time, stroking his beard.

"But then, if you end it all, you don't get to fulfill your mission in this life . . . And maybe that mission is simply to survive sitting alone in a cage for years, rotting away, until you die naturally. Maybe by then you will have learned something, grown spiritually, somehow . . . That's the bigger goal anyway. Our Higher Selves don't worry too much about physical discomfort."

Rostam pushes the button on the sink, stands watching the water run. "Besides," he continues, "if you kill yourself ahead of time, you'll just have to basically go through the same shit again—only worse, usually—in another life, in order to accomplish what you originally set out to do . . . which wasn't to suffer, necessarily, but to *overcome* suffering." He looks over. "You understand what I'm saying?"

Harden nods. He does understand. It's a philosophy discussed in one of the books—or many of them, he's not sure at the moment.

Rostam resumes his slow, metronomic pacing, back and forth. "I knew a few guys who did commit suicide in there . . . One I met afterward. As a ghost . . . Killing himself hadn't solved anything, of course. He was *still* miserable; only more so, because now he couldn't do anything about it . . . He wouldn't listen to me and go to the Light . . . It's like he *wanted* to be miserable: penance or something . . . He created his own prison . . ."

Harden thinks he gets the message. "You don't have to worry about me," he says. "I'm not going to kill myself. I can handle it."

Rostam sniffs contemptuously. "What you've experienced here is nothing. This is the Ritz-Carlton compared to what *real* prison is like—compared to what I went through." He stops and points a finger. "You're lucky you've got this place to yourself, for one thing. Let me bring in 'Big Pimp,' or 'One Punch,' or 'Crazy G,' the booty bandit, to keep you company twenty-four/ seven. You'll be trying to drown yourself in the toilet within a week." He sneers. "Put you in a real prison, they'd make you somebody's bitch."

Harden has no doubt he's correct. You don't spend over twenty years in the courtroom and not learn something about prison conditions. "You're right," he says, "I'm not made for prison."

"Like I am?"

"I'm not a criminal."

Rostam's jaw goes slack. He stares. "You are the *biggest* fucking criminal!" he yells. "How many lies have you told in the courtroom? Each one is a crime. How many other innocent people have you sent to prison? To their deaths? How many excessive sentences, just to make yourself look good, look 'tough on crime'? You think you're above the law, like it doesn't apply to you? You're not a criminal?!"

Rostam looks ready to explode. In a fury, he reaches out and grabs the back of his chair, swings it high over his head as he steps forward.

Harden throws up his arms to protect himself, having fallen to his side on the bunk, his knees tucked into a ball. He knows he deserves a beating—he's been expecting one—but now that it's at hand, he begs for mercy: "Please! Please! I'm so sorry! So sorry . . ." His eyes are tightly closed behind his arms. He shakes, waiting for the hard metal chair to come crashing down—onto his head, his arms, his back, his legs . . .

But nothing happens. He hears the scrape of the chair as it's placed roughly back on the floor. He hears Rostam sigh heavily as he sits down.

Harden opens his eyes and peers out. Rostam is sitting closer than before, elbows on his knees, head in his hands. Harden could reach out and touch him, though he doesn't dare. He slowly sits up, scoots over to put some space between them, sits on the edge of the bunk, his feet on the cold cement floor.

After some minutes of silence, Rostam sits back and looks straight ahead at the wall. "I forgave you a long time ago," he says wearily. "You were an A-number-one asshole but you were just doing your job. Overzealous, I thought . . . Though I could never understand why you made me out to be such a horrible person. I didn't have any kind of criminal record, nothing like that, never been in trouble before."

Harden is also looking straight ahead, at the opposite wall, doing his best to slow his breathing, calm his still madly beating heart. He recalls the trial well—and his motivations. He had portrayed Rostam as a monster, all to better boost his own image as a "savior to society." Now it's *he* who needs saving. From the corner of his eye, he sees Rostam raise his hands then drop them listlessly into his lap.

"All those other things you accused me of," Rostam goes on, "without any evidence whatsoever . . . It's like you just made it all up . . . And the jury believed you; they believed every word. And why shouldn't they? Why would you lie? After all, you were *the* district attorney, sworn to uphold the law, the county's paragon of truth and justice."

Rostam stretches his legs and sinks lower in his chair, rubs his face with both hands. Sighs. "But I forgave you. It was either that or eat myself up with hatred for the rest of my life. And carry it into the next . . . Hell, I was more upset with my 'defense' attorney than I was with you." He laughs softly, and Harden can see him glance his way. "Now *she* was *really* hard to forgive, let me tell you."

Harden has no idea how this will end, but it looks like he's out of any immediate danger. Any "noble" ideas of taking the beating he deserves are out the window (not that he *has* a window). He says a silent prayer of thanks to whomever may be listening.

"You, however," Rostam says, "'Lord, forgive them, for they know not what they do.' Right? That was my reasoning." He shakes his head slowly. "But now . . . Now I don't know. I had no idea . . ."

They sit in silence for a long time.

Harden knows that nothing he can say, no apology, no matter how heartfelt, is going to change matters. He had already resigned himself months ago to the possibility of his never leaving here alive, and now he's certain of it. He continues to focus on his breathing, trying hard to quell the dread rising up within him, threatening to make him break down and cry. He tries in vain to find the still, deep pond inside.

Suddenly, after what has felt like forever, he hears Rostam laugh. Harden is startled from his solemn introspection and looks over.

"You knew!" Rostam bellows. "You *knew* I was innocent all along! Ha! Without a doubt. Amazing. It all makes sense now." He sits chuckling to himself. "Well played, my man, well played."

Harden doesn't know what to make of this sudden change in attitude. Rostam is still reclined, legs out, hands folded across his stomach, looking Harden's way now, grinning, shaking his head in amusement. He actually looks *happy,* Harden thinks.

"Mr. Harden—Wait, is it all right if I call you Dave?"

Hardon nods. "Uh-huh." *The man's insane.*

"Dave, I think it's about time I tell you why you're here."

Rostam sits up in his chair, turns it to face Harden more directly. He's smiling, totally at ease now.

"You're going to love this," he says.

22

"YOUR JOB WAS TO DEFEND ME."

"It was to *represent* you, which is what I did, meeting all of the requirements set forth by law."

Rostam glares at her from across the tiny room. The last thing Gloria wants to do is ruin any chance she may have of ever leaving here, but she isn't about to apologize for his being sent to prison.

"To represent me would have been doing what I asked you to do," he says, "which was provide a defense."

Oh, here we go. "Like your 'witnesses.'"

"For starters."

"Who was it? His 'assistant'? I checked. Navarro didn't have any female assistants, not one, not even a secretary. He was a chauvinist. Females were never privy to his business, apparently."

"My friends, Jessica and Kevin. I told them everything."

"Then why didn't they come forward?" Gloria asks. "They knew you'd been arrested, didn't they?"

"They were probably afraid."

"I don't blame them, a pair of dope heads like yourself."

"I told you where to find them."

Gloria has spent long enough this past year to remember most every aspect of the case. "A restaurant, is that right? Was I supposed to wait there every day for them to show up?"

Rostam throws up his hands. "They *worked* there!" He's yelling at her now.

"You're right," she says, trying to appease him, "I should have gone to the restaurant. I should have gotten them to testify. I'm sorry." It would have been a complete waste of her time, of course.

"And the hotel workers. I spent a week in that room. I could have pointed out at least three or four who would have recognized me easily."

"And what would that have proved?"

"That I was telling the truth!" Rostam cries. "That I was there the whole time! That I couldn't have been in Bay Town, dumping the body, like that guy said he saw me do! It's, like, twenty miles away!"

"Mr. Rostam, please remember: you were in the county jail. I couldn't just let you out to go find some workers at some hotel. Or was I supposed to bring them into the jail one by one so you could pick them out?"

"Ms. Thomas," Rostam leans forward in his chair, threateningly. What? Is she supposed to be intimidated by that stun gun he keeps waving around? "You know damn well that any investigator could have spent one day at that hotel, showing my photo to employees who might have seen me there. It hadn't been that long after my arrest; there's quite a few who would have remembered me and the woman—*especially* the woman. We partied in that room every day for a week. Someone from room service would have remembered me for sure."

"And could they have kept track of your movements? You could have easily left the hotel and come back."

Gloria sighs heavily. She has to make him understand her reasoning why she could never have helped him the way he wanted her to. It's like explaining something to a child. "Mr. Rostam, this was the problem I had from the beginning. No matter how badly I may have wanted to help you, I'm not going to present false or misleading evidence to the Court. It goes against my professional ethics. Being a defense lawyer does not mean I do my best to let guilty people go free."

Rostam looks fit to be tied. He's obviously not used to dealing with a woman of character, with morals. Not all of us are hookers and drug addicts, Gloria wants to tell him.

She's preparing herself for the outburst which is sure to come, when Rostam stands and kicks his chair aside. She flinches, despite her self-control so far.

He paces beside the opposite wall, plainly trying to master his anger. Then he finally stops to face her. "You see, Ms. Thomas, that's the problem *I* have had since the beginning of all this. You have always assumed I'm guilty. From the very first time we met, you never once gave me the benefit of the doubt."

Gloria matches his steely gaze. She has nothing to say to this. She always thought him guilty because he *was* guilty. There's nothing he could have said or done to change that. The evidence against him was overwhelming.

"There's just one thing I want to know," he continues, "and then we can put all of this behind us forever." He takes a step forward and peers at her intently. "Did you know about the video? The one from the hotel?"

Gloria blinks, tries to recall what he's talking about. But she's never heard of a video from the hotel, or from anywhere else for that matter. She shakes her head. "No."

He continues to stare. It's unnerving. Does he think she's lying?

"I'm sorry," she says, "was I supposed to?"

His face finally relaxes and he nods. "Yeah. You were. But it's not your fault."

Rostam retrieves his chair and sits again beneath the shelf. He tucks the weapon into the pocket of his jacket.

Gloria's curiosity is aroused. "What video?"

"It's from the hotel. It shows that I was there the whole time, that I never left. It proves that I could never have killed him."

She's sure this is a lie. Any evidence like that would have been presented during the discovery process, in the beginning. This is simply a clever attempt to manipulate her, to get her to second guess herself, to admit she was wrong. She's not falling for it.

"I see. Well, then you can just use this video footage in your appeal."

Rostam snorts. "You're something else. Just amazing." He waves his hands in the air in a bizarre gesture and settles further into his chair, crosses his arms petulantly. "Let's change the subject," he says. "What's past is past. As far as I'm concerned, you're forgiven."

Oh, this is rich! I'm *forgiven? Ha!*

"What matters now," he says, "is that *you* are able to forgive *me.*"

She can't help herself: "Only Christ can forgive you for what you have done."

Rostam cocks his head and looks at her slantwise. She pulls herself up straight, defiant, looks him fiercely in the eye.

"Tell me, Ms. Thomas, what do you think of the books I've given you? You've read them all, right?"

"Yes, I have. Every one."

He's waiting; she knows what he wants her to say.

"Well, do you like them?" he asks. "Have they helped you in any way?"

This is where she has to be careful. Whatever his plans are for her, it has to do with his books. She needs to cooperate but at the same time stay true to her faith, to her Lord.

"Yes, they're very interesting. I had no idea such books were available. Thank you."

Such trash should be burned, she's thinking.

"Do you have a favorite?"

Gloria has to think about this, but there are probably no right or wrong answers. "I'd have to say *The Power of Now.* It was very insightful." It's one of the few she's actually read cover to cover. Well, mostly.

"About living in the present moment at all times," Rostam says. "It's easier said than done, isn't it? Especially in here."

" . . . "

"And the meditations the book suggests. Have you tried them at all?"

"Yes, I have," she lies. "It's been very helpful."

She's not sure exactly what meditations he's talking about, but she *has* been spending much of her time in quiet contemplation and prayer lately. She prays mostly for her release from captivity, and for Rostam's change of heart. And she prays for her children, of course; and for Dwayne, the damn fool, if he hasn't already killed himself with the pills and drink by now.

Rostam points to the book beside her on the mattress. She had quickly put it there when she heard the doors being opened, to impress him, to assure him she's been reading diligently. "What about the latest," he asks her, "*A Course in Miracles?*"

"It's . . . a bit difficult to follow. And a lot to digest . . . But I'm getting there."

Rostam nods sagely, so full of himself. "Yeah, it's pretty intense. A lot of people have formed study groups to better understand it . . . Have you checked out the 'Workbook' section yet?"

Gloria has no idea what he's talking about. "Yes, very impressive."

"What about the author? Pretty cool, huh?"

Something in her expression must give her away.

He says, "I take it you don't approve. You don't think it's Him who dictated it, do you?"

There's no point in lying about it. "No, I certainly do not."

"You don't think the spirit of Jesus Christ is still alive?"

The impudence! "Of course He is. He is the Son of God. He can never die."

"You don't think He still performs miracles, then? You don't think He could have spoken to this woman? Given her His message this way?"

For seven years? "It was a demon, obviously. She was possessed."

Rostam smirks. "Preaching love and forgiveness? You think a demon would do that?"

"'Satan himself can be transformed into an angel of light.'" *Second Corinthians 11:14.*

Rostam rolls his eyes and shakes his head, feigning ignorance. As a servant of Satan himself, he knows the truth of what she's said. "Well, I at least hope you'll give the book a chance," he says, "listen to what He's got to say. It's some powerful stuff—probably the best teachings on forgiveness you can ever read."

He looks around her room now, around her feet and under the bed, turns in his seat to scan the shelf behind him. "What about the CDs? What do you think?" He's all smiles now, like an eager child—like a mischievous brat, more like.

"I like them. The music is very relaxing." Gloria hasn't touched the second and third to arrive; she hasn't listened to them at all since that first time. She's too smart for that now.

"Notice anything different?"

He's so transparent! "No, not really . . . It puts me to sleep."

Rostam is studying her skeptically. She tires of his scrutiny and looks away; but there is absolutely nothing else in the room to look at, so she settles on the books above his head.

"Gloria—May I call you Gloria?"

"That's fine."

"I want you to know that I respect your devotion to your faith."

This is a surprise . . . Until she can see by his face that it's just another ruse to sway her, to eventually convert her to *his* religion, as she knows has been his plan all along. She returns her focus to the colorful row of books on the shelf.

Give me strength, Lord.

"I also follow Jesus's teachings," Rostam says. "And not just those in the *Course* but in the Bible, too."

Gloria gives him just the quickest of glances; she can't bear to look at him anymore, this liar and manipulator, this cold-blooded killer. A sociopathic criminal proclaiming to be a Christian! It takes every ounce of her self-control to keep from giving him a piece of her mind.

"I'm telling you this because I'm sure you have your doubts about some of what you've been reading—especially about reincarnation—am I right?"

She nods, afraid to say or do any more. She knows this is where he's going to try to persuade her, to convince her.

"But at least you *have* read the books," he says. "I have to admire you for that. A lot of people wouldn't. They might say it goes against their religion to even consider the subject . . . Or they might be afraid of being wrong all these years—that there might be something more than what they've been taught, than what their parents believed."

Gloria knows he is trying to get a reaction from her, but she'll be damned if she lets him succeed. She'll speak her mind at some point, but she'll do so from a position of strength, not weakness.

"So, from what you've read so far, would you say there's some pretty good evidence that it's true—that our souls do keep coming back from time to time?"

"No, I would not."

"Oh? What about all those children who spontaneously recall their life before this one?"

Gloria bites her tongue.

"Or what about all those people who've described their previous lives in detail under hypnosis?"

"It's the work of demons."

"Ooookay. As in, it was demons who made them say these things, or demons describing their own past lives on Earth?"

"There is no greater deceiver than Satan and his minions." She comes close to accusing him of being one himself but keeps her mouth shut just in time.

"So having millions of people all over the world—millions of people throughout history—describing their past lives is one of Satan's master plans?"

Gloria doesn't like his tone. He's ridiculing her beliefs, she can tell. She refuses to honor him with a response.

"To what end?" Rostam asks. "To trick us into what? Behaving more responsibly? More lovingly? To learn that how we live each life actually makes a difference? That we keep trying to become better? That we're not just these physical beings? I don't get it."

It's obvious there is nothing she can say to this man; he wants to argue for arguing's sake. But he'll have to settle for arguing with himself. She won't give him the satisfaction.

"Demons!"

Now the insolent fool is laughing at her!

He'll pay for this, she thinks. He'll pay on Judgment Day. And she will be there at the right hand of the Lord to witness Rostam suffer in the fires of Hell, as he deserves.

He chides: "Was it demons who made Jesus ask his disciples who people thought he was in a former life? Was it demons who made Jesus claim that John the Baptist was Elijah, reborn? Was it demons who—"

"Don't you dare!" Gloria shouts, shaking her finger at him. "Don't you dare presume to know what Jesus meant by that! You are hardly a man of God. Just the opposite. Who are you to interpret the Bible? I'm surprised the pages don't burn at your touch."

"And was it demons who made John speak of reincarnation in the book of Revelation?"

"He did no such thing."

"'Him that overcometh will I make a pillar in the temple of God, and he shall go out no more.'"

Gloria scoffs at this. "What does that mean? Don't tell me *you* understand. The Bible is clear: man is appointed one life to live before Judgment."

"One life," Rostam says.

"That's right."

"Okay, if death is the end of life, what is life the end of?"

He thinks he's so smart. "Life isn't the end of anything; it's the beginning."

"You sure? You didn't first exist in another form?" He holds up a hand to stop her. "But you're right: life *isn't* an end, just like death isn't an end either. There is *never* an end. There's only a change in form, in energy. It's a cycle. When we die here, we just return to where we came from. And then we can come back anytime we want—just like we did this time."

"God, the Father, creates each life. He endows each of us with the Holy Spirit in the womb, at conception."

"Right, God creates everything. But *we* are as much God as anything else. Even more so: we're like extensions of Him—like flames from the greater fire, so to speak—His co-creators on Earth."

Oh, Lord! Spare me! Of course this megalomaniac would have a God complex. "God has no need for 'co-creators,'" Gloria says. "He created the heavens and the Earth, and He created each one of us to find those worthy enough to serve Him. We're given this one life to prove ourselves, before we are called to stand before His Son. Where *you* will stand and be judged someday," she reminds him.

"Where does it say that in the Bible?"

"Hebrews 9:27." She hasn't taught Sunday school for so long for nothing.

"And who wrote Hebrews?"

"Paul."

"You sure?"

"There's been some debate, but yes, I'm sure. What does it matter?"

Rostam smiles smugly and leans back in his chair, folds his hands upon his stomach. "Isn't it interesting how so much of the New Testament was written by this one man—how *one* man's opinion shaped an entire religion. It's almost like you worship *his* views more than Jesus's."

"You're an idiot," Gloria says heatedly. "That's not true at all. You have no idea what you're talking about."

"Oh, no? Including your Hebrews, Paul—who never met Jesus, by the way, except as a bright light, supposedly, on the road to Damascus—Paul wrote *fourteen* of the twenty-seven books of the New Testament. That's a lot, I'd say. Basically half . . . And whatever he says goes, apparently, to this day. This one man, so long ago, was able to—"

"That one man was Jesus Christ," Gloria retorts, "who died on the cross for our sins."

Rostam raises his eyebrows at her. "Did *He* teach that? No. Again, it's someone else's idea that took hold. Jesus wasn't killed to pay for our sins; he was killed because he was chasing the money lenders out of the temples; he was a threat to Joseph Caiaphas, who was getting rich on temple funds. He was a Kabbalist. And like John the Baptist, Jesus was a righteous Zealot who wasn't happy with the status quo. He was a rebel. And he pissed off the wrong people."

It's all Gloria can do to stay seated, to stay silent. She would like nothing more than to throttle this irreverent fool. She can feel the steam rising within her, her hands clenching and unclenching in her lap.

Rostam holds up his hands in defense. "Look, Jesus was a great man, there's no denying it. There's a reason he's remembered, and there's a reason he should be emulated. But his teachings were simple. They were all about love and forgiveness and treating others as well as yourself; about how the kingdom of God is found within each one of us, and not through the Church. Just another reason he was killed."

Gloria can't remain quiet any longer. Her voice is tight with anger as she says, "'For God so loved the world that He gave His only begotten Son, so that the world through Him might be saved.'"

"His *only* son? Jesus said we are *all* 'sons of God.'"

She pays this no mind. "'The Blood of Jesus Christ His Son cleanseth us from sin.' Can *you* do that? Can anyone else? It's through His Blood we are Redeemed."

"Why his blood? Why not his teachings—his example?"

"His teachings? All right: Jesus said, 'I am the way, the truth, and the life: no man cometh unto the Father, but by me.'"

"Right! Exactly!" Rostam sits up straight now in his chair. "Jesus is supposed to be a role-model for us. He taught that we could *all* become Self-realized, just like he did. But the Church distorted this. They put all this emphasis on the crucifixion— on his blood, on the cross—like that's all that matters. Because having Jesus take responsibility for our 'sins' takes karma out of the equation. That's where all this 'dying for our sins' business comes from: people against the idea of karma and reincarnation. Like Paul. Paul was a *lawyer,* for Christ's sake! . . . No offense. No pun intended."

"He was a tent maker."

"Who could read and write so well in Hebrew, Greek, and Latin? Who was also a Roman citizen? No, he *visited* some tent makers. His family—"

"Paul was a saint. His words were inspired by God."

"Right, a lawyer and politician turned saint; happens all the time." Rostam makes a derisive noise. "So I guess you're of the view that his writings—like all the rest of it—are the literal 'Word of God.'"

"The Bible declares that it is the divine Word. Two Timothy 3:16."

"Circular logic. Gotta love it. You don't think the Bible has been edited and changed countless times throughout history? Especially during the beginning? Hell, the Church itself couldn't even decide if Jesus was a god or a man or both until, like, the fifth century or something. And then they had to change everything to reflect their decision. It was all politics."

Gloria has heard variations of this argument before, from many people, both in and outside her own church. She's sick of it. "It makes no difference," she says. "The message remains the same. Every word is divinely inspired. Any changes to the original scripture were done with God's approval, with His guidance. There's a *reason* why the Bible is written the way it is today."

"You know, that's something I have a problem understanding," Rostam says. "If that's true, then why are there so many discrepancies? Why in the Gospels, for example, does John say that Jesus was crucified the day *before* Passover, where Mark says it was the day *after?*"

"That's ridiculous. You know nothing." Gloria's patience is wearing thin. To think for one second that a convicted criminal and drug addict can know more about the Bible than she does is preposterous. "If you would only give me a Bible, as I've asked you to do so many times, I could show you where you are wrong. You're not reading it right, obviously."

"Tell that to professors of religious studies all over the world," Rostam says haughtily. "But I will; I'll get you a Bible, I promise—just for you. I used to have one just like it."

"I prefer the King James version," she says. "It's the only correct one, based on the ancient Assyrian."

"Don't worry, it'll be in there."

Gloria can't stand his arrogant attitude. She wishes he would just quit talking, at least tell her something meaningful, like why she is here.

"I can give you at least a hundred different discrepancies in the New Testament," Rostam persists, "but I'll spare you—Well, just one more—maybe two, since we're talking about Paul and all."

Gloria rolls her eyes, bemoaning the fact that she is truly a captive audience of this pontificating ass.

Rostam: "In Galatians, Paul says that, after his conversion on the road to Damascus, he did *not* go to Jerusalem, but in Acts he says it's the *first* thing he did. Why is that?"

Gloria sighs. "I'd have to see the—"

"Right, right, of course. Here's a better one: Why does Luke say that Mary and Joseph returned to Nazereth after Jesus's birth, but Matthew says they fled to Egypt? . . . Is that the 'Word of God'?" Rostam asks mockingly. "Was God confused that day?"

Gloria can't believe her ears. "You blaspheme!" is all she trusts herself to say. She squeezes her eyes shut to rid him of her sight, squeezes her hands into fists to keep them from shaking.

"And you undoubtedly know the story of the adulteress, in John, right? 'He who hasn't sinned cast the first stone,' and all that?"

Gloria shoots him a look. Rostam's supercilious grin is of the Devil himself.

"But it never happened," he says. "The story is absent from all the oldest known texts. It was added sometime in the seventh century or so. It was a popular moral tale around that time. Like in other instances."

She turns away from him, disgusted, notices the door has been left slightly ajar. The thought of running flits across her mind for the briefest instant.

"So, were the persons who added that and other stories later *also* divinely inspired?" he jibes. "And what about the 'Shepherd of Hermas' and all the original stories that were *removed*?"

From the corner of her eye, Gloria can see Rostam wave, trying to get her attention. She ignores him. As far as she knows, he's making all this up. It might sway or confuse someone else— someone less sure in their walk with Christ—but not her. She has been in His presence.

Gloria turns back and looks directly into Rostam's eyes, puts as much force as she can behind her words: "Mr. Rostam, you are wasting your time. There is nothing you can ever say that will make me change my mind. *Nothing*. I know what I know and I don't care what you think."

She stares him down, unblinking.

And this seems to do the trick. Rostam finally shuts up; he drops his gaze to the floor and sits unmoving, his hands held contritely in his lap.

Gloria closes her eyes, the silence a palliative for her frayed nerves.

Until: "I know . . . And that's what's so sad," she hears him say. "As long as you people believe that the Holy Bible, or the Holy Qur'an, is the one-and-only, indisputable 'Word of God,' this world will remain at war with itself." He sighs audibly. "We're in a new age of enlightenment. But fanatics and fundamentalists like yourself, on both sides, are hijacking the planet, holding the rest of us hostage with your outdated and, frankly, erroneous beliefs . . . There is no one religion better than the other—especially when you're *all* screwed up."

Gloria's temper flares. She's had enough. She's sick of Rostam's company, as much as she once craved it; she's sick of his belligerence and the garbage he's spewing; she's sick of his condescension and being treated like a dope; she's sick of his lies and deceit; she's sick of this God-forsaken prison cell.

"What is your *point?*" she nearly screams. "What does any of this have to do with you kidnapping me and holding me against my will? Of locking me in this—" She stands and gestures wildly at the paltry space around her. "This *hellhole?* Why are you forcing me to read all these damned books? Do you honestly expect me to change my religion for you? If you do, you're out of your damned mind!"

Gloria can see she's surprised him. The coward has his hand in his jacket, reaching for his precious weapon.

And she's surprised herself: This anger feels good! *Just let the arrogant bastard say anything else about the Bible!*

Rostam holds up his hands, pats the air in a placating gesture. He's speaking to her softly now, carefully. As he should. "Gloria, all I'm asking you to do is open your eyes. There's a big difference between faith and *blind* faith. There are so many other scriptures out there besides the Bible. If I told you that Jesus himself preached about reincarnation, you wouldn't believe me, but it's true. The *Pistis Sophia* is one of the most beautiful collections of his teachings. And then there's the Gospel of Thomas, the Gospel of Philip—many others."

Gloria paces the length of her bunk, a hand to her suddenly aching head. She has no idea what he's talking about. What other scriptures? There are no other teachings of Christ . . . Are there? . . .

"And that's just in Christianity," Rostam says doggedly. "There are many other spiritual writings and teachings in other religions, many much older. And what's cool is that, no matter what culture or religion you study, including Christianity, there's *one* underlying truth they all share."

Gloria stops her pacing and looks at the man. His eyes are pleading with her to listen. She puts her hands on her hips, waits for whatever crap is sure to come next. He's determined to lecture her, so she might as well let him; she's through trying to reason with this fool. Maybe she'll at least find out where he's coming from, what his agenda is. Hopefully.

"And that truth is that we are all spiritual beings," Rostam says, clearly glad to have her attention. "Originally, we *ourselves* created these physical bodies, in order to experience the physical world. Our mission—individually and collectively—is to learn and grow through experience. And no matter how difficult life can be sometimes, we keep *choosing* to come back—to work on different issues, try different things, become more loving, which is what it's really all about."

He holds out his hands now, as if in offering. "This is why *Love* is the fundamental teaching of every religion . . . This is why Jesus and Buddha and Krishna and Zarathustra and countless others over the ages have all been such wonderful teachers; they *embodied* the spiritual ideal; they became fully-realized human beings here in their physical bodies; they could transcend the physical world. And they wanted the rest of us to do it, too." Rostam reaches out and clutches the air between them in his fist. "We *can*, Gloria!" he says excitedly. "It's totally possible!"

Standing there only a few feet away, Gloria stares in disbelief at the man before her—at this convicted killer and kidnapper who has uprooted her whole life and imprisoned her in this metal box for over a year. He touts love and forgiveness and spiritual enlightenment, like some sort of wayward preacher— a mad prophet. There is an energy about him. His eyes seem to shine with genuine compassion as he sits there smiling so warmheartedly at her.

He really is crazy. There's no doubt in her mind anymore. But it's equally apparent he means her no harm.

The anger she felt only a moment ago is now gone, and it's left her feeling drained. If there was a battle to be fought here today, she's lost, she can see that plainly now.

Is this how Satan works, then, she thinks, *through pretensions of Godliness in the minds of the wicked?*

Gloria sits dejectedly on her bunk. With an effort she pulls her eyes away from this strange man she had earlier wanted to strangle with her bare hands. She gazes around the small cell that has become her entire world.

"I just want to go home," she says quietly at last.

"You will," Rostam says. "I promise . . . I promise."

23

DANI'S EXCITED. She's actually going to experience a past-life re-gression like she's been reading about. And from what Josh says, she's going to be experiencing a *lot* of them over the coming months.

The point of the sessions is "forgiveness," he says—the same thing her new book, *A Course in Miracles,* is all about.

At first Dani had been intimidated by the sheer thickness of the book; it would take her forever to read the whole thing. But later, after perusing the "Workbook" section in Part Two, she realized it isn't meant to be read all at once, but slowly over the course of a year, or longer. Josh says some people treat it like their Bible, studying it intensely or just picking it up whenever the urge arises.

Being able to talk with Josh about all her books has been wonderful. Though mostly she's the one doing all the talking, so overjoyed to finally be able to express her views and ideas about it all to another person. But Josh doesn't appear to mind at all; he's a good listener and seems genuinely interested in what she has to say. It makes her feel smart for the first time in her life.

And she *is* smart now, she knows. After all, it's not important to know everything, only the important things.

Josh has been really good at answering all her questions, too. Her first had been a big one:

If the same souls keep coming back to reincarnate, why is the world's population always growing? She once heard on TV it was up to, like, seven billion-something people now.

And what he told her made sense:

All souls were created at the same time, he said, but only the smallest fraction of the smallest fraction of them all came to Earth (helped *create* the Earth, actually). And our planet isn't the only place souls go; there are lots of other worlds and dimensions and realities and whatnot. The Earth's population is growing, Josh said, because more and more "new" souls are wanting to experience it physically for themselves, since there's always so much to learn and do here. Not everybody has been here hundreds or thousands of times already. Also (and she had read about this), sometimes our Higher Self chooses to put its Consciousness into more than one physical body at a time; so we can easily have one or two other people running around out there.

There have been a lot of other questions, too, and still plenty more, but the one Dani hasn't asked is when she'll be set free. She's pretty sure it will be after they've completed whatever it is to do with all the past lives they've shared together, but she can't be certain. Really, she's a little afraid to ask, not knowing if she'll like the answer.

Plus, she's a little afraid to leave. Where will she go? What will she do? How will she survive on her own? She tries not to think about it too much.

Right now she just wants to enjoy the few hours she has to spend today with Josh. He can only come every four days, since he has to visit with the others, too. (Dani knows all about them, of course: she's seen them often in her nightly travels.)

This is their second session. The first had been "regular" hypnosis, testing her receptivity and getting her used to the process.

"I was really impressed with your level of concentration last time," he's telling her now. "I think we can go ahead with the regression work today, what do you think?"

"Okay," she says eagerly, "I'm ready." Then, as an afterthought she immediately regrets: "How did Santos do?"

Josh's expression says it all. "Oh, we're having a bit of trouble getting started. Our last couple a meetings haven't gone so well."

"He doesn't want to do it, does he?"

"Nope, not really. But I'm hoping he comes around. In fact, I'm counting on it."

Dani doesn't think so: she knows Santos all too well. It's been a long time, but unless he's become a totally different person, she knows he will never give in. Santos isn't somebody who does things to help other people. And he isn't somebody you went up against—ever. But she just nods her head; Josh will find out for himself, eventually.

"I can tell you don't think he'll do it," Josh says. "But don't worry"—he smiles slyly, taps the side of his head—"I've got an idea."

Josh is sitting in his folding chair at the head of her bunk. He's brought a cushion with him this time. And a digital recorder. He hands her a small microphone. "Just clip it on, like this." He demonstrates with his own. Both are connected to the recording device with wires. "You ready?"

"Uh-huh." A tiny bit nervous now, Dani lies back, reclining on the big, fluffy pillow he brought for her last week.

"Once we reach a sufficient level of hypnosis," he says, "before we do anything else, I'd like to try something with you. You remember the book *Healing Lost Souls*?"

Of course she does. It's about spirit releasement, or "exorcism." The subject fascinates her. She had no idea it was actually real—and so common. But to have it done to herself . . . "Uh, yeah . . ."

"Usually people with a history of addiction have some sort of entity attachment, you know? I know I sure did."

"You did?"

"Yep. Lots. And it took some work getting rid of them all on my own, let me tell ya." He laughs. "But together we can take care of it quickly, today, all at one time." He must see how tentative she is. "It's something that's good to get out of the way, before we get into your past lives," he says. "We don't want to confuse any of their memories with yours, you know what I mean?" He puts his hand on her arm, gives her a reassuring smile. "But who knows, maybe there'll be no one there."

That book had been a real eye-opener, but it also frightened her a little. Now she's afraid to face whatever demons may still be possessing her. But Dani knows she can't back down; she has to go through with it. She stares up at the ceiling. "Let's find out," she says with more confidence than she feels.

"Great. It shouldn't take that long; and then we can just move right into the regression part." Josh picks up his notepad and pen from the floor. "However, the whole thing's gonna take at least a few hours. You need to use the restroom or anything?"

She shakes her head. "No, I'm okay. Can I go in the middle of it, if I have to?"

"Sure, no problem."

Dani can hear him take a deep breath and let it out slowly, and her body automatically follows his lead.

"All right, you can keep your eyes open for now," he begins. "You can look forward or upward, focusing on a specific point or off into space. Take a deep, cleansing breath, inhaling peace and relaxation, exhaling any worries or tension . . . Keep your arms and legs uncrossed and your hands and feet apart; let your arms rest by your sides . . ."

Already, just the sound of Josh's voice is lulling her into trance: a posthypnotic suggestion from their last session, he explained to her earlier. *It's working.*

"We're about to embark on a fascinating journey into the deepest recesses of your mind, where you will fully connect with your superconscious—your soul mind—and experience yourself as the eternal, spiritual being you really are . . . This journey has been taken by the fortunate few for thousands of years. It's an 'initiation' of sorts into the 'Mysteries.' It's a perfectly safe and natural experience . . ."

Josh told her he'd read this script so often to his fellow inmates in prison that he memorized it. She hopes he knows what he's doing.

"As a guided meditation, this is like a dance, where I lead and you follow, with both of us participating and creating the experience together. So your attitude is important, your openness and willingness are important . . . To make the most of it, simply relax and let your subconscious take over. You can accept or reject anything given to you. You are in complete control. This is something only *you* can do for yourself . . .

"So, if you're ready, please join me now in taking a nice, deep breath—the deepest breath you can take—and *hold* it . . . Then *slowly* let it out . . . Good. Once again: a real deep breath and hold it . . . Then let it out slowly . . .

"Very good. Continue breathing deeply and smoothly, focusing on the relaxing sound of my voice. Just relax comfortably . . ."

It's easy for Dani to relax. She'd worried the first time about falling asleep, but Josh assured her that wouldn't happen. Ideally, he said, her body would fall asleep but her mind would stay alert and aware—much like when she leaves her body at night.

"Now, I'm going to count down from ten to one," he continues, "and with every descending number, I want you to slowly blink your eyes . . . Got it? Slowly close and then open your eyes, like in slow motion, with every number . . . *Ten*—do it *slowwwly* . . . Nine . . . Eight . . . Seven . . . Six . . ." Dani is finding it harder to open her eyes each time. "Five . . . Four . . . Three . . . Two . . . and *one*. Now you can just close your eyes and keep them closed . . ."

SHE'S FLOATING in a tranquil sea of Consciousness—of "beingness," simply being—listening to the soothing sound of Josh's voice:

". . . Just remember the breath. A nice, deep breath completely relaxes and focuses you anywhere, at any time . . . Breathing, relaxing, focusing your attention automatically. Your focus and concentration are like a laser beam cutting through metal . . . You're focused, you're relaxed, breathing deeply, smoothly . . .

"Simply let your mind drift, listening to the pleasant sound of my voice, which is soon to become a comfortable feeling in the background, my words blending into one another and flowing into your mind naturally, so that you're free from having to pay attention to the words, as your subconscious understands them anyway . . .

"Pictures, images, impressions, feelings will all float easily into your mind in response to my questions and instructions . . .

"All right. Now, to bypass the conscious mind, so there's no need to even think of an answer, we'll use finger signals from time to time . . . To answer 'yes' to a question, move your left thumb; to answer 'no,' move your left pinkie finger. Do you understand these instructions?"

"Yes," Dani replies softly. At some part of her mind, she's aware of her thumb also responding.

"Good. Now listen closely: I'm addressing any beings attached to Dani in any way. I want to speak with you . . . Are there any beings present?"

To Dani's amazement, her thumb twitches.

"The strongest of you come forward now," Josh commands. The mellow cadence and tone of his voice are gone, replaced by a no-nonsense manner that brooks no reproach. "What is your name?"

He's answered with only silence.

"Do you *have* a name?"

Her pinkie finger rises and falls.

"Speak to me. Why are you here? What is your purpose?"

In Dani's mind, there forms a feeling-picture of "need," of "want," of "fear of doing without." It's like a condensed cloud, absent of any color or light, blacker than black. It seems to have a consciousness independent from her own.

"Speak up," Josh orders, "or I will destroy you."

"You cannot."

Oh my God! Dani thinks. It's her own voice, but deeper than she's ever heard it, flat with no intonation. But it's not her speaking.

"You're right, I cannot," Josh says. "But I am aligned with powerful beings of Light who can . . . You're aware of these beings, are you not?"

Dani's thumb jerks.

"You're scared of the Light, aren't you?"

The voice says, "No," but her thumb says otherwise.

Raising his voice, Josh declares: "I call upon the Forces of Light to help me! . . . Do you see them? They're all around you now! By their power, I cast an unbreakable net of Light around you! You can't escape! . . . I'll squeeze the net tighter if you don't cooperate!"

"No!" Dani can feel its nervousness, its fear.

In her mind, giant beings of brilliant golden-white Light now surround the demon. A fine net of Light shimmers around the dark form squirming beneath it.

"Why have you attached yourself to this woman?" Josh asks.

"It is why I exist. I was told to."

"By who?"

A beat, as if it were thinking. "By that which created me."

"Do you know who or what that is?"

Another pause. "No."

"So you're just following instructions blindly," Josh points out. "What were you told to do, exactly?"

The answer comes immediately this time: "Feed."

"Feed? On what?"

"Hunger."

Dani feels the intense, all-consuming craving of heroin addiction wash over her. It makes her sick; she gags; it's all she can do not to throw up. A flash of the worst withdrawals condensed into one instant . . . And then it's gone . . . It was a horrible reminder of the pain she once suffered—of the life she once lived, every day, for years.

"Are you hurting this woman?"

"Yes."

"Then it's time for you to go."

"I cannot."

"You can. There's a way," Josh tells the demon, the entity, the "thought form," whatever the hell it is. "I want you to look deep within yourself . . . What do you see?"

There's no answer for a full minute or so. Longer. Dani sees what it sees: total darkness . . . then the tiniest spark of light at its core, barely discernible.

"Light . . ." It says this hesitantly, unbelieving.

"Yes! That's right! Light!" Josh is clearly excited. "You are *also* a being of Light, just like those who surround you. *Everything* is Light, ultimately."

"No . . ."

"It's true. Look to the Forces of Light now. Ask them. What are they telling you?"

Dani can see the radiant beings beckoning to the creature.

"They want me to come with them," it says. "I cannot."

"You can! Focus on the Light inside you. It's growing bigger now, isn't it? It is! And soon it will fill you completely . . . Let me know when it does that."

Dani watches in disbelief as the black cloud begins to glow faintly from within, then brighter and brighter.

"It is done," it says at last. There's a feeling like happiness associated with it now.

"Before you go," Josh orders, "I want you to look for any other dark entities, like you once were, that are attached to Dani . . . Do you see any?"

Numerous shifting, black forms appear, all with their own agendas, none to her benefit.

"Yes."

"Speak to them; communicate with them however you can. Tell them what you've learned—what you've discovered for your-self—about the Light . . . Tell them to look within themselves as well."

So very slowly, every one of the alien beings changes to a little ball of shiny white Light.

"What do you see?" Josh asks. "Are they doing it, too?"

"Yes . . . It is done."

"Excellent! Now take them all with you. Go with our bless-ings. Go with the Forces of Light now."

And with that, Dani sees the once dark entities merge with the larger, brighter beings around them. And then they're gone.

The benevolent Forces of Light are out of sight now, but Dani can still sense their presence. She knows that all she has to do is call for them and they'll come again.

She can't say she feels any different after the experience— "cleaner," maybe, "lighter"—but she knows she's much better off because of it.

"Tell me with the fingers," Josh says. "Are they gone?"

Her thumb moves in the affirmative.

"Now, are there any other beings attached to Dani? If so, speak up. I want to talk with you."

"I'm here," says a timid voice through Dani's mouth. She can sense somebody hiding, peaking around the corner, showing themself for the first time. She can barely see the person, but at least it is a *person.*

"And who are you?" Josh asks.

"Mary."

Mary! Of course! That's her real name. It's Mariah, her best friend and "sister" from Barry's stable of girls, the one who'd been killed so tragically. Dani can see her clearly now: her hair is done up like it always was; she's wearing her favorite red dress; she looks confused, uncertain, a little afraid.

"Mary, do you realize that you're attached to Dani now?"

"Umm, I guess so . . . She's my friend."

"Do you understand that you're no longer in your physical body—that you died?"

Dani can sense Mariah's sadness at his remark.

"Yeah . . . I know. But it's okay. Dani's still here."

"Why did you attach yourself to her?"

It takes a moment for Mariah to answer. "What else was I supposed to do? I didn't know where else to go . . . And I really needed a fix." Dani's heart breaks. "Do you have one? I *really* need a hit. She hasn't been scoring at all lately. I don't know what's going on."

"Mary, Dani doesn't do heroin anymore, or any drugs," Josh explains. "And your being attached to her doesn't help you—or her. In fact, it's not good for either of you . . . Wouldn't you like to go somewhere where you can be happy for a change? Wouldn't you like to go home?"

"Home? I don't have a home . . . Dani's my home now."

"Mary, watch what happens."

In his louder, authoritative voice again, Josh says, "In the name of Love and Light, I call upon Mary's family and loved ones and any other caring spirits . . . Is there anyone willing to help Mary cross over to where she belongs? . . . If so, come now."

Above Mariah, a sky of misty, white clouds appears, backlit by a silver glow. A small, frail-looking girl in Hello Kitty pajamas is there waving, smiling down, holding out her hand.

It's her sister. The knowing just comes to her, and Dani can feel Mariah's delight in seeing her again after so long. She'd died so young.

"Maggie! Oh, Maggie!" Mariah reaches up, begins to leave, but then pulls back. "Can I go?" she asks plaintively.

"Of course you can," Josh says. "Go with our blessings. Be happy."

"What about Dani?"

"She'll be okay, don't worry about her. She loves you. You'll see her again someday, I bet."

Mariah's smile lights up her face. "Okay! Goodbye, Dani!" She rises up, and when she reaches her sister, they disappear along with the clouds.

Wow! Dani is blown away. It's still hard to believe. Has Mariah been with her this whole time? Looking back now, had she ever sensed Mariah's presence?

Her thoughts are interrupted by Josh again:

"Are there any other beings attached to Dani? If so, speak up now."

Her thumb twitches. There's a pause. Then the words come slowly, with a sigh, with a feeling of great reluctance: "Yes. I am the last."

An almost familiar face, like a mirror image, takes shape: a young woman with long, auburn hair, worn loosely over her shoulder; large, brown, doe-shaped eyes; a distinctive, narrow nose; a tender smile . . . She seems to be looking directly at her, as if she knows that Dani can see her now.

"Who are you?" Josh asks. "What is your name?"

The woman's smile grows. She opens her arms wide, as if for a hug.

And without a second thought—as if guided by instinct—Dani is diving into those arms and embracing the woman with all her might, holding her tightly, like she'll never let her go.

The images come flooding in—memories long forgotten or repressed: She's five, she's wearing a light blue dress; it's a Saturday, all the kids are playing in the street outside; they've just returned home with the groceries; Dani's a big girl now, so she gets to help put things away; she's standing on a stool, reaching into the cupboard, when the bad men come; she's grabbed roughly and carried away, slung over the man's shoulder, kicking, pounding on his back, her cries unable to drown out the screams coming from inside.

The memory ends there.

Then there's the woman's voice in her head:

I've never left you, Daniella, my love.

It touches Dani's heart, mind, and soul.

"My name is Isabella," she hears herself say. "I am her mother."

24

"FUCKING SLOP."

Santos slings his empty tray at the door. Every once in a while he makes it into the slot, but not this time. He gets up and kicks it through.

Tonight's meal really wasn't too bad, considering. A spicy chicken and rice dish with a thick, homemade salsa on the side. Not enough of it, though. It's never enough. He hasn't felt full once since he got here.

Santos pats his stomach. All the better, he supposes; he's lost the gut. He's in the best shape he's been in since his twenties, when the Syndicate first recruited him—if that's what you want to call it.

His work for them had always felt more like slavery. Especially in the beginning. Before, running with his own gang, he'd been his own boss, calling the shots—not somebody's number cruncher and errand boy. It wasn't until he was finally put in charge (and proved himself worthy of the responsibility) that he felt like he did when he was younger and ruled the *barrio*. But even then he had to grovel before *los Generales*.

Santos knows he'll never be put in such a position of power again. (That is, if he ever gets out of this shit hole, which is looking highly unlikely right now.) Nobody who lets himself get nabbed like he did has much of a future in *La Familia*. It doesn't matter how successful he was at running things, or how much money he made them all; he'd be stuck now in some room not much bigger than this one, keeping the books for some low-rung lieutenant like Avilla.

That's why he plans to go it alone when he's free. *Solo.*

He has more than three and a half million dollars in his Antigua account—$3,661,817.94, to be exact, given a 5.2% annual interest rate over the past thirteen months since the last time he checked, including fees. Out of all the various accounts scattered throughout the Caribbean that Santos kept track of, only this one he has direct administrative control over. All it will take is sending the account number and pass codes—by e-mail, snail-mail, or fax—and he can have any amount and a debit card sent to him anywhere in the world.

He's thinking Argentina, somewhere just outside of Buenos Aires. The cattle business, a sprawling *hacienda*. He has it all planned to the last detail.

His abduction, he now thinks, may have been a blessing in disguise. The Syndicate has to think he's dead by now, so he's free to do whatever he wants. Well, not quite free—not yet.

Santos has racked his brain trying to come up with a way Rostam might let him go, without having to go through his *loco* hypnosis bullshit. Either the asshole is dead serious and really does want Santos to relive his "past lives" and "forgive" Rostam's sorry ass, or it's an ingenious ploy to get into his head and get access to the new pass codes. Either way, the guy is seriously nuts. And Santos has to admit, this scares him a little. There's no telling what Rostam might do once he had him under hypnosis.

At least the fool hadn't sent him a book this month.

Though the CD arrived on time: the same kind as before, but different. Santos is glad he didn't trash the CD-player like he'd wanted to when he first got it. He likes the strange music. It's very relaxing. He's never been able to listen to the whole thing all the way through; he always seems to zone out during the first half hour or so, falling asleep with the headphones on.

He's pretty sure the music is the reason he's been having such incredible dreams lately. He flies every time now and has the wildest adventures. But what's weird is that it's like he's really awake and really there, not asleep at all—not like in a regular dream. Plus, he can remember everything that happens in them.

Santos yawns. Maybe he'll listen to a CD now. He's feeling very sleepy all of a sudden, much earlier than usual.

He lies down, thinks of reaching for the CD-player on the floor but it's too much trouble. His last thought is one of mild surprise.

HE AWAKENS SLOWLY, as if from a depth, his eyelids fluttering, strobing light into his brain. Color and form take shape into that of Rostam's face close above his.

Santos starts, and with a sudden surge of panic, comes fully awake. But he's unable to sit up or lift his arms. He's strapped down; he can feel wide bands across his chest, his waist, his legs.

Before he can utter a sound, Rostam is covering his mouth and nose with one hand, pressing down, using the other to grip his head to hold it still.

Santos feels utterly helpless as he struggles uselessly, his neck muscles straining, his eyes bulging painfully in their sockets.

Rostam's look is grave, but there's no animosity there. He's at the side of the bunk, bending down, putting his weight into his arms, which shake at the effort.

"You're going to die now," Rostam says. "But only for a while."

Santos screams behind the man's hand. He's unable to refill his lungs. The terror he feels is absolute. There's nothing he can do to stop this.

His eyes are locked on Rostam's as the darkness comes creeping in.

"It's for your own good," he hears him say.

* * •

WHEN THE BLACKNESS RECEEDS, Santos's arms and legs, now free, lash out at nothing. The fear and panic are still strong inside him.

Then he's standing. And Rostam is beside him.

Without hesitation, Santos swings his fist at Rostam's head with enough force to knock it into the next world. But he misses somehow. He swings again and again—shouting, cursing—determined to turn this cocksucker into a bleeding, pleading mass of pulp. But Santos's fists go right through him. Over a dozen blows have no effect. It's as if the man is a ghost.

Santos is raging, but he pauses long enough to see what Rostam is staring down at: It's *him*—Santos—lying strapped to the bunk, as still as death, his eyes wide and bloodshot.

What the fuck—?

He renews his attack, tries to tackle Rostam this time, but just stumbles through his unsolid form. He aims a well-placed kick to Rostam's lower back, hard enough to cripple him for life. Again to no effect.

And again Santos's eyes are inexorably drawn to the exact replica of himself lying there.

What is this? Is it really him? It can't be. He looks fucking ... dead!

Rostam looks at his watch, bends down to undo the straps at the body's feet.

Santos kneels beside the bunk. He looks carefully at his own face and goes to touch it, the scar half hidden by beard. But his finger passes right through, as if his head is merely an illusion.

"Impossible." His voice is like a hollow echo.

Rostam is close beside him now, removing the wide strap around the chest and shoulders, the type used to cinch down loads on trucks.

"What the fuck have you done?"

But Rostam doesn't answer. As Santos somehow knew he wouldn't.

The *pinche cabrón* has killed him! Now he knows for sure.

This is some kind of after-death dream or something. It's just like his flying dreams, where he's still really awake. Or maybe this whole thing is just a dream—a bad one so far.

Well, fuck it, then, he thinks, *let's fly!*

Instantly he's soaring straight up through the ceiling, then hanging high in the night sky. The stars are out in full. A crescent moon shines little light but Santos can see clearly. His senses are alive. He can hear and *feel* the treetops swaying in the breeze blowing around him—*through* him. He can smell and *taste* the forest and fragrant earth. He's full of limitless energy.

Directly below him is the building he just left. He dives back down and circles it twice. There are boarded up windows on three sides, and in the front are two cozy rooms lit by lamplight. He passes through the wide double doors and zooms around inside, taking everything in.

This must be where Rostam lives.

He flies through the inner wall separating the rooms from the back of the building, sure of what he'll find.

But past an empty space and blur of wood, straw, and metal, Santos finds not his own prison cell but another. In it lies a black woman, sleeping on her side.

Dios mio! How many does Rostam have in here? Who is she? She must be from the bank in Antigua: she looks Jamaican. What has she told him?

He quickly flies through the opposite wall, where there is yet another cell.

Dani! He hasn't seen her in years, but it's her, definitely—older, and somehow even more beautiful than before. She's in bed, wearing her own set of headphones, listening to a CD. Her eyes are closed; she looks asleep.

Santos can't believe she's here. He goes to strip the covers off her but his dream hands can't do it. He is so fucking horny, seeing her like this; he hasn't had a woman in so long. He jumps on top of her, paws at her, squeezes her, pumps her with his hips, until finally realizing how fruitless it all is. His desire is overpowering but has no outlet.

Fuck!

He strokes her neck and exposed shoulder. *Dani,* mi ruca, *what are you doing here?*

She had loved him once, he knows. There was a time when she would have done anything for him, no matter how badly he treated her. He would have liked to have kept her longer, but she had to go to somebody else after Navarro disappeared.

And that's when Santos finally sees the connection. *Of course!* Rostam is also punishing her for the part she played. It's revenge, after all.

Or does the psycho need "forgiveness" from her, too? Santos still doesn't fully get what Rostam had tried to explain; but how can he when the guy is so fucking insane? He wonders where his money fits into all this. Dani couldn't know anything, could she . . . ? No, there's no way.

Who else does Rostam have prisoner? he wonders.

Again, Santos flies through the opposite wall, only to end up outside. He does an about-face and reenters at the other corner of the building—into still another cell.

This time there's an older, white guy curled up under his blanket. Santos doesn't recognize what little he can see of the man's gray-bearded face. But he must be involved, too, somehow; there has to be a connection, a reason he's here.

Santos passes through the next wall and comes face to face with Rostam again, kneeling beside the body, fiddling with some things laid out on the floor. As he watches, Rostam raises a large hypodermic needle, gives it a few taps, and ejects a thin stream of clear fluid.

He's going to make it look like a drug overdose!

Santos wants to be angry, but already he feels somewhat removed from the scene, as if the body there is no longer him but a friend he once knew. There's a tinge of sadness, but more than anything else is the feeling of elation at finally being free.

I'm free!

Then without any conscious thought of doing so, Santos is rocketing through the atmosphere—higher and higher, faster and faster. Soon he is circling the planet, oceans and continents alternating beneath him in various shades of blue, brown, green, and white.

The joy he feels now is like nothing he has ever experienced before. The only comparison is his flying dreams, but this is on a whole new level entirely.

Soon, without noticing exactly when or how, the Earth is gone, as are the stars, the moon, the sun. Santos sails through a dark void toward a circle of brilliant light in the distance, a magnetic pull drawing him closer. The light appears as an infinitely bright white "hole," with concentric haloes in gradating shades.

Santos enters the light quickly, willingly, sensing it is what he is supposed to do.

Inside, it's like speeding through a luminous tunnel, with no frame of reference to indicate how fast he is really going.

Then abruptly his vision is in every direction at once—three hundred and sixty nth degrees; there is no longer any front, back, left, right, above, below—only *sight*. And as if on an infinite array of television screens surrounding him, Santos's life is playing out before his eyes. Nothing—*not one thing*—is being missed between his birth and his death. He sees and reexperiences everything he has ever done—every thought, every emotion he has ever had.

What is even more astonishing is that he is able to experience all this not only from his own point of view, but from that of everyone he has ever interacted with. Every hug and kind word, every kick and curse, he can feel from each person's varying perspective, as if it were happening to him instead . . . *All* of it . . . every little thing.

The understanding and empathy Santos garners from this is etched onto his soul forever.

There is so much he has to atone for, he realizes. There is so much yet to learn, so much yet to do. He has so much unfinished business to take care of, so much to make up for. He has no idea how he'll ever be able to set it all straight. A thousand lifetimes won't be enough.

Each aspect of Santos's life review happens simultaneously, each "screen" reliving a particular moment in time. And then it's over almost as soon as it began. His whole life in a holographic nutshell.

His flight rushes on.

Eventually, Santos exits into a place of fluffy, white clouds; soft, golden light; a wispy mist drifting in the background. It's *exactly* how he always pictured Heaven to be. Not that he honestly believed in God or anything. He's amazed the place actually exists. He almost expects to find—there!—the Pearly Gates.

A tall, shining figure is approaching from that direction. *Are those wings?* Santos doesn't know what to do. Kneel? Prostrate himself? Stand at attention? But as the person gets closer—and it *is* a person, he sees, wearing a long, white robe, not an angel as he first thought—Santos's anxiety completely disappears. Waves of love wash over him. He recognizes the woman faintly as someone he should know but can't quite place. Her appearance is undefined; it's more a familiar presence she exudes. A soft, silvery blue aura surrounds her.

"Welcome," she says, smiling, holding out her hands. "You're home early."

THE CRUSHING WEIGHT of physical existence is the first thing that registers. Then a burning pain that sears him to the core, as Santos's lungs inflate with their first breath in four minutes and twenty seconds. Someone is beating a kettle drum wildly in his chest.

His eyes are met with a dim and murky light compared to what was before, the colors dull, almost nonexistent.

Then once again, as if from another world, another lifetime ago, Rostam's face is hanging there in front of him, filled with concern.

"Thank God!" the prick says. "You're back!"

25

"GOOD JOB. NOW LET'S monitor the flow."

Erin keeps a watchful eye as Mallia tapes the intravenous needle in place and arranges the clear plastic tubing carrying the patient's blood to and from the UV/ozone treatment unit on the bedside cart. With the flick of a switch, the machine creates a gentle suction, drawing the viscous, red liquid slowly upward. The apparatus glows with a blue ultraviolet light from inside. A large, three-by-six-inch window lets them see the blood's progress as it fills then passes through a pint-size cylindrical chamber, where it is saturated with ozone before being returned to the body.

This is the first step in her Big Sleep protocol. The patient is not yet in a coma but simply tranquilized, asleep "naturally."

The usually dark, burgundy-colored blood that enters, no matter how toxic, leaves the unit a bright fire-engine red, saturated with oxygen and as healthy and pure as can be possible.

The ultraviolet light disinfects the blood by destroying all harmful bacteria and other impurities. Erin thinks it is nothing short of miraculous that a spectrum of *light* can heal this way, targeting only what is alien and harmful to the body's system. Ultraviolet light has been used for decades to purify water, so to her it only makes sense to do the same for blood, which consists mostly of water—as does the rest of the body.

Next, the ozone hyperoxygenates the bloodstream with super-charged oxygen molecules. Because pathogens, including cancer, cannot survive in such an oxygen-rich environment, the treatment helps heal the entire body as these high-powered oxygen molecules are transported throughout the system.

Done repetitively, Erin believes, the combined treatment can be a cure for any disease, if caught early enough.

Unfortunately for Gavin, that isn't the case. His pancreatic cancer was already too far gone when he arrived at the Center seven months ago. Still, the dual method had cleaned and healed his system to such a huge degree that he felt better than he had in years. Every one of her patients says the same thing afterward.

Why, then, isn't this treatment used more widely? It's the question she's been asking herself since she first discovered the procedure. Some people blame a conspiracy: a real cure would put a dent in cancer-industry profits, which are astronomical. But Erin doesn't go so far as that; she blames widespread ignorance and complacency.

Erin isn't a medical doctor—she's a researcher, primarily. Still, she's attended many of the same courses and has worked side by side with physicians while in graduate school. She knows most medical students don't learn a thing about nutrition or "alternative" therapies while in school: they're taught only the "party line"—what mainstream medicine and the big pharmaceutical companies want promulgated. The status quo is just fine for them—until the next big miracle drug comes along. But as far as Erin is concerned, the miracles are already everywhere within nature; we simply have to use them.

Satisfied that everything has been done to perfection, she removes her latex gloves and face shield. (When working around blood, especially that of high-risk intravenous drug users, it makes sense to be ultra safety conscious.) She leaves Mallia to clean up and sit with the new patient for the three hours it will take to cycle through the body's blood supply at least once.

Four hospital beds line the walls, with space for four more someday. Only one is empty. Sunlight streams in upon their occupants through the many tall windows in the room.

Stephen, Erin's newest intern, is performing manual lymph drainage, a type of massage therapy, on Mrs. Graham, a sixty-four-year-old realtor, grandmother, and Oxycontin addict soon to be finished with her Sleep—soon on her way to becoming a *former* addict.

Erin is blessed to have five interns from the local community college's physician assistant program working part time at Fresh Start. She's more than happy to offer some of the hands-on experience they'll need to graduate. She's forged a good working relationship with the school and they're always quick to fill an open intern position at the Center. Once she gets the second floor completed, and rooms and equipment for twenty-plus more beds, she'll be able to take every available student they have. As it is now, she has to turn some away: Fresh Start is a popular place. Not only is it interesting work and a laid-back atmosphere, but the healthy food is all you can eat. Erin knows that many of her interns work extra hours just to get fed, and she doesn't mind one bit.

Finding good interns in the psychology department, on the other hand, has been more of a challenge. Working successfully with drug addicts and alcoholics takes a special kind of person—usually someone who has "been there and done that"—to offer any kind of meaningful advice. Most often it's only these people with similar experiences that an addict will even listen to. To be an effective rehabilitation counselor, Erin has found, having a warm heart and good intentions simply isn't enough.

Fortunately, however, there are many people who have faced the horrors of addiction and overcome their inner demons, and who now counsel others to do the same. And fortunately for her, they're more than happy to do it for free.

A good number of qualified counselors work for the Social Services department. This is where she met Donna. Donna has been faithfully volunteering at the Center since it first opened its doors, three years ago; and she's been invaluable in attracting others of her high caliber as well.

As much as Erin would like for Donna to join her permanently at Fresh Start, she knows that now is not the time to do so—not without the ability to accommodate more patients, or the ability to pay her a decent salary. And certainly not with the potential for Josh's project to put them *all* in prison.

"Hey, you guys, I'm going to go check on the mail. After that I'll be in my office, if you need me."

She says this quietly, knowing that her patients, although asleep, can still hear and register sounds subconsciously. For this reason, soft, uplifting music is played for her "sleepers" throughout most of the day.

Josh's suggestion of having her patients wear individual headphones has merit. All sorts of material, not just music, could be played. A patient could wake up speaking Mandarin if they so choose. Plus, there are the Hemi-Sync programs that induce out-of-body experiences. Josh's reasoning is that since they're already out-of-body much of the time anyway while in coma, they might as well make the most of the experience. It's something she'll have to give a try someday—with the patients' permission, of course—for research, if anything else.

Erin's office is right next door. She stops there to grab her coat and a few pieces of chewy caramel from the antique crystal bowl on her desk—one of the few things left of her mother's. The sight of half a dozen unfinished grant proposals lying there sends her hurrying right back out again.

The Big House's main room and communal living area is festooned with Valentine's Day decorations. A handful of patients are gathered in front of the television, watching *What The Bleep Do We Know?* for the hundredth time, one of the many educational films kept on hand. Mr. Carol, as he prefers to be addressed, is reclined in one of the beanbag chairs in the corner, absorbed in a book. The usually hyperactive Perry is standing at the easel, by a window, calmly painting what looks to be an abstract horse—or maybe it's a giraffe. Two other patients, Craig and Carla, are playing at the pool table recently donated by a local pub. Erin's pretty sure there's a budding romance going on there; it wouldn't be the first time it's happened at the Center. She waves as she heads out the door.

Outside, the sun is a fuzzy golden ball behind a white-gray blanket of low clouds. It's a bit nippy but the crisp, clean air is a pleasant change from the stuffiness inside. There's maybe a foot of snow in the courtyard. Narrow trails lead to her house ahead, into the forest to the right, and past the garage to the left, where twin tire tracks—half filled with new snow—wind through the trees and down to the main road.

Erin whistles and calls for the dogs, then waits before making the trek alone without them.

Passing the garage, she decides to check on her other furry friends.

Of the five remaining buildings, the garage has had the least remodeling done to it. She's not sure what it had been used for before. The longer wall facing the courtyard has been removed, creating a drive-in lean-to of sorts with room enough for up to twelve vehicles parked two rows deep. The roof leaks, the windows are boarded over, and the whole place lists a little to one side; but it gets the job done. Erin is dreading the day it collapses on everyone's rides.

The north wall is home to a small colony of bats, here before she arrived. They're in hibernation now, hanging in one large, quivering mass. Josh has hung a stretch of canvas to afford them some privacy and warmth, and the parking space closest to them is always left empty out of consideration. The bats are loved as much for their mosquito-eating skills as for their nightly acrobatic displays during the rest of the year. They are as much the Center's pets as Honey and Pooch and the multitude of chickens, ducks, and geese in the Long House—not to mention the growing family of raccoons living under her veranda. Josh had even been talking about setting up some bee hives, too, this summer. But it looks like that won't be happening now.

As she walks down to the mailbox, Erin thinks over the Josh problem.

The Fed's surprise visit has really shaken her. For the past many weeks she has been having nightmares of being carted off to prison or having bloody shoot-outs with the police. For over eighteen months she was convinced they had gotten away with the escape scot-free. Always the optimist, she did her best to put the continued possibility of Josh's capture out of her mind. Then, in a single evening, reality had come crashing in. What before had become an abstract notion, an unimaginable risk, was now a clear and present danger. She was hit head-on with the feeling of losing everything at once, and the realization that she had ruined her life completely.

And for what? A mistaken sense of loyalty to her spiritual soulmate.

No, it wasn't a mistake to help free Josh; she will never regret that decision. But helping him perpetrate his outlandish scheme—his all-important "project"—is a different matter entirely. It means so much to him, she knows, but it has to come to an end. His three-year time frame will have to be cut short.

Frazier, thank God, was convinced that Gavin is "Trip"; but he'll be back, he said. Josh can't stay much longer.

Erin would sure like to know who it was who raised questions about Josh's presence at the Center. But in the end, she knows it doesn't matter. His spiritual hypnosis was bound to attract attention at some point, regardless. It may have been excited reports from one or more of her patients that first intrigued Worthing, or whoever it was who notified the authorities. If that's even how it happened. The Feds may have just had their feelers out, keeping their eyes and ears open for any suspicious activity here, who knows? The bottom line is that it's just not safe for Josh to stay. The sooner he can leave, the better.

To his credit, he's been doing everything he can to wrap things up before he goes, spending every day working with one of his four guests at a time, for as many hours a day as possible. At the rate he's going, Josh plans to be finished within six to eight more weeks—it's hard to tell, he says. They'd had to go much further back in time than he anticipated. And even covering four or more lifetimes a day . . .

It's a good thing Santos is finally cooperating now.

Hell, it's a good thing he's *alive!*

When Erin thinks of how close she came to being a party to murder—even of someone as despicable as Santos—she wants to scream and pull her hair. Josh had explained it to her so matter-of-factly afterward, as if what he did should be standard treatment for unruly patients. She'd come close to slapping some sense into him. "What if it didn't work?" she'd shouted in his face. "What if he hadn't come back?"

Josh was shaken, she could tell. He was desperate, he said.

Crazy more like. The fact that his gamble had paid off doesn't excuse the sheer idiocy of it, not to mention the immorality. Ending an incarnation prematurely is *never* an option, no matter what the circumstances. It was the first time *she* ever had to lecture *him* about the spiritual facts of life. She hopes it will be the last.

Gloria is also apparently on board now. Though Josh has said he's caught her "cheating" a few times, only pretending to be in trance. Erin knows it takes a person's full cooperation to be deeply hypnotized, but she honestly can't see how anyone could resist Josh's deep, mesmerizing voice and smooth induction techniques. When they had worked together, just hearing his voice and a touch on her left wrist had put her immediately into an altered state. Someone like poor Gloria must be fighting a battle within herself; she must be afraid for some reason, perhaps due to her religious conditioning. Erin has felt sorry for the woman since she arrived. She hopes the regression work helps her.

She hopes it helps them all. How will this experience affect them, change them? she wonders. Will it be for the better or for the worse? How will the knowledge that they will never really die shape who they are today? Will it make a difference?

And what will become of them when they're released? And they *will* be released soon.

At least they'd better be.

THE TALL, BRICK MAILBOX at the intersection is covered with the same new snow that fell two days ago. Spiraling little birds' tracks decorate the fluffy dome.

This is Erin's first mail collection since Thursday. Friday's snowfall had kept her inside, drinking hot cocoa and watching a *South Park* marathon with her patients—laughter being the best medicine, after all. She's glad to see the main road has been plowed since then.

Inside the box are more letters than she expected, and it only takes a quick shuffle to see why: bills. It's that time of the month again. *Aargh!*

She's fumbling with her tall stack of mail when a vehicle slows and pulls up alongside her.

"Get anythin' good?"

It's her neighbor, Milo, at the wheel of his familiar, beat-up, red pickup. He's rolled down the passenger-side window to talk with her.

"Just bills," she replies, sticking a handful through the open window. "You want some?"

Milo holds up his hands in surrender. "No, thanks. Just checkin' to see if you could use somethin' from town. You doin' all right on whatchamacallits?"

Milo has had his parcel of land for as long as Erin has hers, ever since the Shepherd family—Russ, mainly—sold the land (or donated it, in her case). Milo, his brother, Jem, and their two wives have started a "farm," growing shiitake mushrooms on the fallen and decomposing tree trunks throughout their property, as well as ginseng and a variety of wild berries. Erin's pretty sure they also grow a little weed, which is a slightly more profitable crop. They've had each other over for dinner many times and become friends.

After ascertaining that she doesn't need anything from town, Milo gets to his real reason for stopping: "Hey, Erin, you have any surveyors out here this weekend?"

"No, why?"

"Well, I don't mean to scare you or nothin', but there was a couple a fellers walkin' 'round your place, out back. Snoopin', it looked like. Both of 'em had binoculars." He pauses to spit a stream of tobacco juice out his window. "I spied on 'em myself awhile, asked 'em what they was doin'. Said they was surveyors, but it didn't look so to me. No tools to speak of. No truck, neither. Too well dressed. Figured 'em for cops—*federales* more like." He leans closer across the seat and scrutinizes her for a moment. "You know, if there's ever anythin' we can do to help you, you just let us know, right?"

Erin's mind is reeling. She nods back vaguely. "When was this?"

"Just yesterday. Me and the dogs followed their tracks in the snow. They come through our piece by the bridge, to get to yours. Don't know if they'd been up there before or not."

"Thanks, Milo, I appreciate it."

"Just thought I'd let you know," he says. "Listen, Erin, if you got anythin' goin' on, I'd quit it. You know what I mean?"

"Yeah, I do. I will. I mean, I don't think we have anything to worry about, though," she lies.

Milo looks concerned. "The last thing we need around here is them kind pokin' their noses where it don't belong . . . And I'd sure miss ya."

Erin knows what he must be thinking. They've joked about her LSD research as a grad student; and she's shared the fact that, for a couple of years now, she has been experimenting with a new drug: Ibogaine, a psychoactive substance first found in a plant in Africa but now cultivated all over the world. Like LSD, it's an hallucinogen with both psychedelic and dissociative properties, as well as anti-addiction ones. And like LSD, taking it can be an intensely transformative experience. Erin is convinced that Ibogaine is yet another naturally occurring drug that can help people come to terms with behavioral problems like addiction from a higher, "spiritual" perspective.

She would love to conduct a legitimate research project with Ibogaine, but she faces one major hurdle: Again like LSD, it's classified as a "Schedule One" controlled substance: illegal in the United States. She's been waiting two years for letters of approval from the FDA and DEA that are not likely to come. Despite her previous success, without the backing of a major university, such permission probably won't be granted.

Not that that's stopping her. She's been able to procure supplies of the drug from both Canada and Mexico, where its therapeutic use is legal. She's been experimenting with herself and a small handful of patients, with their consent.

Dangerous? Not at all. Illegal? Yes, of course. Just add it to her growing list of other offenses, right after kidnapping, and aiding and abetting a known fugitive.

"It was probably nothing," Erin tells her friend, forcing a smile. "But will you keep your eyes out and let me know if you see them again?"

Milo gives her a dubious look and scoots back behind the wheel. "Sure will. Me and Jem'll both keep our eyes peeled. We don't want no trouble, but we sure as hell won't let nobody come trespassin' on our land, neither."

They wave their goodbyes. *Thank God for good neighbors,* she thinks as Milo drives off.

Erin considers this news as she walks back uphill. What had the Feds seen, if anything? For that's surely who it must have been—maybe even Frazier himself. But why? Apparently he didn't buy Gavin's impersonation, after all. Or maybe they're just following up on their lead, going through the motions . . . How many times have they been here? she wonders. Watching . . . Or maybe it wasn't the Feds at all . . . But that's just wishful thinking, she knows. Who else could it have been? Certainly not surveyors.

Gavin has kept to his bed lately, so if they've seen anyone besides her patients, it would have been Josh. Fortunately, the two men look somewhat alike: both are about the same height and build, and both have beards. From a distance they could be the same person, she thinks, especially in winter clothes.

Erin's worry level has just been upped a notch. The only thing keeping her from running all the way home is the thought that if the Feds actually knew Josh was here, they wouldn't have hesitated to arrest him by now.

Or me.

The safest thing to do is keep both men out of sight.

They also need to release Josh's guests as soon as possible. But how, without attracting unwanted attention? How closely are they being watched?

It's too much to think about. All Erin has done lately is worry, and she's tired of it.

Soon, she tells herself. Soon it will all be over. Josh and his project will be gone and she can get on with her life, without this weight constantly hanging over her. She's done her part; he can't ask any more of her. She wishes there was a way he could stay, but it's just not possible.

For weeks they've discussed where he should go, what he should do. Seattle's out of the question: they'll be looking for him there. Forget Texas. Erin knows he's leaning toward Minneapolis-St. Paul: good people there, he says. All he has to do is get on the bus from Springfield. He still has almost a thousand dollars left. He can do it; he'll be fine. Or so she keeps telling herself.

He's not my responsibility, damn it!

Then why can't she stop feeling that way?

With the idea of forgetting one trouble by focusing on another, Erin sorts through the bills as she walks, opening and glancing at each one in turn.

The largest amount due is the loan payment to Mountain Valley, of course, Worthing's bank. Nothing new there. Except for the much higher interest rate he surprised her with at the first of the year—nearly double.

Next biggest is from Yarborough and Sons, a local construction company kind enough to self-finance much of the initial work required to get the property up to code, like installing the new water, sewage, and gas lines, and repairing the road. Their interest rate, too, is a bit steep, but the extra financing had been a godsend at the time.

The third largest bill is from Jake's, a local hardware and landscaping store, which is still only too happy to lend her credit. The owner has an obvious crush on her, and Erin feels ashamed at having taken advantage of this every time she sees how high her balance has gotten.

Add on all the utility and credit card bills, and the grand total is a daunting sum.

Erin sighs. She can't dip into her personal savings this time. There's nothing left. Royalties from the book, as meager as they were, have ceased to trickle in these days.

She doesn't see how she'll be able to cover the mortgage this month and still manage to pay the utilities . . . Without a new influx of paying patients . . . It's something Erin can't bear to think about. She knows Worthing wouldn't hesitate to foreclose on the property. It's probably something he's looking forward to.

Aside from the bills and some junk mail, a square, cream-colored envelope stands out. Erin had assumed it was a Valentine's

Day card from Donna and saved it for last, but now she sees the return address is from Virginia. She doesn't recognize the name of the sender.

Inside is a wedding invitation, along with a short, handwritten letter. She stops to read it as she makes it to the top of the hill, the buildings just in sight through the trees.

Thank you so much, the letter begins, *for saving my life.*

Erin quickly looks to the signature: "Tina," with a heart over the "i."

Do you remember me? Tina asks.

Of course she does. It's from a girl Erin treated about three years ago, only weeks after Fresh Start first opened. She'd been in bad shape, covered in cuts and bruises; recently raped; addicted to meth and cocaine, the worst combination. She had been so young, only seventeen, and already so damaged. Someone had dropped her off in the middle of the day; no idea who.

You helped me even though I couldn't pay. You let me stay for four whole months.

The poor girl had needed to stay at least that long. Afterward, she went to live with her aunt in Ohio. Erin had found the woman on the Internet and arranged everything, then called to make sure Tina arrived safely. That was the last time she had heard from her.

I wanted to let you know that I made it. I'm doing real good. I live in Roanoke, Virginia now. I'm a married woman! (The invitation is a little old. Sorry.) My husband is a wonderful man. You would love him! He is an artist, like me.

Tina had discovered her love for painting at Fresh Start. She had a natural talent. They painted the Big House that summer, and while everyone else tackled the outside of the building, Tina painted lovely flower and vine murals in each of the ten bedrooms downstairs. Erin's patients since are always commenting on the beautiful designs. She's glad the girl—a woman now—has found someone to love, who shares her passion.

I can never thank you enough for what you did for me. I think about you all the time. I hope you are as happy as I am.

The letter ends with a big heart and some Xs and Os. And a postscript:

We named our little boy Aaron. It's not the same but close enough. This with a smiley face.

Tina's letter is exactly what Erin needs right now: a reaffirmation of her hard work and dedication. She rereads it as she walks, fondly remembering the person who's life, she believes, she truly did save. It was at a time when Erin felt like she didn't know what she was doing. Besides the Big Sleep treatment—a full fourteen days back then—she didn't really know what else to do. So she had simply loved, had simply shown she cared. She listened a lot, cried a lot, provided a safe and supportive environment away from drugs and alcohol and the pressures of the outside world. And gratefully relied on people like Donna—former addicts with a newfound purpose in life. All of it together seemed to work.

A squeal and some shouting from up ahead make her jump. But it's only a few of her patients having a snowball fight in the courtyard. Erin tucks the mail into her coat pocket and picks up her pace.

Only weeks ago, each of the three now playing in the snow had been considered hopeless cases, in and out of rehab clinics repeatedly over the years. Erin knows they are finally on their way to being rid of their addictions forever, and this makes her happy and proud.

Watching them now is a further confirmation of her life's work. Her research—her approach—has real importance, and it's worth the struggle for recognition. She's going to do whatever it takes to keep the Center going and to see that her methods are made the gold standard for treatment around the world.

In this moment, Erin realizes that—more than Josh, despite their spiritual connection throughout the ages—it is the countless addicts and alcoholics in the world who most need her help right now. *They* are her real purpose in this lifetime. They are her larger, *extended* spiritual family.

With gratitude, Erin looks to the sky and sends a prayer to her parents, wishing them well, thanking them both.

It had taken many years to forgive her alcoholic father for the car accident that took them from her so suddenly. But she understands now that their death was the impetus for what has become her mission in life. It had been their part to play—their "sacrifice"—and she more than appreciates it.

By the time she arrives, more have also come out to join in the snowball fight. Erin scoops up a double handful of snow and runs into the middle of the fray, laughing as she's pelted from all sides.

26

PROPPED UP WITH PILLOWS, the quilted comforter tucked tightly around him, Gavin looks peaceful as he sleeps, his mouth slightly open, snoring softly.

It's a bit chilly in the room, so Josh crosses over to shut the window, startling a pair of birds at the feeder on the sill. The sun has risen high enough to shine directly into his eyes and he blinks at the sudden glare. He leaves the curtains open, takes his usual seat beside Gavin's bed.

The man who single-handedly saved both his and Erin's lives at the beginning of the year has recently lost the strength to care for himself. Josh has become Gavin's chief aid and de facto nurse. When he's not working with his guests—usually for four- to five-hour periods at a time—he's taking care of his friend.

They have moved Gavin to the spare bedroom in Erin's place. Here there is more privacy and he has access to his own bathroom. It has a full tub, which Gavin takes advantage of almost daily now. Josh has to laugh when he thinks of the last time they tried a sponge bath in bed. *Won't be doing* that *again soon!*

Josh has never had to do anything like this before—the cleaning, wiping, turning, dressing, all of it. And Gavin has never had to succumb to such things. It had been awkward at first for the both of them. But they've since overcome the initial embarrassment and now think nothing of it, often laughing at the absurdity of it all.

Gavin is in a lot of pain, Josh knows, but has been refusing the morphine and other pain medication Erin has made available. He's done his best to be drug free, he says, and intends to stay that way. That's the whole point of his coming here, he reminds them. He wants to live his life to the fullest—however short it may be, including whatever pain it may bring—not dulled or masked by narcotics. Gavin has explained that, despite many periods of intense discomfort, he is sometimes able to transcend the pain and reach a state of being he calls "euphoric." And the more often he experiences it, the easier it is to return to and maintain.

They all know it won't be long before Gavin dies; they'd known since he arrived in July. Josh is happy that, in spite of his initial reluctance, Gavin has embraced the idea of a continued existence on the "other side." He's read many of the books on the "required reading" list, plus a few more. The latest, *Hello From Heaven,* sits on his bedside table, beside the lamp and the ever-present glass of water. Together they've been trying to come up with a good way for Gavin to contact Josh after he dies, before he "crosses over," so to speak—just for kicks, for Gavin to have a little fun before he goes. They haven't settled on any one thing yet, but Gavin is leaning toward embodying a little bird—a blue jay, to be precise—and attending his own funeral that way.

Honey comes over and nuzzles Josh's hand, and he happily obliges her with a quick rub down. Pooch is lying in the open doorway, quietly gnawing on his new Frisbee; it has to be broken in just right. Josh knows the dogs really lift Gavin's spirits, so he brings them for a while each day. They're all waiting for him to wake up.

In the meantime, Josh decides he'll do some energy work, a little "spiritual" healing. His goal isn't to "fix" anything in particular but to raise Gavin's overall vibration level. The extra, "higher" form of energy will be used however Gavin's different levels of consciousness—including his body—see fit.

The first step is for Josh to raise his own vibration level. And because the highest vibration on the physical plane—on any plane—is Love, the easiest way to do this is to "fill" himself with Love.

He begins by closing his eyes and taking one slow, deep breath after another until he has calmed and quieted his mind somewhat. After so many years of practice—of "programming" himself—this occurs almost always on the fifth breath.

Then he visualizes a bright, golden white ball of light shining in the center of his body. With each breath, this ball of light—like a miniature sun—expands, growing bigger and brighter, until he can "see" and "feel" it extending outward all around him by a few feet. In his mind he *is* this brilliant, intelligent, conscious being of Light. And his sole function is to Love.

This is as close as he can come to imagining his true spiritual Self.

With a thought—that's all it takes—Josh sends a shining white beam of Light to Honey by his side, an easy target to feel love for. This powerful light envelopes the dog, and her entire being begins to resonate with its higher frequency. Again, Josh can visualize this occurring in his mind's eye. Without having to look at her, he knows that Honey can physically and psychically feel this loving energy.

Then, keeping each beam of Light attached to its intended subject, Josh sends one now to Pooch, to Gavin, to Sheila, to Donna, to Erin, and to every one of her patients at the Center. All he has to do is think of them and they're surrounded by the same Light and Love.

This divine energy doesn't come from him but *through* him—from the infinite Source of All That Is, by whatever name. He is simply an extension of this Source.

Josh holds this focus of attention for a while, concentrating easily on these people (and animals) he knows and cares about.

Then, with a thought—just a thought, albeit a more expansive and limitless one—he sends his Light to every other person in the world—to every being, no matter what form.

This is the tricky part, because in doing so he becomes unbound by space and time. He is no longer a limited physical being at that moment, but a limitless spiritual one. As a being of Light, by sending his energy to every corner of the Universe, in every direction, he essentially becomes as infinite as the Universe itself. His Light and Love are all-encompassing; and for that brief moment, Josh knows what it truly means to be One with God.

WHEN HE FINALLY OPENS HIS EYES, Gavin is awake and looking at him patiently. Both dogs are on the bed now.

"You always wake me up when you do that," Gavin gripes.

"Sorry."

"It's like being plugged in to a bloomin' high-frequency generator."

Josh himself can feel his entire body humming right now. He's filled with enough energy to race to the top of the mountain and back.

"It's supposed to put a little wood in your johnson," he says. "I know how much you like that little Spanish nurse from the college."

Gavin gives a snort.

"But, hey, if you don't appreciate it . . ."

"If it wasn't for you, I'd have been dead when I was supposed to be," Gavin says. "When my money ran out." He holds out his hand to shake. "Good to see ya, mate. You been here awhile?"

"Not too long."

"How'd everything go last night? The bugger give you any trouble?"

"Nah. He's like a whole different person now. Haven't heard him cuss even once. It's kinda scary."

He and Erin had told Gavin everything that night, after the Fed had gone. They owed him at least that much after what he did to help them; it was a heroic act he pulled off.

Gavin had been worried when he saw the stranger enter the house, he said. He could tell that Erin wasn't too happy to see the guy; and the gun and badge displayed on the man's belt didn't bode too well for her, either. So Gavin had left the beginning of the festivities next door and snuck in behind them to keep an eye on things. He managed to hear most of their conversation from where he stayed hidden in the bathroom. Impersonating "Trip" had been a gut instinct, an inspiration, he said. And once he walked in there, there was no turning back.

Josh has since spent many hours talking with his friend about life in prison and his life before. Gavin has never once questioned his innocence.

He has, however, seriously questioned Josh's reasoning behind his project. Telling him about it, too, had been unavoidable. Josh didn't want to lie to him, and his lengthy, daily "appointments" away had to be explained somehow. Gavin was shocked at first, to say the least. It was suddenly just one surprise after another.

"Has he described what he went through yet?" Gavin asks.

"Not yet; not everything. Very little, actually. I think he's still trying to process it all." Josh shrugs with his hands. "I can only imagine it was similar to what other people go through. That was the whole point. I don't know if it was a full-blown transcendental NDE, like in *Backwards,* or not. But he did say that he saw his spirit family, and recognized me there. Didn't mention anyone else, though."

Josh knows Gavin understands what he's talking about. In addition to all he's been reading lately, Gavin has also experienced a few of his own past-life sessions—as well as a single life-between-lives session, which is plenty.

Gavin is gazing wistfully as he strokes the dogs' fur. "I remember the folks I met when we did my in-between," he says, "my 'family' . . . It's hard to understand how they can be your best friends in one life, and then the biggest assholes you ever met in the next . . . Like Fallon." He gives a slow shake of his head, smiling. "He was so happy to see me . . . and me him . . ."

"Yeah, it's wild, isn't it?" Josh says. "But sometimes our enemies can be our best teachers . . . You were close, though, right? Before?"

"Lots of times. More than not, I think . . . He was my little brother once, remember? Under Stalin. We froze to death."

"Oh yeah." Josh remembers that session well. Gavin and his two brothers had been conscripted into the Soviet army. It had been a short, sad life, full of hardships, as many are.

"I'll be seeing them again soon, won't I?" Gavin is still lost in thought, clearly recalling his hypnosis experience as a soul between lives.

"Yep. They'll be proud of you, man." Josh's attitude is that physical death is just another part of an eternal life and should be embraced—celebrated even. "Think of the homecoming you're going to get. All the beer you can drink."

This gets a wry laugh and brings Gavin back to the present.

"No, mate, I think I've learned my lesson on that score. Life's better without any of that—here or there . . . I'd sure like to get laid, though. I can still do that, can't I?"

"So they say. You can do whatever you want at first." This has been a frequent topic lately. "It'll all be in your mind, though, just like everything else. Heaven or Hell, it's your choice." Josh does a two-second rumba in his seat. "I, for one, will be spending my first couple a years singing and dancing." He still hasn't gotten enough of that in this lifetime; it's something he's going to have to remedy before he dies.

"Oh yeah? A regular Justin Timberlake, huh?"

"You haven't heard me sing? I don't believe it! Oh, I could have been a star! Listen—"

"No, no, no!" Gavin's chortling quickly turns to a grimace.

"Hurts to laugh, huh?"

"You got it . . . Tell me something sad . . . Let's talk about your love life."

"Ouch! That hurts."

Now it's Josh's turn to gaze wistfully as he thinks about his most recent tryst with Sheila: They'd gone walking at midnight because of Erin's warning of Feds in the woods, bringing blankets and a basket of late-night treats. He sang to her under the stars . . . and made her cry . . . from happiness, she said.

"Actually, you know, I gotta say that's the best thing I have going for me right now." And the most heartbreaking. Josh would like nothing more than to take Sheila with him when he leaves, but he knows it's not possible. Or a good idea: it's not conducive to his plan. "Saying goodbye is really going to suck."

"Yeah, I know how you feel," Gavin says glumly. "I'm afraid I've fallen a little head-over-heels myself. For our little pint-sized angel of mercy."

"Who, the Spanish girl?"

"No, you dolt!" Gavin looks astounded at Josh's cluelessness. "It's Erin I mean."

"Oh, right." How can he put this to him gently? "Uh, you do know she's *gay*, right?"

Gavin rolls his eyes, keeps them pointed at the ceiling. "Like I give a damn about that. You think my heart cares one whit whether she's gay or not? Christ! I *love* the woman, that's all I know."

"All right, all right, you've got a point. I love her, too. Madly."

"There's lots of different kinds of love," Gavin lectures, waving his hands feebly. "Not everything has to be physical, you know . . . I mean, sure, I'd love to see her butt-naked and riding me like a cowgirl, but we have a deeper relationship than that."

Josh nods, keeping a straight face. "I understand, believe me. Sometimes I think lesbians are God's way of helping us treat women like something other than sex objects. Erin is a blessing in disguise."

"Hear, hear. You don't know how right you are, my good man." Gavin's mouth may be set in a solemn frown but his eyes are cracking up.

Josh hands him the glass of water from the nightstand. Gavin takes it and sucks greedily at the straw.

"Aahhh. I'm sure going to miss you, my friend," Gavin says, smacking his lips. "But I'm going to miss her a whole lot more . . . You don't mind, do ya?"

"No, no, of course not, not at all. I'm gonna miss her, too . . . I wish I never had to leave."

And he wishes he didn't have to lie to her about where he's going. But it's for her own good. If something ever happens and she's forced to, she can honestly say that Minneapolis was the last place she'd heard him mention. Not that he knows she wouldn't lie for him again if she had to.

Instead, it looks like he's heading to the first place many expats—and ex-cons—go, seeking anonymity: Mexico. Obtaining false identification and work should be fairly easy in the right places. And what little money he has left will last him a whole lot longer down there than in Canada, his other option. Remaining in the States, with its hyper-surveillance and data-tracking, just isn't a good idea.

But he and Erin can still stay in touch: there's always encrypted e-mail. And one day she'll be able to visit him, wherever he ends up.

This sudden attention from the Feds has really scared him. Of course they can't be sure that's who it was Milo saw spying on them—if that's even what they were doing—but it's the most logical assumption, especially so soon after Frazier's visit.

The smartest thing, Josh knows, would be to leave immediately—take his guests on a long drive and drop them off somewhere, far away from the Center. But he is *so* close to accomplishing Stage Two, even if it has been much more rushed than he would have liked. It's just too important to abandon everything right now, without obtaining a *complete* forgiveness from any of them.

One more month, that's all he needs.

Josh has found that the root of their problems with each other go way back in time, further than he ever thought possible. And as he already knew, it's a different pattern with each of them.

"Go back to the beginning of our negative relationship with each other on Earth," he'd instructed them all, in turn. "Go back to when we first began to have the problems that have carried over to today."

Harden had been the first. He described a life in the distant past, when he and Josh were cave men, essentially, living in a mountainous region somewhere alongside Neanderthals and different species of ape men—none of whom would survive the coming ages. Josh had fought Harden over a territorial dispute, claiming his women and children and sending him into an exile he didn't long survive. That's when the cycle of revenge began with him. Harden was to repay Josh in their next life together, three hundred years later.

His and Gloria's troubles started more recently, as ancient nomads traversing a nameless desert. Gloria had been a ranking clan leader and Josh his female slave who suffered degrading abuse at his hands, until finally succumbing to suicide. Josh had recalled glimpses of this life himself previously, while in prison. As the girl's spirit, he haunted the caravan, keeping watch over her younger sister—Erin now—until she, too, took her own life.

Dani's first recollection was of a happy life together as young lovers, until Josh left one day on a trading mission, never to return. Eventually, word got back to her that he preferred to stay in the rich lands across the mountains separating them. She felt abandoned and dishonored, and though she later took up with other men, she never forgave him, and carried her resentment to the grave.

Santos's account had been really interesting. Together they lived in a highly technological society of crystal-powered "computers" and giant airships that traveled along beams of light, many thousands of years before such things were supposedly conceived. Josh had been a pretty bad character apparently, arguing for the enslavement of a much older race of people, who valued their spirituality over the technological mind-set of the more recent, "advanced" race of mankind. Santos had been one of these ancient peoples. He tried to organize a revolt—an escape back to their lands, now mostly flooded—but too few had the will to fight. Josh and his group had Santos tortured to death publicly as an example to others of his "class."

And so *their* discord was sown.

Since these initial sessions, Josh and his four guests have covered a lot of ground, flying through the centuries. The pattern is obvious: an eye for an eye, a tooth for a tooth, from one life to another. Though it's not always successive; often many other lifetimes will have passed before they're brought together again to balance the scales.

Also, another pattern has emerged, in line with what Josh has read from his books: They have all been returning to Earthly life more and more often. Where each may have waited hundreds of years before incarnating again, it's now more like fifty, or twenty, or even immediately sometimes. When asked why, from their superconscious's point of view, Josh is told that less time between lives is required to process their experiences on Earth; and that so much more is always needed to be learned from the physical realm, as nowhere else are such lessons and experiences possible; and that, typically, the more lives lived, the more that needs to be balanced—not only individually but collectively, as nations, cultures, religions, races, and so on. Also, often a person incarnates not for their own personal reasons so much as for the greater good, for the way their life may affect the bigger picture.

Josh well enough understands the universal laws of reincarnation. But despite *their* souls' apparent needs or desires to return, he's confident he can make this life on Earth his last. He estimates he's lived at least twenty thousand lives on this planet as a human being. He has done and been it all: male, female; black, white; young, old; rich, poor; wise man, fool; killer, saint; hero, coward; pauper, prince; merchant, priest; genius, dunce; gay, straight; repulsive, attractive; loved, hated; happy, sad; healthy, sick; blessed, cursed; good, evil . . . When is it enough? Or will there *always* be something new and different to experience?

Josh knows that as long as his soul feels there is a reason to return, it will. So he's negating every motive he can think of.

As far as he knows, from his own past lives he's reviewed, these four souls are the only ones he has any real issues with. And to have them all together at one time like this is an opportunity he simply can't abandon—not when he is so close.

Once they have forgiven each other, there won't be any reason to reenact the melodramas they've been foisting upon one another for far too long. He'll have broken the cycle.

And with enough work on himself—on his own attachments and desires—he will finally be able to escape the Wheel of Life.

"Hey . . . Hey, you in there?"

Josh snaps to attention.

Gavin is leaning forward, his arm out, straining to reach him. "Hey, man, you all right?"

"Uh, yeah. Yeah, I'm okay." Josh regains his bearings, gives his limbs a shake. "I, uh—I just go away sometimes, you know? It's no big deal."

Gavin settles back into his pillows. "Mate, you were *away* for, like, three minutes. Just staring, like a zombie . . . You promise me you're not on something?"

"Yeah, yeah, I swear." Josh is upset—not with himself, necessarily, but at his inability to understand why he keeps spacing out all the time. It almost cost him his life, with Santos. "Erin thinks it might be a mild form of epilepsy or something. But really, it's got to be all that time I spent alone in solitary, meditating, leaving my body, I don't know. It happens all the time." He sighs. "What's weird is that I don't *remember* anything. It's not like an out-of-body experience at all, or even a productive trance." He throws up his hands. "But, then again, who knows? Maybe I'm communing with spirits and don't even know it. Maybe my etheric body is on some kind of 'secret mission' it can't tell me about." He laughs unconvincingly.

"Wow." Gavin still looks concerned. "You were really outta there. Nothing I said even registered. It was like you were deaf. I was about to shake the shit outta you."

"You haven't got the strength to shake your wiener."

"Ah, *touché!*" He makes a face, squirms a little. "Speaking of which, I think I might need to put you to work here for a minute."

"'Number one' or 'number two'?"

Gavin pushes gently at the dogs, coaxing them up and off the bed. "Blast it, man, speak plainly! I gotta take a dump, all right? . . . And we'd better make it snappy."

"Righty-O. Your wish is my command."

Josh pulls back the many layers of covers, gently pushes his friend forward and gets his arms around his middle, braces himself: even with such rapid weight loss recently, Gavin is still a pretty big guy.

As he lifts, Gavin says mildly, "What, you going to just drag me there?"

"Huh? Oh. Shit . . ."

Josh lets go and grabs the wheelchair from the corner of the room. With a fair amount of groaning and cursing from both sides, they manage to maneuver Gavin into it.

Josh rubs his back theatrically. "Damn! We need to just keep you in this thing."

"You're lucky I'm so regular," Gavin grumbles. "Once a day sure beats the hell outta three, don't you think? Or should I start eating prunes?"

Josh laughs and the dogs run ahead as he pushes Gavin out the door. "Is it bath day?" he asks.

"Damn straight. Every day is bath day now."

"You want bubbles?"

27

"AND WITH ANOTHER DEEP BREATH, you are once again at the River of
Time . . . As you float along serenely, your mind detaches more
and more from the present, and you are able to see and move in
any direction . . . Orient yourself now so that the past is ahead
of you and the future behind . . ."

Harden is not consciously listening to Rostam's words. His
subconscious took over almost immediately after being inducted
into the trance state—second nature to him now. His normal,
waking consciousness will act as an interpreter between the
"worlds," helping him to understand what he sees, speaking when
asked questions, translating things into modern-day language.

"Now, when you're ready, move forward to the *next* lifetime
we need to visit in order to understand our current relationship . . ."

He is well practiced at this, having already explored so many
lives during eleven other sessions.

Prior to this, Rostam had conditioned him with two separate
days of regular hypnosis—or so he said, because Harden can
remember none of it. He is, however, able to vividly remember
the next session which followed, where he had been regressed
for the first time—first to his childhood.

He was instructed to visualize a descending staircase, where
each step represented a year of his life. They had moved rapidly

down the stairs to the age of fifteen, to an "important event" that occurred then. And to Harden's utter astonishment—felt in that part of his waking consciousness still connected to his present-day ego—he *was* fifteen again. He was there, looking out through the eyes of his younger, fifteen-year-old self, reexperiencing the sights and sounds around him as was recorded in his subconscious mind. Even more incredibly, he was able to reexperience the exact thoughts and emotions he'd had at the time. Even his voice took on a different tone.

For some reason, his subconscious chose a heated argument with his best friend, Ruben, who had cheated on a final exam at school. He could recall every word said on both sides. He could *feel* the anger within himself, *see* the surprise on his friend's face. He could *taste* the peppermint candy in his mouth and *smell* the stockyards across town. He could *hear* the tractor in the field. He could *touch* the brim of his hat. He was *there* again in every way, only with a watcher this time—a silent witness: his now adult self.

Afterward, listening to the entire session recorded onto a CD, Harden wondered at this remarkable ability to recall so much detailed information. It was only later, after reading the following month's book, *The Field*, he was led to understand that memory doesn't exist solely in the brain but within a field of consciousness separate from the physical body, where even the smallest details are recorded—even things the physical, waking consciousness filters out by necessity.

During that same session, he had stepped down to even younger years—ten, six, three, one—remembering significant events at each age. Then finally he was in his mother's womb, able to reexperience not only his own thoughts and emotions but many of *hers* as well. And in this way, Harden could see how—even at such an early stage—he had been subtly influenced by her own hopes and fears and expectations.

From there it was a simple matter of traveling from the womb through an imaginary "tunnel of time" into his most recent past life—again to an important event.

"Look at your feet," Rostam had told him when Harden first found himself in another place and time. "What are you wearing on your feet, if anything?"

With so much that was different bombarding his senses, that simple instruction had helped focus and ground him. The image was as clear as if he were there: "Boots . . . black work boots . . . with black laces."

"What else are you wearing? Look and see. Feel the material. What are you wearing around your waist, if anything?"

"Um . . . a belt . . . It has all these . . . A uniform, it's blue, dark blue . . . I have a hat . . . and a badge. A gun! I'm a cop! A police officer!"

This had been graduation day at the police academy. The year was 1912. His name was Franklin Carter.

They had quickly gone to the last day in that life, to the moment of his death.

"My side, I'm bleeding . . . Oh my God! I've been hit . . . Mack's coming, too—No! Oh no! McCloud!"

"Go outside yourself," Rostam had instructed him then. "You feel no pain, you have no fear. See yourself objectively, as if watching a movie on a screen . . . What's happening now?"

The action was so fast, so intense, it was hard to relate. "It's a massacre . . . They have tommy guns . . . Warehouse was supposed to be empty. I thought Cole . . . Walked right into it. A trap . . . I'm behind a crate, crawling, but . . . shot again . . ."

After a considerable pause, while Carter had stared disbelieving at his dead body, Rostam said, "Hold on, stay with me. You have now died and left that body . . . What are you thinking, feeling?"

"The lousy bastard! I was so close!" His soul, if that's what it was, had risen and was hovering near the warehouse ceiling. "I can see him now. He's—You son of a bitch!"

Harden—or Carter, his spirit—had then tried everything he could think of to take down his nemesis, Eugene Cole, notorious booze smuggler and cop killer. But of course it was no use.

Some time later, after finally realizing he was really dead, his thoughts had turned to matters of the heart:

"Nadine, she's gonna kill me . . . Little Janey—Jack . . . What are they going to do without a father? . . . I'm so sorry . . ."

Harden briefly recalled visiting his family and trying to comfort them, staying with them through his funeral.

He'd shadowed Cole for a while. Watched him die.

But these things had only been touched upon. The whole point of that first past-life exercise had been to get in touch with Harden's spirit self, his superconscious, following his death. From that perspective, he had an almost unlimited knowledge of not only that life but *all* of them.

"Looking back on the life you just left," Rostam asked, "who did you know then that you know now, in *this* life? . . . Who today is Cole?"

Rostam's face had immediately flashed in Harden's mind. And after first dismissing this (his conscious mind's latent interference), the image remained and he had to accept it. "You," he said cautiously.

Then—still associated with the life of Franklin Carter, Special Agent, U.S. Department of Justice, Bureau of Prohibition—a violent anger had risen up within him. He wanted to strike out at his enemy, Cole, now sitting beside him in a different body, in a different time.

"When did we first start having problems with each other?" Rostam asked. "Go back to the time when our adversarial relationship first began."

It had taken a bit more prompting, but soon Harden was reliving a life as a primitive man, identical to today's *Homo sapien* in every way, only hairier—and telepathic. Rostam was encroaching on his territory, his women, his food. It hadn't ended well, with Rostam getting the upper hand. And so began their cycle of retribution.

Now, forty-one shared lifetimes together behind him, Harden is once again soaring over the River of Time toward the next life in the series, its beginning and end demarcated by a soft white glow.

". . . Go to a scene that best illustrates the problem . . ."

But Harden already knows what to do.

He drops quickly down into the slow-moving "river" and is suddenly face to face with an Egyptian, a black man, a sailor like himself. The man is dead, or near enough so it makes no difference. He hangs from an outcropping of rock in the cave, stripped of his clothes, his body streaked with dried blood. This man is nothing, he knows; it is the one hanging beside him—the captain—who is worth the ransom. And for this reason he has been beaten less severely.

"What's happening? What do you see?" Always the Voice directing his attention, his thoughts.

"Έχουμε Yusuf. Είναι αξίζει μια περιουσία."

"Speak in English, please, so I can understand you."

There is the subtle shifting of gears. "Okay."

"Please repeat what you said before. What's happening?"

"We have Yusuf. He is worth a fortune."

"Who is he?"

"He is a trader, a . . . *Karimi*—there is no word in English. He is captain of the . . . *Wind Dancer*, from Alexandria."

"Why do you have him?"

"His people will pay to have him returned."

Yusuf's bruised and battered face is lit by a flickering torch nearby. He will have scars to remind him of this time.

The old man should not have been so disrespectful. Not to me.

"Who are you?" the Voice asks. "What's your name?"

"My name is Nerio Kolossi. I am captain of the . . . *Osprey*, out of Limassol. But home anywhere on the Sea."

"So you're a pirate."

". . ."

"Is that right? You steal ships, kidnap people, hold them hostage. Isn't that what a pirate does?"

"We are the Hunters of the Sea. We are respected and feared everywhere . . . They know of us in Alexandria and Constantinople, as far away as Sicily and Tunis . . . I have a wife in Tunis . . ."

"Why did you kidnap this man? Why not someone else? Is he special?"

What a ridiculous question! "Yes, he is special. He is very wealthy." The old man's ship alone will be worth its weight in silver.

"Where are you? What are you doing?"

"The Bay of Rest—our name for it—east of Cape Kiti. There is a sea cave here. No one knows of it; it is well hidden. It is a base for us, one of many."

The cave is very large as these caves go, with room in the water for half a dozen small boats, and space for much storage in its branching tunnels. The twenty-two men have enough supplies and stocks of food and water to hold up inside for months, if necessary. A considerable treasure—saved from nearly a decade of plundering and ransom—is also hidden deep within its caverns.

"I am waiting for Zaccaria and his men to return with the answer. They are late . . . I am worried."

"What country are you in? I take it you're in the Mediterranean."

"No country. The isle of Cyprus. It is ruled by no one, though Bulgaria, the Byzantine Empire, lays claim . . . Yes, the Sea . . . the Mediterranean now."

"What year is it?"

"Year? I do not know . . ."

"Who is the ruler of the Byzantine Empire right now?"

"Comnenus. I do not—Isaac. Isaac Comnenus."

"Okay. Go now to the next moment we need to see to understand," says the Voice. "On the count of three, you will be there: one—two—and *three*. What's happening? What do you see?"

Only a few torches are guttering along the walls, having lasted all night. Light pours into the central cavern of the cave through several large vents in the ceiling. Also pouring in are men, sliding and swinging down ropes, knives between their teeth, cutlasses at their sides. There is fighting on the boats, on the ledges, in the tunnels. His band is greatly outnumbered and are being cut down mercilessly. He has no choice but to flee, swimming out underwater.

"We are being attacked! I have been betrayed! . . . My men are dying . . . I must go."

"Who's attacking?"

"I do not know . . . Sailing men, like us . . . They have a ship, but . . . I do not understand . . ."

From his vantage point in the rocks, half-submerged in the water outside the cave's entrance, he can see the *Sorceress*, a well-known merchant vessel out of Alexandria, anchored close to shore. Its distinctive red and yellow flags crack in the wind. Why its captain would want to attack the very men who have captured his chief rival, he has no idea.

"What's happening now?"

"I am swimming . . . I—Damn! I am seen . . . Being chased now, a long boat . . . There are men on shore . . . I am lost."

"So you're captured?"

"Yes. Eventually."

"Then what happens?"

He is taken aboard the merchant ship. Dripping wet and bound, he stands before its captain, a giant of a man, whose side and leg are freshly bandaged.

"I am taken before Ghazi."

"Who's he?"

"Nasir Ghazi. A trader, a *Karimi,* captain of the *Sorceress*. He led the attack against us."

"What happens then?"

"He . . . He orders his men to hold me . . . for Yusuf."

Unresisting, acknowledging his defeat, he is led to the mizzen mast, where nails are driven through both his hands, high above his head. Blood trickles thinly down his arms onto his neck and chest.

"Does Yusuf come?"

"Yes."

"What does he do?"

The old man is supported by two of his surviving crew, they themselves barely able to stand. And through the puffy, purple slits of his eyes, Yusuf stares, unblinking, as the men around them offer their own creative suggestions as to what to do with their vaunted prisoner.

At last, with the barest hint of a smile on his ruined face, Yusuf raises his dagger.

"Oh God! No! No! AAARGH! AAAYY!"

"You feel no pain, you have no fear," the Voice instructs. "What's happening?"

The memory of the searing pain lingers in his skull. "He takes my eyes . . ."

"Ouch!"

". . . and then my tongue . . . my thumbs . . ."

There is a silence as he relives the excruciating terror from a distance, somehow removed . . . The cauterizing of his wounds . . .

"So, do you die?" the Voice asks.

"No. I am not so fortunate."

"Oh. What happens next?"

"I am put aboard *Wind Dancer,* in the hold . . . We sail to Alexandria."

"Then what?"

"Uh . . . I am given to a man. I am to work for him . . . A beggar. I am a beggar now. In the streets of a strange city."

As instructed, he feels no pain, no fear—only the deepest humiliation. And sorrow. He chokes back a sob.

"All right," the Voice says, "go now to your last day in that life, to the moment of your death . . . On the count of three, you will be there: one—two—and *three*. What's happening? What do you see?"

"I cannot see; I am blind . . . I am being beaten, kicked . . . There is laughing . . . Children. It is children . . ."

Rising up into the air, suddenly able to see again, he watches as a circle of school kids pelt a filthy beggar with stones. He doesn't recognize the thin, ragged figure as the virile sea raider he once was. He's not sure what has just happened.

But the Voice confirms his suspicion: "Okay. Now that you have died and left that body, I want you to look back on the life you just led, and tell me: Who do you know now, in your current life, that you knew then? Who today is Yusuf?"

Myriad faces come into view. The most prominent: the boson aboard the first ship he sailed as a boy, who took him under his wing and showed him the ropes, how to be a man—now Ruben, his childhood friend; his first-mate aboard the *Osprey*—now his son, Sean; the Turkish crewman who saved his life more than once during many fights at sea—now a defense attorney in his courtroom, a black woman, Thomas is her name; the "beggar king" in Alexandria—now the demented wretch he sent to prison for arson several years ago; then, looming above them all, is the wealthy trader, Yusuf, his face morphing into the man he knows today:

"Rostam. Joshua Rostam."

And now—with a foot in both worlds, both lifetimes, just far enough removed from the personality of his former self—Harden makes the connection: "It's *you*." Rostam is the Voice.

A familiar, righteous anger suddenly builds, ebbs, then fades into the background—still there in strength but connected only to that part of himself who was Nerio Kolossi. The anger flares again momentarily at the sound of Rostam's voice:

"Okay, good . . . Can you find it within yourself to forgive Yusuf?"

"No! Never!"

"Can you at least understand why he treated you as he did?"

Well, yes . . . Nerio would have done the same thing himself, had he been so cruel . . . And he was, come to think of it. "Because I took his ship, his goods. Because I killed his men, beat him, tortured him . . . shamed him."

"Connect with the highest aspect of yourself," Rostam says now, repeating words the part of him that is Harden recalls hearing many times before. "Relive the scenes you just visited, but from Yusuf's point of view. Do this as rapidly as possible. Tell me when you're finished."

A blur of images, thoughts, emotions rush by. He is no longer Nerio, the Cyprian bandit, raised on the Sea, taught to fight and to steal for everything he had; but Kahlil, who grew up on the streets and wharfs of Alexandria, learning how men traded goods, made money. He is no longer captain of the *Osprey* but *Wind Dancer.* He experiences the brutal attack and boarding of his ship; his being held captive, abused; the rescue by his long-time friend and adversary; the justice meted out to the villainous rogue who perpetrated the vile deed, death being too good an end for such scum.

He experiences all of this—every detail—in a moment outside of time and space. For just this instant, he is accessing Universal Consciousness, All That Is, the Oneness all beings share. His Higher Self—that particular aspect of God—has given him this unique glimpse into another's soul.

And as much as he would love to bask in such awesome omnipresence, it is over all too soon.

"I am finished," he says.

"Okay, good. What do you think?" Rostam asks. "Can you forgive Yusuf now for what he did to you?"

"Yes, of course. I only hope he can forgive me."

"He has. *I* have. You're forgiven. Completely." Rostam's voice is like a soothing balm on an old, festering wound. "Now, with the same level of understanding, look back on the life you just left and forgive everyone and everything in it. From a higher, spiritual perspective, realize that your purpose in that life was to learn and grow; and you accomplished that goal."

The entirety of that lifetime is held up before his mind's eye like a crystal sphere, washed clean and polished to a shiny reflection. He has no regrets, no remorse, no debts to pay or collect. All is as it should be. All is forgiven.

After a lengthy silence, Harden's attention is once more brought to task:

"Okay. And now, with a deep breath, let's once again return to the River of Time . . . On the count of three, you will be there, floating peacefully on to the next lifetime we've shared, that we need to understand . . . Ready? One—two—and *three* . . ."

Here we go again.

28

AND IF YE WILL RECEIVE IT, *this is Elias, which was for to come.*

Unable to stop herself, Gloria scans the same passage in some of the other versions beside it:

And if you are willing to accept it, John himself is Elijah who was to come.

And if you are willing to accept what I say, he is Elijah, the one the prophets said would come.

And if you believe them, John is Elijah, the prophet you are waiting for.

"They're all basically the same," Gloria says.

She's no longer surprised. Everything else she has read so far of the various versions are nearly identical. She can't see how the King James version is really any more superior, as she's been told all these years. Though it does have a certain poetic style the others lack.

True to his word, Rostam has delivered her a Bible: *The Contemporary Parallel New Testament,* with eight different versions, old and new, laid out side-by-side. It's not at all what she would have preferred, but she can't complain too much: he's finally given her something she enjoys to read.

With it also came the latest "Book of the Month Club" selection. But its title alone is enough to put her off: *The Holographic Universe.* Obviously a science book explaining away God's hand in Creation—just like those that promote evolution over Intelligent Design.

Last month's book, *The Field,* also had a scientific bent—no doubt making the case that God is nothing more than a field of energy or something. As usual, the book's introduction had been enough for her. She's not about to pollute her mind with any more of that heretical garbage. It was a mistake to have read as much as she has.

Fortunately, Rostam hasn't quizzed her at all on anything in the books, only asked her opinion. And her reply is always the same: "Very interesting." He wouldn't like what she really has to say; and there's no point in upsetting him needlessly.

Rostam is sure to ask her about the new Bible when he comes again, and Gloria knows she won't be able to hold her tongue. She's already found three other passages that refute reincarnation.

Just let him try to quote scripture to me again, she thinks. She's prepared to fight him now on every point.

Except for maybe the one she just read. She has to admit, it does sound like Jesus was talking about reincarnation. But there has to be some other explanation. Elijah and John the Baptist were special. Maybe it only applies to prophets or important figures.

The Bible had come with a note and a list of passages Rostam wanted her to read. Gloria had flushed it right away, but that first passage remained stuck in her memory. She's glad that was the only one: she isn't about to entertain any more of his deluded ideas.

Gloria sets the heavy book aside for the moment, lies back to rest and to think (two things she has been forced to do way too much of lately, if you ask her).

She doesn't understand why so many people have such convoluted ideas about the Bible and what it's really saying. Her own parents still live in ignorance. They don't believe in musical instruments in church, for example, which for her is an absolute necessity. They also believe the Bible strictly forbids public displays of affection, like hugging or kissing in church, which is sheer nonsense, of course. Doesn't the Bible mention Jesus himself kissing Mary Magdalene? Or his mother? She's sure it does. It's something she'll have to look up later.

It had taken Gloria nearly half her life to finally break free from her parents' influence and find the one true faith within Christianity. She was raised to believe the Church of Christ was right in all ways. But then one day, shortly after her sixteenth birthday, she had gone to a Sunday evening service with a friend. (It was an Episcopalian church, she recalls, or maybe Lutheran, or Methodist, she's not sure—one of those radical, liberal sects at any rate.) And the experience had changed her life. Such beautiful and uplifting music! An organ, guitars, a flute once! People hugging and kissing in the aisles!

Gloria hadn't been able to tell her parents, but in her heart she could no longer belong to their church. She began attending as many Sunday evening services with her friend as possible. And when the time came to leave home for school in Austin, she went wild, exploring as many different branches of Christianity as she could find, including a brief, crazy stint as a Jehovah's Witness. Each purported to be the best, to have all the answers (except for the Unitarians, if you could even call them Christians). But it wasn't until law school in Houston that she was finally able to stop her searching.

Gloria smiles fondly at the memory. Being baptized in the Baptist Church had felt like being found after wandering lost in the wilderness. It was a real community, and she had been welcomed with open arms. It had been when she met Dwayne, who attended church regularly back then. She attended the adult Bible scholarship classes and began really studying the Word for the first time. And later she began teaching the children's classes herself—something she greatly enjoyed and continued to do for nearly fifteen years.

Her eyes cloud over as she thinks of her students and the youth choir she worked so hard to organize. She'd missed their first concert over a year ago. And she's going to miss her second Mighty Gospel competition soon. She wonders how everyone is doing, if they've managed to get along without her.

Krunk! Pop! Squeak!

Gloria freezes, suddenly overcome with dread, as she always is when the doors are opened.

No, not today! He's not supposed to come until tomorrow. She had been looking forward to a day of peace, just reading her Bible. Rostam is doing this on purpose in order to throw her off.

But she hasn't been faking at being hypnotized lately. As much as she might try to fight it sometimes, she always succumbs in the end. Her mind begins to wander, and then she just drifts off into la-la-land. Often she doesn't feel hypnotized at all, until she's suddenly in another person's body, in another time.

Gloria has recalled so many supposed "past lives" for him since they started. She knows that's what he wants, what makes him happy. Rostam has told her repeatedly that once they get through them all she can go home. There can't be that many left. How many more must he subject her to?

The last life he made her see was a cruel one—the character he made her play a Muslim soldier. She was fighting in a Holy War against invading Christians at a fortress on the coast of Syria (northern Israel today). They finally won the battle after many weeks of fighting, but victory had been stolen from her—*him*—personally. He was killed while looting a church. An imam—his own teacher, who the soldier had the regret of knowing all his life—ordered him to stop and replace everything he had taken. But there was so much to be had! So many gold and silver idols of the infidels! He refused, of course, and the imam had ordered his immediate death at the hands of his fellow warriors.

Gloria had then imagined staying on at Acre for what must have been months afterward. The carnage was unbelievable! As a restless spirit, the soldier walked amongst the bodies of men and horses alike stacked several feet high where they had fallen. It was inexcusable what the imam had done to him, and the soldier did everything within his limited power to hurt the "holy" man. However, the best he could do was haunt his dreams, and even this he did ineffectually. He vowed to get his revenge someday, perhaps when the imam himself died and passed over to the soldier's lonely, ghostly realm.

Gloria hadn't been at all surprised to later recognize the imam as Rostam in this life. In every episode he puts her through, they are at odds with one another in some way. She doesn't know what he's trying to prove. Sometimes *she* is the "bad" guy, sometimes *he* is; often it's both. And every time, Rostam asks for forgiveness.

He's forgiven her, he says. Can she forgive him? Of course, of course. After all, it isn't real.

She knows Rostam is putting these thoughts into her head somehow. But the sights and sounds—the *smells!* for God's sake—are all so vivid. The sensations are all so convincing.

She's spoken languages she's never even heard before (though they're probably not real).

And the various incredible scenes and scenarios she finds herself in! Such intricate dramas! Such details!

Plus, the *emotions* she's felt at times are overwhelming. Happiness, sadness, fear, anger, joy, jealousy—they are as real as any she's ever experienced before. She's both laughed and cried herself to tears. How do you fake something like that? How does he do it?

But it's the *thoughts* that really confuse her. They're so distinct. It's as if she owns them. She has knowledge of things she never had before—that she has no possible way of knowing. And the *memories*—a whole lifetime's worth! Each life's totally different. Where do they come from? There's no way they can be hers.

Unless what she is experiencing are truly her past lives . . .

But that's impossible.

Only someone as warped and diabolical as Rostam could produce such elaborate fantasy. He's placing it all there within her mind for her own wild imagination to act upon and expand. It's all an elaborate trick. It has to be.

And it's making her just a little insane.

"Hello, Gloria." Rostam has his folding chair in one hand, his recording device and notebook in the other.

"We don't have a session today, do we?" she asks.

"Is it okay if we do? The more we can get through, the sooner we can get this finished, put it all behind us."

"But why are you here early? We were on a schedule: every four days."

It looks as if he's about to say something but then changes his mind. "I thought maybe we could wrap it up sooner, you know? Maybe in a couple a weeks. What do you think?"

Gloria hates these sessions. She can't stand having to "relive" these farces—as many as four or more at a time. She hates her mind being filled with such troubling theatrics. Even more, she hates the doubt and confusion they always leave behind. She honestly doesn't think she can take any more of it. But what other choice does she have?

Rostam had told her when they started she would have control over the sessions herself, she could stop at any time. But that's not true. Once the "past-life" action starts, there's no turning back: she's totally engrossed—entrapped—within the story each time, waiting to see how it will end.

"I don't—Do we have to? I was going to read my Bible."

"Oh yeah, that's right! What do you think? Pretty cool, huh?"

Gloria picks up the weighty tome and places it on her lap, begins flipping through its pages, finds one she'd marked earlier.

She clears her throat and reads aloud: "John 9:1. 'And as Jesus passed by, he saw a man which was blind from birth. And his disciples asked him, saying, Master who did sin, this man, or his parents, that he was born blind?'" Gloria stops and meets

Rostam's eyes for a second. "Now listen: 'Jesus answered, Neither hath this man sinned, nor his parents: but that the works of God should be made manifest in him.'

"You see?" she says. "Jesus told them how wrong such thinking was. It's another example I promised you. I have more."

Rostam sets up his chair at the foot of her bunk and sits, his back to the doors, their knees almost touching. "Some people also say that passage demonstrates how the concept of reincarnation was common knowledge," he says. "The disciples were obviously familiar with it or they wouldn't have asked the question. And Jesus doesn't berate them for it but simply explains that, in this case, karma wasn't the factor, but 'fate.'" Rostam smiles and spreads his hands. "Some scholars say that Jesus here is essentially acknowledging reincarnation. He isn't condemning the idea, I don't think."

Gloria's jaw clenches as she bites her tongue. Rostam's condescending tone is infuriating. She quickly thumbs through the Bible's pages again. "I'd like to know who these so-called 'scholars' are you keep referring to."

"Bart Ehrman, for one," Rostam says, "head of Religious Studies at the University of North Carolina. He's written a lot of good books. Or Philip Jenkins at Penn State and Baylor. Bruce Chilton at Bard College. And then there's Elaine Pagels at Princeton, probably the most well-respected authority on—"

"Job 7:9," Gloria interrupts loudly, tired of his rambling. Those names mean nothing to her. Just because someone is a professor somewhere doesn't make them an expert. And she's sure there are plenty of professors who would agree with *her* instead. She reads: "'As the cloud is consumed and vanisheth away: so he that goeth down to the grave shall come up no more.'"

He doesn't look so smug now. "Another example," she says. "Shall I continue?"

Rostam holds up a hand. "Were they talking about the physical body or the soul? It's not clear."

"It couldn't be any more clear," Gloria says, exasperated. "When we die, it's over. The scripture doesn't lie." She again begins turning pages. *Unbelievable!* He'll always have some nit-picking argument to make, no matter what she says.

She finds another marked page. "Psalm 115:17. 'The dead praise not the Lord, neither any that go down into silence.'"

Rostam just looks at her stupidly, obstinately. "Any more?" he asks.

"Not at the moment. I'm sure to find many if I cared to look."

He points to the Bible in her lap. "You might wanna try Psalm 90. It's all about dying and being reborn again. Like 'newly sprung grass,' or something like that."

Gloria sniffs and closes the book.

"There are actually more passages in the New Testament that are pro reincarnation and karma than con," Rostam says. "Have you looked up any from my list?"

"No, I don't need to."

"That's too bad . . . But, oh well." He claps his hands together once and smiles. "Let's not argue about it anymore. We'll just have to agree to disagree, as they say, all right?" He bends to pick up his notebook and recorder.

Gloria gives a shrug. That's just fine with her. Some people can't stand to be proven wrong.

"I'm glad you like your new Bible," Rostam says, handing her the little microphone. "I just wish you would read the other books I gave you."

She can only stare back. *How does he know?*

Rostam chuckles. "It's obvious, Gloria . . . But don't worry. It's too late now, anyway . . . Let's just get started, shall we?"

"What do you mean, 'It's too late'?"

He looks flustered and takes some time answering. She's caught him at something, she's certain.

"Oh, nothing, nothing." He waves the question off. "You and I are almost finished here, that's all."

Then why does he look so guilty? And "finished"? She doesn't like the sound of that word. That's the second time he's used it. You discard something you're finished with. You finish something off when you kill it . . .

"You ready?" he asks.

Gloria nods slowly, still working through the implications of what he said.

"You want to lie down? On your pillow?"

"No." She closes her eyes. "Let's just get this over with."

"You sure?"

She opens her eyes briefly to glare at him. "Yes."

He apparently got the message: "All right. Let's begin by taking some slow, deep breaths . . . By the count of five, you'll have reached a deep state of relaxation, as deeply relaxed as you've ever been before . . . *One*—a nice, deep breath and *hold* it . . . letting it out *slowly* . . ."

Impossible! Already Gloria can feel the tug of sleep coming over her. Has she become so conditioned that she's powerless to stop it? It's his smooth, silky voice. She wishes she could just plug her ears.

"*Two*—with each deep breath, you're becoming more deeply relaxed . . ."

She's going to fight it this time with everything she's got, she decides. He may win in the end, but she can show him that his power over her isn't absolute. Make him work for it.

"*Three*—each inhale filling you with peace and relaxation, each exhale releasing any tension or worry . . ."

Despite her determination, Gloria can feel that familiar, soothing sensation spreading out to her limbs, like a drug. She flexes her hands and feet to stave it off. *Did he notice?* With an effort, she opens her heavy eyelids a crack to look out. Rostam has his own eyes closed, too, as he usually does at this point. She gives her arms a slight shake, opens her eyes and mouth wide to stretch her face.

"*Four*—your body and mind relaxing more and more with each breath, into that pleasant, comfortable state you know so well . . ."

Eyes closed, back in a posture of perfect serenity, Gloria's heart is suddenly pounding. *The door!* He's left it open! And she hasn't caught a glimpse of his stun gun in weeks . . . Does she dare . . . ? *Yes!* She may never get another chance. But how? When? It has to be soon, before she slides unknowingly into trance, as is sure to happen eventually.

"And *five*—with another deep breath, you are so deeply relaxed, so utterly at peace, your mind so quiet and still, you feel yourself floating now . . . floating higher and further toward the River of Time in the distance . . ."

She is sure Rostam's eyes are open now, checking her for signs of hypnosis, judging her level of relaxation. She relaxes her face as best she can, relaxes her shoulders, breathing slowly, smoothly.

He knows, she frets. He's been quiet too long.

"On the count of three, you will have reached the River of Time and be floating there upon it . . . One—two—and *three:* you're there now."

No! Gloria fights the image in her mind. She knows she's not fully hypnotized, but she can feel that floaty sensation taking over. She can see the River of Time—her own, personal conception of it—flowing irrevocably beneath her. She needs to act now!

"Good," Rostam says. "Now, as you rise up high above the—"

Without another thought, she moves: She rotates at the waist, picks up the Bible beside her with both hands, and stands, swings it with all her might, arms outstretched. She catches a quick glimpse of surprise on Rostam's face as the Bible connects with the side of his head. The *THUD!* fills the room, and the impact sends a shockwave coursing up her arms.

She totters there a moment as Rostam sways then sags in his chair, his eyes large, a hand coming up to ward off another blow. His legs have slid forward against hers, so she quickly jumps aside.

She steps behind his chair, raises the Bible as high as she can, and with a primal scream, brings it crashing down upon his head.

Rostam slumps to the floor, as if dead.

Gloria drops the Bible and flees.

She slips through the crack in the doors to find herself in a tiny, dark space. There's another narrow opening into a lighted place beyond. She slams the steel door shut behind her, slides a bolt there into place to secure it. Then she squeezes out through the gap, the walls on both sides scratching her skin and grabbing at her clothes.

Now she is in a T-shaped corridor paneled with sheets of plywood. There is only one way out: a closed door. *Damn!* She didn't think to check Rostam's pockets for any keys; she hopes the door is unlocked. And that there's no one on the other side.

She puts her ear to it and listens. The knob turns easily.

The door opens into a small living quarters: a bedroom/bathroom combination. There is another door in here, and through it is a much larger room, like a cozy library, or study, with bookcases and plants and two mismatched recliners. A set of large, double wooden doors are to her left. The open windows, their curtains moving fitfully in the breeze, show her a beautiful spring day and surrounding forest.

Gloria gasps at her first sight of the outdoors—of freedom!—in well over a year.

She looks around her for anything she can use. She has no shoes and she'll need some if she has to walk very far. She spots Rostam's familiar, blue, fleece pullover hanging by the doors and grabs it, puts it on; she may need it later this evening when it gets cooler. She searches both rooms. Finding no shoes, she puts on the three pairs of thick, woolen socks from a shelf of clothes. Any padding and protection at all will help.

The whole time she's there, Gloria keeps expecting Rostam or someone else to run in and stop her, grab her. She has to remind herself that he's safely locked away for the time being, just like she was for so long. All that can help him now is an accomplice, which she is sure he has. She remembers the pretty woman in the construction cap and orange vest who flagged her down; she may be here somewhere. And there may be others she has to avoid.

Gloria knows she needs to get away quickly before she's spotted. And she'll need to get some distance from here before she's discovered gone.

Outside, a dirt road passes by. Left or right, which way to go? She heads right at a fast pace, choosing the direction going slightly downhill. As she walks, her eyes continuously scan the forest around her and the road ahead. She wants to run but knows she is in no shape to do so. Plus, she needs to conserve her energy and strength for whatever challenges await her.

She hasn't gone far at all when she catches sight of some tiny figures on the road a ways away. They've just rounded a bend and are moving in her direction.

Oh my God!

Gloria stops in her tracks. She knows that if she can see them, they can see her. She doesn't know what to do. Go the other way? Into the forest? The thin, widely-spaced trees offer no cover; she can't hide there.

Now it becomes clear what the smaller figures are: *Dogs!*

She has no choice now. She turns and runs. She can hear the dogs barking furiously in the distance, a voice shouts for her to stop. She doesn't dare.

In no time she's passing the building she just left, sparing it only the briefest glance. There's no way she can go back in there! He'll never let her go, now!

Gloria winces at the painful stones beneath her feet. She begins to cry, sobbing in ragged breaths, gulping for air. There must be somewhere she can hide . . . But she has no real hope of finding safety. She knows all is lost, and cries all the harder for it.

Still, she keeps running. She can't bear the alternative.

Her lungs ache with the exertion. There's a terrible stitch in her side. Her legs are sending shooting pains for her to stop. But she staggers on, as fast as she can go.

The dogs' barking is getting louder, closer.

Then Gloria sees another building in the distance, its faded wooden walls and roof blending in with trees around it. It sits at a turn in the road ahead. Maybe she can hide there, she thinks frantically, or at least escape the dogs.

If she can get there in time.

With renewed determination, Gloria picks up her pace, the pains in her chest and legs and side and feet screaming in protest.

Coming closer, it looks like someone's home: a small, fenced-in yard; tall windows with open shutters, overflowing planter boxes on their sills; a set of brightly painted doors, ajar.

She's nearly there.

Gloria risks a glance behind her as she runs. One mangy beast is ahead of the other, its fierce teeth bared in a snarl. She stumbles and cries out as she almost falls.

Then she's crashing through the rickety wooden gate and barging through the doors of the house.

The commotion is instantaneous. She's assailed by screeching and squawking from every direction. A storm of feathers and fluffy down rises up swirling around her. And Gloria's momentum carries her even further into the cacophonous maelstrom. She screams and spins about, hitting at the wildly flapping creatures flying up from under her feet and launching themselves off the walls. She's being attacked from all sides.

"Stop! Stop! AAAYY!"

Now she's being pecked and bitten painfully by two huge, honking, gray geese, their enormous wings beating the air, sending up even larger clouds of dust and feathers.

She has no idea where the exit is. Screaming hysterically, she runs into some low platforms along the wall, hurting her knees and scattering chickens and nests everywhere. She attempts to throw herself through an open window but is repelled by the wire mesh covering it.

Abruptly, the honking geese chasing her disappear. But the frightful noise around her increases a hundred-fold as the dogs begin barking inside.

It's all too much, and Gloria collapses to the dirt floor beneath the window. Golden rays of sunlight illuminate the particle-strewn air around her. She curls up in a protective ball, whimpering, as she waits for the first of the dogs to tear into her flesh.

"Oh, Lord, help me, Jesus! Help me, Jesus!"

"Woof!"

"AAAYY!"

Eyes held tightly closed, Gloria cringes and cries out as the animal licks the tears from her face.

29

"NO! YOU CAN'T GO!" Dani cries out, suddenly overcome with the rawest of emotion, the most heart-wrenching despair. "You can't leave me!"

Her name is Sarah MacPhearson. She is eighteen. Her lover of nearly two years—the father of her unborn child—is holding her at arm's length as she pleads with him in vain.

"What about—What about the baby?" Her hands press upon her stomach, upon the slightest bump beginning to form. "You can't abandon your own child!"

"I've told you," he says, "it is not my decision to make."

How calm he looks, she thinks, how totally unaffected by the news he brings.

"I can go with you," she pleads tearfully. "No one has to know."

"No, that would not do. I'm to be accompanied by my father. We go to Wilmington in the morning. We sail from there."

So soon! "How—How can you do this? How can you do this to me? Don't you love me?"

He looks irritated with her now. "Of course I do, Sarah. You know I do." He grips her shoulders painfully, shakes her. "How many times must I tell you? I have no choice in the matter. I lose everything if I go against their wishes."

Their wishes. His parents' wishes, she knows, are for their eldest son to marry into a family as wealthy and prestigious as their own. Having the daughter of a Scottish fur trader and Cherokee medicine woman for a daughter-in-law doesn't interest them in the slightest.

"But, Richard, we don't need them! We can go away! My father will help us, I know he will!"

She reaches for him but he catches her hands, holds them tightly between his own. It's as if he doesn't want to be touched. *How can he be so cold?*

Richard shakes his head and looks away. He can't even meet her eyes. "No, I must go," he says tonelessly.

"Oh! I hate you!" she shouts, anger instantly replacing her despair. "You *want* to go!"

"It's my future," he says, raising his voice, looking fiercely at her now. "Why can't you understand that? I have an obligation to my family to make something of myself. Do you actually think I would choose poverty over a life as a gentleman? I am to be a member of society."

Sarah can't believe what she is hearing. "You liar! *I* was to be your future! *We* were to be your family! . . . How can you? . . . *Oh!*"

She aims a kick at his shin and connects, muddying his breeches and eliciting a curse. She struggles to pull away, but he still holds her hands painfully in his, away from him, as if he knows she'll pummel him if she gets the chance.

"I despise you!" she screams in his face. "Go then! Go to hell for all I care! "

Her subsequent attempts to kick him are futile, so she quickly leans forward and sinks her teeth into the back of his hand.

"AAAHH!"

Richard yells in pain and tries to jerk his hand away, but Sarah holds on like a terrier. Until he finally pushes her away with such force that she falls to her side on the ground.

"Damn you!" He stands above her, alternating between sucking on the wound and looking at it with horror. Blood runs down his wrist and onto his shirt and the cuff of his fine new coat. His lips are smeared red. "Look what you've done! You stupid girl!"

Sarah has never seen him so upset. He takes a step toward her lying there in the mud, and she instinctively places a protective hand over her belly and scoots away.

Their argument has drawn onlookers, mostly women doing their shopping or visiting the apothecary where Sarah's mother works inside.

"Mr. Whitley!" someone calls out.

Richard pulls his furious eyes away from her to scowl at the crowd. Then, as if embarrassed, he casts her a final, disgusted look and stalks away, holding his injured hand before him.

"Go ahead! Run away, you coward!" Sarah yells at his back. "You are no man! You're nothing to me! . . . To the devil with you, Richard Whitley! Go on!"

Richard only quickens his pace and is gone around the first corner.

For the longest time she looks unbelievingly down the empty street. As if he will suddenly reappear and come running to her, tell her how wrong he was; how he would rather spend his life with her and their child than with anyone else; that he's sorry; that they will leave together tonight, if that is what she wants; that he will always love her. Forever.

Then someone is there, helping her to her feet. Two women, supporting her as they guide her up the steps. Her mother, appearing in the doorway with a worried look, reaching out to catch her as she falls . . .

"I — I MUST FAINT. I don't know," Dani says softly, deeply affected by the girl's emotions.

"Okay. Now move forward in time," Josh instructs her. "Is there anything else you need to see, in order to understand? Do you ever see Richard again?"

There is a long pause as Dani processes so much information flowing through her mind, so many memories flitting by. Then: "Yes."

"All right. On the count of three, you will be there, fully present in the next moment you need to experience . . . One—two—and *three* . . ."

SHE STANDS BEFORE THE MAN she thought she would never see again. Her candle and the dim lamplight from his room cast quivering shadows across his handsome face, made more so by age. She hesitates, her resolve weakening at the sight of him so close. But then she is past him, with no resistance, as she had hoped—as she had known from his greedy eyes following her from the dinner table.

She stands with her back to him at the desk and blows out her candle, tries to summon the courage that had brought her to his room.

Richard's hands encircle her waist. She turns to him, searches his face—for what? Love? Remorse? Regret?

"Sarah," he murmurs.

"I knew you would come back . . . When they told me, I . . ." She dips her head, worried her true feelings will show.

Richard lifts her chin and she can see the naked hunger in his expression. He kisses her.

Unbidden, the passion Sarah felt as a young girl comes rushing forth from a spring long buried inside her. She's torn between the burning love she once felt for this man and the all-consuming hatred that plagued her for so many years when he left.

She gives in to both as they make furious love again and again throughout the night, Sarah using her teeth and nails and fists, as she herself is taken savagely.

Much later, in what must be the very early morning, she lies sore and bruised beside him, listening to the slow, even rumble of Richard's snore. Sure that he's asleep, she gets dressed by the lamp, which has remained dimly lit all night.

This done, her torn clothing arranged as best she can, her long hair reasonably fixed and coiled atop her head, Sarah stands beside the bed, staring down at the most loved and most hated man of her life. She removes the knife from the pocket of her dress and holds it uncertainly. Light glints off the blade.

She'd tested its sharpness in the kitchen earlier; there's no doubt it can easily cut his throat or puncture his heart, as she planned. She holds the knife's edge close to Richard's sleeping face. He looks so peaceful, almost smiling, snoring contentedly.

Sarah tries to summon the anger she has harbored for so long. But something has changed during the night. Her emotion has been spent. Also—although he never said he was sorry (they hadn't spoken much at all)—she could sense the regret within him. He'd held her tenderly at one point, stroking her arm, her breasts, her face, gazing soulfully into her eyes. Now she can't bring herself to perform the final act.

Minutes go by and she imagines a dozen different ways she can use the knife growing heavier in her hand. Then, with a soft moan and snuffle, Richard turns away, his naked back exposed to her now.

It would be so easy . . .

But: *Enough.* Sarah straightens and drops the knife back into her pocket. She will let him live. He's not worth the trouble it would cause. She may not have gotten the revenge she sought, but she finally has closure.

Making to leave, she spots the small canvas satchel on the floor, beside Richard's boots.

Perhaps she's found a way to hurt him, after all.

"THEN WHAT HAPPENS? What do you do?"

"I go to the carriage. It's been waiting for me all night, behind the—Oh! The poor horses! They need to be fed and watered."

"What happens to Richard?" Josh asks. "Do you see him again?"

A pause as Dani moves through time. Finally, so quietly: "No."

Josh clears his throat. "All right. Now let's go to the last day of that life, to the moment of your death. On the count of three, you will be there. You will feel no pain, you will have no fear . . . One—two—and *three:* you're there now. What's happening? What do you see?"

HER DAUGHTER, JULIA, sits sobbing in the grass as James pulls Sarah toward his waiting horse. Julia's new husband stands impotently beside the woodpile, an axe in his hand, not daring to interfere.

Sarah herself isn't crying, though inside she is full of grief, distraught at the chain of events and afraid of what her enraged husband might do. Her lip is swollen and bleeding from where he hit her a moment ago.

Standing beside his horse, she pulls her arm away defiantly, and James hits her again, knocking her to the ground. Through the dizzying haze, she can hear Julia screaming at her stepfather. Then Sarah is being lifted and thrown over the back of the horse, the saddle horn digging painfully into her side. James mounts behind her and rests the large, heavy bag she had packed on top of her.

Then they're riding away at speed. Sarah can hardly breathe with the jostling of the horse below and the weight of the bag above. She tries to reposition herself but it's no use; she has to endure the discomfort and pain for however long. Soon they are galloping, and she can feel herself ready to pass out from the abuse and lack of air.

She wakes lying on her back, in the still-wet grass. There's a sharp pain in her side, the thick taste of dust in her mouth. James is cursing loudly nearby. Interlacing tree branches tremble in the rain-swept sky above.

Where are we? Where has he taken me? What is he going to do?

A sudden weight falls on her chest, accompanied by the unmistakable clinking of coins.

"You *did* take them!" her husband roars. "What else have you done, you harlot?"

Sarah rolls to her side, away from him, the satchel of coins hitting the ground damningly beside her. Bile rises in her throat and she throws up her meager breakfast of this morning, wipes her mouth on her sleeve.

"Did you have congress with that man?" James shouts behind her. "Did you abase yourself beneath my very own roof?"

The kick to her backside is so hurtful and so unexpected, Sarah lets out a cry.

"No!" she lies.

"What is this, then?"

Her missing anklet, a recent anniversary present, falls to the grass only inches away from her face, its silver chain twinkling at her. She'd noticed it gone three days ago, while bathing at her mother's, washing the smell of sex from her body. She had known then, with dismay, exactly where she lost it.

Hearing of the duel, Sarah had quickly left her mother's house, where she told James she would be staying, the evening before. She'd then fled to her daughter's new home in the country. She didn't think James yet knew where Julia lived, as he had refused to attend the wedding or speak to his stepdaughter since.

But she was wrong.

If only I had left last night . . . But the previous night's storm would have made traveling on the roads perilous, if not impossible.

"I should kill you for what you have done!" James says vehemently, landing another ferocious kick to her legs. "Because of you I have murdered an innocent man! A friend!"

"Please! Stop!" Sarah cries. "Just let me go! You never have to see me again!"

"You want to leave? Well, you shall not be returning to *my* house, I can assure you of that! You have dishonored not only yourself but me as well! My family!"

This time the kick catches her in the side as she tries to turn away. She has never felt such pain and it takes her breath away. She lies curled in a ball, gasping for air.

After a few blessedly silent minutes, having recovered slightly, Sarah begins to crawl slowly across the grass, away from her incensed husband pacing nearby.

Her scream catches in her throat as James is suddenly on top of her. He pushes her to her back and straddles her, rips open the top of her dress, her underclothes beneath, exposing her breasts.

"What's this?" he says hoarsely, slapping her hands away, grabbing one arm tightly. He pokes at the bruises and bite marks still covering her chest. "What are these? *He* did this to you? Did you enjoy it? Is *this* what you like?"

She struggles to get out from under him, to push him off her. But he is too heavy, too strong, too determined to punish her somehow.

His fist stills her for a moment.

"You have one final duty to perform, woman, before I leave you to your own devices," he says, breathing hard.

Sarah doesn't even recognize her husband now—the caring man who once pitied her and her young daughter and taken them in, who had loved her and treated her with kindness and respect. Instead, she sees an enraged beast with the cruel eyes of a stranger.

He's possessed!

Spittle flies from his mouth: "Act like a whore and you shall be treated like one, I say!"

The crushing weight on her stomach lifts as James kneels on the ground and forces himself between her legs. He pulls down his breeches, pushes up her dress.

Uselessly trying to smooth it down, Sarah's hand brushes up against something in her pocket, pricking her through the cloth. She fumbles through the folds, finds the knife, and lashes out at the most obvious target above her.

"AAAHH! God *damn* you!" James reaches down and his hand comes away bloody. "You evil witch!"

Sarah swipes again, carving another deep gash in his groin.

He howls in pain and rage, and seizes her fragile wrist as she goes to strike again.

Sarah screams as her bones snap and the knife falls from her grasp. Her vision goes dark, bright lights dancing in her head.

"Why?" she hears him cry out in anguish above her. "I *loved* you!"

Sarah opens her eyes. She's surprised to see tears running down his face as James plunges the knife into her chest.

"OKAY. NOW THAT YOU'VE DIED and left that body, look back on the life you just left . . . Who did you know then that you know now, in your current life? . . . Who is Richard?"

Like so many times already, Josh's face comes to the forefront of Dani's mind, this time superimposed over Richard's.

"You . . ." she says softly, still shaken. "The same . . . soul."

"Who today was your husband then? Who killed you?"

Now there comes the clear image of somebody she really hates to see—somebody she's been fortunate enough not to have had any problems with in other lifetimes she's visited—somebody who had usually been neutral, or a friend and ally, up to this point.

Dani hopes this doesn't mark the beginning of a new pattern in her lives. If so, she'll have to find a way to warn her future selves somehow.

"Santos," she says, his face leering at her from the darkness. "Emilio Santos."

30

THE NUMBERS ARE GONE. Santos lies staring at the ceiling with its all too familiar marks and patterns, willing the numbers to come.

But it's no use. Ever since he "returned from the dead," his once savant-like ability—his coveted genius—has eluded him.

For almost three months now, he's tried in vain to solve the most simple exponential equations, to create the most basic series of primes—something he's done since he was a child. And already he's forgetting what that was like. The numbers are no longer there for him, no longer his friends calling him out to play, but just empty, utilitarian symbols devoid of any life. Their special magic is gone.

It's almost a blessing, he tries to convince himself. There's a quietness now, a stillness to his mind Santos has never experienced before. At first it felt like something missing, something lost, but now lately, more like something gained: room to breathe, to ponder, to think without overanalyzing, without always applying the numbers and logic and probabilities. As a result, he's become something of a "philosopher," contemplating the meaning of life for the first time. He's even caught himself daydreaming, something he never used to do, or lost in abstract thought for hours on end.

Brain damage? That had been his first thought. Rostam told him he was physically dead for over four minutes before he could be revived. The *tonto* had shot him up with some drug to make his heart beat again; and when that didn't work fast enough, had to give him CPR. Santos's chest had ached for weeks.

What a fucking crazy thing to do! If Santos had any doubts before about Rostam's genuine lunacy, that insane stunt proved it. *The guy is completely nuts. He's out of his fucking mind.*

But Rostam does know what he's talking about, apparently.

This whole past life thing is absolutely amazing, Santos has to admit. *It's incredible. It's blown his mind totally wide open.* What he'd thought before to be nothing but the deluded ravings of a madman have proven in fact to be true. *Who would have thunk it?*

For more than ten weeks now, over fifteen sessions, he and Rostam have covered sixty-two different lifetimes they've shared. And these just the adversarial ones, supposedly. From ancient Atlatia, to Africa, to Asia, to Europa, to the Americas, they have traversed the globe through the ages, probing the depths of Santos's subconscious.

And superconscious, though not to the extent Santos experienced it himself, alone.

He thinks on it often; and the memory of his time in "Heaven" is as vivid to him now as as if he was there again.

Following the initial welcome by his friend and guide—a being of Light like himself, who he's known forever—they had gone to a place of "energy restoration." There, Santos's soul was showered with a sparkling waterfall of pure Love and Light—a reconnecting with his Source . . . There are no words to describe how wonderful it was; nothing on Earth can even begin to compare . . . He felt renewed and invigorated, more unquestionably alive in spirit form than ever in his human body. Any residues of Earthly worries or trauma were instantly washed away.

Then he and she (for although his guide no longer projected herself as a female, or as any kind of form but a radiant ball of silver-blue Light, Santos still thinks of her that way), they had sat for a short "talk" about his most recent life. How did he think it went? Did he accomplish his goals? What could he have done differently? . . . Of all his experiences in the spirit world, Santos has been spending the most time since then reviewing this one, going over their conversation again and again.

He hasn't come to any conclusions yet. He realizes, of course, that there are plenty of areas for improvement in his life, but he isn't beating himself up over anything.

In light of all he's learned during the course of revisiting his many lifetimes with Rostam, Santos understands that, most often—as in this life—his purpose is nothing more profound than simply "being," simply learning and growing through experience. However, he knows that, at the same time, he is meant to be a *force* during this life as well—not "bad," not "evil," but definitely not "good" either—for others to have the opportunity to *react to* and develop themselves in relationship to. It's a necessary role; and it's the one he chose this time, his contribution to the great play—the great, ongoing drama—of human existence.

As he's since reminded Rostam: where would he be today if Santos hadn't put him in prison? Still a pathetic drug addict? Dead? How spiritually enlightened would he have become without Santos's influence? And he knows Rostam agrees; it's an extremely valid point.

Santos had seen "Rostam" at the next stop on his journey on the other side. His guide had led him through a "Grand Central Station" for incoming souls, then down numerous branching "corridors" of translucent energy, where groups of souls were gathered in countless bunches, like grapes on a vine, for as far as the eye could see. Approaching his own spirit "family," Santos could feel their many familiar frequencies of vibration resonating with him, guiding him like a collective beacon. He was met by a semicircular array of different colored lights—white, pink, and yellow. Rostam's soul—the part that always remains; bright yellow with a light-green aura—had been the first to greet him, "embracing" him enthusiastically. And as he did so, the memory of their entire history together came rushing over him at once:

They went back far, far before their meager time on Earth, before there *was* an Earth. They are more than just spiritual brothers, they are individual aspects of the same Being: two fingers on the hand of an infinitely-limbed God, helping Her to create the Universe and All That Is. Everything they do for themselves, they also do for Her, for it is through *them* that She knows Herself, that She experiences Herself in that form. This is their ultimate purpose.

And it was through this awesome reunion with his spiritual brother—this trip down an infinitely winding memory lane— that Santos first became aware of his own individual importance in the Grand Design: His experiences—at every stage, regardless of the world or plane or dimension he's in at the time—are special and unique to himself alone, contributing to the Source (his *Highest* Higher Self) that singular perspective that would otherwise have gone unknown. His soul may be only a drop in the ocean that is God, but it's an essential one, as they all are.

Such are the thoughts that have occupied Santos's mind since his "death."

Had he stayed dead, Rostam tells him, he would have encountered many other things: vast "libraries" and "schools"; "vacations" to other worlds, other realities; and more "counseling" than Santos could possibly imagine or even want—all in preparation for his next life on Earth—or wherever.

But he obviously wasn't meant to stay.

After checking in with his spirit family, Santos had been led by his guide to what Rostam calls the "Council of Elders," a small group of purple-colored light beings—the only ones he saw of that color. He stood before them just long enough to hear "Hello" and "Goodbye," essentially. He was to return to his physical incarnation, they told him; it was not yet his time to come "home."

And in the next instant, Santos had come alive in a body about two hundred pounds too heavy, Rostam's *loco* mug looking down at him.

Oh, fuck, had been his first thought.

KRUNK! POP! SQUEAK!

Rostam's early. They're not due for a session until tomorrow. But, hey, better to get it over with. This one may be their last; or if not this one, the next for sure. They usually explore four or five lifetimes at a pop, over a span of anywhere between four hundred and twelve hundred years. They've had a lot of ground to cover, since their "negative karmic relationship" began about forty-five thousand years ago.

But Santos doesn't mind; he enjoys the sessions. If anything, he's been getting one hell of a history lesson this way. It's even better than the Travel Channel.

The last lifetime they reviewed was in 1417, during what had been called the "Great Schism" in Europe, when the Church had three popes, all claiming true legitimacy. Santos had backed Urban VI, in Rome, Italy—Rostam, Clement VII, in Avignon, France. They knew of each other through letters, but met only briefly at a place called Constance, in the Western Empire, for a big meeting to finally resolve the matter. There, the two of them had argued for weeks, agreeing only that the fool, Otto Colonna (soon to become Pope Martin V—go figure), would make a mockery of the papacy. Then Rostam, the dumb-ass, had tried to poison Urban and his gang, but only ended up killing Santos instead, who was one of four who drank the wine intended for the pope's supper that evening. It was an excruciatingly painful death he remembered, and he's glad he didn't have to relive it fully again.

As usual, they had talked about it afterward, while Santos was in spirit form, and "forgave" each other.

He's tried to tell Rostam that all this forgiveness bullshit isn't necessary anymore, ever since their full-contact spiritual reunion during his NDE. But according to Rostam, it's not that simple—it's a subconscious thing, he says. He's adamant about going through the whole past-life process and resolving the various issues in each one. But as far as Santos is concerned, they're both forgiven already. Forever. He's seen the bigger picture.

If Rostam could just understand that, as spiritual beings, we are all automatically forgiven for anything we might do on Earth, he wouldn't need to carry the karmic baggage he's packed for himself. Ultimately, it's only *himself* he needs to obtain forgiveness from.

Instead, Rostam's karma has become his dogma—a self-fulfilling prophecy.

But, then again, hey, what do I know?

"ON THE COUNT OF THREE, you will be there, in a scene that best illustrates the problem we want to understand . . ."

He wants so much to fly off and explore on his own, but Santos is kept tethered to Rostam's captivating voice, keeping him focused and on track.

"One—two—and *three:* you're there now . . . What's happening? What do you see?"

HE IS STANDING IN A CLOUD of gray smoke, his arm extended, a dueling pistol in his hand. The recoil from the blast reverberates throughout his body.

A woman screams. Voices are raised. As the smoke clears, he can see Whitley—for that is the man's name—lying in an unnatural position on the grass.

He feels no remorse, only the remnants of anger and humiliation—and a small sense of satisfaction.

This is by no means the end of the problem, he knows. He must find his wife and question her.

"Why did you shoot him?" Rostam's voice, ever present in the background.

"He insulted my wife . . . He insulted me . . . This was a duel. A matter of honor . . . I could not—It could not stand."

"Is he dead?"

A pause. "Yes."

"Oh. Okay. So I guess that's it, then . . . Where are you?"

"Collingswood Green."

"What town, what country?"

"Charlotte. The United States of America."

"North Carolina?"

"Yes."

"Do you know the year?"

"Yes . . . It is 1796."

"What's your name?"

"James Hiram Burke."

"All right. Very good. Let's go forward now to the last day of that life, to the moment of your death . . . On the count of three, you will be there . . ."

HE STANDS BEFORE a freshly dug grave, looking in, his stark reflection on a black pool of water from last night's storm. He holds the reins of his horse in one hand, the small satchel of coins in the other.

He is so tired. He would like nothing more than to lie down in this grave and be done with it, but his own family's plot is in another section of the cemetery. He will have his own grave shortly, he knows. In spite of his efforts, the blood has refused to stop flowing in a thin sheet down his leg.

Whitley's funeral is today—in a matter of hours, most likely. Burke would have liked to be there, to pay his respects. Not to apologize, necessarily, but to at least let the man's parents know their son had not died with dishonor. His once boyhood friend deserves at least that much from him.

He tosses the money bag into the grave. It lands with a muted splash, shattering his reflection.

"Your coins, sir." He cannot bring himself to say he is sorry.

He moves his horse away, finds that he is too weak to mount.

"Come on, Beauty." He leads her down the path to where his grandparents and his father and his youngest sister are buried, to where he himself will be interred in a matter of days—alongside Sarah, when her body is eventually found not far from here.

He doesn't quite make it.

31

RICHARD WHITLEY, 1762 – 1796, Beloved Son, Patriot. The etching has eroded but the lettering is still clear. A pair of angels in the corners of the headstone keep watch over the grave.

"Well, here it is," Erin says.

It wasn't very hard to find. An Internet search on Charlotte's local historical society's site had produced the name of the cemetery, along with a map listing the various names buried there and the dates.

A three-hour flight from Springfield had gotten her here. It maxed out her last credit card but was worth the expense: it would have taken at least fifteen hours to drive—something they may be doing later anyway.

If Josh is right, there's a small treasure in rare gold and silver coins buried beneath her feet.

Erin's listened to the pertinent sections of the recordings herself, so she's on the same page, more or less.

"But what if someone saw the bag lying there and took it out before they buried him?" had been her first question.

"There's a good chance they didn't," is Josh's view. "It was probably covered in mud, or under water. And from what they both said, it wasn't that big, like a small purse or something, with a strap."

Erin thinks there's a fifty-fifty chance of it still being there. Pretty good odds, actually.

She stomps on the ground a few times, testing the packed earth. How much work would it be to dig up a grave? she wonders, not for the first time. She could help, probably, but there's no way she can do any of the heavy digging or lifting. She's just not physically strong enough. And climbing in there? No way. Josh would have to do almost all of it himself.

How deep does it go? Six feet, like she's always heard? And what would they find? After two hundred-plus years, there can't be a casket left. Or the canvas sack. Or anything but bones, most likely. Or at least one would hope.

Erin looks guiltily around her. She can't believe she is seriously contemplating this. It's absurd. It's insane.

No, it's desperate, she acknowledges. She has vowed to do whatever it takes to keep the Center going. And if this is it . . .

At least, as Josh has reassured her, it's his own spirit they would be disturbing, so there's no worry about "waking the dead" in this case.

But assuming it's even possible, how long would it take? They would have to get in and get out in one night—in about five or six hours. That's it. From around midnight to five in the morning, she figures, at the latest.

On the plus side, the grave is in a fairly secluded part of the cemetery, near the center, away from both the fence and the entrance. And the few largish mausoleums around the site would at least partially block them from most directions. Plus, the cemetery itself is out of the way, in an older, residential part of town. There's not much traffic. There's a pretty good chance no one would see them. Though they would probably see their lights.

Or should we even use lights?

And maybe a new moon would be best to work by, under the cover of darkness. The next one should be in about two weeks, she thinks, eight or nine days after Easter.

Erin marks the date in her mental calendar, as if she's already made up her mind to do this crazy thing.

"Crazy or stupid," she says, walking away.

Lightly treaded paths wind their way through the old cemetery. The grass is neglected, parched and yellow and too long in many places. There's not much vegetation; only a dozen large oak trees stand as sentinels, clusters of bushes here and there along the rusted iron fence. The rest is wide open. Nothing much to shield them from prying eyes as they dig but the mausoleums and a few tombs and small monuments scattered about.

Maybe the best thing she can do is keep watch. Which again begs the question: How is Josh going to manage basically doing this by himself? He's a strong guy, sure, he's in shape; but it's wishful thinking—ridiculous even—to think he can do so much work in so little time, on his own. They're going to need some help, that's all there is to it. But who?

Milo and Jem are the first (and only) to come to mind. Erin is ninety-nine percent certain they already flout the law, growing Mary Jane. But could she ask them to go grave robbing with her? A thousand miles away? What reason could she give? A share of the profits? They're not even sure what's down there, exactly, if anything.

Although they do have a pretty good idea.

According to Santos's second session reviewing his life in Charlotte, Burke had seen a good number of the very first gold coins minted in the United States—the ten-dollar "Eagle" and the five-dollar "Half-eagle"—as many as ten each, perhaps more, all from Whitley's own purse. There were also at least ten of the new silver dollar coins, minted only a short time earlier. Santos (as Burke) also mentioned seeing a few privately issued gold "doubloons"; but these, he recalled, Whitley had taken from his waistcoat pocket, so there's no point in counting on those to be included.

Burke had only glanced inside the satchel when he found it in his wife's bag; he hadn't counted the coins. But he did notice there were both gold and silver pieces inside.

However, more than likely, they've surmised, not all of the coins Burke saw at the table still remained in the bag when it went into the grave. By Dani's account, Sarah had spent a full day and two nights at her daughter's. And as Gavin said, "What mother wouldn't share at least half what she stole with her own child?" Not only that, but Sarah had also gone to her mother's that morning after leaving the hotel.

Taking Dani once again to that time in Charlotte proved this to be the case. Sarah had divided the loot three ways, giving most of the gold to her daughter. She kept for herself: seven gold pieces (four "heavy," three "light") and nine silver ones.

Not the great treasure they first hoped.

Or is it? Research on the Internet showed that the 1794 silver dollar is an extremely rare and valuable coin. It's estimated that only about one hundred and forty have survived to this day. One in good condition recently sold at auction for $175,000.

To think that only *one* coin could pay off all her loans makes Erin giddy. A second would completely refurbish the Big House and allow her to buy most of the medical equipment she needs. She could create her "Dream Center" and afford to hire permanent staff.

With only one of these silver coins, Josh could set himself up with a new identity—a new life—anywhere.

But that's not all: A 1795 gold Eagle in decent condition can land $120,000, or even *twice* that, on the open market. A Half-eagle from the same year, up to $80,000 or so.

Figures like these make digging up poor Mr. Whitley a tempting proposition indeed.

At the entrance, Erin examines the gate there: a tall wrought-iron archway with a pair of ornamental swinging doors. At one point it had been secured by an ancient locking device with a giant keyhole, but now a heavy length of chain and rusty padlock hang from one of the open doors.

The fence itself is about five feet high, with spikes like skinny arrowheads running along its top. It surrounds the entire cemetery. As does a cracked and narrow sidewalk.

Erin decides to take a walk around the perimeter to look for other possible ways in or out, like maybe an unlikely gap in the fence. She also wants to inspect the neighborhood grown up around the place over the past two centuries. It won't take long: the grounds are even smaller than she expected to find, only three short square blocks.

Directly to the south, across from the entrance, is a small park about the same size.

Along the west side, across the street, is a long row of small, old, one-story homes. She sees only two people outside, down the entire length of the street—one an elderly man working on his car, the other a young, pregnant woman gardening. Soft classical music floats out of a curtained window.

A nursery and landscaping company takes up the entire northern border, much of its property, it seems, covered with small greenhouses. Two workers are stacking heavy-looking sacks into the back of a truck; both stop to watch her pass by; one waves. She returns the greeting and keeps going. It's likely no one will be there during the night, she thinks; definitely a good thing.

Along the east side are more old homes, looking like so many cozy cottages. A church dominates the last block, on the corner. Its doors are open. There's not a soul in sight, though organ music comes from inside.

According to the historical society, the church was built in 1849, the same year the Mint finally opened their Charlotte branch. No doubt Whitley's unfortunate demise slowed things down a bit.

Having circled back to the cemetery's entrance, Erin takes another look at the gate's chain. Someone from the church must be in charge of opening and closing it each day. The padlock looks to be the weakest link.

Shouldn't be a problem.

She cuts through the park to reach her rental car left a couple of blocks away.

She has just one more errand to run before heading back to the airport.

As she walks, Erin compiles a list in her head: They'll need a pair of heavy-duty bolt cutters, for one thing; a pick axe, maybe; some shovels (she can do her part to help, even if they can't find someone else); work gloves, certainly; a couple of hand trowels; buckets; rope; a stepladder . . . Many of these things they already have at the Center.

Gavin mentioned getting or making some kind of sieve to sift the coins from the dirt once they reach bottom. It's a good idea. Still, all the coins should be in one spot. Hopefully they didn't sink too far down. The biggest obstacle Erin can see is getting to them in time.

In more ways than one.

If the coins are there to be found, she needed them, like, last month.

If she can't come up with enough money soon, Worthing has threatened to start foreclosure proceedings. Erin knows he can smell blood in the water. Already, even more of his investor friends have been tramping around her property unannounced, taking a look around—"surveying." No wonder he had refused her request for refinancing.

She is officially sixty-four days overdue on the mortgage. She was barely able to cover the utilities and operating expenses last month. Her other bills are also overdue and must still be paid.

Of the thirteen patients at the Center right now, only five are able to pay. It's just not enough. Unfortunately, those who most need the treatment, usually aren't able to afford it.

But what is she supposed to do? Accept only those with money? Turn away someone who's suffering, when there's an empty bed available?

It's been a quandary for Erin since Fresh Start first opened its doors. She wants to help people and advance science, not run a business. Without donations or grants, without the second floor finished, without Worthing's cooperation . . .

There is only one thing she can think of. And she would *really* hate to have to play that card. But the man may leave her no other choice. He refuses to even meet with her now.

Worthing's wife, Yvette, had shown up on Erin's doorstep in the middle of the night last summer, asking—no, demanding—to be admitted. Secretly. For free. She had been dropped off by her obvious lover (a much younger man), both strung out on speed and who-knows-what, already up for days. She stayed a whole month before returning home from her "spa vacation in Hot Springs."

Erin still has a copy of the admittance form with Mrs. Worthing's signature. She still has the lab work, the records. Donna as a witness. Photos, video.

Erin would hate to betray the woman's trust. But desperate people do desperate things . . .

And these are desperate times indeed.

32

EVERYTHING IS READY TO GO. The sun is preparing to go down at last, lighting up the sky a golden violet-blue.

Josh stands with his hands on his hips, admiring his creation—the result of three days' work: a dense, intricately stacked pyramid of wood, five feet high, its base six feet wide by nine feet long. The lumber is stacked in stair-step fashion up each side, creating a three-by-six plateau on top. Gavin lies there, wrapped tight in his chosen "burial" shroud: his favorite set of sheets—dark blue with little stars, moons, and comets.

Getting him up there had been the tricky part. The four of them are still covered in sweat from the effort.

It's an unseasonably warm spring day—the hottest Easter on record—and much to Josh's delight, the women are wearing shorts and not much else. Everyone is barefoot, enjoying the feel of the newly sprung grass in the meadow, half a mile from the Center.

Erin and Donna arrived a short time ago with the dogs and their "man of the hour," kept cool these past few days in the bathtub filled with ice. They've also brought a cooler of drinks and the evening's picnic dinner, including a peach pie (Gavin's favorite) made special for the occasion.

Sheila has been helping Josh all afternoon make the final preparations.

He'd spent the entire first day hauling the old plank flooring from the Long House to the clearing, in Erin's pickup. It had been stored piled against the back wall inside the chicken coop since he pulled it up exactly one year ago this month. There was more than enough to do the job.

The second day, yesterday, was spent building his masterpiece. Josh used a handsaw to cut the lengths of wood to just the right size, then built them up around the pyramid's core: twelve large bags of charcoal stacked side-by-side, three layers high. He's not sure if this will make a difference or not, but it seemed like a good idea at the time—a touch Gavin might have appreciated.

Today, he and Sheila used a hoe and rake to create a wide circle of bare dirt around the structure, so no grass will catch fire. They also put up some temporary bracing of plywood sheets on all four sides, to keep the stacked timber in place while everyone helped to get Gavin situated on top.

Josh has just removed the plywood and set it aside. He supposes he could have left it on, but he likes the step-pyramid look—the aesthetics of it all—much better this way.

Right now the whole thing stands outlined against the beginnings of a glorious sunset. It's a fitting send-off, he thinks, for a good man. A good friend.

Josh wipes the sweat from his brow as Sheila hands him an ice-cold bottle of brew (well, root beer, which tastes better anyway). She's drinking the same. They tap their bottles in silent toast to a job well done. He pulls her close and they stand holding each other, gazing west.

It doesn't take long before Josh can feel that certain itch he gets whenever he's alone with Sheila outdoors. "Hey, there's still plenty of light left," he says slyly, motioning with his head to the trees.

"No!" She laughs, pushing him away. "This is a solemn occasion."

"It's a celebration!" He catches her by the waist with his free hand.

"But he's watching."

"Let him. Gavin loves a good shag. He's probably been waiting for us to do it all day, I bet."

"No, I mean he's watching us right now." She stops his advance with her cold drink against his chest. "Here, bend down."

Huh? Josh lowers his head obediently; he can feel her rustle his hair.

"See?"

Perched on Sheila's finger in the twilight is a large, bright blue butterfly—the same one (it must be) that has been fluttering around them all day. Earlier, Josh had named it "Gavin," joking that it was his spirit animating the insect: "A lot easier than a bird, I suppose."

But now, so many hours later, with it still close by, it doesn't seem so far-fetched anymore.

Josh holds his face only inches away, the beautiful creature's spotted, blue wings moving slowly up and down.

"Of course!" he exclaims. He finally gets it. What better symbol for metamorphosis, for change, into something greater—freer—than it was before.

"Gavin, you did it!" he says. "Way to go!" He points at it sternly: "Now, hold on a minute; don't go anywhere."

He straightens, cups his hands to his mouth: "Erin! Donna!" There's a laugh to his voice. "Come quick! You gotta see this!"

"JOB WELL DONE. You did good, my man. You may have screwed up, like we all do at some point, but you picked yourself up and finished your life strong. You overcame. You transcended suffering. And you made a difference. You made my life better by knowing you . . . Thank you, my friend . . . Until we meet again . . ."

There's only the slightest breeze to fan the flame in his hand as Josh touches the burning taper to the pyre.

Erin goes next, lighting the opposite side, her lips moving silently. The big blue butterfly that had taken refuge in her cleavage, clinging to her bikini top, is now gone.

Then Donna and Sheila each take their turn, tossing their wicks, mouthing their own goodbyes.

The flames spread quickly across the kerosene-soaked wood, encircling the pyramid's base and rising up its sides in thin, transparent sheets. Josh knows this superficial fire will soon ignite the many fuel-filled balloons placed strategically throughout the structure, so he encourages the others to move away with him.

On top, little moons and stars sparkle orange-red in the dusk. Snaking wisps of fire rise up and dance around Gavin's shrouded form.

A dull explosion goes off from within, then another, followed by a series more. And in less than a minute, there is a roaring inferno, its flames leaping ten, twenty feet into the air, Gavin's body hidden within a swirling tower of fire.

Whoa! This is way more than Josh had expected. The searing heat pushes them back, sends them all running, shouting out in surprise—the dogs barking, joining in.

Josh is awestruck by the blaze. Even from here, he can feel the waves of heat being thrown off. And the sound! Like a howling, crackling, exultant wind. A veritable fountain of glowing red sparks fills the sky: a million fire fairies, too high, too ethereal, to ever touch ground.

A hand on his shoulder. He turns to Erin's beaming face lit by the flames. He bends down and plants a big, wet kiss on her lips.

"That's from Gavin," he says loud enough to be heard over the fire.

"Thanks!" Erin's eyes are wide and bright, like her smile, her pupils huge: an open window to her soul. She gives him a tremendous hug, then pulls away, shouts, "He would have loved this!"

"He *is* loving it!"

"Right! You know he is!"

They stand arm in arm, watching Gavin's body burn, the flames ravenous and higher still.

Josh wonders if the light can be seen by anyone else. He hopes no one calls the fire department or Forest Service. What they're doing is illegal, he's sure, and the last thing they need is for the Law to interfere.

Only the four of them there, all close friends, know that Gavin is dead and gone. To the temporary residents of Fresh Start he was just another patient under special care, rarely seen, and won't be missed.

Tonight, most all the patients are gathered in the Big House for movie night, preceded by a talk from Donna's boss about the social services and resources available to them once they leave the Center. He's sort of "babysitting" this evening.

Mallia, only a few weeks away from graduating from the physician assistant program, is watching over the two newest patients "asleep." She and the few other interns who occasionally cared for Gavin have been told he left for a hospice in Little Rock.

All in all, Gavin's death will go unnoticed and unrecorded by anyone, especially by the authorities, as per his wishes.

It was Gavin's own idea, one Josh hadn't even considered: Upon his death, Josh was to assume Gavin's identity. His driver's license, his New Zealand passport, his credit cards are all Josh's now—not to mention his car and watch and the few clothes he'd brought with him. So, for all intents and purposes, as far as the law is concerned, Josh is now Gavin Oliver Dumbrowski.

He likes his new initials but can see why Gavin had foregone the last name.

There's a bit of a discrepancy between Josh's appearance and that of Gavin's photo IDs; but the beard helps matters some, and he can always wear colored contact lenses or tinted glasses until he's able to get the listed eye color changed from green to gray (a typo originally, he can say). Their height and weight were about the same: he shrank an inch and lost thirty pounds, if ever asked; but he doubts anyone will notice.

Josh's only real worry is being fingerprinted. So that's just something he'll have to do his best to avoid. Plus, there's always DNA testing if it ever comes down to it.

And then there's Frazier. He took Gavin's name and numbers, knowing that Gavin didn't have long to live. If he were to ever compare Josh's face with the man he met in Erin's kitchen . . .

Best to just stay out of the way and under the radar. Indefinitely. Preferably outside the country.

Nothing has changed, really. But Josh couldn't have asked for a better new identity. He's extremely grateful to his old friend. He sends him a big "Thank you" now, as he knows he'll be doing often throughout the years to come.

With any luck, Josh thinks hopefully, he'll have enough money soon to start over again properly somewhere. That is, if the coins are there to be found, if they can get to them in time, and if they're not caught in the process. A lot of *ifs*.

Milo and Jem are out; they can't help. "Growing season" has begun and they can't risk any problems with the law, especially not now; and especially not doing something so outrageously foolhardy. Losing their hard-earned property, they said, wasn't worth *any* amount of money. They think he and Erin are nuts.

So Josh has a problem. And he doesn't particularly like the only solution he can come up with. Nor does Erin. But what other choice do they have?

The day after Erin's return from the cemetery in Charlotte, Josh had dug a "practice" grave. With Gavin's coaching and encouragement from the sidelines (his final day on Earth), it had taken Josh seven hours of nonstop digging to create a hole six feet deep, six feet long, and three feet wide. After the first four feet down, he was exhausted.

Even taking into account all the time and energy he'd spent removing rocks that won't likely be at the gravesite, Josh figures he won't be able to do it in the time they've allotted: 11:00 p.m. to 5:00 a.m. And he hasn't yet factored in the time it will take to find the coins.

He *has* to have help with the digging—someone with real muscle—if they're to have any chance of success. They may just have to put their plan on hold if things don't work out.

Josh would wait to try to find the ideal partner for the venture (if there is such a person) if he wasn't so pressed for time. Frazier could be back any day to check on "Trip" and his presence at the Center. Josh has to leave *soon,* especially now that Gavin is dead.

And especially now that his project is complete. It's time to wrap things up. It's over. There's nothing left to do now but let his guests go free.

Fortunately, he's been able to achieve forgiveness with all of them—for each and every lifetime they've shared where there has been reason to forgive. He's accomplished his goal.

With only one minor exception: Gloria. She refuses to forgive him for his conduct in *this* life. In closing his old accounts, it seems he has opened a new one. He's been struggling to come up with a solution.

Josh knows that by accessing one's subconscious and super-conscious, one essentially bypasses the ego and all of the hang-ups and baggage associated with it—like *pride*. Without pride in the way, it's a fairly easy thing to forgive and to accept forgiveness. So, although it may have been time consuming, it hadn't been difficult, once each person had the opportunity to see the whole picture and understand the complex and often hidden dynamics of the situation from a higher, egoless, perspective, following their death in each life reviewed.

But the waking consciousness has a mind of its own. No matter what one may come to terms with and "think through" subconsciously during hypnosis, the return to the waking state and its human personality can still be fraught with peril if deep-seated, negative attitudes and emotions—like hatred and prejudice, for example—are not dealt with rationally on that same waking level of consciousness. For this reason, hypnosis is not a cure-all.

Much of this "negativity" is simply habit—an *addiction*—being so used to, or dependent upon, a particular attitude or emotion that one is at a loss without it. For instance, no matter how much a person may purport to dislike melodrama and conflict in their life, they still seem to do whatever they can to create it, or foster it, thereby feeding on the flood of emotions—anger, despair, shock, grief, whatever—that comes with it. It's *exciting*, regardless, even if not recognized on a conscious level. Or like stress: despite its many negative consequences—both physical and mental—many people thrive on it, seemingly addicted to the chemical cocktails their nervous system produces in response.

In Gloria's case, though, Josh thinks, it's the feeling of *self-righteousness* she's addicted to. She simply can't admit she's been wrong.

Despite all the evidence, despite having personally revisited dozens of past lives she has lived before, Gloria still flatly refuses to believe in the continuous cycle of death and rebirth. It's like she's wearing a conceptual straightjacket—addicted to her beliefs.

By making the conscious decision to forgive Josh for what he's done in abducting her for a greater purpose, she would be essentially admitting there *is* some validity to his methodology, and would therefore be admitting to at least the possibility—if not the actual truth—of reincarnation and karma.

During her own life-between-lives session, which all four of his guests went through in the end, Gloria had been in direct contact with her superconscious self—her soul—even more so then in other sessions. And in this state, although she didn't condone Josh's behavior, she had at least understood why he did what he did, and had forgiven him for it, completely. So on *that* level they have no problems, which is what's most important anyway. But Josh can't help but worry that Gloria's conscious resentment might fester over the years to the point of eventually creating a "blemish" on her soul, and a new need for revenge, which might force him back into yet another lifetime with her.

But he's done all he can do. It's time to "Let go and let God," as they say.

Thankfully, the others are totally on board, achieving forgiveness in this life as well as the rest. "It's all good," as Harden says now. "No worries." He's become a regular prison monk, as he likes to call himself these days.

Everyone is looking forward to being free again. However, Dani admits to being a little fearful of what awaits her out there; and Josh is sure Santos shares her anxiety. He can't blame them; he feels the same way himself. It'll be a fresh start for them all.

As if reading his thoughts, Erin gives his arm a squeeze and leans into him. "It's all going to work out," she says encouragingly.

He nods and squeezes back, puts on what he hopes is a brave smile.

But she's obviously not convinced. "We don't have to do it, you know. We can live without the money . . . If there is any."

"I know." And he does. "But it would sure make a difference, wouldn't it?"

Erin looks away to where Donna and Sheila stand watching the fire. "Yeah, it sure would," she says at last.

THE PYRE BURNS STEADILY, no longer the explosive conflagration it once was. It still has several hours of life remaining, and still more as an eventual heap of glowing embers. Gavin's once earthly body has become indistinguishable from the coals.

Night has also settled in. A half-full, waning moon hangs idly behind a single slow-moving cloud.

Honey and Pooch, lying to either side of where Josh and Sheila have spread their blankets, both prick their ears to a sound only they can hear. They sit up and incline their noses to the sky.

Josh can see Sheila shares the same sense of anticipation, but he can only shrug in response to her questioning look.

Honey begins it first: a low, keening howl, rising higher in pitch as it goes on and on. Pooch joins her on the second refrain—four in all—both dogs ending on the same beat, as if they'd rehearsed for this moment. Then both simply lie down as before, muzzles on paws, eyebrows jumping, watchful expressions seeing into the night.

Josh had raised dogs for many years before moving from Washington state to Texas, and he's never witnessed a display like this one. It clearly meant something to them. Was this their own send-off for Gavin? What had they sensed, seen?

Sheila whispers in his ear: "Wow."

Her sweet breath on his face, her touch, her sensitivity and caring—her very being: Josh is going to miss her terribly. He would cry now if he hadn't shed all his tears in prison.

How can I leave this?

He keeps telling himself he's doing it for her own good, that it's not fair to her to have to live her life with him always on the run. But if he really does care for her, he thinks, doesn't he at least owe her the truth? Shouldn't he at least explain to her why it is he has to go? . . . And shouldn't he at least allow her to make her own decision about whether she wants to stay with him, or not?

Yes, of course. And if he's to be honest with himself, this is what he is afraid of. She could say no. She would *probably* say no. She might lose all respect for him, knowing what he's done; who he used to be. But, then again, it's respect he has to show her, first and foremost, isn't it? It's respect for the truth he so adamantly avows to serve. He's been a coward for not telling her before now.

Tomorrow. He'll tell her tomorrow.

Or maybe he should wait till next week, until after they return from Charlotte. One coin could change everything. Just one coin could give him and Sheila the chance at a real future together. Maybe.

But is that really what he wants? Does he want that attachment, that dependency, that ball-and-chain? Isn't his freedom from the Wheel more important than a single relationship . . . ?

He pulls the blanket higher to cover Sheila's bared shoulder. He kisses her brow, nuzzles her hair, inhales the scent of her he has so come to love. Sighs.

Could it be love? No. It can't be . . . Not again . . .

No, *never* again. It's a good thing he's leaving. He was just setting himself up for another fall. He couldn't bear another heartbreak like before.

Josh shakes off his sadness, turns his mind to the more pressing business at hand.

Seven more days. So much to do before then.

One last project. Boom or bust.

PART FOUR

Si non caste tamen caute.
(If you can't be good, be careful.)

~ St. Paul

33

"'**BUT, MOM, BILLY WANTS SOME** ice cream, too,' says Sue," says the reading machine in his lap as the wand passes over the book's page.

"Fuck Billy," says Santos. "*I* want some ice cream."

His reading lessons are going well. He hates to admit it, but he's grateful for this time left alone; he wouldn't be caught dead seen doing this by anybody—a grown man using a toy made for kids. But, hey, it works. It's just like having somebody reading to him as he follows along. And lately, Santos has found himself reading out loud without even using the thing. He's figuring this shit out! Soon he'll be reading as good as anybody else.

He'll have to. If he wants to find a job, that is. But what other choice does he have now?

When the numbers went, they *all* did. No matter how hard he tries, Santos can't think of even the first digit in his offshore account. He'd never once thought to write it down; there was no reason to; and it was best that way, in case somebody were to ever find it.

So now all that money is gone. Irrecoverable. There were millions, that much he does remember—along with the bank's name in Antigua, and the name of the woman who used to help him over the phone: Renata. But with a pass-code-protected numbered account, just his claim to the money isn't going to help him. He's screwed, plain and simple.

Santos has already said goodbye to his dreams of a cattle ranch in Argentina, or to any aspirations at all of leading the good life someday.

He can't even think about returning to the Syndicate. What good would he be to them now? He'd be made somebody's front man or money collector. No, not even that—they'd probably transfer him, have him moving drugs like a mule, taking all the risks, expendable now. He's better off on his own, no matter what.

And Consuela and her family? His father-in-law? *Adios amigos.* There is no way he's going back to that house and be subjected to their pity, to their inevitable scorn. Besides, she's probably already gotten a divorce by now and moved on after all this time. He's supposed to be dead, right?

So it's off to work he'll go. Doing what, Santos doesn't know. But he can still make it out there. He's still a smart guy, even without the numbers. He'll find something to do. He's in good health and in better shape now than he's been in twenty years; he can do anything a thirty-year-old can do.

And who knows? Once he learns to read and write good, he may just go back to school. Not *real* school—he's not stupid—something vocational. Become the chef he's always secretly wanted to be. His father had been a chef, or so he was told.

In the meantime, he'll do whatever it takes to get by—dig ditches if he has to. Anything but crime. He's done with that life. It doesn't pay in the end—in the *long* long run. He knows that now.

Santos's near-death experience has changed him forever. He's still deeply affected by it. Not a day goes by where he doesn't think about what he saw and did in the afterlife. He's extremely grateful for the experience, no matter how fucked-up the circumstances. He only wishes he could have stayed longer, experienced even more.

Now it's his life review that plays most often in his mind. All his mistakes, all his regrets: he doesn't want to repeat any of them.

All the good things he's done—too few and far between—were such a pleasure to see again, especially from the other people's points of view. He hopes to add many more positive experiences like those to his résumé. There's still plenty of time left to do so.

The guilt Santos had felt then, reviewing some of the worst things he's done, was enormous. But he's surprised it wasn't the so-called "big" things that troubled him the most. Instead, it was the little things he never gave any thought to, like ignoring a friendly greeting, saying something cruel to an employee, or even just talking unkindly behind somebody's back. All these thoughtless, "inconsequential" instances added up, and pained his soul deeply when seen from the other side.

It makes him wonder how much of what he does on Earth is a result of his worldly personality—his ego—calling the shots, without any consultation with the "man upstairs," his "higher" self. It seems now, in retrospect, having seen his entire life played out before his eyes and visiting his true home, that all the hardest lessons he's learned (or *not* learned, as the case may be) have been because he didn't pay attention to the quiet voice inside him, the constant "witness" who has probably seen the same stupid shit unfold time after time again throughout many lives.

Santos has since pledged to do the best he can to live from the heart—his soul—and not the head. He wonders if poverty will make this any easier or harder to do.

Krunk! Pop! Squeak!

Maybe today is the day he leaves. Rostam had said it would be soon. Santos is looking forward to seeing the world again. With new eyes.

"Hey, man." Rostam brings in the smell of the outdoors along with his folding chair. He's gotten a lot of sun in the week since he last visited. He nods at the Leap Pad device in Santos's lap. "How's it going with that?"

"Good. I love it. I'm knocking 'em out." Santos holds up an accessory book beside him: *Winnie the Pooh*. "I'm gonna jump to the highest level tonight, just to try it. It's like I already know how to read, you know? All I needed was for somebody to show me. Watch!"

He picks a line in the current book at random, and without using the wand, he reads: "My fav—fav-or-ite-it . . . My favor-ite fla-vor is s-t-r-a-wa—Fuck! Hold on . . . Stra-wa-ber-ree—Strawberry!" He reads the whole thing, faster this time: "'My favorite flavor is strawberry, says Sue.' Check it out!" He laughs, knowing that to Rostam it's no big deal.

"All right! Pretty cool, man." Rostam actually looks impressed. "Not bad for—what?—a week? Five days? I knew you'd like it. I saw the ad for that and thought it was a pretty good idea."

"I don't know how the hell they get this thing to work," Santos says, "but it's *fantastico.* It's like magic or something. It's too bad it only works on these books, though, or I could read yours."

"Yeah, no kidding. I think they've even got something different that translates languages that way now, I'm not sure. A lot has changed."

Rostam sets down his chair in the usual spot by the door. Santos hopes this isn't going to be another hypnosis session: they're done with all that. Or so he thought. He appreciates the company, though.

"What's up?" he asks.

Rostam hesitates, shifts in his seat: not the easygoing confidence he usually displays. Something's up.

He better not say—

"You're not going back to the Syndicate, right?"

They've covered this already. "*Si.* I don't need them anymore."

"And you're pretty much done with crime in general, right?"

"Right." *Where is this going?*

Rostam chews on his lip, wrings his hands as if unsure how to proceed. Finally: "But what if it wasn't a crime against anyone? Or not even a crime, really, but only in the eyes of the law, you know what I mean?"

"Like nobody gets hurt."

"Exactly! More like a moral, ethical thing than a criminal one."

Very interesting. "Well, I guess it would depend on what it is, then."

Rostam pauses, clearly thinking to himself.

Santos is going to give him all the time he needs. *This should be good,* he thinks.

At last, Rostam leans forward, elbows on his knees: "Mr. Santos, I've got a proposition for you."

34

DANI'S HAND MOVES SMOOTHLY across the paper, her pen making a faint scratching sound as she fills the page of her journal. She's writing faster than she normally does, in a neat script—more like printing—nothing like her own girlish loops and whorls.

The words are also not her own.

At first she hadn't been aware of what she was doing, until she noticed the different writing style flowing from her pen. *Why, this is strange,* she thought without stopping. She'd been jotting down a few of the day's thoughts on her reading, when the words just suddenly appeared.

When her hand finally stops, poised over the paper, Dani doesn't know what to do. She lays down her pen and stares at what she just wrote:

Hello Dani,

I am your guide and protector. It was a pleasure to meet you the other day. Though, of course, we have known each other forever.

I would like to help you in your earthly life, if you are willing, which I believe you are.

I am available for you anytime. Simply call for me and I will be there, wherever you may be.

Feel free to ask me any question and I will do my best to answer it for you. We can communicate freely here, in your journal.

Let us begin now, shall we?

Dani rereads it several times.

"Is this for real . . . ?"

It has to be; she wrote it herself . . . Didn't she?

·Her "guide and protector," it says, "a pleasure meeting you" . . .

The only "person" it can be, she thinks, is the being of light she was reunited with during her final session with Josh. Not the short session most recently, where they revisited her tragic life in North Carolina again, but the much longer life-between-lives session at the end, after all the others.

Then, Dani had remembered (reexperienced, really) her time in the spirit world before choosing her present life. She'd met her guide, somebody she's known forever and ever, since the Beginning, somebody so close to her that he's aware of *everything* she does—her every *thought*, even—while on Earth. And he hadn't judged her at all (nobody does there, she learned), but only gave her some "coaching" where needed.

She'd never thought for a second they could communicate like this while she is "down here." She's not sure how to go about it.

Dani picks up her pen. And with a sort of curious trepidation, she writes in her usual childish scrawl: *Hello. It is very nice to meet you.* She adds: *again.*

She places the tip of her pen on the paper and waits . . . Nothing happens.

She closes her eyes . . . Still nothing.

"Oh! A question, that's right."

She gives it some thought, but it doesn't take long: *When am I going to leave here?* she writes.

Immediately her hand skips to the next line, and the answer comes in neat print: *Tomorrow. Early in the morning. Prepare yourself.*

"Oh my God!"

Dani hesitates only a second this time: *What am I going to do?*

Again, the answer comes instantly: *You must find others like yourself. They will be your friends. They will help you.*

A feeling of elation washes over her and she laughs out loud. *This is so cool!* It's incredible!

"Friends," she says. That sounds nice. She can definitely use some of those . . . And it looks like she has a good one here with her right now.

She writes, *What is your name?*

You may call me whatever you like.

For some reason, Dani pictures a tall wizard with a long, white beard and colorful robe, although what she recalls from her final session was simply a bright blue ball of light . . . Should she call him Merlin? No, too cliché. But it needs to be something wise-sounding, for sure—like Solomon. No, too "religiousy" . . . Alexander? No . . .

What about "Bob"?

The thought just pops into her head, as (it's funny when you think about it) most thoughts do.

Bob. She likes the name—very unpretentious, and friendly sounding.

May I call you Bob? she writes.

Yes. Thank you. It is a good name, her hand writes again. If it wasn't in such a totally different script, Dani would think she was just talking to herself.

What do you mean by "others like yourself"? she asks. *Who is that?*

Those people who are psychic and who are aware of the greater reality. This is who you are becoming now.

Where are they?

They are everywhere. Their number is always growing.

Dani's a bit disappointed with this response. It's too vague, not really like any help at all. But maybe she's not being specific enough. She tries again:

Where can I find them? Is there any place I should go?

Yes, her guide answers. *Go to the Lily Dale Assembly in Lily Dale, New York. You will find many people like yourself who will help you. You will make many friends there.*

Tears well in her eyes, she is so happy. And so relieved.

Thank you, she writes with a trembling hand. *Thank you so much.*

Dani closes her journal, lays it carefully beside her. A tear rolls down her cheek, unnoticed.

She takes a long, measured look around her tiny room, her eyes coming to rest upon her cherished row of books on the shelf.

"I'm gonna have to take you guys with me."

35

SQUEAK! POP! KLUNK!

Gloria stares at the pile of clothes at the foot of her mattress. It's the same outfit she wore on the day she was abducted.

It still hasn't registered yet; it feels like a dream. She had been sleeping only moments ago, woken by the too-early light and the sound of the doors being opened.

"It's time to go," is all Rostam said. And then he was gone. That's it, nothing more.

She knows she should be ecstatic at the news, but all she feels is a sense of dread.

Where is he taking me? What is he going to do with me?

She can't believe Rostam will simply let her go. Now that he has gotten her "forgiveness," what is to keep him from killing her? Who knows how a madman thinks?

Gloria sits up and reaches for the clothes, pulls them to her.

The blouse is on top, a lovely patterned pink she had worn for the first time that day; it went so well with the suit. Her bra and panties and hose are next. She holds them up; these won't fit her now, she knows, none of it, she's lost so much weight. Then there's the matching skirt and jacket, her slip in between. But where is . . . _Here it is!_ Her beautiful silk scarf is in the pocket.

But what about her purse? Her wallet! Her phone! Her watch and jewelry! She checks the jacket's pockets again but finds nothing else.

Damn him!

Rostam has stolen everything of value, of course. She shouldn't be so surprised.

Furious, Gloria throws back the covers and gets out of bed. She picks up the shoes he left on the floor and sets them on the mattress with the rest.

It's such a nice outfit, she thinks. She'd worn it special for her big meeting that day . . .

The recollection of how she had been duped—of how she had gotten her hopes up only to have them so cruelly dashed—infuriates her all over again, as if it happened yesterday.

"Damn him!" she says.

Damn him to hell! She should have killed Rostam when she had the chance.

Hands clenched into fists, shoulders bunched, arms twitching at the memory of it all, Gloria relives hitting him with the heavy Bible, imagines beating him to death with it this time, kicking him, stomping him to smithereens . . . Then she could have waited for his girlfriend to come looking for him and killed her, too. Instead of being caught like that . . . She hadn't been thinking straight at the time. She panicked. If only she could do it all over again . . .

Gloria ponders the Bible on the shelf, where it has sat untouched since that day. It's not a true Bible, she thinks; it's corrupted with false translations, false words, and she wants nothing more to do with it. But it can still make a good weapon . . .

She'll try to take it with her, use it when she gets the chance.

Having laid out her clothes—such foreign objects to her now!—Gloria washes in the sink. She hurries, not knowing how much time she has left to get ready.

Home! The very idea makes her heart race. Until she remembers that she most likely has no home to go to any longer.

The enormity of the difficulties she will soon be facing (if she really does make it back) hits her like a punch to the gut. Her knees sag and she has to sit sideways on the toilet, rest her head in her hands.

"Oh, Lord, what am I going to do?" she moans.

The church.

Of course. The thought instantly calms her. Her friends will help her. They'll know what to do. They'll help put her life back on track, reunite her with her children.

Oh, how happy she will be to see her kids again! And Dwayne, too, she admits grudgingly, if he hasn't drunk himself to death by now.

Gathering herself, Gloria sees that Rostam has also left the breakfast tray in its usual spot by the door. And something else catches her eye.

Oh! There's her purse. She quickly goes over and looks inside: her wallet, watch, jewelry, phone—everything is there. Even the money.

She checks the phone: it's dead, as she expected it to be, but it's still a disappointment.

Gloria sits at the foot of the bed, opens her wallet to the pictures of her kids. There's Michaela and little Gabe, their happy faces smiling back at her. These would have been taken about two years ago, she reckons. How much different they must look now! Michaela will be almost thirteen, Gabriel eleven. She's missed over sixteen months of their lives!

And Rostam wants her to understand why he did what he did. He wants her forgiveness in *this* life as well. Ha! Never! It wasn't just *her* life he ruined. She'll make him pay for the grief he's caused her babies. She won't rest until she sees him back behind bars, where he belongs. Or dead in the ground.

But that depends on if he really does let her go today. Either way, she may still be able to escape somehow; she almost did it before. She needs to keep her eyes open for the right opportunity. She needs to keep her wits about her, keep up her strength.

Gloria gets her spoon off the shelf and sets the tray of food in her lap. It's the usual: two hard-boiled eggs, some oatmeal, raisins, an orange, and a large blueberry muffin.

My last meal in this God-forsaken place.

The realization makes her anxious to get going. It may be her last meal, period.

She finishes the eggs, oatmeal, and raisins quickly and eats the muffin as she gets dressed. She puts the orange in her purse, saving it for later. She has the feeling this is going to be a very long day.

Anything can happen.

36

IF HE TILTS HIS HEAD BACK, Harden can just make out the step up into the vehicle. It's a van or SUV, he thinks, from the glimpses he got out of the sides of the glasses. The lenses are completely blacked out, rendering him virtually blind. He can see only slivers of light and color around the edges. The frames are tied securely to his head in back; he can't move them, he's tried.

"Watch your step," says Rostam at his elbow, guiding him carefully. Harden reaches his cuffed hands forward as he climbs in and haphazardly grabs on to a seatback in front of him.

Rostam gives him a gentle shove, says, "To your left. There's someone else there, sharing the seat."

He sits clumsily, holding the seatback for support; his thigh bumps the person beside him. "Oh, excuse me."

"Dave, meet Gloria—Gloria, Dave. Though I think you guys already know each other." Rostam seems to be in good humor this morning: there's an animation to his voice. No doubt he is equally glad this is over, finally.

Harden is surprised someone else is present. He's embarrassed at first to be seen in such a condition, but then it occurs to him that she may also be similarly bound. If this is the case, then it proves his long-held suspicion that he was not Rostam's only captive. He had never come right out and asked.

"Hello, Gloria," he says as nonchalantly as he can muster. "Beautiful day for a drive, isn't it?"

He gets an incoherent mumble in response.

Gloria? Who do I know named Gloria? She must work in the courthouse, or be involved with Rostam's case somehow, or— *Aha!* Rostam's defense attorney. Of course. Gloria Thomas.

Wow! So this is who he recognized so many times in previous lives!

Harden hopes they will have the opportunity to discuss her own experience. Has she been here the same amount of time? What does she think of Rostam's "program"? He has so many questions he would like to ask her. Just knowing that another person has shared his ordeal—the same life-changing process— makes him feel even better about the whole thing.

"Excuse me, Dave." Rostam's voice is directly in front of him. "I hate to do this to you, man, but rules are rules." He lifts Harden's wrists and removes the right cuff, then pulls his left hand aside, cuffing him to his neighbor. "There you go."

Their chained hands rest heavily on the seat between them. "Well, I guess we're stuck with each other now, eh, Gloria?"

No response. She seems almost lifeless beside him. Maybe she's sleeping.

After another minute of silence, there is a lilting whistle outside the open door. "Come on, guys! Up, up, up!"

Harden feels the car jostle to the sound of scrambling claws and eager panting. He's assailed with snuffling dog's breath from the row of seats ahead and he has to laugh, pulling his face back from the first curious snout, then two.

Gloria shrieks beside him and pulls away, taking his arm painfully with her. She sets to whimpering pathetically, likely cringing in her place. Harden tugs gently until their cuffed wrists rest once again on the seat between them.

With his free hand, he pets one of the dogs, marveling at its silky coat, its satiny-soft, floppy ears, the surprising strength of its tongue licking his hand—reveling in the experience of contact with another creature. He laughs out loud.

"Hopefully she'll go to sleep soon." Rostam is speaking to someone outside.

Harden can't hear the response, but it is clearly a woman's voice. There's more conversation he can't make out.

Then Rostam again, closer now: "Bye, Dani. I'll miss you. Take good care of yourself, now."

"I will." A different woman's voice, softer, higher pitched. "Thanks, Josh. Thanks for everything. I really mean it."

"I wish there was some way we could keep in touch, but . . . you know."

"Yeah, I know. I understand. I'll be okay, though. I have some-place good to go, I think."

"Good, good. Here . . . It's not much, but it should get you a bus ride to just about anywhere. And a room for a couple a nights . . . I wish I could give you more, but . . ."

"That's all right. Thank you . . . Bye, Josh."

"Bye, Dani."

A lengthy silence follows. Harden can hear only the dogs, shifting around on the seat in front of him.

Is she another captive being set free? he wonders. It sure seems like it.

Then someone is getting into the front passenger seat, by the sound of it: probably her, Woman #2.

Soon Rostam is back: "Take it easy, Dave. I really enjoyed getting to know you better and having the chance to work things out."

"Me too, Josh. I'm glad we're square now." Over the past few months, Harden has come to actually like and respect this guy. "Can't say I'll miss you, though."

Rostam barks a laugh. "I don't blame you!"

"Stay out of trouble."

"I'll do my best. Goodbye, brother."

Harden smiles and waves blindly with his free hand. "See you on the other side."

"You bet . . . Goodbye, Gloria!" Rostam calls out.

"Bye now . . ." She says it so softly Harden doesn't think Rostam could have heard.

Then he must be talking to the dogs: "Okay, you two, take care of mama now. Be good. I'll see you guys later."

The door slides shut.

Another minute goes by, then someone is getting into the driver's seat. "Drive safe," he hears Rostam say. "You too," is the reply: Woman #1.

And then they're moving, traveling over slightly uneven ground. The air coming in through an open window up front is full of the green growth of spring—a woodsy smell. It contains the slightest grit of dust Harden savors in his mouth. Oh, how he would love to *see* all of this after so long! He catches blurs of green and brown and blue through the slits in the sides of the glasses.

Soon, he tells himself. Soon he will be pulling up in a taxi to his home. Soon he will be rolling in the lush, green grass of his lawn and diving into the crystal-clear water of his pool. Soon he will be kissing his beautiful wife, holding his lovely daughter. He shudders in anticipation, a shiver of excitement runs up his spine.

Sixteen and a half months. So, so long. Far too long to be kept locked in a cage.

Harden can't help but shudder in an altogether different way when he thinks of all the poor souls he has sentenced over the years to *ten-times!* that amount of time—and for things of relatively little consequence, like drug possession and theft . . . Perhaps there's something he can do about that now.

Since his own incarceration, Harden has experienced himself as a cop and a criminal, a killer and a saint. He has a good deal of empathy and understanding now for *both* sides of the coin.

He has no idea exactly what he is going to do when he gets home, or if he will even return to the courtroom. But if he does, he vows, it will be to be *smart,* not tough, on crime.

THEY HAVE BEEN DRIVING ALL DAY, with only two stops to use the restroom, and that only by the side of the road, off the main highway. Unfortunately it makes no difference to Gloria, who has wet herself repeatedly. Some of her urine has soiled his slacks, no matter how he's tried to move away. The stench is nauseating, in spite of the open windows.

Although he has been kept plied with water, he's had only a candy bar to eat since breakfast. He's famished.

He's dozing upright when Harden feels them slow again and exit the freeway. Then it's another ten minutes or so of stops, starts, and turns before they park and the engine is shut off.

This feels different than the stops before. He can hear city noises outside.

There's some movement inside the van, the driver's voice speaking softly: "Look out, now . . . Excuse me, Honey . . . Oops!"

And then she is only inches away, it seems: "David? Gloria? How are you guys doing?"

"I'm all right," Harden says. "The wrist is a little sore, though."

There's no answer from Gloria. He's stopped expecting any.

"Gloria?" the woman says louder. "Gloria?"

Still no response.

"David, do me a favor, will you? Give Gloria a shake. No, wait, here, lift your hands; let me get those things off you."

Harden raises his wrist to the top of the seatback in front of him, the dead weight of Gloria's limp arm hanging beneath. The sudden release from his attachment to her is liberation enough. He rubs at the chafing left behind.

Gloria's arm falling seems to have woken her up. Harden can feel her stir beside him. "Wazzit . . . ?" she says groggily.

"All right, listen up," the driver says. "I'm going to let you out in just a second. But please don't try anything funny, because I'll still have the Taser gun pointed at you the whole time, okay?"

"Okay," he says.

"We're at the bus station in Atlanta. You both have enough cash of your own to get tickets to Houston, or wherever else you want to go. If you try to use your credit cards, it'll probably alert the police, I don't know, it's your call. But if it were me, I'd just want to get home first. You know what I mean?"

Harden can only nod. The idea of finally going home is overwhelming. He's afraid he may start to cry.

"Now, David, I'm going to ask you to please take care of Gloria here. Get her on the bus with you, okay?"

"I will."

"Good. Thanks. She's a little out of it right now, but she'll be all right in a few hours or so. You ready?"

Harden nods, filled with anticipation; he feels like a child going on a special trip. He laughs nervously. "I am *so* ready."

"Hold on," she says. Then, apparently to the dogs: "You guys stay put."

The sliding door opens and Harden's nose wrinkles at the wave of exhaust fumes—an extremely foreign (but welcome) odor to him now.

"Come on," the woman calls from outside. "I know it's hard to see, but help Gloria out, too, will you, please?"

Harden slowly and carefully climbs out, pulling Gloria with him. She follows without a sound.

Another voice, Woman #2: "Don't forget the books!"

"Oh yeah."

The two women in front had kept up a constant dialogue during the drive, but Harden wasn't able to hear anything they said over the music on the stereo.

He feels something pressed to him.

"Here you go, David. Josh wanted you to have this. It was supposed to be your book this month; it sort of slipped his mind."

"Thanks," Harden says, meaning it. He wants to say more but chokes up with sudden emotion. He thinks of all the incredible books he's read during his captivity and how they have changed his life. He'll need to replace all those he left behind.

"I think you'll really like it," she says kindly. "I sure did; it's one of my favorites. It's sort of famous in certain circles."

Another book is handed to him. "Please give this one to Gloria, later."

"Of course." He holds both to his chest; tries to smile but is too anxious.

"Okay, good. Now, just move over to your left a little . . ."

Harden bumps into the van.

"Oh! I'm sorry, your *right!* Sheesh! Sorry about that."

He shuffles to the right, holding Gloria by the arm.

"Okaaayy . . . Stop, right there, don't move."

He hears the van's door slide shut.

"All right, you guys are in a safe spot. You can take your glasses off, but give me a minute to drive away first, okay?"

Harden nods, pointlessly; he knows she is already gone.

Another door slams, the engine starts, and with a double tap on the horn, she drives away.

He's able to remove the glasses by inching them up in front and back in turns. He does the same for Gloria, who hasn't said a thing since they left the vehicle. She's obviously been drugged: she has that sleepy, glossy look to her eyes.

They're standing in a covered parking area. It's dusk. Humid. Harden can see the entrance to the bus depot directly across the street from them, moths swarming the bright, overhead lights, people milling about outside.

Did everyone wear such colorful clothing before? he wonders.

Woman #2 is already gone.

Dazed, as if in a dream, Harden reaches for Gloria's hand. She takes it docilely, like a child.

"Come on, Gloria," he says. "Let's go home."

Together they step back into the world.

Wait!

Harden almost forgot the books he'd set on the ground. He goes back alone to pick them up.

They're each the same title: *Ask and It Is Given*.

37

THE EARLY MORNING SUN is straight ahead on the horizon. The highway hums beneath him. It feels so incredibly good to be behind the wheel and on the road again after so long—almost fourteen years.

Josh can't believe how luxurious cars have gotten since the last time he drove. Gavin's Honda seems more like a Mercedes to him. Even Erin's beat-up old pickup had been a big step up from what he was used to before his arrest, simply with the advances in style and technology.

It's not hard for him to stick to the speed limit. Everyone else on the Interstate is practically flying past him on the left. *Christ! What's the hurry?* he thinks. If anything, he has to remember to accelerate every now and again.

Music plays on the stereo—something Gavin had left programmed—a cross between Celtic folk and classical. He likes it a lot.

"Fuck! Can we please change this shit?" Santos has been quiet until now.

"What do you prefer? Heavy metal?"

"Anything but this whiny flute and fiddle crap." Santos turns back to his window, where he's been watching the world go by. "This shit's getting on my nerves."

"All right, let's see what else we've got here . . ." Josh pushes one of the many buttons on the stereo—a marvel to him. A Gregorian chant emits loud and low from the speakers. He turns up the volume, looks over at his passenger and smiles.

"You have *got* to be fucking kidding me."

Button number three produces a mellow jazz tune. Santos stares at the stereo between them for a full minute before nodding his approval.

They've been driving for only an hour so far. *Fifteen more to go.* Josh sighs. It's going to be a long trip.

After a few miles, Santos reaches over and turns down the volume a bit. "I've got a question for you," he says. "What happens if the coins aren't there?"

Josh and Erin had discussed this at length, coming to only one conclusion: "Well, then I guess we're screwed."

"What the fuck am I supposed to do then? You gonna leave me in Charlotte? Put me on a bus to Houston?"

Josh is surprised. "What do you mean? You don't want to go home?"

Santos reclines his seat a few notches, crosses his arms. "That's not an option anymore."

"Oh? Why not?"

"Nothing you need to worry about . . . Let's just say things wouldn't be the same. Not like they used to be."

"You mean the whole giving up the life of crime thing."

"Yeah, that's right." Santos snorts loudly, sits fuming with some inner demons for a while. Then: "You think I have any power with them anymore? Well, I don't. Not now . . . I'm not sure I ever really did."

Josh has to keep his eyes on the road. "Leave, then. Just grab your stuff and go."

Santos gives a bitter laugh. "You don't know what the fuck you're talking about. They *own* me. It's *La Familia.*"

"Don't tell them. Start all over again someplace new. You've got your own money, your credit cards—"

"I've got shit, you dumb-ass! My wife is Consuela Vargas. Daughter of Manuel Francisco Vargas. You know who he is?

He's big—big!—in the Syndicate. You don't think they haven't gone through my bank accounts by now? My property? She'll do anything he tells her to do. They've probably already started looking for her next husband. Shit, they've probably married her off by now. To Ortega, or some other fucking prick."

Josh doesn't know what to say; the guy may be right; Santos knows more about that world than he ever will.

"Besides," Santos goes on, "if I showed up now, they'd just try to get rid of me." He looks out his window, mumbles something like, "Without the numbers . . ."

"What's that?"

"Nothing. Never mind. Forget I said anything, all right? I'll figure something out."

"Well, you've got, like, almost two grand in your wallet. That's a start, at least." Josh has less than a third of that amount. He'd thought about adding Santos's cash to his own for only a second—maybe two.

Santos humphs. "That's nothing," he says and settles into his seat.

They ride on in silence for a while before Santos speaks again: "You're not worried about me jacking you for the coins? If they're there?"

Josh has thought about it, of course; he would be an idiot not to. But the way Santos has clearly changed since his NDE, the way he's gladly cooperated and forgiven all their previous lives together, has given Josh hope. Maybe Santos really is the new man he claims to be.

Even so, Josh isn't going to be taking any chances. He and Erin both will be keeping a watchful eye on their temporary partner in crime.

"I'm not worried," he lies. "Besides, we already know I can kick your ass."

Santos chuckles at this. "Yeah, you got me there . . . Not that I hadn't already fucked *myself* up." After a considerable pause:

"I guess you learned to fight dirty like that in prison, huh? You bulked up, too. You're not the scrawny junkie you used to be."

Josh can't help but take a perverse pride in his hard-earned martial skills. He chides himself for it now.

"What, you knew me?"

"Saw you once, from a distance. Before. Then later, on the news."

"Oh yeah. I forgot about that."

Josh thinks for a moment, looking back, wonders if he even wants to get into this. "Unfortunately, in prison, too many people take kindness for weakness," he says. "I learned that the hard way . . . But I wasn't about to stop being a nice guy, so I had to get tough, too."

From the corner of his eye, he can see Santos nodding his head in appreciation. Or maybe just thinking.

"Here's one that's really been fucking with me," Santos says after a minute. "How'd you know it was me that killed Navarro? I know Dani didn't tell you a goddamn thing . . . Did she?"

"Nope, never said a word, never mentioned your name. She had me convinced she worked for Navarro."

"She did. As his whore."

Josh lets that go. He already knows; he and Dani had talked over everything in depth. "You know who *did* tell me, though?" He's looking forward to the reaction this is going to get. "The guy you sent to kill me, on Coffield."

He lets the silence go on and on. And as he does, Josh remembers the violent episode vividly: the wiry Hispanic kid coming at him in the showers, catching him totally unaware; the shank piercing his side once, twice; catching the third strike with his forearm, closing the gap, kneeing the punk in the groin, dropping him; then, in a rush of fear and rage, pounding the fool's face repeatedly into the cement floor as the onlookers cheered, as both their blood washed down the drain.

He had spent a full day in the infirmary before being sent back to his cell to recuperate. The kid wasn't so fortunate: he was shipped to a medical unit. And he hadn't told Josh a thing; he never had the chance. It was the kid's friend, a fellow gang member, who came to him weeks later with the information: someone named Santos, from Houston, had ordered the hit. It wasn't too difficult to learn more over time: the prison was full of Mexican gangs—and snitches.

"Well, you can't blame me, can you?" Santos says finally, a touch of saccharin, of caution, to his voice now. "You were my one loose end. Besides Dani. And she wasn't about to say shit; I took care of that." He drums his fingers loudly, nervously, on the armrest. "I knew you were telling your side of the story; writing letters to the Court, the papers . . . Somebody might have listened to you one day, put the pieces together."

Josh really can't blame him; he understands. He's already forgiven Santos for everything a long time ago. He'd forgiven everyone involved, years before his escape. It's the "System," the corrupt and uncaring injustice system, he is still having a hard time forgiving—may never forgive, he fears.

"No, no chance of that ever happening," he says. "Once those cuffs are on you—unless you're rich and famous—no one listens to a word you've got to say anymore." He scoffs. "'Innocent until proven guilty' is a myth, a platitude."

Santos looks over. "Nobody's innocent."

THE MILES GO BY, the scenery changing from low-lying mountains to flatland to rolling hills. Jazz is replaced by world beat is replaced by silence.

"There was something like twenty grand missing. You take it?"

"Yep."

"Thought so."

• • •

THEY'RE LEAVING CHATTANOOGA on the long bridge over the Tennessee River, their car's shadow stretching infinitely before them, when Santos says, "What if it didn't work? When you killed me."

Josh looks over, blinks, tries to focus. He'd been lost in thought, in a trance of sorts; he's amazed he's been driving this entire time, as if on autopilot. "Huh?"

Santos's seat is even more reclined than before; his eyes are shut. "What if I didn't come back?"

It takes a moment for Josh to realize what he's talking about. "Uh, it would have ruined the whole project, I suppose . . . No, definitely . . . And we wouldn't be here now, that's for sure; we wouldn't have found out about the coins." He shrugs, gestures to no one but himself. "But it was a risk I had to take. I mean, you weren't cooperating at all. What else was I supposed to do?"

Silence. Then: "Don't worry; I'm not mad at you."

"Ha! You should be grateful. A lot of people would die to have that kind of experience. Literally." He laughs at his pun.

But Santos doesn't seem to have noticed. "I don't feel so bad about all the people I killed, now," he says after a while, his eyes still closed. "Now I know they're in a better place—that I never really killed them at all . . . Did them a favor, actually, if you think about it."

"Yeah, right. Maybe you were *meant* to kill them for some reason. Payback for another life, or something, who knows? . . . But, then again, you could have interfered with their mission, stopped them from completing whatever it was they were set out to do . . . You could have created some seriously bad karma for yourself, man."

Santos has nothing to say to this. "I'm not afraid to die now," he remarks after another long pause.

"Yeah, I know what you mean," Josh says. "When you experience yourself like that—as what you *really* are; so much more than this"—he plucks at his arm—"this *meat suit*—it changes the way you feel about everything."

"I'm kinda looking forward to it."

"Death?"

"Yeah."

"Well . . . first you gotta finish whatever you came here for, you know? Whatever lessons . . . Get your heart and mind right."

"Easier said than done."

"Yeah, no kidding."

Josh watches as a truckload of cattle odoriferously passes by with a muted roar. It's followed by the usual line of passing cars. The passenger in the last one flips him off. Josh waves.

He says, "You know, a wise guy once said, 'My secret is that I don't mind what happens.'" He lets that sink in for a moment. "I think he was talking about forgiveness—about forgiving everything to the point of not being bothered by it anymore . . . I think that's what he meant. I think that's the key."

"Like I said," Santos growls laconically, his eyelids at half-mast, glancing over, "easier said than done."

THE SILENCES BETWEEN THEM have grown more comfortable throughout the day. Josh's thoughts are wandering again when Santos, appearing lost in his own musings out the window, says, "Why didn't I go to Hell? I should have."

"Uh, did you believe in Hell?"

"No, not at all. But I sure as hell didn't believe in Heaven either."

"That's why," Josh explains. "We *create* everything we experience. With our minds—our consciousness. By ourselves or as a group. There and here. Wherever. In the spirit world, whatever we *expect* to see at first, we do. Until we eventually realize it's all just a product of our imagination; and then we can see the Reality behind it all."

"I saw the Pearly Gates," Santos says. "And an angel."

"It's what you expected to see, I guess. Some people see Jesus. Or Muhammad. Or Elvis."

"It was Radha, my teacher."

"That his name?"

"It's a *she*. Or at least to me she is."

"Cool."

Time ticks by along with the miles. It's obvious that Santos finally wants to talk about his near-death experience. But Josh is going to flip the script: act like he doesn't care. He reaches for the stereo.

"Hold on." Santos puts out his hand. "What I don't understand—What I've been trying to wrap my head around since then is—" He looks to Josh, perplexed. "There's no punishment, is there?"

"Nope. Unless you create it for yourself; unless you think it's what you deserve, or something. Guilt or whatever . . . Ultimately, only we judge ourselves. But that's plenty: we're our own worse critics."

"Then what's stopping me from raising hell on Earth? From killing and taking and doing whatever the fuck else I want?" Santos puts his seat up, animated now. "If I'm never going to get punished for anything I do here, why don't I just live it up while I can?"

"You were doing that anyway, weren't you?" Josh points out.

"Because I didn't know any better. And I didn't give a rat's ass. I thought this was the only life you got."

"But you *did* know better, didn't you? On *some* level, at least— your 'conscience' telling you, maybe—ever since you were little; *especially* when you were little—you *knew* you were supposed to be a good person. Am I right? And you knew this instinctively, without anyone having to tell you. Because your soul knew better."

Santos lets out a snort, looks out his window.

"Anyway, now you know that you keep on living, that this life is just one of many," Josh says. "That's why it's so important to learn this stuff. Now you know you're *never* really going to die—you'll still be you, no matter what. And anything and everything you do, or even *think* about, will eventually come back to either bless you or bite you on the ass someday—if not in this lifetime, then in another one down the road."

"Karma," Santos mutters.

"Yep. 'God shall not be mocked; whatsoever a man soweth, that shall he also reap.'"

Santos remains quiet for a long time. "You didn't answer my question," he says at last. "If there's no punishment after death, what's the point of being good while we're alive? Just karma? Just the fear that it's gonna make things worse for you later? . . . What if karma is just some more man-made bullshit you're putting all this importance on? Like you said: you believe in it, so you end up making it true. Maybe if you just stopped believing in karma, you wouldn't have any reasons to come back."

Now it's Josh's turn to sit in silence for a while as he contemplates his answer. He'd once had the same thought himself, many years ago.

"No, I wish it was that easy," he says. "Karma's the rule, whether we like it or not—whether we believe in it or not. It affects everyone the same way: atheists, Muslims, Christians, Jews, Hindus, whatever. They all report the same thing.

"But, anyway, the point isn't to be 'good,'" he goes on, "it's to learn and grow—to *evolve*, spiritually. And being good all the time doesn't let us experience everything there is to learn, you know what I mean?"

"So it's okay to be bad once in a while."

"Yeah, sure, if you don't know any better . . . 'Perhaps some of us have to go through dark and devious ways before we can find the river of peace or the highroad to the soul's destination.'"

"Uh-huh. Well, 'dark and devious ways' never brought me any enlightenment," Santos says. "I had to *die* first for that. I never learned shit being bad but having a good time and getting what I wanted."

"Most of the time, being 'bad' is just being *ignorant*," Josh says. He'd had this same conversation with many of his fellow prisoners over the years, mostly those riddled with guilt for their crimes. "We're not born in 'sin,' but ignorance. We don't know any better because we're so immersed in the physical. We put our egos in charge. But our Higher Self *always* knows better; we're just out of touch with it . . . And in a way—up to a point, at least—we're *supposed* to be out of touch with it while we're here. It's how we learn."

"What are you talking about?"

Josh uses his favorite analogy: "It's like this: Some billionaire, all right? Like Bill Gates. You put him in the slums to find out what it's like to be poor, he's not going to really learn anything. Because, in the back of his mind, he always knows that he can go home to his mansion, or wherever, anytime he wants. You see what I'm saying? . . . But if you took away his *memory*—his true identity—for a while and stuck him there, then he'd *really* experience what poverty was like. He might actually learn about real worry, real fear, real despair. Or real friendship, maybe. He might learn about charity and the gratitude that comes with it, from the *other* side of the fence. Or the feeling of overcoming an 'impossible' challenge. Who knows?"

It's getting late, the sky a dusky purple. They're passing a large sign for a rest stop and a place to eat, up ahead.

"You hungry?"

"Yeah, let's eat, I'm starving. And I gotta take a leak."

Santos seems to be mulling over what Josh has said. As they exit the freeway a mile later, he says, "When we did that life-between thing at the end, and I got to meet my spirit family, or whatever you wanna call them, again . . . it was the same people—'beings,' whatever—I met when I died *this* time and came back." He laughs softly to himself as he remembers. "Both times they gave me a hard time for being such an asshole. But that was for, like, one second; it was nothing, really. And then they just welcomed me home. And showed me love . . . so much love." He shakes his head, unbelieving. "It's like all the bad shit I'd done didn't matter to them, so long as I learned from it."

He turns to Josh with a troubled expression, plainly exasperated. "But that's the thing: I *didn't* learn from it, did I? I came back *again* as a crook. From a booze smuggler to a bookmaker—a fucking gangster both times. How come?"

Josh pulls into a parking space in front of the truck stop's diner. "I don't know, man. You picked this life for a reason, though." Then the obvious occurs to him: "Maybe that's why. You didn't learn enough from the time before, like you said. After all, we keep working at it till we get it right."

He shuts off the engine and leans back, sighs, thankful for the break, for the chance to stretch his legs. He looks over at his passenger, the former violent career criminal who looks genuinely concerned now for the fate of his soul.

"The important thing is will you get it right *this* time?"

Santos stops to contemplate the question as he's getting out of the car, his face dimly lit, half in shadow.

"I don't know," he says finally, shaking his head. He looks Josh dead in the eyes. "Honestly? I seriously fucking doubt it."

38

FREEZE! HANDS IN THE AIR! She would love to do it, but they probably wouldn't appreciate the joke. Especially not right now, with just their heads sticking up above the ground and no way to make a quick escape—trapped in the very hole they've dug for themselves. Besides, she couldn't make her voice deep enough anyway.

Officially, Erin is the lookout. She's to give a shout if anyone comes poking around—maybe intervene if necessary. But it's been hours already and it's plain to see they won't be disturbed. So she's been helping with the grave, hauling out five-gallon buckets not-quite full of dirt on a rope. Her arms ache. And she has blisters on her hands, in spite of the gloves.

Now, though, she's taking a much-deserved break—a couple of minutes, no more. She sits atop a three-foot-square, white marble monument some ways away (the resting place of a Mr. and Mrs. Monaghan, 1823. *Did they die together?*). It has a good view of the entrance, just in case. They'd locked the gate behind them but you never know: someone might notice the new padlock and call the authorities. Better safe than sorry.

Their escape route is on the north side of the cemetery, where they've hacksawed off five of the pointed spikes from the fence. They can use the stepladder to climb over if they need to. Their cars are also parked on the northern side.

Pshht! goes her new can of cola. Erin rarely drinks soft drinks but this is her sixth for the day. She's wired. And strung out. She hadn't slept well the night before, and she's been going hard at it all day. She can use the caffeine and sugar right now, not that her nerves wouldn't keep her up and on edge by themselves, in her state. She drank the first of a case in the car, on the way up from Atlanta. No point in stopping now.

She'd spent over seventeen hours on the road today in a rented van, including three rest stops to eat and to walk and water the dogs. After dropping off her charges, it had been a relatively quick four-hour drive to Charlotte. She made their eleven o'clock rendezvous at the graveyard just in time.

Now she is exhausted, both physically and mentally.

Finally—*finally*—Josh's project is over and those people are out of her life forever. Well . . . almost.

Santos had been clearly shocked to see her when they met tonight. But he recovered quickly enough. She can tell he hasn't forgotten, or forgiven, the devious role she played in getting him nabbed. They greeted each other from a distance, and not once has she let him get too close.

However, he and Josh seem to be on good terms, so she's been doing her best to be friendly.

But Erin still doesn't trust him. And never will, despite Josh's assurances that the man has changed his ways. She believes Santos really did see the Light during his near-death experience, but she doesn't think that by itself is enough to erase a lifetime of mental conditioning. And in Santos's case, it was all bad. She can't match the notorious gangster she met in the club on New Year's Eve a year ago with the veritable saint Josh has been describing to her lately. But perhaps he'll prove himself tonight.

Just to be on the safe side, though, she's packing the Taser in the waistband of her jeans. And if that doesn't work, there's always "Plan B."

The Taser sits right beside her now as she takes her break. It's rubbed a raw spot in her side after all the sweaty work.

The heat wave has continued, even in this part of the country, and all Erin needs tonight is a light blouse—dark, like the rest, to blend into the shadows. A large bandanna covers her hair. She knows her white face probably sticks out like a sore thumb, but she isn't about to blacken it in this heat. Let someone think she's a ghost—a floating head—if they spot a glimpse of her.

Josh and Santos could have safely worn all white, had they chosen to, because now they're both covered from head to toe in dirt. Their eyes are bright in their bearded and begrimed faces, catching and reflecting what little light there is of the nearly-new moon, a sliver, which still casts everything in a muted, spectral white. Erin is surprised at how well she can see by it, even at a slight distance, now that her eyes have adjusted.

She's glad tonight is almost over, too. They've made quick progress and are at least an hour ahead of schedule. They're working steadily, without speaking. Barring the occasional string of obscenities from Santos, she doubts anyone from the sleepy neighborhood surrounding them has heard a sound. From where she sits, she can barely make out the whisper of their shovels.

They should be almost there. The soil is much more moist than they had expected, due to some recent spring rains, and it makes the digging easier. Working together only a couple of feet apart, the men have already dug nearly six feet in less than four hours.

She is just thinking about returning, when there's some commotion, a sharp cry from Santos.

Erin hops down and runs to the grave. When she gets there, Josh is crouched down, holding what looks like a bent stick. It's a rib.

"All right," he says calmly, "let's see what we've got here . . . Erin, lower the light, will you, please."

She obliges, retrieving the large, box-like emergency flash-light from their bag.

Far below the rim of the grave, Josh switches it on to its low-est setting and sets it in the corner. The dark, freshly-dug walls seem to absorb the light, giving the inside of the grave a dim, ethereal glow.

With his hands, Josh digs below him and comes up with an-other rib bone, apparently broken off from one of their shovels. He snaps it like a twig, looks to Santos kneeling in the corner. "We can still use the shovels until we get most of the bones cleared, but we need to be careful. We can't go damaging the coins in any way." He stands up. "Let me switch with you; I'll take that end."

Santos is silent for once. He moves to the foot of the grave and makes the sign of the cross, touching his forehead, heart, and each shoulder in turn.

That's interesting, Erin thinks. He isn't Catholic, is he? It must be a universal gesture now, to ward off evil. Yet another religious superstition based on unnecessary fear.

"Maybe you should use the trowels," she offers, "just to be safe. Everything has probably settled by now; the coins could be mixed in with the bones."

Santos looks up at her with naked animosity. He clearly doesn't appreciate her input.

She meets his belligerent stare. "You okay?"

He nods brusquely and looks away.

"Good idea," Josh says. "We'd better be as careful as we can at this point." He gives her a grin. "You up to hauling some more bucket loads?"

"Sure." Erin smiles back bravely, her palms already aching at the thought.

"Could you get us a couple a bottles of water, too?"

"You got it."

When she gets back, both buckets are already full and the men are busily unearthing pieces of skeleton with their hands.

Erin again hauls up and lowers one bucket after another, taking a few steps either left or right to dump their contents. The ones with mostly bones are lighter, and the rope doesn't hurt her hands as much.

"Don't worry, man, it's just an old version of me," she hears Josh say light-heartedly. "I'm sure he doesn't mind if I don't."

As the buckets come up, Erin has time to examine their contents. The bones are uniformly brown and picked clean by whatever micro- or not-so-microorganisms that do such things. They're hollow, fragile. Touching them doesn't bother her nearly as much as she expected it to. Most she easily recognizes from her anatomy classes, years ago: tibia, fibula, femur, ischium . . . *There's a vertebra . . .*

"Alas, poor Richard. I knew him well, Santos."

To Erin's morbid delight, Josh is kneeling amidst the debris with Whitley's skull held contemplatively in his hand. Santos is definitely not amused.

When she laughs, Josh tosses the skull up to her and she catches it without thinking. Its lower jaw is gone, of course. It has a surprisingly nice row of teeth, only one or two of them missing in back.

"Save that for me, will ya, Erin?"

"What? Are you serious?"

"Sure. How many people do you know who can point to a skull on their desk and say, 'That was once me, in a previous life'? How cool is that?"

She gives an exaggerated shiver. "All right, I'll put it in the bag."

"Wait, hold on." He stands and hands up the lower jaw portion, all its teeth but a molar also intact. "Gotta make it complete, you know."

Erin puts the pieces together, turns the smiling skull to face him. "Joshua Rostam," she moans in her best ghostly voice, "I curse you for a thousand lifetimes for disturbing my grave and stealing my coins."

He laughs. "I'm *liberating* them, buddy. Returning them to their rightful owner. The latest edition of him, at least."

Erin goes to put the skull in the bag, still chuckling at their irreverent antics.

"Hey! Do we have anything to wrap it in?" he calls out from ten feet away. "To protect it?"

Sheesh! "No, I'll just leave it out for you, then," she replies over her shoulder, trying not to be too loud: who knows who could be walking around outside the cemetery at this early hour.

Then they're back at it, working silently as before. And soon Erin hauls up the last bucket of scraps. There are no more bones to be found. They'd also come across a metal belt buckle, half a dozen large buttons, four brass handles to the former casket, and many of what must have once been coffin nails.

But still no coins.

If they're even here.

It's the fear she's been afraid to voice all night. She knows Josh refuses to entertain the idea.

She watches him comb the bottom of the grave with his fingers. "I think we'd better just use our hands from here on out," he says. "Even one scratch could really mess them up—reduce their value." He turns up his face, gives them both an encouraging look.

"Whatever you say, boss."

Santos's tone is friendly enough, but Erin still can't shake the feeling of unease she has about him. Not for the first time (or the hundredth) she wishes they didn't have to involve him in this at all. But what other choice did they have? It was either him or postpone the whole thing indefinitely.

Now, though, seeing how close they may be to finding the coins, she has to admit it was the right decision.

"They've probably settled since they buried him," Josh says. "Remember, it was a puddle of water when you threw them in."

"It wasn't me, it was Burke," Santos says.

"Aw, same thing. You know what I mean."

Josh works his hands into the moist, loamy soil, beginning at the far corner of the grave. They had dug it a little wider and longer than what they figured necessary, just to be sure.

"Where's the ladder?" Santos says gruffly. "I need to take a whiz."

Erin had moved it aside to empty the buckets. She bends down and pushes it to him along the ground. It's only a four-foot stepladder, but it's heavy. "Here you go."

Santos takes it easily and props it against the wall, quickly climbs out.

Erin can hear him watering the grass nearby. She wonders what he would do if he came back to find her down there in his place. She hates the idea of him finding the coins before Josh. But she keeps her distance: she feels safer with Santos below her, in the ground. When he returns, Erin takes her seat at the lip of the grave, closest to Josh.

Josh is digging quickly but carefully, turning up the upper-most six to eight inches of soil. Santos does the same from his end. The minutes tick by slowly as both men inch toward one another on their knees.

"Could they have sunk deeper, somehow?" Erin finally has to ask. Her impatience has grown to match her excitement.

As if in answer, Santos makes a noise of surprise. Eyes wide, he plucks a large coin from the ground and holds it close to his face. The dim light barely reflects off its surface: it's clearly silver, though tarnished a dull gray.

Erin sits amazed, too stunned to speak.

"They're here!" Santos says hoarsely. He flips the coin to Josh, who also appears shocked into silence.

Santos again reaches into the earth, and with an exultant laugh, pulls out another coin. Gold this time.

With a barely contained "Whoop!" Erin jumps up from where she's been anxiously waiting. She does a celebration dance, shaking her hips and pumping her arms in jubilation.

Yes! We're rich! We're rich we're rich we're rich we're rich!

When she returns to the grave, Josh is sitting back on his heels, holding two silver dollars in the palm of one hand, a freshly uncovered gold piece in the other. Santos stands behind him, inspecting his own gold coin, spitting on it to clean it off.

Erin wants to jump in there with them but knows there's no room. "Let me see, let me see, let me see!" she half pleads, half commands, like a child.

Josh looks up and beams at her through his mud-caked beard. "We did it, Erin! We did it!" He has tears in his eyes.

"Here." This from Santos, who is grinning at her altogether differently. He flips the coin to her, high in the air, spinning in the dim moonlight.

She has to take a few steps to catch it with outstretched hands. Its heavy weight surprises her. She turns away from her own shadow to see it better, catches a glimpse of Santos from the corner of her eye.

"No!" she screams, heedless of the noise.

In agonizing slow motion, Erin watches Santos raise the stepladder in an arc above his head, then swing it down with a sickening thud.

Josh! She rushes to the grave, sees him lying crumpled on his side. Santos is raising the ladder yet again.

"No! You'll kill him!"

The face Santos turns to her is twisted full of hate. "That's the idea," he says coldly. But he's stopped, the ladder held shoulder-height.

Erin thinks fast. "What about me?" she cries. "Don't you want *me*? Don't you want to pay me back? Fuck me?" She can see by his sudden change in expression that she's on the right track. "Well, come on then, tough guy! You going to just let me get away? Let's see what—"

She turns to run at the same instant Santos swings the ladder. But she isn't quick enough: it catches her behind the knees, sending her crashing to the ground, on her side.

She's still too close to the grave. Charged with terror and adrenaline, Erin quickly crawls away, feels his hand close around her ankle. She kicks out blindly with her other leg, hears him curse as she pulls her ankle free.

She scrambles forward, reaches for the Taser at her side. But it's not there.

Oh my God! Where is it? Did I drop it? She thinks frantically, recalls her little dance, then: *The monument!* She left it there. *Shit!* There's no way she can get to it in time.

Not daring to waste a second looking behind her, Erin lunges for the bag of gear only a few feet away. She has to get ahold of a weapon of some kind.

But just as she reaches it, Santos catches her leg again. She digs wildly through the bag, taking it with her as he pulls her to him along the ground. Then he's roughly flipping her over.

In her panic, Erin grabs the first thing at hand and swings it at Santos's blackened face. Whatever it is cracks loudly against the side of his head, and with a groan, he falls heavily to the side.

She looks at the object in her hand: Whitley's skull. *Thank God!* It's now missing a few more teeth.

She's up and moving before Santos has a chance to grab her again. She has to get to the Taser. She can make it; it's not far.

There is no way she's going to let that psychotic animal get his hands on her again; it would be his every violent, sexual fantasy come true. And she would suffer horribly for it. If she survived at all.

There it is!

The monument is only thirty feet away, now twenty—she can see the soda can on top—when Santos tackles her from behind. His momentum sends them skidding across the grass, Erin on her stomach, her chin bouncing painfully off the ground.

Before she can catch her breath, Santos has rolled her onto her back, straddled her waist, pinned her arms to her sides. His eyes are wild, crazed. He's breathing heavily.

"Oh, you've got this coming, bitch." He rips off the bandanna covering her hair.

"Wait, wait! Okay!" she gasps. "I'll do it! I won't fight you!" With a supreme effort of will—against her every instinct—she goes limp, unresisting.

It's had the desired effect: confused him just long enough. Time for "Plan B."

Erin screams at the top of her lungs.

Or tries to before Santos's meaty palm cuts her off. She struggles in vain against his powerful grip. Then he has her by the throat, choking her. Now she can't breathe, let alone scream. She claws at his arms, but her nails are cut far too short to do any damage. It feels like she'll soon black out . . . but, then, maybe being unconscious would be the better alternative.

"Nobody can help you now, *senorita*," his filthy face inches from her own. Blood trickles freely from a place above his ear.

With his free hand, Santos rips open her blouse and grabs her breast, hard. He pulls at her bra strap, which won't break but only cuts into her skin. To her instant relief, he releases her throat to use both hands to undo the clasp in front. She's able to take a deep, rasping breath—but that's all.

Santos attacks her bared breasts with his hands and mouth. Erin grabs two fistfuls of his scraggly mane and wrenches his head away, only to be dealt a hammering blow to her solar plexus. It takes her breath away more completely than his choking ever could. She sees nothing but blinking stars on a field of black. She wants to throw up. She would curl into a ball if she was able, the pain is so great.

"You think you have a choice what's gonna happen to you?" he whispers harshly in her ear. He reaches down and grabs her crotch, begins working at the snaps of her jeans.

She can't see him clearly. He's only a dark blur, a crushing weight atop her, an overpowering force of evil she is helpless to fight against.

Well, so much for "Plan B."

She spits at him, showering them both.

Santos grabs her chin. "You think you can treat me like—"

"WROOF! WROOF!"

"Aaargh!"

Santos's weight suddenly shifts and is gone. *Thank God!* Erin can hear him struggling a few feet away.

"Aaah! You fucking mutt! AAAHH!"

"WRUMPF! WRUMPF! WRUMPF!"

Honey!

Erin blinks away the haze, fights back the nausea rising up within her, rolls to her side.

Santos is on the ground, fighting both dogs now. Pooch has his jaws locked around Santos's upper arm, shaking it fiercely. Honey keeps lunging in to bite at his legs, his arms, his face, keeping the man constantly swinging and kicking to fend her off.

Erin musters all her strength and starts to crawl slowly toward the monument. The pain in her gut is immense, debilitating; it's still difficult to breathe.

Behind her, one of the dogs cries out in pain. Then again, weakly. She can't look. She has to get to the Taser. She rises to her feet, staggers and falls, gets up again. She hears more snarling and snapping, more yelling and cursing, another canine yelp of pain.

But she's there! She pulls herself up with effort, sways, grabs the Taser still lying on the marble top.

Yes!

Erin turns and her wrist is caught painfully by Santos, standing there, glowering at her, blood running like a faucet from a nasty bite to his cheek, his shirt bloody and in tatters. He twists the Taser from her hand.

Their eyes lock for a hopeless moment. A quiet sob escapes her.

Then he hits her again in the stomach, and she collapses like a rag doll, her wrist still held aloft in his Herculean grip, her shoulder stretching in its socket.

"Wrumpf!"

Erin raises her head enough to see Honey standing defiantly before them, unsteady on her feet, teeth bared in a snarl.

Oh, Honey, don't! It's too late.

Santos lets go of Erin's arm and she accordions to the ground, doing a face plant in the grass.

"Where the fuck did you come from, dog?" she hears Santos say. "How the fuck did you get in here?"

Honey growls.

"You wanna attack me again, you piece of shit? You wanna save this lady here?"

The Taser goes off like a sizzling cap gun. Honey's howl is pure agony before she finally goes quiet.

They gave their lives for me, Erin thinks.

And in the next instant she is filled with a strength—a power—not her own. Her pain is gone; her despair, her fear are gone. She opens her eyes with total clarity, sees Santos standing beside her.

She acts without hesitation: Lying on her side, she brings both knees to her chest, then kicks out with all her might, connecting with Santos's knee. She can almost feel the ligaments snapping at the impact.

"AAAHH!" Santos screams as he falls. He almost lands on top of her, clutching his knee with both hands. The Taser is nowhere in sight. "Oh, *FUCK!*" he shouts, writhing in pain. "God *damn* it!"

Erin rolls away from him. And with renewed hope for escape, she clambers to her feet.

But as she takes her first stumbling step, Santos catches an ankle and she goes to her hands and knees on the ground. She tries to crawl forward but he pulls hard, laying her flat. She kicks and connects once, twice, three times before he finally manages to capture that leg, too.

Santos pulls her to him slowly, seemingly climbing her, as she struggles futilely, her miraculous burst of energy all but spent.

There's no point in screaming anymore. His hands are at her waist, her shoulders, and then he's forcing her onto her back yet again, absorbing her frenzied blows, until he finally manages to pin her arms above her head.

He lies atop the length of her, his terrible, bearded, bloody face resting on her own, cheek to cheek. His chest heaves and he moans in pain. Erin struggles to breathe under his crushing weight.

They lay like this for an interminable period; and eventually he goes quiet.

But as soon as she thinks he may have passed out, Santos says softly, almost tenderly, "Don't worry, *mi ruca,* I'm not gonna kill you. Not now . . . I'm gonna take you with me. Keep you somewhere safe. For a long, long time . . . Like you and your boyfriend kept me . . . Won't that be nice? You'll like it, I promise you."

Erin is not afraid to die. But she *is* afraid to be tortured at the hands of this beast. Despite her resolve, she breaks down and cries.

"Good, that's good," Santos croons. He kisses her hair, her face. "That's my girl. Just let it all out."

She can't stop crying, no matter how she tries. All hope is gone.

Soon Santos raises up and rolls to the side, releasing his hold on one arm. He trails a finger down her cheek, her neck, her breast. Erin shudders in disgust.

"We have a special connection," he tells her. "We're related, did you know that? You're my sister . . . We're soulmates." He takes her chin and turns her face toward him.

Erin meets the cruel eyes of her killer. She summons the courage to make peace with her death. It can't come too soon.

"Will you forgive me?" Santos says. He holds her gaze, chuckles dryly. "Of course you will . . . Better luck next time, right?"

He sits up and, favoring his knee, cursing under his breath, still gripping her right wrist tightly, he scoots back against the

wall of the monument, rests his head against the marbled stone—
a stark contrast: filthy black on white.

"So much for your luck, huh? You remember?" He smiles
grotesquely, his lips split and swollen, his teeth stained blood
red. "You really had me going there; got me all riled up . . . And
we're gonna finish what you started, believe me, *mamacita*."
He winces and rubs his knee. "But first we're gonna get my
coins."

The flat of the shovel catches Santos square in the face with a
reverberating *CLANG!* Eyes wide in surprise, his nose smashed
to a ruin, it takes a moment before he slumps sideways to the
ground.

Dani stands to the side of the square block, the shovel raised
high for another strike. She waits to see that Santos isn't moving
before lowering it. "I thought he would never get off you," she
says, staring down at his body.

With a cry of relief, Erin pulls her hand away. "I didn't think
you were going to come!"

Dani looks to her. "I was scared," she says simply.

Erin pushes herself away from Santos's unconscious form,
scrabbles back, attempts to wipe the thick layers of now-con-
gealed blood from her face. She stares at the vile creature who
would have surely killed her. Eventually.

"I understand," she says.

Dani helps her to her feet, supports her as she takes a few
tentative steps. Erin presses a hand to her aching stomach; she
hopes there isn't any internal damage.

Oh my God! She grabs Dani by the arm. "Have you seen Josh?
How is he?"

"He's at the bottom of the grave. I don't know, he wasn't
moving."

"We have to help him!"

Halfway to the gravesite, Erin stops. "Wait." She looks back
to where Santos lies. "What about him? What if he wakes up?"

"Hold on," Dani says calmly, already retracing their steps, "I'll take care of it." She swings the shovel up to rest on her shoulder as she goes.

Erin finds Josh sitting crookedly against the far corner of the grave, as if asleep. The ladder is propped up against the side.

"Josh!" she calls out, dropping to her knees.

He starts, dazed. "Huh?"

"Are you all right?"

"Erin . . . ?" He looks up, puts a hand to the back of his head and makes a face. "What—Are you okay? Where's Santos?"

"Uh . . ."

Clang! The sound carries easily. She cocks her head to listen. *Thwack! . . . Thwack! . . . Thwack! . . .* Then silence.

Erin begins to lower herself over the side. "Oh, I think he's gone ahead without us."

PART FIVE

Be confident of this very thing, that He who has begun a good work in you will carry it to completion.

~ Philippians 1:6

39

"COME ON, DAD, IT'S TIME to clear out. Lunch is almost ready." Sean briefly places a hand on Harden's shoulder before he goes. The gesture is appreciated.

Harden begins collecting the papers covering the table, stacks them in various piles. At his feet are scattered half a dozen white, cardboard legal boxes full of such papers: writs, affidavits, depositions, appeals, photographs of evidence, transcripts of trials, letters to the Powers That Be. Even in today's digital age, the legal system is awash in a tsunami of paperwork.

Though far from being finished, he's happy to stop for the day; he has been hard at it all morning.

His son now a safe distance away, the hummingbirds return, darting in and hovering at the feeder under the table's umbrella. It had been Harden's own idea to put it there. After many weeks of tentative forays into his territory, the beautiful, tiny birds have become used to his presence, sometimes alighting briefly on his head and shoulders as he works intently on the cases before him.

He's been spending most of his time outdoors, working diligently at the patio table by the pool or enjoying leisurely walks with Allison around the neighborhood. Since his "incarceration," he has a new appreciation for fresh air, sunshine, and wide open spaces.

Harden has a new appreciation for *everything* in his life now. It's like being born again and seeing the world through fresh eyes.

He isn't drinking anymore, that's for sure, hasn't touched a drop since he's been home, doesn't have it in the house. He had even attended a few AA meetings someone recommended, opting instead, however, to go it alone. He has already come so far and his will is strong. He's a new man in every way.

Harden credits his continued success at sobriety to his meditation. He still meditates every day, for an hour each morning and often at night, before bed. It centers him, focuses him, helps him stay connected to the Higher Self he experienced while in hypnosis. It gives him inspiration and insight into matters of importance. He can't imagine his life without meditation in it now. How much harder it would be! How much harder it *was!*

His wife had been amazed at the changes in him when he came home—is *still* amazed—and not just at the physical ones. Seeing it from her perspective, he would be, too. He simply doesn't think or act the same way anymore. He's more thoughtful now, for one thing, more considerate, more loving.

Allison is at the grill with their daughter-in-law, Stacy, in town with Sean and the baby for a few more days.

Though not allowed to assist in their efforts in any way, Harden did get a peek at the menu earlier: tofu this, tofu that, a whole bushel of grilled vegetables—and a thick, juicy T-bone steak for him, in honor of the day. His nostrils flare, taking in the savory smoke as he walks past, carrying an armload of boxes with his laptop case balanced on top.

"Howdy, ladies. Y'all sure you can't use some help with that?"

His wife waves a dripping basting brush at him. "No! You just git!"

"I like you in my apron," he says to her suggestively with a wink before he goes. "You should wear it more often."

Until today, he hadn't let her or any woman near his grill. But times change. People change.

Allison and Stacy have been clearly enjoying themselves all morning, cooking, talking, fussing with the baby. They seem to genuinely like one another. And Harden has to admit, he likes her, too—left-wing liberalness aside.

Hearing about his newfound interest in metaphysics and parapsychology, she brought with her something to further his studies: *Ramtha: The White Book*—her "graduate work," she calls it. She's an occasional student of the school.

He, Sean, and Stacy have stayed up late each night since they arrived, discussing all he had learned while he was away. They've read some of the same books, the more well-known, and are on the same page, more or less. His son had been intrigued to hear about their many past lives together. He and Stacy both plan to have some regression work done when they return home to L.A.

Harden has tried to convince Sean to stay, to move back to Houston; but they've made a life for themselves in California now, his son says, and that's where they'll remain. However, with their relationship repaired, both men have vowed to visit each other often.

Cutting through the kitchen, Harden rests his load on the counter's edge long enough to snag a big chunk of cucumber salad, then a carrot to carry with him in his teeth. Bowls of salads and trays of hors d'oeuvres line the countertops. The Lansfords and Montgomerys will be coming by later with their broods to eat, swim, and watch a movie.

Why must holidays be the only reason to visit and celebrate each other? he ponders on his way to the den. *Every day should be as special.*

On his desk lies the work cut out for him: hundreds of former cases he oversaw and prosecuted as district attorney, and some more recent ones as district judge. He has amends to make, many wrongs to right—though he knows there are some travesties of justice he won't be able to fix. For some, it is simply too late.

Also, for everyone in Texas, he's going to do whatever it takes to get the state's sentencing guidelines changed. "Five to Life," for example, isn't a guideline, it's a license to punish indiscriminately, to lock anyone up and throw away the key.

Harden is an appeal attorney now: the bane of his existence and "enemy" of his office only a few short years ago. But being on the opposite side of a deliberately unjust system is a challenge he is looking forward to. It will be a difficult yet rewarding career. It's the very least he can do. It's what he *has* to do now. *Pro bono,* or for minimal pay.

He's given it a lot of thought. If they have to sell the house and make some changes to their lifestyle, then so be it, that's what they'll do. It will be good for them to downsize a little.

Surprisingly, Allison has been very supportive of his decision. This might be a good time for her to go back to work, she says. He can tell she's excited; she has already spoken with a realtor.

The woman amazes him. Harden knows how very fortunate he is to have her by his side.

"What's up, Pops?"

"Well, think of an angel!"

"These things are *heavy!*" Allison drops one of his boxes down beside him. "Thought I'd give you a hand."

She drapes her arms around his neck as he takes her waist in his hands, pulls her close, and kisses her precious face.

"It's so good to be home," he murmurs, their foreheads touching.

"It's good to *be* your home."

LATER THAT EVENING, surrounded by friends and family, Harden cringes at the sight of himself on television. In the studio, they had made him wear makeup, despite his protests. But the blue pinstripe does look good on him, he has to say. Hair's perfect. He only wishes now he'd kept the beard.

The Morning Grind, with Charlene Sheara. Deferring to his guests, he's relented to watching his appearance on the program yet again.

On screen, Harden sits beside his fellow "victim" in the ordeal, Gloria Thomas. She looks equally well-dressed and made up, a wig replacing the natty dreads he had last seen her with.

"And you were held for how long?" Charlene asks with practiced concern.

"Sixteen and a half months," Gloria responds quickly, "almost a year and a half."

"That's incredible! And you were all by yourselves, alone, this entire time? You had no contact with each other at all, is that right?"

"Yes, that's right," Gloria says. "I had no idea anyone else was there. For the first twelve months—the first year!—I was totally by myself. Rostam wouldn't even speak to me through the door."

"I can only imagine how afraid you must have been."

"I was terrified!" Gloria is on the edge of her seat, her hands barely contained in her lap. "But I had my faith in Jesus. He sustained me. And he saved me in, the end."

"Judge Harden—"

"'Mister,' please," he interrupts politely. "It's just 'mister' now, thanks."

"Mr. Harden, can you tell us about Rostam's purpose in abducting you? What were his reasons for doing all this? Did he ever say?"

Harden at home tunes out at this point; he's seen it too many times. It's a farce. Ms. Sheara had known the answers to all her questions prior to the interview, of course. There were to be no surprises.

But one: No one on the show had been prepared for Harden's *support* of Rostam's project, for his belief that more people could benefit from such an experience. Most of his thoughts on this and on reincarnation had been edited and removed.

He catches the eye of his daughter, Claire, across the room. She's sitting on the floor, with her niece in her lap. She's had the baby all afternoon; it's his turn. He motions for her to come and relinquish her charge.

"Happy Father's Day, Grandpa," she whispers as she hands over the wide-eyed little bundle of joy, a string of bubbles forming on the infant's lips.

"Do the police have any leads?" asks Charlene on the giant screen that will thankfully soon be playing a movie Harden had missed this past year—one of many.

"The FBI is handling the case because we were taken over state lines," Gloria says. By this point in the interview—much of it never shown—she has scooted perceptibly away from him on the couch, distancing herself from the brainwashed turncoat at her side. "They know we were kept in North Carolina, somewhere near Charlotte. There were dry-cleaning slips from there in our clothes' pockets, and the place has confirmed that they did clean the items. But I probably shouldn't—It's an ongoing case."

"He cleaned your clothes?" Charlene acts surprised.

"Yes. Before he gave them back to us. They were probably in some filthy place the whole time. Honestly, I can't believe we got them back at all. Though he stole my money and jewelry, of course."

Harden doesn't believe Rostam would have done that; nothing of his own was missing, including his cash and Rolex. He should have spoken up at this point, he knows; he should have called her on that. But it wouldn't have done any good anyway. The media wants to focus only on the villains, not the saints.

His phones had started ringing off the hook with requests for interviews after this one, until he finally had the numbers changed. Reporters still get past the gate's security to pester him at home. But the commotion will die down at some point. It always does.

Charlene had directed only one more question to him specifically: "What do you plan to do now, Mr. Harden, now that your life has been spared?"

On the television, it shows a close-up of him giving this a moment's thought. The answer, he recalls, had just come to him: "Keep reading, I suppose, keep meditating, keep learning more. Try to be the best person I can be—without knowing it." He's surprised they left that in.

"Er—What about you, Ms. Thomas?"

The Lansfords and Montgomerys—their own children and grandchildren visiting for the weekend—all congratulate him for his performance on national TV. They had missed the original when it aired last month.

Then, cartoon over, it's blessedly time for the feature film.

Angela coos softly in the crook of his arm, holding tightly to his little finger, staring fixedly into his eyes. It's just an impression, but Harden can sense his own grandfather's presence in her gaze.

"Welcome, little one," he says, acutely aware of the inherited wisdom of her soul. "You need anything in this life—anything at all, I mean it—you can count on me . . . You know this, don't you?"

She makes a face, and his nose is immediately assailed with her answer.

He has to laugh.

40

"'**FINALLY, MY BRETHREN,** be strong in the Lord, and in the power of his might . . . Put on the armour of God, that ye may be able to stand against the wiles of the devil . . . For we wrestle not against flesh and blood, but against principalities, against powers, against the rulers of the darkness of this world, against spiritual wickedness in high places.'"

Gloria sits listening to Reverend Jenkins, not in the choir, where she belongs, but in the pews with the regular folk of the congregation. She misses her lofty view. Maybe she can join them next month, after she's been to a few practices. All but one of the songs she's heard are new. They've moved on without her.

The problem, really, is that she doesn't *feel* like singing right now; she has too much else going on in her life as it is. Being in such demand, being so popular all of a sudden, has its drawbacks.

The interviews alone are taking up all her time, although they're becoming less and less frequent as the weeks go by. The money she's earned from them has been a godsend. Every little bit helps these days.

With *His* help she will be able to purchase a home again some-day. And move out of the cramped, smelly apartment they're in now—although it definitely beats that women's shelter where she was forced to stay, those first few days back in the city.

She can't believe Judge Harden had just dropped her off at the police station like that. They thought she was crazy.

Thank God for her friends in the Church. They were quick to act when they finally learned of her plight—when they finally discovered she was *alive*. And thanks to them, her children had been well taken care of in her absence. Tamara and Rochelle, and even Reverend Jenkins, had fought the State for custody, never letting the kids spend one night in a state-run facility. They were so very fortunate. The Lord had watched over them all.

Gloria opens her purse, takes out a slim notebook and pen, jots a note to herself: a reminder to thank Judge Strickland for her compassion.

Putting the notebook away, she spies the small white box she received in the mail. She hesitates, then quickly makes up her mind: She takes it out and sets it on her lap. Waits.

Michaela gives her a questioning look.

Gloria takes her daughter's hand in hers and holds it tightly against her side. She would have her arms wrapped around both her kids right now if she knew it wouldn't embarrass them. Not a day goes by since her release that she doesn't thank the good Lord for their being reunited.

The children have fared pretty well, considering. Much better than she has herself. Having to change schools has probably been the toughest thing for them—that and thinking their mother had been killed, of course.

She catches Gabe playing with his new phone, one of the many gifts they've received since her kidnapping and return became public knowledge. She nudges him with her elbow and it instantly disappears. There isn't the slightest bit of guilt on his smiling face. She'll have to do something about that.

Gloria has to keep reminding herself that giving is what makes people happy. But there is only so much charity she can take; it's humiliating. During her many interviews, she emphasizes the Church's support and downplays her own situation. Still, the packages and checks keep arriving. Some stranger has even set up a fund for her and the kids; but whether she'll ever see a cent of that money is anyone's guess.

By far the best thing that has come from her sudden notoriety is her new job: Simons, Olivetti, and Burns. Family law. During her training, she is supporting both the divorce and child-support divisions—areas she has personal experience in now.

Using the firm's computer system and national database, Gloria knows she will eventually track down Dwayne and the disability checks he has so cowardly absconded with. To do that to his own children . . . it's criminal. There is a special place in Hell reserved for such reprobates. And addiction is no excuse; she's heard that one too many times already. Every man she has to sue for back child support now has her ex-husband's face for inspiration. She hopes he chokes on his pills, overdoses, winds up in the gutter somewhere.

The police haven't been any help at all in finding him, of course. They don't care one bit. He's one of their own, after all, retired or not. They're probably hiding him, protecting him from her.

Well, they'd better.

And the FBI has been just as useless in finding Rostam. The best they can do is shake down dry-cleaners, test the soil on her shoes . . . Dog hair! How does that help them?

Gloria wishes she could have remembered details of the trip to the bus depot in Atlanta, but she'd been drugged, her mind swept clean. The orange in her purse was tested and found to have been injected with scopolamine, the "Devil's Breath," a terrifying drug from the jungles of Columbia, which renders people zombies. It proves that Rostam's reach stretches even farther than anyone thought.

Only *she* knows how cunning, how diabolical—how mad—he really is.

He had almost broken her, had almost gotten her to believe in the lies he was feeding her—of reincarnation, of "karma." He had come so close to driving her insane with his full-day hypnosis sessions. She's lucky to have any mind left at all, to have any memory of her *real* life, today.

Gloria is still astounded at how clever Rostam was in convincing her she'd lived before as other people. She can still recall exactly what it had felt like to be in those bodies, experiencing everything they did, thinking everything they thought . . . What had almost persuaded her, in the end, was how seemingly *normal* each life was, in spite of whatever drama it contained. And the smallest details . . . things that couldn't have been picked from her brain, pulled from her own memories . . .

Yes, he had almost succeeded in brainwashing her. Almost.

Gloria gives herself a shake. It isn't right to be having such thoughts, especially not in church.

She pats her daughter's hand. Everything is going to be okay.

Many people, including her children, have suggested she see a psychiatrist after all she's been through, go to group counseling maybe. But teaching Bible School again has been the best therapy she can imagine. The familiar lesson plans, the familiar stories, the familiar well-thumbed Bible she's had since law school: even only once a week, they're bringing some sense of normalcy to her life, something to anchor herself to in a stormy sea.

The collection basket is finally making its way around. Gloria had earlier given the kids a few dollars each to put in. It's important for people to see that they're giving back, that they're not shirking their obligations, that they're getting back on their feet, as strong and as capable as before—with or without a man in the house, with or without charity.

She opens the thin, square box in her lap, takes out the folded slip of paper inside, reads it for the last time.

Please forgive me, it says.

She crumples the note in her fist.

When the basket reaches her, Gloria upends the box and the large, shiny coin drops in with a satisfying plop. Then she watches as her son's dollar bills cover it up.

To think that Rostam would try to *bribe* her for her forgiveness! The audacity! The man is shameless. She can honestly say she hadn't once considered it, hadn't once even touched the money he sent her. She wasn't about to sully herself in that way.

And to think she could be bought for a *token!* No matter how antiquated it might be. Was he trying to send her a message? Was he mocking her?

Gloria knows she should have sent the coin to the FBI. But she also knows it would have been pointless. The Church will make much better use of it—purchase some candles, at least. The FBI will have to make do with the box and the padded envelope it came in: registered mail, postmarked Miami.

Miami . . .

The memory comes again, unbidden: She is a conquistador, a knight of the Order of Santiago, under the command of Pedro Melendez, who they must soon find. Their ship landed weeks ago. Now they ford the limitless marshes of southern Florida, in search of Fort San Mateo. Their company is lost, sick, and starving. Men are dying each day, including the precious friars they are charged to deliver. And he will soon follow, without some food, some fresh water.

The armor he wears is unbearably heavy and suffocating in the heat; it slows him down. But he dares not remove it: it is the only protection he has against the savages who inhabit this new land.

The tall grass parts and there one stands now: a woman, virtually naked, dark skinned, muscular. Over her shoulders is slung a small deer, or some other kind of strange, dead animal. Without a word, she drops it heavily to the ground.

Their eyes meet. He stands transfixed, uncertain. He knows he should raise his weapon and fire, yet . . .

Then, with an almost imperceptible nod, she is gone, as if she had never been.

For the next two weeks, their mysterious benefactor leaves them such food when they most need it. Still men die, but not as before.

Others have seen her, too. But only *he* has looked directly into her eyes every time.

In them, Gloria recognizes Rostam—who he was then.

She hadn't relived this life with him under hypnosis. And there are other lifetimes she has been recollecting on her own—where she and Rostam weren't in opposition but had *helped* one another.

As much as she wants to believe that these are nothing more than a "posthypnotic suggestion" planted in her mind by her former captor, Gloria has her doubts. And it's these doubts which plague her when she's left alone with her thoughts.

"'And to you who are troubled, rest with us,'" Reverend Jenkins intones. "'When the Lord Jesus Christ shall be revealed from Heaven with his mighty angels . . . In flaming fire taking vengeance on them that know not God, and that obey not the gospel of our Lord Jesus Christ . . . Who shall be punished with everlasting destruction from the presence of the Lord, and from the glory of his power . . . When he shall come to be glorified in his saints, and to be admired in all of them that believe in that day . . .'"

Gloria believes. Of course she does. She *does* believe in that day. He shall return. And when he does, she will be resurrected and stand by His side. Nothing has changed.

Nothing has changed . . .

"'. . . That the name of our Lord Jesus Christ may be glorified in you, and ye in Him, according to the grace of our Lord Jesus Christ.'"

"Amen! Hallelujah!" Gloria shouts, standing, oblivious to her neighbors, banishing her thoughts, her doubts. "Hallelujah! Praise Jesus!"

And as one they sing.

41

ONE MORE TIME! **BUT FIRST,** a hot dog. With everything.

Dani is soaking wet as she leaves Splash Mountain in search of a concession stand. Every man in the vicinity, it seems, has to eyeball her chest, their heads swiveling as if by some innate programming. Even with a bikini top worn under her shirt, her "girls" must be in stark outline to either side of her bag's strap.

Oh well, let them look; it's harmless enough.

Hot dog in hand, she finds a bench parked mostly in the sun, miraculously empty—probably because everybody else is seeking the shade or air-conditioning in this heat. But Dani is loving the feel of the sun on her skin, already a chestnut brown this summer. She can't get enough of the outdoors after being cooped up inside for so long.

She sets her water bottle on the bench, beside her, to also absorb the sun's rays. Water and sunlight, both so essential to life.

Dani watches the crowds go by as she relishes her meal, spots of mustard ignored on her nose and chin. So many people! She's heard there are even more during the winter months, tourists by the thousands flocking down from the north. She's glad she came when she did, but any time of year would have been just as special. An added bonus will be seeing the super-deluxe fireworks display tomorrow night, put on for the Fourth.

Her new friends couldn't believe she wanted to head to Florida in the middle of summer, and understandably, no one wanted to come with her. Besides, the summer months are the busiest for them up there, seeing visitors from all over the world.

Bob, Dani's guide, had been right: Lily Dale was the perfect place for her to go. She's found more than friends there, she's found her calling in life. Bob has been more than willing to help her contact other spirits with messages for their loved ones still embodied on Earth. While at Lily Dale she has been learning to become a "medium." And she's been learning so much more.

She had come straight from Charlotte on the bus that day. Worried about her future, scared of facing the world on her own, having no idea what she would find, Dani had shown up with nothing but the clothes she wore, a bag of books, and a few old coins.

Thankfully, more than one person there had been "told" she was coming and so were ready to receive her with open arms. It was unbelievable, surreal, and such an incredible blessing that she'd happily cried herself to sleep that first night.

She hadn't really believed either Josh or Erin when they told her how much the coins were worth. But after a week, through the Assembly's own attorney, Dani learned she was now rich. Beyond her wildest dreams. Under proper management, the lawyer assured her, she would never have to worry about money—or her future—ever again.

The first thing she did was lease a cottage at Lily Dale: a place to call home. She's promised to spend every summer working there. But for now, she has some places to visit, some goals to fulfill.

Orlando, Paris, Rome. Bucharest, Romania, the land of her heritage. Her ancestors were gypsies from there, her mother's spirit had imparted before she left for the Light. Her people had been shunned and abused and ridiculed for their beliefs, for what they knew to be true. The ignorant masses had been afraid and called them "witches" who consorted with the Devil. So they were exiled, sent packing all across Europe, retaining their knowledge for centuries until it was finally beaten out of them. Dani wants to pay her respects, walk the same land she's recalled walking on before, in other lifetimes.

She's excited about traveling overseas.

And about having the means to do so.

But the money itself doesn't mean much to her; she knows that what really matters, money can't buy. For her, its best use is helping other people.

One thing she's been able to do so far (though it may not seem like much to somebody on the "outside") is rescue a handful of girls from the street—girls like she once was. She's made special trips into the city with this very goal in mind. And, with their acceptance, has placed them all in rehabilitation centers, paying for a four-month stay. When they're ready to leave, a bus ticket to anywhere in the country will be waiting for them. Along with three thousand dollars.

She plans to do more. But one easy thing she can do now is fund other nonprofit rehab centers and programs for "lost girls." It's something she's been looking into online. Fortunately, there are many good organizations like these being run in every major city, and in some not-so-major places, too.

Another, smaller, thing Dani has been doing—her own, personal "mission from God"—is leaving behind copies of her favorite book wherever she goes. Her bag always contains at least a few. She'd made arrangements with the book's publisher for hundreds of extra copies of *Journey of Souls* to be sent to her in New York. She leaves them in taxis, shops, restaurants, at bus stops, the park, everywhere. She'll leave a couple in her hotel room when she heads to the airport in a few days.

And a crate of books will be waiting for her in Paris, when she lands (the French version, of course).

Finished with her lunch, Dani picks up her water bottle reverently. *The elixir of life!* With a few deep breaths, she centers herself, clears her mind, pictures her friends at Lily Dale, inspiring a feeling of Love. Then, as she's recently learned to do, she sends this loving energy to the water held between her hands. It doesn't take much, only a few minutes of focused intent to make a big difference. But she keeps it up for longer; it feels good to do, and it energizes her as well.

Dani has a new respect for water now. She's learned through reading *The Hidden Messages in Water* and other books (much of it research way over her head) that water is greatly affected by Consciousness, by *thought*. Brackish water, for example, can be made pristine by loving intent alone. Hard to believe, but true; it's been scientifically proven again and again. But at this point in her education, nothing surprises her anymore.

Also, since our *bodies* are made up mostly of water, it doesn't take a scientist to see how thoughts can affect our health. So these days, Dani sends positive thoughts and intentions to her body, as well as to the water she puts into it.

Now, as Dani fills herself with Love, she sends it not only to the water but also to her friends at Lily Dale, to Josh and Erin, to Barry and her "sisters," to the spirit of her mother, to Mariah, and, yes, even to Santos.

She regrets the karma caused by killing him, but not the act himself: the asshole deserved it. And she had to save Erin; it was either her life or his. But in the final analysis, Dani knows, it was murder, plain and simple. He was still alive when she came back to him; she could have tied him up and left him there. But taking off his head had seemed like the right thing to do at the time—the safest course. No doubt she'll be seeing him again, in some shape or form, some other time around, to pay for it.

A shadow passes by in front of her, then another that stops, blocking the sun. She opens her eyes.

A little boy, no more than six or seven, stands looking at her worriedly. "Do you have an aspirin?" he says. "My mom's head hurts."

"Don't, Brandon, come here." The woman reaches blindly for her son. She's taken the seat in the shade to Dani's right. She looks pale and holds a hand to her forehead, her eyes squeezed tightly shut.

"Migraine?" Dani asks.

The woman nods once, teeth clenched in pain.

Dani has to ask: "Can I help? I really think I can; I've done it before."

She's cast a quick, disbelieving glance. "Nothing you can do . . . Need my medication."

"You don't have it?"

"Hotel."

"Oh . . . Here, drink this." Dani hands her the now warm but energized bottle of water.

"Thanks." The woman drinks some of it down, hands the rest to her son. "Don't worry, sweetie, I'll be okay." She closes her eyes again, grimacing.

After a long moment's hesitation, Dani scoots closer. "Let me do this." Without waiting for the poor woman to beg off or relent, she takes her gently by the shoulders and turns her, places her hands at each of the woman's temples from behind. Having "charged" her hands only a short time ago, they still retain a fair amount of energy (loving energy, healing energy, it's all the same), and Dani can feel their higher vibration in relationship to the woman's head.

She closes her eyes and once again summons the familiar, universal feeling of Love, focusing now on the woman at her side, intending to do only what's best, whatever that may be.

After a minute, she becomes aware of the boy; he's standing up on the bench, behind her, watching what she is doing.

"You wanna try?"

He nods uncertainly.

"Okay. Here." Dani moves to the edge of her seat, motions with her head for him to pass behind her. "Get in the middle, okay?"

She lifts one hand for a second as the child steps between them; she encircles him with her arms. "Now put your hands under mine." He does so. "Now close your eyes."

After a while she asks, "You feel that?"

"Yeah, uh-huh . . . What are you doing?" There's an awe, an excitement to his voice.

An enormous amount of positive, healing energy is running through Dani's hands. It's coming from the Source all around them; she's just tapped into it. The process, which began with breath work and visualization, is now operating on intent alone. She could easily keep it up all day.

"I'm sending her a whole lotta love," Dani explains. "You love your mom, right?"

"Uh-huh."

"Good, then you do it, too, and we'll make her all better. Now, keep your eyes closed and take great-big, slow breaths. Send her all the love and happiness you can."

"Okay."

The boy still hasn't moved after five minutes. He hasn't made a sound.

Dani can tell that the woman's body—her head, at least—has begun to resonate at the same high frequency. She knows intuitively that the woman's pain has lessened considerably and will soon be gone.

She carefully takes her hands away.

She leaves them there with a copy of *Journey of Souls* in her place, the colorful "For You! Pass it on!" bookmark sticking out, plain to see. They'll be fine.

Dani blissfully weaves her way through the throng of fellow Mouseketeers, keeping her eyes open for a place to buy another bottle of water. It feels wonderful to have been able to help somebody like that.

Approaching the Magic Castle, she stops in her tracks.

Oh my God! There she is!

Dani just stands and stares dumbly, watching, for the longest time. Then she's digging through her bag.

"Excuse me! Excuse me!" she says, running up to an elderly Japanese couple. *They're good with cameras, right?* "Will you take my picture? Please? Just for a second?"

The man gladly accepts her camera, smiling back at her, happy to be of help. The woman offers to hold the bag for her as well.

"Hi!" Dani exclaims breathlessly a moment later. She doesn't know what else to say. She feels like a little girl again.

"And what's *your* name?" asks Cinderella.

"Dani? Uh, Daniella."

"Oh, that's a beautiful name! Like a princess!"

She can feel herself blush, speechless before her childhood idol.

"Would you like our picture taken together?" Cinderella asks. She raises her arm, smiling brightly, welcoming Dani to her side.

Dani ducks underneath, wraps her arm around Cinderella's waist, beams at the couple holding her camera. Or at least she thinks it's them—she can barely see a thing through her tears.

42

"UH . . . ERIN?"

"Hold on one second." She finishes a last note for the evening shift: a reminder to stop Mr. Fuller's flow of propofol entirely every two hours to check on him. This will bring him out of his sleep temporarily. He's brand new, and as a chronic alcoholic, needs special attention at first.

Mallia is fussing with the stereo again. It's a neat system; it controls up to ten different channels of programming at once. And with eight beds now—eight sets of headphones—that's plenty. But it's been acting funny lately.

"What's up?"

"Did you change the program for Mrs. Huang?" Mallia asks, perplexed.

"Nope."

"I could swear it was on *Claiming Your Self,* but now it's playing *Wave II.* Look." She points to the chart on the wall. "You sure you didn't change it?"

"Positive." Programs have been mysteriously changing by themselves a lot this past week. Erin whistles eerily. "Maybe we have a ghost."

"You don't think . . ." Mallia waves her hand, taking in the sleeping figures along both walls.

Erin shrugs. "Could be. I've heard that only ghosts can control electronic devices, but, then again, being out-of-body is a little like being a ghost, isn't it? Aren't both in the astral plane? Or is it the ethereal? . . . I'll have to ask Josh."

"Oh . . . Well, then, should I change it back?"

"Nah, let them have their fun. They know best anyway. And if it *is* a ghost, maybe they're communicating with it somehow. Maybe it's trying to help things . . . Or maybe it's just being a butt."

Mallia shudders. "Scary thought."

"Why? Ghosts are still just people, right?" Erin pats her on the shoulder as she goes. "I'm going to go check on the progress upstairs. They're supposed to be through sometime today."

"Okay. Will you tell Conner to come here, if you see him?"

"Will do."

Conner is one of the many new interns. Thankfully, Erin had been able to talk Mallia into staying on full time as her chief assistant and Fresh Start's new Admissions Director—with a fat salary to go along with the title, of course. She's taken on much of the new-patient workload.

Outside the "Sleep Chamber," Erin is met with the hustle and bustle of various work crews and delivery persons. Since the sale of her coins, it's been nothing but non-stop action and progress around the property. She is finally creating the Dream Center she has always wanted.

She and Josh had gone their separate ways, leaving Charlotte. He took both their coins to a numismatist—a rare coin dealer— in New Orleans.

Her three silver dollars, being in such excellent condition (preserved like new), had sold quickly, for even more than she hoped. The gold pieces had taken a little longer to sell, but the wait was well worth it: The Eagle alone brought her $245,000—a new record for that coin. The money had been wired to her account in Eureka Springs.

Needless to say, Worthing about shit his pants. All her outstanding loans and debts were paid in full. And Jake at the hardware store had received a special bonus: dinner and a great big hug and kiss in appreciation. Following that, Erin had transferred all her funds to Mrs. Gardner's bank at First Security.

It's a funny thing: now that she has all the money she could ever need, everyone wants to lend her more.

Erin makes her way upstairs. The second floor of the Big House is nearly finished. They'll soon have room for thirty-three guests altogether. More than half of the new rooms are already occupied. And once the pool and bath house are completed next month, people won't have to stand in such long lines for the showers anymore.

Everything should be ready by mid-October, just in time for this year's Halloween party, to celebrate.

On the landing, she almost collides with two men carrying down a long roll of carpet. "Coming through, boss!" hollers the one closest, walking backward down the steps. Erin recognizes Keith, one of her many patients pitching in to help, as usual. Behind them she spots another pair of workers with a similar load.

"Yikes!" she says, retreating. "You guys done already?"

"With this part of it," says the contractor at the other end. "Nothing but the tile to finish now. We should be outta here early afternoon tomorrow."

She's waiting at the bottom of the stairs, out of harm's way, when someone tugs at her sleeve. It's Marilyn, Fresh Start's new Assistant Chef, a septuagenarian dynamo with more energy than anyone Erin has ever met. She's "assistant" in name only.

"Erin, now, I know you asked for only one Boston cream pie for this evening, but Lawrence wanted me to tell you that we've gone ahead and made more for everybody. Is that all right? Good. Now, is it still dinner for two? At eight? Right, don't worry, I haven't told a soul. And we just got in those delicious mushrooms from the neighbors (and a special package for you) so we'll be having those with dinner tonight. Lunch should be ready in about twenty minutes. Would you like to eat with everybody else or at home? I've set up the usual spread for the workers, and some of them are already eating. It's turkey and avocado sandwiches today, nothing special, but there's a really nice pasta salad to go with it I think you'll like—sun-dried tomatoes, lots of basil. You'll love it."

Erin's a bit dazed and it takes her a moment to realize it's her turn to speak. "Can I get a little picnic lunch packed up? If it's not too much trouble?" The idea just came to her. It would be nice to get away for a little while, maybe visit Gavin's meadow.

Marilyn gives her a knowing look. "For two?"

"Uh-huh."

"Excuse me, Erin. Hey there, Marilyn." It's Marcelo Cruz, the elderly contractor in charge of refurbishing the Shed. It's being turned into a meditation and yoga studio. "Ma'am, it's what we talked about before. The truck delivering the flooring this time is too tall for the branches crossing the road. I know you don't want to cut them. May I borrow your truck again, please?"

"Of course, Marcelo. Do you remember where I keep the keys?"

He laughs. "Yes, ma'am, in the ignition." He gives Marilyn a sly wink and a smile. "See you later?"

Erin watches the woman blush to her roots. *Ah, could this be another budding, summer romance?*

But Marilyn pretends to ignore him. "Now, don't you worry about a thing," she tells Erin. "I'll have that ready for you in no time, with maybe a little something extra to go with it. Where will you be? Outside? Good, I'll find you in a jiffy." She's unable to hide her smile as she bats away Marcelo's hand making a grab for her before he goes.

Love is in the air indeed.

Now she had better find Donna, see if she's free for lunch.

On the way out, Erin spies Conner talking to a patient by the library wall—a very *pretty* patient, she notices. "Hey, Conner.

Mallia's looking for you. She wants you with the newbies when you get a chance."

He, too, has that certain twinkle in his eye. "Oh, okay." He smiles bashfully and holds up a book: *Autobiography of a Yogi*. "I was just telling Nichole about how one of the Beatles used to keep a stack of this one at home to give to people, to boost them up. Have you read it?"

Erin smiles at them both. Nichole looks like a totally different person than the strung-out waif she'd been when she first arrived. "That's George Harrison who did that. And yes, I've read every title here, and then some. The library's namesake was my mentor, so to speak. My friend."

The placard prominently displayed reads: TRIP'S MEMORIAL LIBRARY. Multiple titles from Josh's "required reading" list are here for patients to check out. It had been Donna's idea, done in honor of both Josh and Gavin, the Center's two Trips—one at least for a time in the eyes of the law.

Frazier the Fed had commented on it during his surprise visit in June. Erin gave him a copy of her favorite book, *The Seat of the Soul,* as a "go away" present. But he really wasn't such a bad guy: he'd given "Trip" plenty of extra time to pass on, and he was sincerely happy for her sudden success.

Erin had told Donna everything, shortly after her return from Charlotte—as soon as Milo and Jem had finished removing the storage containers, as soon as all traces of Josh and his guests had disappeared. Now that it's finally over, she figured it was safe to share the whole story—not knowing, of course, how Donna would react.

Fortunately, her girlfriend has a very open mind and a high tolerance for stupidity. Donna had known something was bothering her for quite a while but just associated it with her financial troubles and worry over losing the Center—which *were* factors, certainly.

Erin knows she hasn't been the best of company this past year, and she intends to more than make up for it in the future.

Outside, the courtyard is just as busy.

The new garage building, extending deep into the trees, is getting the final preparations made to its large, flat roof—eventually to be turned into an expansive herb and vegetable garden accessed by stairs. All that remains of the old garage is the north wall, out of respect for the family of bats still living there. Carpenters have propped it up and built around it, creating a deluxe bat house—bat *mansion,* more like. Their flying friends don't seem to have minded one bit.

Her own home is also getting a much needed makeover. Most of the work is going on inside, but the scaffolding set up around the perimeter makes the place look like a major construction zone. She'll be glad when it's all over at the end of the summer, only weeks away now.

Pooch sees her and comes bounding over from his place in the shade under the veranda. He's taken over the raccoon's old hideout, all the noise and commotion lately being too much for them apparently. Pooch still limps since his casts were removed, and he may just have a slight limp forever; but he's got all of his old energy and zest for life back, thankfully.

Erin does her best to spoil the both of them now, even more so than before.

Honey is in her usual spot on the front porch. She lifts her head in Erin's direction but is enjoying her massage way too much to bother coming over.

Donna sits in the rocker, a tall drink in her hand, working her bare toes into the dog's shiny, golden fur. Occupying the chairs to either side are a couple of their younger patients, both talking animatedly over one another. Two large coolers of iced tea are on the rail, along with a line of cups for the many workers. Fresh Start's new Director of Psychology looks over and waves cheerfully. Erin's heart leaps and she waves back.

"Come on, Pooch," she says, bending down, kissing his grinning face. "Let's see if mama Donna wants to go for a walk."

Erin is really looking forward to their private dinner tonight. She's thirty-five years old today. She's thinking maybe it's time to settle down.

The diamond has been burning a hole in her pocket all week.

43

"THANKS FOR YOUR HELP, Nate. 'Preciate ya."

Josh hoists the heavy bag of groceries: a few last minute items. How could he have forgotten *chocolate?* He's purchased every candy bar in the marina store. Who knows when they'll find another supply? Nathan has called ahead to Key West for him, asked the store there to have at least a dozen cases of Hershey's Kisses ready to go.

He wonders what else he's forgotten in all the excitement. Things can be shipped to them if needed, he supposes, even if it's to Tahiti or Bora Bora.

Josh can't help himself: he does a little jig in front of the store, kicks up his heels.

Today's the big day! Sailing off into the sunset!

How many years had he dreamed of doing exactly this some-day? From his dark, dank prison cell in Texas, it had seemed like an impossible fantasy. Now he's about to live it.

He's read a lot about sailing, but that's a far cry from actually *doing* it. And these past few months have proven just how nautically challenged he really is. Fortunately, however, there has been no shortage of fellow boat lovers willing to lend him a hand. The sailing community here had readily adopted him when he arrived.

And Josh has had no shortage of people willing to act as crew on his maiden voyage.

He's real happy to have found such a great couple as Brian and Leanne. Both youngsters have sailed all their lives. But mostly they're just a pleasure to have around. With such positive, easy-going attitudes, they should make ideal traveling companions.

They've agreed to come along and show him the ropes until the end of March, three months away, and then he's on his own. Following a lazy stroll around the Caribbean, it'll be through the Panama Canal and on to Hawaii.

Around the world, or bust!

With the sun on his face, a fresh breeze in his hair, and his bag full of candy, Josh makes his way down the dock. He smiles to himself. Laughs out loud. He can't believe how his fortune has changed.

What they received for the coins went way beyond any expectations.

They'd divided up the coins between the three of them: each getting three silver dollars, one gold Eagle, and one Half-eagle. Josh had kept the extra, "funny looking" gold piece for himself.

And it was this one that had made all the difference.

"Brasher doubloons" they are called. Only five were known to still exist. His was dated 1787 and was in very good condition, only slightly used. On a scale of 0 to 70, as used in investment coin grading, it rated a 50—an impressive value. Also, every Brasher has the distinctive hallmark punch of Ephraim Brasher's initials; but only his had it on the eagle's breast, rather than the usual left wing. And it was for this reason the coin had finally sold in September to a Wall Street investment firm for 7.4 million dollars.

Josh had been tempted to deliver Erin's half of the money to her in person, just to see the look on her face; but wisdom prevailed: he simply wired it to her new account.

Followed by an encrypted e-mail. They've been able to keep in touch regularly this way, which is nice, but he misses her. And Donna. He's looking forward to seeing both of them in Hawaii, for their honeymoon.

One day he hopes to revisit Fresh Start and see for himself all of the changes he's heard about. But for now he'll have to settle for the occasional update. He'd laughed himself silly hearing about Worthing "falling" into the pool on Halloween. It's amazing what you can teach a dog to do.

With the satellite equipment and single-sideband radio recently installed on board, Josh should be able to communicate with Erin and the rest of the world from anywhere, even from far out at sea. It will be essential in running his organization:

The TRUTH Foundation—Teaching Reincarnation as a Universal Truth for Humanity—established to rectify the damage done by the Church over the past seventeen hundred-plus years—not to mention by Science, which has practically become a religion unto itself.

The main goal of the Foundation is to increase public awareness. And one way to do that will be to distribute the best books on the subject (sifted from all the nuttiness out there) to public libraries everywhere, including those in schools and in prisons. Another will be to establish college-level courses—Reincarnation 101—at various schools around the globe.

There is already an overwhelming amount of evidence (if not verifiable proof) that reincarnation is a reality, contained in a large number of books; and he plans to use some of these in his courses. But Josh would also like to see more comprehensive textbooks devoted to the subject, like those by Cranston. He plans on contacting many of the leading researchers in the field to put one together. He's already begun work penning the introduction himself.

"Hey there, Tripster!"

"Hiya, Benji!" He waves to the salty dog sanding the rails of his vintage Grand Banks. The old man has lived aboard the same boat for decades, but *Smilin' Eyes* rarely leaves her slip. The few times he's ventured out, he said, it's been only to upgrade to a better marina. And now that he's here, he's not going anywhere.

For Benjamin, it's enough to simply live on the water, messing about in his boat.

He's the marina's resident brightwork expert. Anyone who wants a lesson only has to visit on any sunny day, when he's out varnishing, sanding, then re-varnishing his teak.

Josh is surprised any wood remains. He doesn't understand it. He may be an expert on the universal laws of karma and reincarnation, but he's still clueless when it comes to human nature. Take Santos, for instance: a perfect example. The gangster had completely fooled him into thinking he'd changed after his NDE. Or maybe he honestly had, and something in him just snapped when he saw the coins, made him revert to his old ways of thinking, "addicted" to that criminal mentality.

But it would be naïve to think that was true. Santos had probably schemed to take all of the coins for himself when he first heard of the plan. He was a bad character, that's all there is to it. Bad to the bone. And one out-of-body experience—no matter how profound—wasn't going to change that.

Josh has kicked himself repeatedly after that night. Santos's attitude had been made all too clear: With no punishment in Heaven, why behave on Earth?

Well, he'll learn, eventually. That's what spiritual evolution is all about. Free will. Choices. Cause and effect. And Santos *did* pay for his actions, didn't he? And he'll continue paying in other lifetimes till he gets it right.

At least he probably wasn't as surprised when he died this time. He probably went straight home. With less baggage, maybe. Hopefully.

Josh knows their work together was productive, but he can't help but wonder if his project was ultimately successful in the end. He feels pretty confident that he managed to visit every negative lifetime they all shared, and obtain complete forgiveness for each one. But still . . .

There shouldn't be any problem with Santos: it wasn't Josh who killed him this time. And he'd left things on pretty good terms with both Harden and Dani.

It's Gloria who worries him. He hopes the silver dollar he sent eases some of the suffering he's caused her. But will she hold a grudge? Will she make him come back again someday?

He'll just have to leave it in the hands of the Lords of Karma. He's tried his best, and that's all he can do.

As he approaches the end of the dock, Josh can finally make out his own boat's mast from the vast array of sticks moored around it. The way it tapers and curves makes it look like the boat is already racing in the wind.

There she is, at the end: a fifty-eight-foot custom catamaran, a former charter boat, only slightly used, now outfitted for some serious offshore cruising. *Incognito* freshly lettered on her stern.

It looks like Brian has just finished cleaning the hulls; his scuba gear lies in a puddle on the dock and he stands dripping in his trunks, inspecting something in his hands. Leanne is making other preparations for their departure, coiling the length of thick, yellow cable supplying them with power while ashore. They'll soon be relying solely on their batteries, and the wind generator and solar panels to charge them.

It's like living in a cabin on the ocean, Josh thinks merrily. *A very well-appointed cabin, if I do say so myself.*

"Ahoy, Admiral!" Brian calls out. He smiles and waves, holds up the pieces of decayed metal in his hand. "Replaced the zincs."

"Good thinking. Now, avast, ye maties!" Josh bawls loudly in his best Captain Ahab. "Batten the hatches! Man the sails! Shiver me timbers! Let's get this floatation device moving!"

"Aha! Thar he blows!"

Sheila appears at the rail above him. The sight of her in a sarong and bikini top still takes his breath away. He's going to love this new lifestyle.

"What took you so long?" she asks. "We were about to send out the Coast Guard looking for you."

"Leave without my Snickers? Are you *mad,* woman?" He hands up the sack.

"Oh my God! Did you buy out the entire store?"

"Just the candy aisle. And I got your favorites, look! Twizzlers! And Starburst! Look inside!"

"You're incorrigible," she says, turning to go back in.

"Yeah, whatever *that* means."

Even without the money now, Josh would still be the wealthiest man on Earth with Sheila by his side.

She hadn't batted an eye when he told her about prison, or about his escape, or even about his project. She already knew most of it; she'd recognized the man behind the scruffy beard soon after they met: his face had been all over the news for weeks, only a few months before. She also recognized his tattoos for what they were, where they came from. Besides, she said, any man with such an insatiable appetite for touch—not sex, but simply touch—had to have either come from prison or a cave in the Himalayas.

Like him, Sheila hadn't been looking for a relationship, outside a business one. But, as she put it, there's no denying fate. She believes they were *destined* to be together, that it's written in the stars.

Josh doesn't share her belief in astrology (he thinks it's ridiculous, actually, though he keeps that opinion to himself), but he knows all about Universal Will working in conjunction with their own. Unseen forces are at work in people's lives, whether they like it or not. And he appreciates that fact.

"Thank you," he says meaningfully to no one in particular.

"What's that?" Leanne moves by him up the makeshift wooden stairs to the boat's deck. She has the extension cord in its bag, ready to be stowed.

Josh holds up a finger. "'If the only prayer you say in your life is "Thank you," that will suffice.'"

"Who said that?" Brian is there with the scuba gear; he hands up the dive bag to his wife.

"Meister Eckhart, a famous Christian mystic of his time, like Teresa of Avila. Like all mystics, they sought personal experience with the Divine, one way or another, rather than just taking someone else's word for it."

"Like us," Leanne says brightly.

Both his crewmates had undergone a lengthy life-between-lives session about a month ago.

"Pretty much," Josh says. "But your experiences were more controlled, and much more thorough. Theirs were usually fleeting and unexpected, usually the result of intense prayer or meditation. They really didn't know what to make of them, or how to explain it." He grabs the scuba tank and heads up the stairs. "Most people just thought they were nuts."

Brian says, "Yeah, well, until the other day, I probably would have thought the same thing."

"Not me," Leanne says. "I spoke to fairies when I was little, so I know anything is possible."

Josh looks to Brian, who just shrugs and smiles.

Fifteen minutes later, they're ready to go.

Brian has expertly untied the bow and stern lines and tossed them aboard. Only the spring lines, coming together at one point in the middle of the dock, now hold the boat to shore. He looks up at Josh: "You ready to shove off, cap'n?"

"We all set?"

"Aye-aye. Everything's shipshape."

From his elevated position on deck, Josh takes a look around the slip, takes a last look at the marina he's come to love. Everything looks good. They'll be leaving the wooden steps behind. There's nothing left to be done.

"Well, before we do anything," he says, "let's get the *real* captain up here."

Sheila is downstairs in the starboard hull, *their* side of the boat for now. She's in the library, securing a row of books with a thin bungee cord. It's just another thing he loves about her: she's as much of an avid reader as he is, her mind as wonderful as the rest.

"The crowds are waiting outside to wish us *bon voyage*," he says.

She acts like she hasn't heard. She walks past and closes the door he just entered, locks it, and turns, eyes him seductively as her sarong slips like silk to the cabin floor.

"What's the rush?"

ORION, THE "HUNTER," hangs due south, moving imperceptibly westward across the sky. That must be Aldebaran glowing orange-red above and to the right, the Pleiades beside it. Soon Sirius, the "dog star," the brightest of them all, should be coming over the horizon to the southeast. That's the direction they need to head. Celestial navigation: in spite of all the high-tech equipment on board, Josh is determined to reach Antigua the old-fashioned way. If his calculations are right, they should be in St. John's just in time for Brian and Leanne to fly home, with plenty of leisurely stops along the way.

Why Santos would volunteer his new pass codes while under hypnosis is still a mystery. Maybe it was a guilty subconscious. Maybe it was prescience, a precognition, that he would no longer be around to spend the money. Whatever the reason, Josh is grateful. However much is there should buy a lot of books for a lot of people.

They left Key West an hour ago, one minute into the New Year. Now the moon lights their way, casting its soft white radiance across the rolling, quicksilver waves and expansive deck that will be his home for many years to come.

He's at the wheel in the pilothouse. Only a dim, red light illuminates the chart table, the radar screen the only other thing on inside: no big ships in their path, smooth sailing ahead.

The lovely sound of Leanne singing comes in through the open hatch above him, floating on the same gentle wind filling their sails. Now Sheila's laughter, even more beautiful music to his ears.

He can see them at the bow: Sheila lounging with some pillows in the netting, a drink in her hand; Leanne sitting with her legs crossed on the catwalk, casually strumming her guitar; Brian lying on his stomach with his head out between the anchors, watching the twin hulls slice through the water, where dolphins had been playing earlier in the day.

He'll join them soon enough; but for now, Josh is enjoying this quiet time alone. He needs to wait for Sirius to show him the way. Plus, he's had something of an epiphany and is still mulling it over.

He had been so worried about falling in love again. But he was wrong. Love—romantic love, that is—isn't something to be avoided or feared, he realizes now, even when it causes such pain and heartache as he'd felt as a young man. It's not an "attachment" or a desire to steel oneself against, practicing needless self-control. It's not frivolous or unnecessary. Instead, it's something we're here on Earth to experience, to enjoy, to learn.

Life is a school, and love is the lesson.

Gavin had been right: there are lots of different kinds of love. And romantic love is really no less important than love for humanity, or for one's friends and family, or for nature, or for art or music—or for God.

But *real* love, regardless, is unconditional: it doesn't require someone to love us back; it doesn't require anything, period. There's no reliance or dependency involved, no "addiction," no obligation, no control. There's nothing to be afraid of.

And there's no reason for it to draw us back to Earth, unless . . .

Of course . . .

It's what he's known all along: love is simply our nature as spiritual beings; it's what we are *supposed* to do. And what better place—what better opportunity—is there to express love in so many different ways? Where else is it more *needed* than here?

As Josh ponders this, an idea strikes him:

Maybe he's been thinking about all this the wrong way. Maybe he's been putting too much importance on the wrong thing. Maybe coming back isn't supposed to be about resolving his karmic issues . . .

Maybe it isn't about himself at all . . .

Whoa . . .

It's as if a light goes off in his head, and Josh can see everything clearly for the first time:

"Graduating" earthly existence isn't about escaping the Wheel. It's about discovering the true reason we're here and then *living up to that truth*. It's about choosing to come back, not for ourselves, but to dedicate our lives to selfless service to others—to loving others.

He's shaking his head, laughing to himself—*at* himself. *Now* he gets it!

He blinks, focuses. There's Sirius, shining brightly, already well above the horizon.

Oh, shit.

Josh makes the necessary correction, pointing the bow at where the star most likely made its appearance. He ties off the wheel to keep the boat on course (he's not using the autopilot either; it's all connected). Now it's just a matter of tuning the sails.

Outside, the salty sea air is invigorating and he fills his lungs with it. As he pulls the lines and works the winches, Josh considers his own change in course.

For the first time in years he's rethinking his grand plan.

Life—on the physical plane, that is—really isn't so bad when you've got love in it. In fact, it's pretty great.

And surprisingly, it's not the receiving, he's found, but the giving of it, the feeling of it, the *being* of it that's the best part.

He could get used to this, he thinks. He may just have to "reenlist," after all.

Besides—he still has a lot to learn.

EPILOGUE

THE DINGHY SKIPS ACROSS THE WATER, with Stanley at the bow. Their destination is only a minute away, anchored offshore.

He's scowling because he hates being told what to do, especially by a woman.

He's surprised to have seen her there; he wonders how much she knows. She obviously doesn't have a problem taking care of his girls while he's gone. Hell, she'd already started feeding them.

And what a looker! That is one hot mama if he ever saw one. Only about twenty years too old for his taste: Once they hit puberty it's time to cut 'em loose.

Stanley considers himself a connoisseur of young pussy. He's tried 'em all, from Mexico and Panama to the Philippines and Vietnam. But the best by far are right here in Thailand. They aim to please, that's for sure. Pretty little girls can be found anywhere, but the Thais' sweet disposition makes them all the more enjoyable. And in demand.

After so many years of living here full time now, he can instantly spot the ones who'll give the most bang for the buck. It's an essential skill in his line of work. His visiting clients, from all over the world, expect him to deliver every time. And he always comes through. That's why he's known as "The King" of sex tourism in this country.

The dinghy slows and comes up alongside the yacht, one of those big catamaran sailboats, the kind he could never afford, even if he wanted one. The kid—a local beach rat—holds them steady as Stanley climbs aboard the steps built into the rear of the hull.

The man is waiting for him outside in the cockpit. He's wearing his usual faded red swim trunks and nothing else. It's hard to believe this long-haired, tattooed hippie is a millionaire.

Stanley holds out his hand, all smiles now, and greets his new friend. "Howdy, Trip!"

"Hey, Stan. How's it going? We all set for tonight?"

"Ready and rearin' to go, hoss. Hope twenty-eight is enough for ya. Couldn't get any more than that on such short notice. Had to borrow a few from some friends." He waggles his eyebrows. "None over twelve in the bunch, guaranteed. Maybe even a virgin or two for the right fella."

"Ah, that's great. The more the better," Trip says. "You get them all new dresses, like I asked?"

"Sure did. Wasn't too hard. Church had boxes of 'em. They all look great."

"Good, good. You're the man, Stan. What would the sex trade here do without you?"

"Huh?"

Trip waves him inside, the cool air beckoning from the open door. "Come on in," he says. "I suppose you're ready to get paid for all your hard work."

"Hell yeah!" Tonight's soirée is netting him a fortune. The man's business associates are set to arrive this afternoon.

"You wanna drink?" Trip asks.

STANLEY'S FIRST THOUGHT when he wakes is that he's starving, like he hasn't had a solid meal in days. He reaches for a cigarette on the nightstand, pats the empty air . . .

Huh?

He can tell immediately he's not at home—or anywhere else he knows. It's a tiny, bare room; unpainted, corrugated steel walls; a set of cargo doors; a sink and toilet in the corner; a shelf.

He swings his legs off the bunk, realizes he's naked, his body covered in a sheen of sweat.

Jesus Christ! What the hell did I do last night?

He tries the doors; they're locked. He pounds on them. Calls out. Listens . . . Nothing.

He lies on the cement floor, peers through the slot. A large water beetle scurries out, startling him.

Where am I? What the hell is going on?

He slates his thirst at the sink. The water is hot, like everything else in this damned metal box.

On the shelf are a few small items.

Over here . . . a book.

READING LIST
(GROUPED IN SUGGESTED ORDER, * "REQUIRED")

Mastering Your Hidden Self: A Guide to the Huna Way, by Serge Kahili King

Conversations With God (Series), by Neal Donald Walsch

**The Power of Now: A Guide to Spiritual Enlightenment,* by Eckhart Tolle

Autobiography of a Yogi, by Paramahansa Yogananda

The Power of Kabbalah, by Yehuda Berg

The Seat of the Soul, by Gary Zukav

• • •

**The Field: The Quest for the Secret Force of the Universe,* by Lynne McTaggart

The Biology of Belief: Unleashing the Power of Consciousness, Matter, and Miracles, by Bruce H. Lipton

**The Holographic Universe: The Revolutionary Theory of Reality,* by Michael Talbot

Miracles of Mind: Exploring Nonlocal Consciousness and Spiritual Healing, by Russell Targ and Jane Katra

Adventures Beyond the Body: How to Experience Out-of-Body Travel, by William Buhlman

The Hidden Messages in Water, by Masuru Emoto

The Language of Miracles: A Celebrated Psychic Teaches You to Talk to Animals, by Amelia Kinkade

• • •

The Truth in the Light: An Investigation of Over 300 Near-Death Experiences, by Peter Fenwick

*Backwards: Returning to Our Source for Answers, by Nanci L. Danison

Talking to Heaven: A Medium's Message of Life After Death, by James Van Praagh

Hello From Heaven: A New Field of Research—After Death Communication—Confirms That Life and Love are Eternal, by Judy and Bill Guggenheim

● ● ●

Reincarnation: A New Horizon in Science, Religion, and Society, by Sylvia Cranston and Carey Williams

Soul Survivor: The Reincarnation of a World War II Fighter Pilot, by Andrea and Bruce Leininger

Life Before Life: Children's Memories of Previous Lives, by Jim B. Tucker

*Same Soul, Many Bodies: Discover the Healing Power of Past Lives Through Regression Therapy, by Brian L. Weiss

*Journey of Souls: Case Studies of Life Between Lives, by Michael Newton

*Destiny of Souls: New Case Studies of Life Between Lives, by Michael Newton

Memories of the Afterlife, edited by Michael Newton

Healing Lost Souls: Releasing Unwanted Spirits From Your Energy Body, by William J. Baldwin

Regression Therapy: A Handbook for Professionals (Two Volume Set), edited by Winafred B. Lucas

● ● ●

Ask and It Is Given: Learning to Manifest Your Desires, by Esther and Jerry Hicks

**Seth Speaks: The Eternal Validity of the Soul,* by Jane Roberts

Ramtha: The White Book, by JZ Knight

A Course in Miracles, from the Foundation for Inner Peace

How many have *you* read?
Give us your feedback on these and others like them at
www.EscapingTheWheel.com

AUTHOR'S NOTE

THE EARTH IS MOVING at 1,000 miles per hour as it rotates on its axis. The Earth is also traveling at 66,000 mph as it orbits the sun. The sun and solar system are whizzing along the edge of the Milky Way galaxy at 481,000 mph. And the Milky Way is clocking 1,350,000 mph around a cluster of other galaxies that make up our expanding universe.

Add to this the fact that every single part of your body is in motion, and every atom in it is a mini-galaxy, dancing and whirling at *incalculable* speeds.

There is much within the physical world that cannot be measured, and Science can only guess at such things.

Measuring most any aspect of the *spiritual* world is also beyond the capacity of physical science. A different set of laws exist, as do entirely different realities beyond our comprehension.

For example, there is much we cannot see. And because we cannot see it, many think it does not exist. However, visible light is only the tiniest fraction of the electromagnetic spectrum. We are surrounded by invisible things just as real as the visible. This includes beings with consciousness and intelligence, like ourselves. It includes other worlds and dimensions.

Each of us can experience these things personally, or learn from those who have.

The books are just a start. Explore within.

* * *

TO EXPERIENCE a past-life/life-before-lives session for yourself, visit NewtonInstitute.org to find a professional hypnotherapist near you. It will change your life forever. Guaranteed.

Another good resource is the National Association of Transpersonal Hypnotherapists (NATH) at HolisticTree.com.

For information about Hemi-Sync, visit MonroeInstitute.org. Their proven methods for achieving expanded states of awareness have been used by thousands of people for decades.

Also, Lily Dale is a real place. Visit LilyDaleAssembly.com.

● ● ●

PLEASE post your review of *Escaping The Wheel* online at your favorite book sites, like Amazon and GoodReads. Thanks much!

Happy reading!

THANKS, MOM. Thanks, Bro, Larry, Sue.
And a special thanks to "Bob" and the gang.

Thanks also to the Human Kindness Foundation
(HumanKindness.org) for putting me on the Path,
and for bringing light into the darkest places.

Most importantly, I thank you, my readers.
Thanks for spreading the word.

Namasté.
The Light within me salutes
the Light within you.

ERIC ARTISAN is a contemporary artist, writer, and book lover. This is his first novel. He welcomes your questions and ideas at Eric@EscapingTheWheel.com

CPSIA information can be obtained at www.ICGtesting.com
Printed in the USA
LVOW11s1322211014

409798LV00001B/1/P

9 781500 561871